"*August Snow* is one of my favorite books that I've read recently . . . This book is so good, I actually put it down, and I briefly entertained the notion of moving back to Detroit."

—Nancy Pearl on NPR's *Morning Edition*

"All of us begin in grace and great promise and, staring at the door left open behind, wonder where they've gone. Stephen Mack Jones knows this, as does his narrator August Snow, as does their battered city, Detroit. Jean Cocteau believed the world is a misunderstanding. We read searching for stories that help us untangle some of that misunderstanding; *August Snow* is one."

—James Sallis

"[A] witty, mayhem-packed first novel . . . Snow's own voice has echoes of Raymond Chandler's. Be assured that when the showdown comes, Snow—an action hero with the heart of a mensch—and his crew prove up to that task."

—*The Wall Street Journal*

"Wonderful." —Nancy Pearl for KUOW Seattle

"Stephen Mack Jones's rock-solid debut, *August Snow*, is powered by the outgoing personality of the title hero and his deep affections for his hometown of Detroit. This author proves himself a natural entertainer."

—*Chicago Tribune*

"Jones, a Detroit-area poet and playwright brings the city, its environs, and its eateries to vital life in a mystery coiled around the contemporary crime du jour of cyber-finance meddling. His is that rare tale that, despite its thriller-level violence, maintains a fiercely warm heart at its core—and ends far too quickly."

—*The Boston Globe*

"[Stephen Mack Jones] has deftly created a unique multi-faceted character in the best hard-boiled tradition, easily enjoyed by those who appreciate quick-thinking, fast-shooting detectives. This is a well-polished first novel with exceptionally strong characters and unexpected plot twists; it's a superb start for a new series."

—*Lansing State Journal*

"Mack Jones's prose is poetic and cutthroat, seemingly paradoxical elements he sees in his Detroit. You should meet this guy."

—*Milwaukee Journal Sentinel*

"[A] polished, gripping debut. Poet Stephen Mack Jones's novel bristles with energy, compassion, humor and a page-turning plot."

—*Minneapolis Star Tribune*

"Compelling . . . strong one-on-one dialogue keeps the story moving. *August Snow* is an entertaining read that gives Jones—and Detroit—plenty to celebrate."   —*Toledo Blade*

"*August Snow* is an absolute joy to read from start to finish; Stephen Mack Jones has infused a real love of Detroit into every page. Characters are full of life, with August being a modern day anti-hero to a T, burdened with responsibility he never asked for but with the moral compass to ensure that he gets the job done regardless . . . We can only hope this isn't the last we see of him."

—*The Michigan Daily*

"[August Snow] is persistent, courageous, true to his friends . . . Now here is an interesting book."   —*Lincoln Journal Star*

"As far as compelling reads, this book is what you want. The book takes the reader into the depths of Detroit, exploring, race, class and the cities that contain it all."   —The Rumpus

AUGUST
SNOW

AUGUST
SNOW

STEPHEN MACK JONES

Published by
Soho Press, Inc.
853 Broadway
New York, NY 10003

Library of Congress Cataloging-in-Publication Data

Jones, Stephen Mack, author
August Snow / Stephen Mack Jones.

ISBN 978-1-61695-868-8
eISBN 978-1-61695-719-3
1. Racially mixed people—Michigan—Detroit—Fiction.
2. Race relations—Fiction. I. Title
PS3610.O6289   A94 2017   813'.6—dc23 2016030513

Interior design by Janine Agro, Soho Press, Inc.

Printed in the United States of America

10 9 8 7 6 5 4 3 2 1

For my family:
Past, Present & Future

AUGUST
SNOW

The house is a narrow two-story, two-bedroom, redbrick Colonial with two and a half baths, hardwood floors and a small kitchen. The focal point in the living room is a brick fireplace framed by bookshelves. At one time the bookshelves were full of the works of Frederico García Lorca, Pablo Neruda, Juana Inés de la Cruz, Octavio Paz and Pita Amor. My mother, Isabella Marie Santiago-Snow, would read to me from her favorite poems, her patient voice flowing like warm Juarez honey.

Of course, in our house, these poets had to share shelf space with classic noir gumshoes, who stood shoulder-to-hardbound-shoulder with the interminably boring and occasionally grotesque: weighty tomes on police procedure and criminal law, rules of evidence and forensics texts complete with coroner photos of humans in various states of disassembly and decay; there were mysteries by Dashiell Hammett, Arthur Conan Doyle and Raymond Chandler and first-edition signed copies of Rudolph Fisher and Chester Himes. And there were the programs from five August Wilson plays we had seen as a family at the Fisher Theatre in downtown Detroit.

After my mother passed away five years ago, the modest brick house in the neighborhood known as Mexicantown, once referred to as "La Bagley," became mine.

"It isn't what it used to be," she'd said of our Mexicantown neighborhood. An ornate crucifix she'd brought to the hospital hung above her bed while clear liquids dripped into her slowly disappearing body. "No one's working. People forced out of homes they lived in for years. Thieves are bolder. Freight trucks cut through neighborhoods where children play in the streets. Sell the house, Octavio. Take the money. Move somewhere else. Forget that place."

I lied and said I would. Then we prayed the rosary.

Neither time nor politics have been kind to Detroit. In Mexican-town, they've been downright cruel.

In the 1940s, the Mexicans came to Detroit for the same reason blacks had abandoned the south a decade earlier: well-paying, steady work in the auto factories. The only color Henry Ford saw was US Currency Green. He didn't care if you were a spic, an A-rab or a nigger as long as you could tighten a bolt or guide a body onto a chassis. Tighten that bolt, guide that body, get paid.

When word got out that working at Ford and General Motors meant good, steady work and good, steady money, more Mexicans came to Detroit.

Contrary to popular belief, Detroit's "white flight" didn't start in the '60s. *Gringos* have always been "flying" out of the concentric circles of Detroit. All in an effort to avoid—well—everybody: The Germans. The Italians. The Irish. Greeks. Swedes. Finns. Blacks. Mexicans. Vietnamese. Now the influx of Chaldeans and Middle East Muslims.

All of us have our angry and fearsome ghosts in this mad American machine.

In Mexicantown, homes once reserved for doctors and wheelers-and-dealers were soon bought for pennies on the dollar by waves of Mexicans in pursuit of something once considered the exclusive purview of white people: the American Dream.

For the love of my Mexican mother, my African-American father bought the two-story brick Colonial in 1978. He wanted my mother to be close to her family, her friends, her culture. He was an anomaly, a black man living in a Mexican neighborhood. But eventually, through no small amount of effort on my mother's part and the occasion of my birth, he was accepted. Toasted with tequila at Saturday backyard parties and prayed for on Sunday at Holy Redeemer Church's Spanish-language mass.

It didn't hurt that my father was a Detroit cop.

I've poured some of my settlement money into bringing this house back to life, even going so far as to buy and refurbish seven other houses on Markham Street. The only house I had demolished was one to the north of me, which had once been beautiful but was beyond redemption after two decades of broken crack and meth pipes, heroin needles, attempted "Devil's Night" arsons, human and animal waste.

A garden on that plot might be nice.

Peppers, kale and cabbage, lettuce and tomatoes.

What's a Blaxican without a garden?

Especially if you can't look with pride on your hard work during the early evening or late night hours, a bottle of Negra Modelo beer or chilled shot of Cabresto Tequila in hand.

While I was away, free-diving to the bottom of various bottles of booze around the Mediterranean and Scandinavia, apparently the city thought it would be nice to replace the stripped and gutted streetlamps with eight new solar-powered LED streetlamps. A mostly ineffectual effort to ward off crime on a nearly desolate street in Mexicantown.

I'd tried to get on with my life after the trial and award. Live my life as a normal citizen. But I couldn't quite shed the knowledge that I'd failed at a job I had loved. A Judas to the apostles in blue. The eyes on me in grocery stores and restaurants, the unrelenting judgment. I was looked at as if there was someone just over my shoulder—an out-of-focus and disquieting figure.

Everybody loves a hero.

Nobody loves a rat.

A woman I'd met in Oslo helped me moderate my drinking. A beautiful young woman with smooth brown skin, a smile like sunrise, and eyes the color of amber. Tatina. She was half-Somali, half-German, a refugee from the perpetual Somali civil war who had seen horrors I couldn't imagine. Somehow her soul had survived, embracing light and exuding warmth. For three months beneath the ice-blue skies of Norway I held her, made love with her, felt my body levitate when she laughed. Her breath on my chest felt like where I needed to be.

It felt like home.

Of course, being from Detroit I've never quite trusted happiness.

So I returned to a city where happiness is usually a matter of finding contentment in an acceptable level of intangible fear, unfocused loathing and unexplainable ennui.

It was early fall when I found myself back in front of my house on the short, twelve-home street of West Markham in Mexicantown. Nestled against the front door was a small package. Before mounting the steps, I stopped and looked around. A well-fed calico cat stopped in the middle of the street and narrowed its eyes at me as if to say, "The fuck you lookin' at?" before stealthily moving on.

I walked up the steps then crouched near the box; it was the size and shape of a shoebox and wrapped neatly in brown paper. Even though I'd been gone for a year, temperatures were still elevated over my testimony against the former mayor and several Detroit cops—now dismissed or imprisoned—who had aided the mayor in his various criminal enterprises. A shoebox wrapped in brown paper could very well be a homecoming gift from anybody who was annoyed that I'd destroyed careers and made off with a sizable chunk of money from a bankrupt city.

After scrutinizing the package for a minute or so, I carefully lifted it.

Too light for a bomb. No tell-tale odors. I unwrapped the box—a discarded Nike Air Max 90, men's size 10 shoebox—and checked for wires. Nothing. Maybe a simple warning inside: A newspaper clipping from the trial with a red X over a photo of me. A stupid note warning me to get out of town by sundown. The clichéd metaphor of a dead rat.

I lifted the lid.

Inside was an empty Skittles wrapper.

I laughed.

At least *somebody* was glad I'd come home.

2

It's getting so a mackerel snapper can't pray in Detroit.

Much to the delight of Lutherans, Baptists, the affluent Catholics of Oakland County and atheists, the Archdiocese of Detroit has closed or merged nearly sixty Catholic churches in the past year, leaving the city's downtown black, Hispanic, elderly and poor Catholics feeling abandoned by a church they had prayed in and tithed to for years. Now, the people who'd suffered the most during Detroit's perpetual slide into financial insolvency felt even more marginalized and afraid.

Sitting tenuously on the threshold of closure were Old St. Anne's, a grand Catholic cathedral built over three hundred years ago, and St. Aloysius on Washington Boulevard, with its rose-colored marble columns and semi-circle "well" revealing the downstairs altar and pews.

Today I went to St. Al's—one, because I like what the Franciscan Brothers do for the homeless and elderly; and two, because, hell or high water, they persist in holding daily afternoon mass regardless of whether one or one hundred worshipers show up. With downtown's recent revitalization, more young white suburban Catholics in Donna Karan and Pierre Cardin suits were taking time out of their lunch schedules to kneel, bow their heads and take communion. Not enough new blood to move the church safely off the closure bubble. But enough for the dioceses to pocket a dollar or two.

At the end of mass, Father Grabowski took me by the elbow and led me to an alcove.

"Good to see you back, August," he said, a smile forming somewhere inside the thick tangle of his full white beard. Grabowski had known my family for years and he was one of the few priests my father actually trusted. "You know you can't buy your way into heaven, though, right?"

I took it he was referring to the two grand I'd dropped into the collection plate, very nearly giving Mr. Lokat, an elderly black layman, a heart attack.

"You need it more than I do, Padre," I said.

Grabowski nodded enthusiastically, then said, "Oh, I didn't say I wasn't gonna take it. In fact if you've got any loose change left, I'll take that, too. I just said you can't buy your way into heaven."

I told Father Grabowski I'd just returned from visiting my parents' graves. Big Jake, the cemetery groundskeeper, a grizzled black bear of a man, had caught me laying down a bag of cashews, Mom's favorite snack, and pouring out a dram of twenty-one-year-old Auchentoshan single malt scotch for Dad on the grass covering his grave.

The old priest nodded. "They're always in my evening prayers, August."

I said, "For what I just dropped in the collection plate, Padre, I'm thinkin' maybe they should be in your morning *and* afternoon prayers, too."

"'And again I say unto you, it is easier for a camel to pass through the eye of a needle than for a rich man to enter the kingdom of heaven.'"

"That's pretty good," I said playfully. "You should write that down."

"Matthew, 19:24," Father Grabowski said with a wide, yellow-toothed grin. "Yet another reason why you'll never be on *Jeopardy*, jackass."

Like most nuns and priests I'd known, Father Grabowski dreamed of being welcomed at the pearly gates by Alex Trebeck.

I pulled an errant ten-dollar bill out of my pocket and shoved it into Father Grabowski's hand. "All I got left. Get yourself a shave, old man."

Unlike the twenty or so other faithful who emerged from the Thursday afternoon mass, I discovered there was a car waiting for me outside. The car—a new, brightly gleaming navy-blue Ford Taurus with blacked-out windows—came equipped with an equally bright and gleaming black driver.

"I prayed for you," I said to the tall, slender and well-dressed driver leaning casually on the hood of the car. His expensive cologne, carried on the early fall breeze, had a nose-tingling, eye-stinging cheapness to it. Any cologne smells tawdry if you bathe in it.

"Oh yeah?" the driver said as he scanned me from head to toe with eyes shielded by a pair of Ray-Ban sunglasses. "Must not've worked. I'm still alive." The movie-star grin on Detective Lieutenant Leo Cowling's chiseled Abyssinian face disappeared, replaced with a well-practiced scowl. Cowling had been practicing this scowl for upwards of twelve years, ever since we were at the academy together. It still needed practice. "See you've been spendin' all the taxpayer's money on threads."

I was wearing a pair of slightly scuffed brown Bjorn loafers, nicely broken in black Buffalo jeans, a grey Nike sweatshirt and brown leather motorcycle-style jacket that had once belonged to my father.

Hardly haute couture, but comfortable as hell.

I was also wearing a stylish Glock nine-millimeter semi-automatic that was secured by my belt in the small of my back. My mother would have been appalled that I'd brought a gun to church. My father, however, would have considered it necessary any day of the week in the city and twice on Sunday.

In the year I'd been away from Detroit, I'd never felt the need for a gun, save for two very interesting weeks in northeastern India. Back in Detroit, old habits reemerged quickly. My Glock was one of several items I reluctantly retrieved from the storage unit I'd packed my life into before I left the country in a concerted effort to die from self-pity and cirrhosis of the liver.

"Danbury wants to see you," Cowling said. "Get in."

"What's Danbury want?"

"How the fuck I know?" Cowling's eyebrows creased over his sunglasses and he took several aggressive steps toward me. "Get in the car, Tex-Mex."

Cowling was maybe an inch or so taller than me and in good shape. I'd seen him in the gym at the 14th Precinct. He was quick and could handle a speed-bag pretty well. On the heavy bag, though, he had nothing, his fists buckling at the wrist.

A solid jab to his solar plexus, a right to his jaw and Cowling would be on his ass watching Disney bluebirds flutter around his head. But it would have been a shame to put him down only a few feet from a house of worship.

"You know," I began, squinting up at the diamond-blue early fall sky, "it's such a nice day, I think I'll walk."

"Don't make me—"

"Do fucking what?" I said, taking a couple steps to close the gap between us. I was already fuel-injected with adrenaline. The key was—and always had been—to know when to fire up the engine and hit the gas. After a couple seconds of hard stares, I smiled at Cowling, then turned my back on him and began walking west on Washington toward Campus Martius.

What's the old saying about not being able to go home again?

3

Lieutenant Leo Cowling was suave, good-looking in a street-thug-hip-hop way. He was well-rehearsed and calculating when it came to knowing who in the local media was most beneficial to the DPD. And to his career. Other than that, he was a waste of a badge. "To Serve Myself and Protect What I Got."

Cowling reported to a man who was his exact opposite. Captain Ray Danbury promoted Cowling shortly after the air surrounding my lawsuit against the department had cleared—as much as such air can clear. Danbury was smart and politically astute. He knew Cowling didn't deserve the promotion; Cowling was at least a pinky knuckle deep in the dirty police inner circle under the former mayor. Petty cash bribes, soft extortion and corralling high-end hookers for a few politicos and business elite for private parties at Manoogian Mansion, the mayor's residence. For my investigation into the mayor's office, I was demoted, then unceremoniously fired. Things got nastier and that's when I filed a wrongful dismissal suit. Didn't want to, but like my father used to say, "The only ground a man ever really owns is the two-square-feet he's standin' on—and God help him if he gets pushed off that."

My lawsuit got the attention of the DA and the State Attorney General—both of whom were implicated at least on the periphery as beneficiaries of Cowling's "ho-wrangling" skills. After I won my lawsuit and collected twelve million dollars, Danbury figured the department and the mayor's office had suffered enough. Adding Cowling to the lengthy list of cops and administration officials given the boot or serving time would only have prolonged the city's suffering and threatened a complete and catastrophic collapse of the department. Nobody wanted the State cops to take over. Even fewer still wanted the FBI's regional office to continue doggedly digging through the city's years-deep garbage.

Better the little demons you can control than the big devils you can't.

Danbury promoted Cowling in an effort to shorten the choke-chain on him.

The walk down Washington Boulevard reawakened an old passion for a freshly made turkey Reuben on toasted rye. I decided to happily pursue the subject on foot.

Schmear's Deli had struggled, barely survived and thrived for over fifty years on Woodward Avenue near the One Campus Martius traffic roundabout. Once the old Kern's department store had been razed and replaced by the modern gleaming glass and steel jewel of One Campus Martius, businesses along the Woodward corridor experienced a revitalization few had ever imagined for Detroit and fewer still thought possible.

Sure, you can still find those who fondly reminisce about Kern's larger next door competitor, Hudson's, and their massive display windows, or the way the thirty-two floors were brightly lit at Christmastime. Or the store restaurant's Maurice salad and garlic mashed potatoes with meatloaf.

Frankly, the young professionals who now command the streets of downtown Detroit mostly either don't remember Hudson's (now a cavernous underground parking garage) or don't give a shit about Maurice salads and garlic mashed potatoes with meatloaf. They just want some buffalo wings or extra spicy Pad Thai while scrutinizing *The Wall Street Journal* and *Advertising Age*, or clicking the Facebook "Like" icon on their iPhones.

The rise of One Campus Martius made it all right for white suburbanites to return to the heart of a city long written off as a hovel of black poverty, simmering racial animosity and perpetual urban decay. The iron-gated wig shops, roach-infested malt liquor bodegas and abandoned office buildings that once made the piously pitying national news reports had suddenly been replaced by international accounting firms, mortgage companies, software start-ups, ad agencies, tony "goat cheese and free-range egg" breakfast cafes and the ubiquitous Starbucks.

Schmear's Deli, a staple through good times and bad, was now surrounded by trendy restaurants and upscale boutiques. In order to compete in the new Detroit business core, Schmear's changed from the small, cigar-scented restaurant with a prominent display of beef tongues to something more appealing to the Monday-through-Friday invasion of tech-savvy iPad-slinging professionals.

The posters of Che Guevara, Angela Davis, Mahatma Gandhi, Malcolm X, Martin Luther King, Jr. and David Ben Gurion that had once yellowed on the nicotine-stained walls of Schmear's were gone. So were the waiters who had chewed the wet stubs of cheap cigars, retired mostly by virtue of age and throat cancer. The scarred, uneven wooden chairs and tables I used to sit at with my mom and dad had been replaced with gleaming stainless steel, and shimmering seafoam green Pewabic Pottery tiles. In place of the yellowed posters were inoffensive acrylic paintings and smiling photographs of Detroit's ethnically varied residents. One of the photos was of me when I was five flanked by my mom, dad and the current owner's barrel-chested, gap-toothed father.

When I arrived, the young professionals were happily finishing their lunches and paying their tabs. Time to get back to whatever people in Michael Kors and Jones New York suits do.

A seat at the counter opened up and no sooner had I saddled up than I heard, "The prodigal son returns!"

Ben Breitler, second-generation owner of Schmear's, was now

in his mid-sixties. With each passing year he looked more like Albert Einstein on a methamphetamine bender.

Ben was wearing a rainbow-colored tie-dye T-shirt with the bold words "Light One Up!"

We embraced and I said, "Hate what you've done with the place, Ben."

"Yeah, well, I hate it, too," Ben said with a dismissive shrug. "But you gotta give the gentrifying class what they want. Adapt or die. So you're back now? For good or just slumming?"

"For a while," I said. "I started renovating my folks' old house in Mexicantown before I left. I'll finish that and then decide what I want to do when I grow up."

"Good!" Ben said with a grin that revealed a couple-grand's worth of West Bloomfield cosmetic dentistry. "Live by example and be an example to live by. Mexicantown's a *great* area! And it's only gonna get better. You mark my words. And as to deciding what you wanna be when you grow up, don't look at me for advice, kiddo. I *still* don't know what I wanna be when I grow up—but somehow I don't think it's gonna be a Jewish deli owner tearing his hair out over the cost of good lox and fucking green tea."

Ben turned and frantically waved for one of his waitresses—a young, spike-haired redhead with imposing, dark eye shadow, koi fish tattoos swimming up her left arm and a silver nostril ring. Emo wasn't normally a look I was attracted to. That being said, Lucy "Tank Girl" Tarapousian had always been the exception to this relatively loose rule.

"Look who's back!" Ben yelled over the departing crowd.

Tank Girl saw me and admonished her new customers to "Talk amongst yourselves." As she walked toward me, she said, "Oh-la, me amigo! Que pasa bangy-bangy?"

"Your Spanish is still god-awful," I said. "But the look is workin'."

Tank Girl gave me a rib-bruising hug and—much to my

surprise and delight—a full kiss. Yet another reason why I enjoyed the ambience of Schmear's. She tasted like good sex or fresh lox. I often confused the two.

Ben, Tank Girl and I talked for a while. Mostly about my year-long adventure in international drinking and a bit about how the city tried to screw me. After a while, Tank Girl wrote down her phone number, address, email, bra size and locations of her latest piercings on a napkin and stuffed it in my inside jacket pocket.

"Text me," she said. "I'm sick of my boyfriend."

"You're back with boys?"

She grinned, shrugged and got back to her famished customers.

"Don't you have a policy about staff flirting with customers?" I said to Ben.

"Hey, *boychik*, if I did, *I'd* never get laid."

Ben wrangled a menu for me: six laminated, colorful pages bound in imitation burgundy leather. It included a list of their bottled waters—domestic and imported, flat and effervescent—and "healthy" smoothies and teas.

"Jesus, Ben," I said perusing the menu. "You really have gone over to the dark side."

"What can I say?" Ben said with a dismissive shrug. "The dark side pays better."

The mayor, city council and at least a third of the DPD had thought the same thing a year ago . . .

4

I ordered the Turkey Reuben "Extraordinaire" with buffalo-seasoned sweet potato fries and a side order of cole slaw complete with chopped walnuts and McIntosh apples. Ben gave me a bear hug, then excused himself.

I was only three bites into my sandwich when a squat black man in his late forties entered the deli. He sported a thick black mustache, round tortoise shell glasses, a nicely cut tan suit and Oxblood loafers. He mounted the counter stool next to me and said, "This seat taken?"

Captain Ray Danbury, Detroit Police Department. The man Cowling was supposed to have delivered me to.

"How's the sandwich?" Danbury said with a wide grin.

"It was good," I said. "Then you walked in."

"What can I say?" Danbury laughed. "I have that effect on people." Danbury was a good cop in a city where good wasn't always recognizable and ethics were often amorphous. His rise to captain had been a slow, arduous one; he didn't play favorites and his politics hadn't always aligned with those of his superiors. But he got the job done. And after the corruption indictments of the last few years, the people of Detroit were finally ready for someone like Danbury.

"You buying?" he said to me. "Word on the street is you got some serious coin."

Danbury ordered coffee black, three sugars and a Jewish Farmer's Omelet: peppers, onions and rough-chopped lox with toasted challah bread. He dug into his food as if he hadn't eaten for several days—which I doubted considering he was twenty pounds over what a man of five foot ten should be.

"You're not gonna invite your puppy in for a bowl of kibble?" I said, staring out at the navy-blue Ford Taurus parked near the Campus Martius traffic roundabout.

"Cowling?" Danbury said, chewing while he spoke. "Don't be too hard on him, August. He's right where I want him and he's happy in his gilded cage." Danbury took another forkful of his omelet. "Besides. Last thing this city needs is another cop trial. You pretty much sealed the deal on that."

"What do you want, Ray? I mean besides my always-illuminating company."

Danbury shrugged. "Heard you was back in the D. Just wanted to say hey's all."

"Bullshit."

"Yeah, you right," Danbury laughed and took a slurp of his diabetes-inducing coffee. "Guess who's been missing you?" He paused for dramatic affect before saying, "Eleanor Paget."

I felt the muscles in my shoulders tighten.

"Yeah," Danbury said brightly. "Shocked the shit outta me, too. But the bitch's been calling my office, the chief's office and the commissioner for the past two weeks asking for you. I keep tellin' her you ain't a cop no more and you off God-knows-where getting your knob polished. But you know what the woman's like."

"I do indeed."

Danbury turned to me and in a quiet voice said, "You think you could slip back in town and nobody'd notice? Hell, man, I knew you was back before you was wheels-down at Metro."

"What's she want?" I said.

"How the hell do I know?" Danbury said. "I'm just a highly paid messenger. And besides. Don't wanna know. Got me enough to worry about, never mind that woman and yo narrow, half-wet ass."

We sat quietly for a moment before I worked up the courage to say, "Why didn't you testify on my behalf, Ray?"

"Because *your* wounds are *your* wounds," Danbury snapped, "and mine are mine. And I don't need anybody reopening *my* wounds and twisting a finger in 'em." After a moment or two, he sighed and said, "You know how much tuition is at U of M?" Then he said, "You're a good cop, August. *Were* a good cop. Always liked you, man. Liked your daddy, too, God rest his soul. But it's been a long time and a lot of rough road between then and now. I got me two kids in college, a mortgage and a wife that likes the remodel on her kitchen which, by the way, ain't gonna be paid off for another two fuckin' years."

I nodded. "I understand."

"No, I don't think you do, August." Danbury pushed his empty plate away. "But, hey, that's awright. You find you a lady who pops you a couple kids and—" Danbury stopped mid-sentence, then said, "Sorry."

I shrugged and said, "It's been three years."

One second.

One bullet.

Two lives.

Danbury finally extended his hand. "We cool?"

Reluctantly, I nodded and shook his hand. "We cool."

Danbury reached into a coat pocket and retrieved a folded piece of paper.

"Eleanor Paget's number. Call it. Or don't. I couldn't care less. But just so's you know: Eleanor Paget can make a lot of people's lives miserable when her calls ain't returned. And Lord knows—my life's hard enough without any more of that woman's shit on my shoes."

Danbury stood and thanked me for the lunch. As he turned to

leave, I said, "Tell Cowling if he ever approaches me like he did outside of St. Al's, I'll put him down."

"Acknowledged and understood," Danbury said with a decisive nod. He left.

I looked at the number written on the piece of paper.

The black emo waitress named Crazy Horse filled my glass with fresh iced green tea, leaned on the counter and, offering a dimpled smile, said, "Feel like eating anything else, champ?"

"Yeah," I said, still looking at Eleanor Paget's number scribbled on the paper. "A bullet."

5

Once upon a time, the mantle over the living room fireplace was crowded with photos of my black grandparents and my Mexican grandparents, baby pictures (mine, cousins and neighbor kids too numerous to remember), my folks' wedding photo, my dad looking intrepid and invincible in his Detroit Police Department dress uniform and my mother looking beautifully languid on the sands of Sleeping Bear Dunes. There was a framed photo of our used 1979 Oldsmobile 98 (Dad loved that car), a Day of the Dead celebration at a local Mexican restaurant and, of course, the Holy Mother Mary framed prayer card.

Over the years the pictures changed: Me receiving my yellow belt in karate at the age of six; grandparents lying placid in their coffins; a family trip to Traverse City; Rusty, a greyish-brown mutt who was my first, only and best dog; my graduations from high school, Wayne State University and the police academy. The number of pictures of cousins and neighbor kids steadily declined over the years as the number of cousins and neighbor kids who went to prison or died increased. The only photos that remained were of the Holy Mother Mary framed prayer card and the 1979 Oldsmobile 98.

Now, there were only two pictures on the mantle: my parents' wedding photo and one I'd taken of Tatina in Oslo.

There were no books yet in the bookshelves.

As I stood in the middle of the empty living room assessing what to do with the house and my life, the doorbell rang and was quickly followed by a knock on the front door. Instinctively, I found myself reaching for my Glock.

I walked to the door and peered out through the high sliver of window: there were two very small elderly women standing at the door, one Mexican-American, one white, both in matching purple North Face bubble coats.

I opened the door and said, "Hi, ladies."

It must have been my delivery since the two women giggled.

"Mr. Snow?" the Mexican-American lady said.

"Yes, ma'am."

"Hi!" she said. "I'm Carmela Montoya. This is my friend Sylvia Zychek." Sylvia gave an enthusiastic wave even though we were less than two feet from each other. "We're your neighbors!"

"We just wanted to stop by and thank you for the wonderful job you did on our house," Sylvia said. The houses I'd bought and renovated on Markham were simply a way to keep myself busy and to feel connected with people without having to actually connect with them. Obviously, these ladies hadn't gotten my memo. "And that man? The Mexican gentleman who's been watching your house while you were away? Oh my, what a nice man. A little scary looking, but really nice."

"We also wanted to thank you for helping bring this neighborhood back," Carmela said. "My son and daughter-in-law didn't want me to move back to Mexicantown, but—well, this is home. It's where I feel alive."

"You're very welcome, ladies," I said.

"Not much," Sylvia said to her housemate. She was craning her neck to peek around me for a better view inside my house.

"What?" Carmela replied.

"I said he doesn't have much!" Sylvia said, louder.

"I just got back from a long trip," I said. "Most of my stuff's in storage."

"Well, you need any help," Carmela said, "you give us a call. Or just come on over. We've always got cookies and cake, sometimes our special brownies and—"

"Oh, she makes the absolute *best* strawberry-filled churros!" Sylvia said.

The ladies thanked me again, turned and began walking away. "The streetlamps?" I said quickly. "When did the city put those in?"

"Oh, it wasn't the city," Sylvia said. "It was some private company. I think it was—"

"LifeLight," Carmela said. "That was the name on the truck. LifeLight."

"They look nice, don't they?" Sylvia said.

I watched the ladies descend my steps hand in hand and slowly make their way back to the house next door. They walked like I remembered people walking in this neighborhood a lifetime ago, with casual confidence, as if this narrow street were the best of all possible worlds.

For whatever reason, talking with the two old girls brought a certain buoyancy to my spirit. Maybe there was hope for this nearly forgotten part of the city. Maybe I was a part of that.

I was also thankful Carmela and Sylvia hadn't mentioned any aspect of my trial. Maybe they didn't know. Maybe they didn't care.

Twenty minutes and one phone call later I was in a suit and on a trajectory toward a world that might as well have been Camelot—or Mars: the northeastern tip of southeastern Michigan, zip code 48236.

Grosse Pointe.

Gringos emerging from beneath the Cobo Hall Convention Center on the Lodge Freeway and driving northeast on Jefferson Avenue are welcomed to the city by a four-ton black cast iron fist. Don't let fellow Mexican-American Robert Graham's beautifully sculpted forearm and astounding fist of iconic boxer Joe Louis scare you: rarely has it actually punched anybody.

I drove past the fist and gave it a respectful nod.

Take that, Hitler . . .

The steel-grey Detroit River churned on my right as I negotiated my white rental Cadillac CTS through mid-afternoon traffic. Past the tourist-friendly expanse of Riverwalk. Past Mariner's Church (like a good Mexican with years of Catholic muscle memory, I involuntarily made the sign of the cross for the lost crew of the Edmund Fitzgerald), and the imposing cylindrical towers of the General Motors Renaissance Center world headquarters.

Further east I passed Belle Isle—alternately known throughout the decades as the jewel in the crown of "the Paris of the Midwest," "Blood Island" and, most recently, Michigan State Park No.101, courtesy of a bankruptcy restructuring deal. Beyond the white cantilevered Belle Isle Bridge, high-rise condos, apartment buildings and motels streamed past. There were low-slung grocery stores and a boarded-up gym where legendary boxing trainer Emanuel Steward had given boxing champions like Lennox Lewis, Wladimir Klitschko and Thomas "Hit Man" Hearns PhD lessons on "the sweet science." Monuments to a once-proud history collapsing in on themselves.

To the right off of west-bound Jefferson Avenue there were still neighborhoods that served as the gateway to hell. Where black children cowered in the corners of abandoned houses reading stolen books from school libraries by the last light of day. Places where the devil was fed his daily dinner by a state that hated its largest city and a country that unctuously pitied those who lived here.

Most of the restaurants and funky bars that had once dotted the shoreline were years gone. Victims of failed real estate schemes, encroaching poverty and a Byzantine city government intent on following the playbook for the fall of Rome.

A few remained, but for the most part the small redbrick, low-lit bars where Sippie Wallace, John Lee Hooker and James Cotton once performed were nothing more than ugly brown fields where feral dogs and the occasional coywolf hunted by night.

Further on and nearing Lake St. Claire was the first of the Grosse Pointes: Grosse Pointe Park, the anteroom of the other northern Pointes. A community designed for those who may have been related to Grandma's money, but kept at a comfortable distance because of a marriage outside of the Protestant faith or to someone not of generations-pure Anglo-Saxon blood.

Next was Grosse Pointe Farms. This is where the patresfamilias of old money live, sequestered in their redbrick and leaded glass mansions, listening to either Mozart or Duke Ellington while sipping their sherry or port and tsk-tsking on the state of modern Detroit.

And then there is Grosse Pointe Estates.

Grosse Pointe Estates, perhaps the second port-of-call for the *Mayflower*, was the epicenter of Grosse Pointe wealth. This was where great-*great*-grandma's money was firmly ensconced. A citadel where whispers toppled empires, expanded territories, or created histories and futures in their image. That "shining city on a hill" protected by the battlements of an arcane real estate algorithm.

This was where old money lived with even older skeletons.

Berlin wasn't the only city to have been divided by a wall; there was definitely a high and near-impenetrable wall between Grosse Pointe Estates and the rest of Metropolitan Detroit, though invisible to the naked eye. It was a wall built from generations of money, power and privilege. This was where the term "ethnic cleansing" took on its subsonic American rhythms and rhymes.

It is easier for a camel to go through the eye of a needle than for a Mexican to enter the kingdom of the Pointes . . .

I eased through the idyllic, meticulously maintained and vigilantly guarded neighborhood, hoping I didn't get pulled over for not quite fitting the narrow Pantone color-scheme in this part of town.

A common mistake uninitiated plebeians make is to park on the winding, tree-lined street and ring the doorbell of the three-story, two-hundred-year-old home less than forty manicured feet away: you've just rung the doorbell of what was once the servants' quarters. Maintaining on-property staff living in separate quarters belonged, for the most part, to a bygone era of dinner in tuxedos and carriages drawn by Cleveland Bay horses. The same era of black serving staff whistling as they carried dinner from kitchen to dining room, the whistling meant to assure their masters they had not sneaked a cheek full of the master's food.

I was pretty sure there were still those who pined for the long-ago days of French Service and whistling Negros.

These days, most of those quarters had been converted to security checkpoints, private offices, power plants, storage or greenhouses. Any servants required by these estates usually found themselves on an hour-long cross-town bus journey to get here, lugging their own plastic buckets of sponges, rags, Febreze, Windex and Pledge.

Another good reason to hope we don't run out of Mexicans any time soon.

"Good morning, sir."

The gargoyle at the gate to Eleanor Paget's estate was a young man with short-cropped blond hair. He was built like a middle linebacker and wore a spiffy black suit, crisp white shirt, black tie and black jump boots, well-polished. It was easy to see the left side of his suit jacket was cut a little wider to favor whatever weapon was holstered on his waist. I figured he had a six-shooter of some sort. Maybe a Smith & Wesson .32. He had the unmistakable look of well-trained ex-military. If he needed more than six out of a barrel to quell a disturbance at the gate he either flunked out of Airborne training or ISIS had just invaded Grosse Pointe in force.

I smiled my most reassuring safe-colored-guy smile, had my driver's license ready and said, "August Snow to see Ms. Paget. She's expecting me."

The security guard returned my smile, quickly compared my driver's license photo to my face while instantly memorizing the information on the license. After a moment he nodded and said, "You're cleared, sir. Welcome to the Paget estate." He pointed at the four-story Federal-style brick structure in the near distance and said, "All you have to do is—"

"I know the way," I said, barely able to hold on to my "friendly-Negro/Mexican-don't-shoot-me" smile. My cheeks were aching. "Thank you."

"Enjoy your visit, sir," the young security guard said.

"That ain't gonna happen," I said.

The things us brown people do to make white folk feel comfy: Inoffensive grins. Slumped shoulders. Downcast eyes. Folded hands.

Résumés.

I slowly wheeled the car along the narrow drive past dogwoods, oaks and pine trees until I reached the circular driveway in front of Paget's sprawling home.

It wasn't quite Lord Grantham's idyllic Downton Abbey English countryside estate, but it was a close runner-up.

Looking at the tall front entrance, I found myself slightly amused. Stuck in the well-manicured lawn near the steps was a small sign: THIS HOME PROTECTED BY DIGITAL DEFENSE HOME SECURITY, A DIVISION OF BLACK TREE CORP. A discreet, diamond-shaped sign you could see on the lawns of homes from Taylor to West Bloomfield. The difference being Black Tree Defense Corporation wasn't your average home security company. They were a major player with the US Department of Defense. The guys the DOD called for contract soldiers in Iraq, Afghanistan and off-book incursions into Pakistan, Syria and Yemen.

Not so long ago in a land far, far away, I'd patrolled as a marine sniper with a few Black Tree guys in Afghanistan. Gung-ho ex-military frat boys without allegiance to anyone or anything, save for their bloated paychecks and eye-popping bonuses. Guys who were one psych eval away from a straightjacket.

I got out of the car and started walking toward the front entrance. Before I reached the cobblestone steps, the tall white double-doors swung open. Standing framed in the doorway was a powerfully built middle-aged Mexican-American man with skin like tanned leather. He was dressed in white shirt, black tie, tan sport coat, black pants and black soft-sole shoes. His ponytail was jet-black and tightly banded.

The man gave me a dispassionate, sleepy-eyed look and calmly said, "I don't recall the lady of the house ordering any black bean salsa, sir."

"Geez," I said. "For a second I thought you were Carlos Santana. Then I remembered Santana isn't built like SpongeBob."

"Welcome home, amigo," the man said, tightly embracing me. "We missed you."

"Good to be home," I replied in Spanish, returning his embrace.

I'd known Tomás Gutierrez since I was a kid. He and my father had been good friends right up to the day my father died. I was lucky enough to inherit that friendship.

Tomás and I went inside. He took my coat and whispered, "She's completely loco these days, August. Sorry you have to be here."

"I don't have to be here," I said. "I chose to come." This was partially true. It was really the damned intractable sense of duty, honor and integrity my father had instilled in me that brought me here.

"Then you're as loco as she is," Tomás said under his breath. Even whispers had a tendency to echo in the massive foyer.

As Tomás escorted me across the expanse of black and white checkered marble, I whispered, "Thanks for looking after the house while I was away."

"You meet Carmela and Sylvia yet?"

"Yeah," I said. "Nice ladies."

"Bat-shit crazy," Tomás said. "I think they're pot-heads. But, yeah, nice ladies."

On the way to the first-floor study, as we passed under chandeliers hanging from the vaulted ceilings, Tomás told me he and his family were sorry for what I'd gone through with the department and that he missed my mother and father. I said I missed them, too.

"Your old man," Tomás said. "He was wise. And your mother? A sister to Madre Maria."

Tomás had been in Eleanor Paget's service for ten years, ever since his failed attempt at owning a restaurant in Mexicantown. The economy had tanked and it had taken his restaurateur dreams with it. He worked briefly for a metal stamping plant in Pontiac, but the Crash of '08 took care of that. The plant was shuttered and Tomás found himself out on the streets with a hundred fifty other former employees. I found him the job at Eleanor Paget's estate.

I briefly wondered if Eleanor had any idea that beneath Tomás's suit and well-groomed look was the body of Ray Bradbury's *The Illustrated Man*. Tattoos that snaked around his arms, winding around his chest and back. Tattoos of tarantulas climbing barbed wire that twisted around Christ's crucifix. Tattoos of ornate daggers in the mouths of rattlesnakes. The strangest of these was a single tattoo on his upper right shoulder of General Emiliano Zapata Salazar.

And of course there were the yesteryear scars from bullets and knives . . .

We reached the study, a bright room resplendent with two-hundred-year old family heirlooms, Persian rugs and an antique Bösendorfer piano I very much doubted Eleanor played. Through the bank of high-arched windows was a distant view of a white gazebo and the low brick building that housed the swimming pool, sauna and state-of-the-art exercise equipment. Beyond that was Lake St. Clair.

"You got some dinero, right?" Tomás said.

I smiled and nodded.

"Then buy up a couple more houses in the 'hood," Tomás said. "Bring 'em back, man. You don't buy 'em then some rich white kid will and before you know it we're all neck-deep in kale smoothies, tapas, Starbucks and Whole Fuckin' Foods."

"Sounds like a plan," I said.

"Goddamn right it does," Tomás said. Then, glancing at the door, he said, "Good luck, amigo. Keep your powder dry."

"I have no idea what the hell that means," I said, smiling at my friend and shaking his hand again.

Before leaving he asked if I wanted coffee and I said I did.

Tomás winked and said, "I'll make it strong. Mexican style. You're gonna need it."

I entered the study and there she sat—the Virgin Queen ready to send another incompetent or conspirator to the Tower.

"Where the bloody hell have *you* been?"

Eleanor Paget was in her mid-sixties. She looked twenty years younger, courtesy of good genes and exceptionally discreet plastic surgery.

"Hello, Eleanor," I said. "Nice to see you, too."

"Oh, don't be impertinent."

A black woman sat near Paget. She was well dressed and about the same age, but without the same easy access to plastic surgery.

"Do you have any idea how many times I've tried to contact you, Mr. Snow?" Paget said, glaring at me. "Any idea at all?"

"Maybe you heard about my legal trials and tribulations?" I said.

"Oh, who cares!" she barked. "Yesterday's news, not even worthy of fishwrap!"

"Calm down, Eleanor," the black woman said.

"Don't tell me to calm down!" Paget barked. "Who are you to tell me to calm down!"

The black woman forced a smile, then said, "I should get back to the office."

"Yes!" Paget screeched. "Get back to the office! Do something that I actually pay you to do!"

The black woman gave me a sheepish look. "You'll excuse me."

She made for the door of the study. Paget rose quickly from her throne and clicked on dangerously high black stilettos across the marble floor, reaching the woman at the door. The two talked in low voices for a moment. Then the black woman gently blotted the trail of tears on Eleanor Paget's cheeks with a tissue and left.

"Rosey," Paget said to no one in particular. "Rose Mayfield. She's—maybe you remember from . . ."

I did.

Paget shook herself out of her momentary stupor and made her way back to her awaiting burgundy leather wingback throne. She sat and crossed her long, smooth legs. Plastic surgeons could do a lot with the human body, but they were limited when it came to legs. Eleanor Paget's legs were original high-end equipment.

Paget recaptured me in her icy glare, drew in a sharp breath and said, "How much would you care to wager my concerns trump your inconsequential public hanging?"

Without embarrassment or gentlemanly aversion of my eyes, I looked at her legs for a good two seconds. It was the type of attention Paget liked. "You've been working out, Eleanor," I said. "You look good."

"Don't play the swarthy Hispanic with me, Mr. Snow," she snapped. "Do you have any idea of the effort I've expended to reach you?"

I'd never been referred to as a "swarthy Hispanic." I wasn't quite sure if I should feel insulted, complimented or simply laugh. "I've been out of town," I said.

A young Mexican woman dressed in servitude white brought my coffee and carefully set it on the small coffee table between Paget and me. The girl—eighteen, maybe nineteen—asked in a soft voice if "madam" would like anything. Paget waved her off.

Before disappearing, the brown-skinned girl gave me a furtive glance, hoping to quickly categorize me as either a "friendly" or a threat to her immigration status.

I lifted my cup of coffee to her and quietly said, "Thank you."

"You're very welcome, sir," the young girl said. Then she made a nearly imperceptible bow to Paget before leaving the study. "Still making people bow to you, Eleanor?" I said after a sip of the coffee. "Isn't that a little antiquated?"

"It always amazes me how people these days categorize civility, decency and respect for social status as 'antiquated,'" she said, still holding me in an unblinking blue-eyed gaze. I was sure any minute I would be turned to a pillar of salt. "To the point," she continued, "I need you to look into something of a delicate matter."

"I'm not a cop anymore, Eleanor," I said. "I'm not even a licensed private investigator. I'm just José Public now."

"I need your help!" she suddenly shrieked, slamming a slender and well-manicured hand down on an arm of her chair. She snapped her mouth shut, drew in a ragged breath and cast her now wet eyes toward a bank of windows that gave expansive views of a green, rolling acreage. Her silence carried a critical atomic weight.

"Do you have any idea—any inkling—how long it took to build all of this?" she finally said. "This empire? Almost one hundred years of hard work. I am the empire now, Mr. Snow. I will not under any circumstances have it taken from me. And I need your . . . help."

Eleanor Paget's business was a private wealth management and investment bank, Titan Investment Securities Group. Her wealthy, erudite great-grandfather had started it in the late 1800s in the heart of Detroit's then-prosperous business district. And it was the bank her now-deceased husband had embezzled from before killing his sixteen-year-old mistress and himself at a riverfront condominium.

The murder/suicide was how I'd first met Eleanor Paget.

Paget spoke to me haltingly about something being "wrong" at the bank. She could feel it; an elaborate maze of obfuscation keeping her from the truth. Board members once opened veins for her. Now they were hushed, insular, evasive. Her new, young, hand-picked chief executive officer Joseph Dylan "Kip" Atchison had once kowtowed to her every wish. Now he was laughingly dismissive of her concerns. Her indomitable command of the business and all who served it had been eroded by a force beyond her influence. An amorphous, shadow command. Something that was quickly and quietly rendering her inconsequential. She wanted me to investigate her bank and the people who had walled themselves in and her out.

"Of course, I'll pay you," she said, as if the mention of money was somehow beneath her stature. "Whatever your price, it will be paid."

I asked her a few questions: Did she have any current bank records at the house? Did she have remote computer access to the bank's accounting system? Were there any staff in particular she had suspicions about? Any customers or accounts raising red flags? Were there any current or pending state or federal bank regulation inquiries or investigations?

She brusquely answered each question: "Yes," "No," "Of course," "How the hell should I know, you stupid man?"

I reminded her that I was no longer on the force.

"How hard can it be to get a private investigator's license?" she said. "Surely anyone who is ambulatory, has citizenship and a GED can get one." She paused and a look came across her face. "My God. You *do* have citizenship and a GED, I presume?"

"Been over the border and out of the cotton fields for about as long as you've been off the *Mayflower*, Eleanor. *And* I'm armed with a sociology degree from Wayne State."

A look of relief washed across her face.

I said I'd talk to a few people I trusted for their expertise and discretion, but beyond that there was little I could do.

Paget's clear blue eyes began filling with tears. Her expertly painted bottom lip trembled. She quickly wiped her tears away, took in a sharp breath and said in a low, hoarse voice, "It appears I was wrong about you, Mr. Snow. I thought you had more spine than those pimps dressed as policemen in Detroit." She stood, looked down at me and said, "Thomas will show you out. Goodbye and good riddance, Mr. Snow."

"I'll get back to you with several names," I said.

"Don't bother."

I offered my hand. She didn't take it. Instead, she walked quickly out of the room.

Classic Eleanor Paget.

6

Tomás met me in the foyer of Paget's house.

"How'd it go?" he whispered.

"Let's just say I don't think I'll be getting an invitation to her Detroit Institute of Arts spring fundraiser," I said.

"Thank God," Tomás said. "Then I'd have to serve your ass *and* the Aryan Nation." As I suppressed a laugh, Tomás said, "You want me to roll down your street after I leave here?"

Tomás was referring to Markham, my street in Mexicantown—the one he'd been patrolling in my absence. A bit of free advice: when someone like Tomás says "roll down the street," it's best to take cover—especially if you have villainy in your heart.

"I'm back and I'm strapped," I said. "My street, my concern."

Tomás nodded. "Don't forget to drop by the house. Elena will have both our asses if she finds out I've seen you and she hasn't."

"How's she gonna find out?"

Tomás laughed. "Wow. You young bucks really are stupid. Women are like their own little NSA listening outposts. Especially Elena."

In Mexicantown, I would have driven past at least ten shoulder-to-shoulder brick or clapboard row houses, several vegetable gardens, a dilapidated convenience store and a small Mexican restaurant in the time it took me to drive from Eleanor Paget's house to the security gatehouse at the entrance to her property.

All I wanted to do was get a burrito and beer, then head back to my house and figure out what to do to make it into some sort of home, however temporary that might be. To hell with Eleanor Paget and the hardships of a life lived in the economic stratosphere. I still had to breathe the pollution wafting in from I-75 South and idling freight trucks waiting for egress to the US or Canada.

Sorry, Dad.

I tried living the chivalrous life you wanted me to back when I was a Detroit cop. And we know how that turned out.

Even so, I'd be lying if I said my cop curiosity hadn't kicked in. As I neared the gate, I pulled to the side of the drive, parked and got out.

"May I help you, sir?" the young security guard said, emerging from the gatehouse.

"Ranger, right?" I said offering my hand. "Mountain Division?"

He took my hand and shook it. His easygoing smile disappeared and his eyes narrowed at me. He repeated, "May I help you, sir?"

"Marine," I said of myself. "Sniper."

The guard quickly sized me up. "Hoo-ra," he said. His name was Frank.

Without going into details, I gave Frank a few inglorious highlights of my visit with Eleanor Paget. I told him that I used to be a cop and he said he knew who I was. I was curious about the estate's security and if Paget had had any recent visitors who raised suspicions. Before I could say anything else, Frank casually rested his hand on the grip of his .32 and was on the phone to the main house.

"Yessir, Mr. Gutierrez," Frank said while keeping me locked in his eyes. "Frank on the perch. Just calling to make sure everything's all right in the nest. I have Mr. August Snow here asking questions about our security matrix. Allow and inform or disallow and notify?" I'm sure Tomás was barely holding it together as he answered Frank. "Yessir. Thank you."

Frank moved his hand away from his .32.

"You got fucked," Frank said, referring to my DPD lawsuit and trial. "Pardon me for putting it that way, man—sir."

Then he gave me the lowdown.

Any visitors who weren't on the standard approved list got cursory background checks.

Goddamn Google.

Frank, who was maybe four years younger than me, told me every visitor to the estate was either automatically logged by a pre-approved keycard issued by Eleanor Paget or entered manually by himself or any other on-duty guard from Digital Defense Home Security. The guards—usually the same two—traded shifts, working Monday through Saturday. Sunday, only pre-approved keycards were allowed access. Any pre-approved keycard could be locked out by Paget at any time for any reason. Two clicks on a laptop and you were rendered persona non grata.

"A chimp could do this fucking job," Frank said. "At least I mostly get to sit inside and do school work. Six months more and I've got an associate business administration degree."

"What's Digital Defense like?" I asked.

Frank shrugged. "Corporate types. Bean counters mostly. Some of the guys—on-site guys like me—they're really into it. Gung ho discharges looking for work. Something they can put their skills to. Other than that it's just migrant work—no offense."

I smiled and said, "None taken."

While we talked, a black BMW edged up to the wrought iron gate. An arm fit with an expensive suit sleeve and monogrammed shirt cuff reached out, the hand waved a keycard at the discreetly positioned electronic reader and the gate cranked opened.

Frank waved at the car as it drove by.

"Aaron Spiegelman," Frank said. "Chief financial officer and president of the board. Self-important, whiny little prick."

I asked Frank about security cameras on the property. Hesitantly he said there were eight. That jibed with what I'd seen on my way up to the house. The cameras recorded 24-7 to four hard discs located in the guard house. Simultaneously the video feeds were downloaded to servers located at Digital Defense's offices in Birmingham, Michigan, fifteen miles away. The only downtime was every second Wednesday or Friday night—kept purposely random—when the recordings were reviewed at the main office and, pending any anomalies, wiped clean in preparation for the next week's recording period.

"Any surveillance in the house?" I asked.

"Don't have a clue. Never been up to the big house. Somehow I doubt it, knowing what an absolute hellhound the old bitch is about her privacy." Frank took a moment to assess me again. Then, quietly reassured, he continued, "It's a little fast and loose with the surveillance cameras. Old equipment. After two years of watching cars drive in and out, leaves falling, snow piling up, grass growing, the lawn getting cut and weeds getting whacked, nobody much cares about maintaining or upgrading the equipment. The guys who review the recordings at home office? Mostly baked. Basic training washouts or tech geek weenies working on their résumés. Black Tree didn't put any money into the system after they bought Digital Defense. Word at HQ is Black Tree's trying to dump the company."

Finally, I asked Frank if our conversation was currently under surveillance.

"Yeah," he said with a nonchalant shrug. "But, I mean, unless you all of a sudden pull out your pecker and I have to shoot it off, this'll get fast-forwarded and deleted at home office."

I told Frank I appreciated his time and his candor.

"Stay vigilant," I said. "Eleanor Paget may be mean as a snake, but like anybody else she deserves to feel safe."

"I do my job. A hundred percent," Frank said. "But I gotta be honest—for minimum wage and healthcare that wouldn't cover the cost of a Band-Aid, I got nothing invested here. I got Wi-Fi in the guard house and most days I just do class work. Six more months and I'm gone. Fuck it."

"Stay strong, Army," I said.

"*Semper fi*, Marine."

On the way back into Detroit proper I made a couple calls to people who were surprised to hear my voice. People I gambled might still be willing to talk to me. The first person I called was a former cop buddy who had since gone private.

"Jesus, August," my former friend said. "Guys find out I'm talkin' to you and there go my contacts at the Fourteenth. Sorry, man, but that's just the way it is."

Another former cop buddy said he'd be glad to look into things, but his doctor had advised against any stressful endeavors. In the time I had been out of the country, he had requested a transfer from his Major Crimes detective sergeant's desk to heading the department's motor pool.

"Transfer saved my life, August," he said. "And my marriage. Not as much money, but I'm down to just three meds a day."

The third told me to fuck off and never, ever call again or else my balls would be in a blender.

Ex-girlfriends.

What are you gonna do, right?

By the time I found myself in the shadow of the GM Renaissance Center, I was hungry. I would try to get a hold of Skittles later. I'd worked with him on locating and recovering Eleanor Paget's embezzled money two years earlier. I'd never met Skittles in person. And unless he called you, contact was nearly impossible. But I had my ways.

I've been to Mexico.

And I've been to Southern California and Texas.

But unless you've taken the Bagley Avenue exit off of I-75 South to Detroit's Mexicantown, you really haven't had good Mexican food.

I took the exit and hoped whoever was following me in the black Chevy Suburban was hungry, too.

I parked behind one of my old haunts, Xochimilco, went in and was seated almost immediately at a small, round table near a faux stained-glass window portrait of Pancho Villa. A petite, full-figured brown-skinned girl with a smile that made me feel instantly buoyant took my order.

Near the front entrance, the hostess held a large black flower-pot overflowing with bright marigolds. She was animated as she spoke to the restaurant's slick-haired manager, who stood with his arms tightly folded across his chest. His dark eyebrows were furrowed and he nodded, his eyes keenly following the hostess's pointing finger. I imagined they were discussing where to put the various pots of marigolds they'd ordered for the Día de los Muertos celebrations.

While I waited for my food and whoever had followed me—presumably government types considering the vehicle and the strict adherence to speed limits and use of turning signals—I thought about Eleanor Paget.

I had been the lead investigator on the murder/suicide that took her husband's life and the life of his sixteen-year-old prostitute. There was really little to investigate save for how much money he'd embezzled and where it had gone. Fifteen million could certainly buy a lot of booze, Viagra and Oxycodone, but I'd been doubtful those were the only expenditures.

Eleanor Paget cared less about her husband and his perverse infidelity with a sixteen-year-old child. She cared infinitely more about where the embezzled money was, and about her reputation and that of the bank. In fact, she saw no distinction between those two reputations.

For a short period, Paget thought she was running the investigation. She went as far as to tell the Grosse Pointe Police, Detroit's former mayor, the Detroit Police commissioner and my captain that she was in charge. Which meant she'd click a stopwatch and we, like mostly black Keystone Cops, should run in any direction she pointed.

It took a while and a few interesting closed-door meetings, but finally Eleanor Paget—at my insistence—backed down.

Through a few legitimate and questionable contacts I'd cultivated, I found Paget's money. At least, what her husband hadn't pissed away on expensive getaways, suites at four-star hotels in Miami and Manhattan, jewelry and clothing for his teenage mistress. And, of course, booze, Viagra and Oxycodone.

Finding the remains of Paget's embezzled money made me a star in her steel-blue eyes. Aside from that, I suspected I was one of very few people who had in no uncertain terms told her to sit down and shut the fuck up. Begrudging respect is better than no respect.

My steak burrito arrived well-seasoned and resplendent with gooey cheese. The aroma was enough to welcome me back to the 'hood.

"*Delicioso*," I told the waitress, spreading my hands appreciatively over the generous plate of hot food. I asked for another Negra Modelo. The waitress smiled and left in pursuit of my second beer.

I was about a third of the way through my burrito and halfway through my second Negra Modelo when a short, athletically built blonde woman dressed in a nondescript two-piece blue wool pants suit with white blouse pulled out the chair opposite me and sat down.

"Mind?" she said.

I gave a welcoming motion to the seat she'd already laid claim to.

The woman—maybe in her early-thirties, like me, and purposely plain, save for piercing blue eyes—tactfully showed me a badge and photo ID: FBI Special Agent Megan O'Donnell, Detroit Field Office.

"Don't remember you from my trial or the Fed's investigation into the DPD," I said. "New in town?"

"Ten months," FBI Special Agent Megan O'Donnell replied curtly. "Missed all the excitement. I assume everything went well since you're cavalierly breaking speed limits?"

I shrugged, cut a small bit of my burrito with the edge of my fork and stabbed it. I held it up for a moment and said, "You ever have the steak burritos here, Special Agent O'Donnell? They're really quite good."

"I prefer Mexican Village. Or Armando's." Two other tremendous Mexican restaurants within a stone's throw. "Something about their margaritas."

"How may I help the FBI today?" I took the small bit of burrito from my fork and tried to figure out why official types always seemed to interrupt my breakfasts, lunches and dinners.

"You just met with Eleanor Paget at her home in Grosse Pointe Estates, 3652 Colfer Pines Drive," Special Agent O'Donnell said. "Mind if I ask why?"

"Mind if I ask why you're asking why?" I took another bite of my burrito. Official types hate it when you continue eating in their presence. Makes them feel not quite as intimidating as they hoped they were. Frankly, they rarely ever are.

"I'm sorry," O'Donnell said with a forced laugh. "Maybe I was unclear. See, I'm FBI and you're . . ."

"The guy who pays your fucking salary, blondie, through a very unfair and Byzantine tax structure," I replied.

O'Donnell sighed. I found myself waiting to see small cracks form in her façade. There weren't any. After a moment, she made a failed attempt at a smile and said, "Let me start over."

"Sure," I said brightly. "Always ready to start over with a beautiful lady."

She seemed unfazed by my charm.

"I would really like to know what you and Mrs. Paget talked about, Mr. Snow. I could, of course, compel you to tell me, but I'd rather we simply had a nice chat. Professional to professional."

"I have no idea what I'm 'professional' at these days," I said. "Aside from drinking." I finished my burrito and second beer at about the same time and sat back in my chair. "To begin with, Special

Agent O'Donnell, I believe Eleanor Paget prefers 'Ms.' or 'Miss' or 'Omnipotent Galactic Tsarina' to 'Mrs.' We talked about her bank. She believes it's being tampered with. She wanted to hire me to investigate the matter, but I informed her I was no longer a member of the Detroit Police Department and neither was I a licensed private investigator and as such any investigation on my part could possibly lead to local, state and federal violations. She graciously thanked me and we parted on mutually respectful terms."

O'Donnell's steel-blue eyes bore into me for a few seconds, then she said, "Paget has never thanked a soul for anything in her life. And she probably ended the discussion by telling you to go fuck yourself."

"Language, Special Agent O'Donnell," I said, feigning shock.

"And the rent-a-cop?" she said. "Wha'd you gentlemen talk about?"

"Our time in the service, him being army, me being a marine," I said. O'Donnell's softball interrogation wasn't helping me push down any guilt I was feeling, courtesy of my father, for having walked away from someone in need. Like them or not. "You serve, O'Donnell? Or maybe you're just some pink-ass Princeton Criminal Justice sorority chick who thinks the FBI is a nice first step to that cushy DOJ appointment."

"Marine," O'Donnell said. "Turkey, Afghanistan and a one-off in Venezuela. Logistics, then Intelligence. First job was getting jarheads the equipment they needed to do their job. Second job was getting rifle-jockeys like you the information you needed to put the enemy in the cross hairs and pull the trigger."

"Anybody ever tell you how absolutely sexy you are when you talk like that?" Rattling O'Donnell's cage for information as to why the FBI had an interest in Eleanor Paget was proving difficult.

"Plenty of times," she said, unamused. "And I've killed 'em all. Now, then. The security guard. What else did you brothers-in-arms discuss?"

"Perimeter security. House security. Recent visitors. Who has gate access cards. And if he'd noticed anything unusual in the past month or so, to which the answer was no." Then I said, "You should give him a holler. Seems the FBI type: Pure of heart, poster boy good looks, gung ho, not all that bright. Plus he could use the health insurance."

"I'll send him an application," O'Donnell said.

I was pretty sure she wasn't going to send him an application.

"Your turn," I said. "What's your interest?"

O'Donnell stood, smoothed out her wool jacket, flipped a business card on the table and said, "You have yourself a nice day, Mr. Snow. Next time, try the Pueblo Platter at Mexican Village. Or the margaritas at Armando's. *Muy delicioso*."

"From anyone else's lips," I said, "the attempt at Spanish would have sounded hilariously patronizing. From yours—honey in the cup of my ear."

O'Donnell stared at me, shook her head and said, "Jesus."

Then she walked out.

I settled the bill, leaving the round, angelic waitress stunned at the five hundred percent tip. I just hoped she wouldn't Tweet, Instagram or Facebook about it.

I sat at the table beneath the stained-glass likeness of Pancho Villa for another ten minutes, pissed at my curiosity and ego for having let the FBI follow me to dinner.

Then again, losing O'Donnell on 275-South would have resulted in my missing out on a really good steak burrito, a couple superior quality Mexican beers and an interesting, if softball, interrogation.

7

Less than a week back in Detroit and I was already on an FBI watch-list.

Probably another reason people were reluctant to visit Detroit.

On my way home, I thought about Oslo and Tatina. How beautiful she was. How wise she was for someone in her early thirties. Then again where she came from, wisdom was a twelve-year-old boy with an AK-47 knowing when to pull the trigger and when not to. Wisdom was an eight-year-old girl knowing how to evade gang rape in a land where rape was public policy. Wisdom was a German medical doctor knowing when to get his Somali wife and mixed children out of a country hell-bent on eating itself alive.

By comparison having an impromptu Mexicantown dinner with a petite blonde FBI agent was a mid-summer stroll through Belle Isle's botanical gardens.

As much as I'd left Norway for fear of falling in love, I'd also come home because of the magnetic draw of Detroit. I missed my parents, good people who had given me all that I had. Who would visit their graves? Who was left to pray the rosary over them as they lay resolutely silent beneath the earth? And who would be there to raise chilled shot glasses of tequila to them when Mexicantown pulled out all the stops on November 2, Día de los Muertos?

"We're not defined by the laws we swear to uphold or the

people we save in the performance of our duties," my father told me at my graduation from the academy. "We're defined by the people we lose. The ones we maybe could have helped but didn't. In this job, that's in your future, son. And when it comes, your mom and me'll be there for you."

That future had come once too often and in ways that shattered my core.

And my parents had been there for me.

When I arrived back in my Mexicantown neighborhood, it was dark and a fall chill was in the air. The new streetlamps were shining brightly. Enough so that I could see two cars parked in the small space of shadows between the streetlamp cones of light. One car was facing east, the other west. A young black man dressed in baggy Adidas sweats and a PellePelle leather coat too big for him was leaning on the latter, talking to the driver.

I turned my headlights off and parked the car a half block away from my house.

Then I checked my Glock. Full clip, one in the snout.

Just as I got out of my car, the neighbor across the street emerged from his house carrying a baseball bat. With a thick Mexican accent, he hollered to the man standing by the car, "What are you doing here? There are children here! Go away!"

The black man standing by the car turned to look at the Mexican man on the porch.

Then he pulled a gun.

Before he could raise and level the weapon, I had my Glock pressed against his temple. The tires of the other car squealed and screamed off into the darkening fall evening.

"Nice night to be somewhere else, isn't it, asshole?" I said.

The young man began trembling. He shifted his eyes to get a look at me, but it was obvious he didn't want to move too much for fear of having his head explode clean off his shoulders.

"Yes, sir," the young man said.

I turned my attention to the Mexican man standing on his front porch with the baseball bat.

"My name's August Octavio Snow, sir," I said to the man on the front porch. "I'm your neighbor across the street."

"Carlos," the man said.

"Nice to meet you, Carlos," I said, still pressing the barrel of my gun against the young man's temple. "It's pretty cold out tonight. Why don't you go inside and get warm. Tell your family everything's all right because it is, okay?"

After a moment, Carlos nodded and went back inside his house, but he stood by the darkened living room window watching me and the young drug dealer.

I turned my attention back to the young black man. "Now, then, what's your name?"

"Jimmy," the trembling young man said. "Jimmy Radmon."

"You sellin' drugs, Jimmy Radmon?"

"Yes, sir."

"Well, not anymore. At least not around here." Then I said, "What are you? Seventeen? Eighteen?"

"Eighteen, sir."

"Eighteen's too young to die, wouldn't you agree?"

"Yes, sir," Jimmy Radmon said. He swallowed hard. "Too young to die."

"Tell you what, Jimmy Radmon." I eased the gun out of his hand. It was an old, battered .32 and light, probably no bullets. "You seem like a smart kid. So here's the deal: you come around here again selling drugs, I'll kill ya. Then I'll toss your dead body in an abandoned house two blocks over and let the rats feast off your corpse. How are you with a paintbrush and power tools?"

Confused, Jimmy Radmon turned his head to finally get a full look at me and the gun that had been pressed against his temple. "What?"

"Simple question: You any good with a paintbrush and power tools?"

"I—yeah—I done some work," he said nervously.

"What's your rate?"

"My what?"

"Your rate," I repeated. "How much you charge an hour?"

"Man, I'm 'bout to shit my mothafuckin' pants and you askin' how much I charge an hour?" he said. "Brotha, I be chargin' whatever you willin' to pay."

"Good," I said stowing both guns away. "Now empty your pockets."

He did: three dime bags of marijuana, couple baggies of coke, couple baggies of crystal meth. All of it now at his feet.

"You're not very good at selling drugs, are you, Jimmy Radmon," I said looking at his car, a rusted-out 1998 Pontiac piece-of-shit.

"Second time out," he said, lowering his head in shame.

"*Last* time out," I said. "You a corner boy?"

"A what?"

"You answer to anybody?"

"No, sir," he said. "Just tryin' to get over's all. Ain't nothin' for niggahs in Detroit."

I took him by his upper right arm and walked him to the middle of the street underneath a streetlamp. Then I shouted, "Hello, Markham Street neighbors and friends! My name is August Octavio Snow and I live at 2324 Markham! I'd like your attention just for a moment!" A few lights came on. A few curtains parted. A door or two cracked open. After a minute or so, Carmela and Sylvia stepped out onto their porch. Four others followed.

"Everybody," I said, "this is Jimmy Radmon."

Carmela waved and said, "Hello, Jimmy."

"Jimmy was going to sell drugs in the neighborhood. I've convinced him to follow another, more promising career path. In a couple days, Mr. Radmon will be painting a few rooms in my house and maybe doing some repair work. If he's any good, I'd like for you to give him a chance. If he sucks, let's just say you won't have to pay his bill. Thanks, everybody. Enjoy your evening."

"Can Mr. Radmon take a look at our water heater?"

It was Carmela again.

I looked at Jimmy Radmon and said, "You know anything about water heaters?" He nodded. "Well, Jesus, don't just stand there—go take a look at it." I pushed him toward Carmela and Sylvia's house. "And remember: I know places where your body would never be found, Jimmy Radmon."

"How much do I charge?" he whispered back to me.

"Don't worry about that," I said. "I'll cover you on this one. A hundred if you fuck it up. Three hundred you set the ladies' water heater right and leave them wanting to feed you milk and cookies. Stay away from their brownies. Come back to my house in two days. We'll talk about the other houses around here that could use work."

He took a few more steps toward Carmela and Sylvia's house before stopping. He half turned to me and in a low, shaky voice said, "Thanks, man."

I spent the next couple days unpacking bags and boxes and sifting through the storage unit I'd rented before leaving on my post-trial international drinking binge. I bought a few pieces of furniture for the house, starting with one of those high-tech select-your-number beds. I added a forest-green leather sofa, a large flat screen TV (what's a home without ESPN in hi-def?) and a nice sound system so I could listen to some of my mom and dad's old CDs and 101.9FM, Detroit's NPR affiliate. Rounding out things, I brought in a few pieces of my old life to make the place feel a little bit more like home: my dad's Arts and Crafts paddle-armrest chair and some of my mother's art.

The former drug dealer Jimmy Radmon had managed to fix Carmela and Sylvia's water heater and I paid him three hundred cash. He said they had more work for him—which I couldn't imagine since I'd already completely renovated the house before flipping it.

"Don't look at me, man," Radmon said with a big, theatrical shrug. "They don't like the kitchen cabinets and they want me to install new ones they done bought."

I laid another couple C-notes on top of the ones in his hand and grumbled, "Those are nice cabinets I had installed, goddammit. There's nothing wrong with those cabinets."

"They women, man," Radmon said. "Old, but still women."

Soon after he left, I made a run to a place in the southern, most-decayed industrial corner of Mexicantown, a building that had once been a shipping and receiving warehouse. The building—cryptically named Rocking Horse—was now mostly revitalized, a small miracle achieved by an influx of artists. Three floors of open-concept artist studios, meeting rooms and make-shift coffee bar and kitchen. Against all odds, the Rocking Horse building was mostly resurrected from the dead, brick by brick, wire by wire. Young painters and sculptors, photographers and guerrilla filmmakers, all at great personal risk, reclaimed the corpse of the building. They battled the rats and swept up the used needles, the shattered brown bottles, the empty malt liquor cans, the vomit and shit, both human and animal.

When I had worked Eleanor Paget's husband's murder/suicide, Rocking Horse is where I'd originally gotten in contact with Skittles. He was considered something of a hacker legend. The Banksy of black hat computing.

I was greeted at Rocking Horse by a young, white, pudgy hippy-wannabe guy with a patchy black beard meticulously making a cup of coffee at the studio's makeshift coffee bar.

"You here for the Kresge thing?" the tubby barista said, a grin peeking through his unkempt beard.

"No," I said. "I need to talk to Skittles."

The bearded barista wasn't very practiced at lying; his eyes widened, he shifted nervously and his furry lower lip quivered. It was oddly refreshing to see such innocence. "Who?"

"Just tell him we need to talk," I said smiling at the man. "Pronto, mi amigo."

Inadvertently, the man nodded.

I left.

Saturday afternoon, I went to the Boll Family YMCA downtown on Broadway. This was a YMCA no one could have imagined ten years earlier, especially in the heart of the city: bright, sleek and spacious, everything the northern suburban private health clubs wanted to be save for diverse and socially responsible. I'd joined soon after returning to the city.

Of course, I was old-school Y and the variety of New Age weight equipment initially confused and angered me. When did weight-training equipment start looking like the torture machines of the Spanish Inquisition?

I was standing in front of a piece of machinery called a deltoid catalytic isometer and trying to figure out just what the hell it was. There were illustrations on the side of the machine showing how to use it. I imagined the illustrations were done by the same half-wit who did instruction manuals for Ikea.

A tall, well-toned, tanned and impossibly vivacious white brunette wearing an array of expensive and revealing spandex offered to help me figure out the machine.

"Frankly," she said slowly, assessing me from head to toe, "I don't think you need the DCI. Your delts look pretty—you know — developed. If you don't mind my saying."

"Thank you," I said. "Your delts are nicely developed, too. So what's your favorite workout?"

After a wheatgrass and apple smoothie that seriously tested my gag reflex, the brunette—a web and mobile apps security customer relations manager named Beka

Something-or-Other—invited me back to her apartment on Woodward Avenue in the redeveloped Midtown area to show me her favorite workout, which involved a lot of pelvic thrusts, squats and lifts. Primal hunger without a modicum of emotional connection. Occasionally during our workout I thought about a dark-skinned woman I'd known in Oslo.

This was nothing like Oslo.

This was a welcome distraction. An escape from myself.

Afterwards I went back to my house, showered and thought some more about Oslo beneath the jets of hot water. Then, in an effort to feel at least partially grounded, I brewed a pot of rich black coffee in my folks' old percolator.

Later that evening my phone rang, but it wasn't my regular ringtone. It was the Four Tops classic *Reach Out.*

I answered it.

"Yo-yo, Snowman," Skittles said brightly. "How's the land of the living and the dead treatin' ya, bro? And you like that upgrade?"

"What upgrade?"

Apparently for sport Skittles had tracked my travels abroad. Amazing the information one credit card can provide. Finding that after a year away I'd booked a flight back to Detroit from Oslo, Skittles had upgraded me to first-class flight accommodations on Delta. Naively, I thought the upgrade was simply a credit card reward.

"Bring me anything from Mumbai, Bruges or Oslo?" he said.

"Smiles and memories."

"Damn," he said.

"I didn't exactly leave here to go on a shopping spree, Skittles," I said. "That being said, I may have something nice for you."

I told him what I needed and how much I'd pay, including his usual required perk: a Costco-sized box of the actual Skittles candy. He seemed genuinely excited, not necessarily at the prospect of hacking into Titan Investment Securities Group's computer system—that was something he could have done after sucking down a bowl of Cambodian hash. No, it was the prospect of actually being paid cash in addition to a few weeks' worth of Skittles candy.

"Thanks for taking the job," I finally said. "Not many people willing to reconnect with me these days."

"You was always cool with me," he said. "Ain't about a thang, Snowman. Just remember: cash be kang. All other suckas can hit the bricks with they dicks in they fists."

"Wow," I said. "Hacker *and* poet. A real renaissance man."

Later, sitting on my new forest-green leather sofa, I looked through family photo albums: My mother and father picnicking on Belle Island. Vacationing in Traverse City and Alabama and south of Mexico City. Their wedding. Me as a baby with my dad's badge pinned to my onesie. Thanksgivings and Christmases. Day of the Dead celebrations in Mexicantown. High school and college graduations. My dad saluting me at my graduation from the academy.

Family albums go better with scotch.

Or a gun.

At around seven o'clock Sunday morning there was a succession of heavy knocks on my door. I did what any citizen of the City of Detroit would do after hearing a succession of knocks on their door at seven o'clock in the morning. I racked one in the barrel of my gun and looked through the narrow windows of my front door.

It was Ray Danbury.

Eleanor Paget was dead.

I felt my heart skip a beat. I fought the urge to make the sign of the cross, partially out of shock and partially out of guilt. I'd blown off a person's real concerns based on their social and financial stature.

Danbury was very interested in knowing where I had been Saturday night. I told him.

"That's it?" Danbury said. "No clubs, parties, orgies?"

"Nope."

"Damn. You 'bout the dullest millionaire I know."

"I'm the *only* millionaire you know." I peered over his shoulder. "Where's Cowling?"

"You kids don't play well together," Danbury said. "I drove myself."

I offered Danbury coffee, which he waved off. Looking around, he nodded his approval. "Needs a lady's loving touch. I'm all about that TV, though."

On the way downtown, I asked Danbury how Eleanor Paget had died. As he guided the unmarked cruiser through northbound I-75 traffic like a seasoned Formula One driver, he told me it had been a single GSW to the head. It looked like suicide, but since this was Eleanor Paget all the i's had to be dotted and the t's crossed.

"And the gun?" I said.

"Oh, you gonna love this," Danbury said. "Remember the gun her husband used to top himself and the girl? The gun I nearly got my ass in a sling for?"

I did. A nickel-plated limited edition Smith & Wesson .38 with a rosewood grip. Before I was able to confirm a suspicion, Danbury, under pressure from Eleanor Paget and her team of lawyers, had released the gun to the family. This was the shit bucket Danbury had alluded to at Schmear's Deli. The mess he didn't want any lawyer—defense or prosecution—poking around in at my trial.

"Same gun," Danbury said. "When I released it to Paget couple years ago, you know what she did?" Danbury paused for dramatic effect then said, "She had a display case made for it. Cherry wood with gold inlay. Italian marble base. Had it in a room off the library. Brass plate underneath. You know what the plate says? 'The Bastard's Last Gift.'"

Danbury exploded with laughter, then he shook his head and

said, "Yeah, buddy-buddy. The rich truly *are* different from you and me."

"I *am* one of the rich now," I said.

"Yeah," Danbury said. "But I know where yo high-yellow ass come from, so you can't be runnin' no bougie game with me, nigga."

8

Through the Wayne County Morgue's autopsy room speakers, master bluesman R.L. Burnside was singing ".44 Pistol."

Eleanor Paget's washed and naked body was laid out on a shimmering stainless steel autopsy table. Lying next to her on separate tables were the remains of three other former human beings patiently awaiting the medical examiner's professional attention.

On the ride downtown, Danbury said Paget's body was discovered in the library where we had met three days earlier. She was found by the young Hispanic woman who had served me coffee. The Grosse Pointe Police Department had followed standard procedure by begrudgingly calling the DPD for professional assistance.

"Most of her head's still there," Danbury said. We were in the viewing room just outside the morgue examination room waiting for Bobby Falconi. Danbury poured himself a cup of road tar coffee that had been cooking for a couple hours. He added three packets of sugar, a splash of cream, stirred with his thumb, then sucked the coffee from under his nail.

"Time?" I said.

"Falconi says late Saturday or early Sunday morning. He'll know more later."

".44 Pistol" was fading out and Robert Johnson's "Cross Road Blues" was fading up as Dr. James Robert Falconi, Wayne County Chief Medical Examiner, entered the viewing room wearing an impeccably ironed white lab coat. Bobby Falconi was a black man in his early fifties who looked twenty years younger. He shaved his head, which made him look all the more imposing, and he had a jagged one-inch scar over his left eye. He would tell you he got the scar in an ugly fight at a strip club on 8 Mile Road. Truth is he got it when a beaker in the Trace Lab exploded.

Bobby was the toughest looking nerd you'd ever meet.

He saw me, grabbed my hand and shook it enthusiastically. On the lapel of his lab coat was a large round pin that bore a photo of a pretty high school girl in cap and gown.

"Well, I'll be damned," he said grinning. "Long time, kiddo."

"Long time, Bobby," I said. I pointed to the photo button. "That can't be Miko, can it?"

"Sure is." Bobby proudly tapped a thick finger on the button. "Off to Julliard in a week. Full ride for viola and composition. You have no idea how weird it is to have a black child who thinks, 'Yeah, boy! Mozart, Brahms and Beethoven! Now *thems* ma *niggas!*'"

"She must get it from the missus," I teased.

Bobby laughed, then his eyes narrowed and he scanned me from head to toe. "Damn, August. Sorry what happened to you, man. Somebody had to take the fall for being honest in this city and, tag, you were it." Then he brightened. "So what brings you and Tubby McGlutton"—he nodded to Danbury—"to my Little Den of Decomp?"

"Eleanor Paget's body," Danbury said. "And don't be callin' me no 'Tubby McGlutton,' nay-gro."

"Oh, please, Ray," Bobby scolded. "You're twenty pounds overweight. You smoke two cigars a day. And I'm sure, like every other over-forty black man who just *has* to show how successful he is in Detroit, you probably have three Courvoisier and Cokes three times a week at the Pontch. Oh yeah, son, I got a cold storage drawer with your name on it." After eviscerating Danbury and taking a breath, Bobby said "Paget's pretty straight-up stuff: GSW to the right temple. Bullet followed an upward ten-degree trajectory and exited through the top right of her noggin. Only bit of weirdness was the force she used to press the barrel of the gun to her temple. Enough to cause pretty deep bruising. Then again, it's weirdness I've seen before. People really angry with themselves. Or some people feel a little more push commits them to the act."

"May I see the body?" I said.

Bobby made a grand gesture. "After you." I led the way toward the cold concrete and steel autopsy room.

There was a rumble of angry voices near the morgue entrance. The doors burst open and five men in suits tumbled in. The man in the lead was Detroit Police Chief Horace Renard, a tall, lean black man with round wire-rimmed glasses. He looked more professor than cop. Renard was followed quickly by Aaron Spiegelman—the man I'd seen enter Eleanor Paget's compound three days earlier as I was talking with Frank the security guard. The other suits carried the water for Renard and Spiegelman.

"This is an atrocity!" Spiegelman shouted.

"What would you have me do?" Chief Renard said calmly. "Grosse Pointe can't handle it. If anything we're honoring a long-standing professional agreement and performing a decades-long courtesy."

One of Spiegelman's lackeys blew his cookies at the sight of naked, dead and mangled bodies. On wobbly legs he staggered out of the room.

"Look at this place." Spiegelman pointed a quivering finger toward Eleanor Paget's body in the autopsy room. "Oh, my God! God! She's—*naked*!"

"That's generally how we do autopsies here," Bobby said to Spiegelman.

Chief Renard gave Bobby a look. Bobby shrugged, crossed his arms over his broad chest and leaned against a bank of body drawers.

"You've got her lying between—what?—a crack whore and some guy who probably got stabbed robbing a liquor store! This is unconscionable!" Then Spiegelman directed his rigid forefinger my way. "And *him*! What's *he* doing here?"

Chief Renard cut his eyes to Danbury. Danbury said, "Mr. Snow was one of the last people to see Paget alive. Thursday afternoon. I find a visit with the dead often shakes the truth out of the living. Once we're done with him, we'll be talking with you, Mr. Spiegelman."

I was about to speak in my own defense when Spiegelman shouted, "She killed herself! It was a *suicide*! Why does—why does anybody need to see her like this?"

"Your concern for her modesty is touching, Mr. Spiegelman," Chief Renard said. "But as I'm sure you know, any time a weapon is involved—suicide or not—we investigate. It's what the citizens who pay our salaries expect of us."

Spiegelman got chest-to-chest with Renard, looked up into Renard's wire-framed eyes and said, "I want her out of this horror show in the next twelve hours, Chief. If you don't meet that time frame, I will involve the bank's attorneys, Eleanor's personal attorney, the district attorney, the mayor, and city council. Am I understood?"

"Clearly," Renard said, seemingly impervious to Spiegelman's threat. "And if you would, please make yourself available for an interview within the next twelve hours, okay?"

Incredulous, Spiegelman caught the eye of a member of his entourage, an older man with a shock of white hair. The man nodded once. I assumed from this quick exchange the man with the white hair was Titan Investments Securities Group's general legal counsel. Spiegelman backed away from Renard, turned and walked out of the morgue with his remaining lackeys.

Renard sighed, lifted his glasses and rubbed his eyes with a thumb and forefinger. "Mr. Snow, under any other circumstance I would shake your hand and welcome you back to the city which wrongfully castigated you. However, in the prevailing situation

I would suggest you give a full statement to Captain Danbury which I will then read with interest and heightened scrutiny. After that, I would suggest you stay easily accessible for any further questioning."

"Absolutely," I said, forcing myself not to salute.

Renard turned his attention to Danbury. "Ray, this could get real ugly real fast. Do what you have to do to close this out quick and clean." Renard peered over the top of his glasses and in a low, calm and intimidating voice said, "And let's have ballistics do a *full* work up on that fucking gun this time, okay, Ray? No games, no politics, no bullshit, n'k?"

"Yessir," Danbury said.

I could feel the prickly heat of Danbury flushing from where I stood.

"Control the press on this thing," Renard concluded.

"Yessir. I'll put Cowling on point."

"And Bobby?" Renard said after heaving a heavy sigh. "Turn that creepy goddamn music off."

Bobby grinned and nodded.

After Renard left, we went into the autopsy room to observe Eleanor Paget's remains, although there was little to discuss except whether Bobby should run a GSR test—for gunshot residue—and a tox screen. The remaining bit of cop inside me surfaced and told Bobby he should run the tests; Danbury gave his cursory chain-of-command approval. It was difficult looking at Eleanor lying on a metal slab. Naked and eternally quiet. It was even harder to look at her and know that maybe I could have done something.

The dead were once again defining me.

9

The 14th Precinct was run out of a once-impressive late-1800s fieldstone mansion on what's known as the Woodward Spine. At one time the precinct was an urban showplace. A proud example of repurposing Detroit's unique architectural past for a promising future.

After decades of Detroit's economic misfortunes, missteps and mishaps—most tied to the dwindling fortunes of the automotive industry, a craven and inept political system and the willful abandonment of the poor and disadvantaged—the precinct started to fall into disrepair. I used to work out of the 14th. And even with the leaky ceilings, warped floors and cracked walls, I loved the place. It smelled like a history of French settlers, horse stables and hard-earned pride.

Now, with the recent opening of the department's new multi-million-dollar downtown headquarters and a rebalancing of the city's shaky spreadsheets, the 14th would soon be an abandoned stone husk.

I spent an hour in Ray Danbury's cramped, drafty office briefing him on the meeting I'd had with Eleanor Paget. He took meticulous notes, as he'd always done. The only point that pricked his ears and gave pause to his pen was my impromptu lunch with FBI Special Agent O'Donnell.

"FBI? No shit?"

"No shit."

"Damn," Danbury said, his eyebrows arching. "And you ain't been back but a minute."

About forty minutes in my phone rang. This time the ringtone was George Clinton and Parliament's "Give Up the Funk."

I asked Danbury if I could take the call. Slightly irritated, he said I could.

"You alone?" Skittles said in a low, conspiratorial voice.

"Yes," I said. "But never lonely."

"I been inside the belly of the beast, man—that Titan bank," Skittles said. "Five fuckin' hours in an amusement park."

"Listen," I said brightly. "Can you call me back in about thirty minutes? I'm right in the middle of something. So call me back and let me know which amusement park you went to." I disconnected. "My cousin Paolo," I said to Danbury, offering no other explanation for the call.

"Paolo?" Danbury said, his eyes narrowed. "I thought I'd met everybody in your family."

I gave a casual shrug and smiled. "You know us blacks and Mexicans. Always an aunt, uncle or cousin in the wood pile."

"'Paolo,'" Danbury said scratching his salt-and-pepper stubble chin. "Ain't that I-talian?"

The fact that one of my first reconnections in the city was with Skittles, a notorious hacker and social media prankster, was the one thing I would hold back from Danbury. And besides, I didn't know his real name, physical description or location, so why bother?

At the end of my interview, Danbury sat back in his chair, thoughtfully swiveling back and forth. The gears were whirling, but soon they would engage.

"That's it?" he said.

"That's it."

He held me in his hard gaze for a few seconds. "No hard feelings?"

I looked at the photos of his children, Marquis and Chantelle, from the gap-toothed innocence of elementary school to the joyful arrogance of college. And there were pictures of his wife, Yolanda, beautiful, smiling, content.

"No hard feelings," I said.

I stood and we shook hands.

Before releasing my hand, Danbury said, "Please don't forget—I know you, August. You like a damned pit bull: teeth sink in, jaws lock and you ain't satisfied until somebody's ass been chewed off. Eleanor Paget is lookin' like a suicide, pure and simple. Ain't nobody's ass needs chewin' off. And whatever guilt you might be feelin' over dead-ass Eleanor Paget ain't gonna put the bullet back in the chamber."

I offered a weak, unconvinced smile and nodded. "Do me a solid, Ray—"

"Oh, I'm supposed to do *you* a solid?"

"Check out a kid named Jimmy Radmon for me," I said. "Black, eighteen, about five ten, five eleven, maybe one forty."

"And I would do this for you—why?"

I shrugged. "Because you think I'm aces?"

Danbury exploded into laughter then told me to get the fuck out of his office.

Before leaving the station I walked back to the morgue. Bobby was in full autopsy gear, walking around the Y-cut open remains of Eleanor Paget and speaking into a digital tape recorder. In the background, Son House was singing "Death Letter Blues."

Bobby stopped recording his notes once he saw me.

"Mind if I don't shake your hand?" I said.

"Lightweight." Bobby took off his latex gloves, pitched them in a nearby medical waste container and gave me a stern look. "You know you're just a citizen now, right?"

"José Blow."

"And providing you with information on this or any other open

DPD case constitutes a serious ethical and legal violation of my sworn duties and responsibilities as the lead coroner for Wayne County."

"Yep."

"Okay," Bobby said smiling. "Glad we got that out of the way."

Bobby warned me a rush job like this might yield very little in the way of revelations. The hole in the top of her head was the obvious cause of death. And the weapon and the display case would likely bear her fingerprints and no others.

"Tell you the truth, August," Bobby said, "this'll probably be a twenty-minute job. Half-hour tops. Save for the lab work. Only question I have is who the hell was her plastic surgeon? Stem to stern, labia to boobs, cheekbones, eyes, hairline. Not that she needed it. Basic bone structure's uncompromised. Tits were mostly transmuscular. Kind of like a new paint job and rims on a cherry '67 Corvette."

"You've been in this job too long, Bobby," I said.

"Yeah, tell me about it."

"She didn't much like people," I said, looking at the quiet repose of her opened body on the steel table. "Frankly, I don't think she liked herself much. Maybe plastic surgery was her way to reshape herself into a person she could halfway tolerate."

Bobby said, "The fuck do I care? All I'm saying is when she opened the chute, she left a Class A chassis with some Grade A aftermarket parts."

"Wow. You are just one classy guy."

"That I am," Bobby said, grabbing my hand and shaking it. "And I think I got a little, you know, hippocampus on your jacket there."

I looked at the tiny glob of grey goo on the sleeve of my coat.

Bobby suddenly bellowed with laughter and said, "It's oatmeal, for crissakes!"

I flicked the glob of oatmeal from my sleeve to the floor, where it no doubt began mingling with a sluice of microscopic human debris.

Even though I knew he would, I admonished Bobby to be as thorough and discreet as possible when it came to Eleanor Paget. Bobby was well versed in the political value and inestimable power of discretion. Even in the bowels of the city morgue, the Lead Coroner for Wayne County had to tread lightly and with no small amount of stealth. Science was science. But politics often times trumped science.

Danbury had a young, fresh-faced patrolman drive me home, an olive-skinned Chaldean kid named Aswan, probably ten minutes out of the academy.

"You like bein' on the job?" I asked.

"Love bein' on the job," Aswan said. "A lot of the shop owners see me, a Chaldean, and they feel comfortable. Like they've got somebody on the inside that'll take care of 'em." He paused, shrugged, then said, "Then again, some of the older ones—especially the men—see me and think *Mukhabarat*."

Halfway back to Mexicantown I was, for whatever reason, given to thoughts of family dinners. Maybe it was Aswan's half-eaten lunch riding between us—a shawarma sandwich and a Styrofoam cup of sweet herbal tea.

I'd been raised primarily on Mexican food—homemade tortillas and enchiladas, chipotle-crusted pork chops and tamale pie with dill and cilantro cream sauce. My mother was an incredible cook and my father was eternally grateful for her expertise in the kitchen.

Of course, there were those few days in a month when she deferred to my father's Alabama homeboy tastes: fried chicken, ribs, collard greens, red beans and rice, coleslaw with chopped apples and raisins and red-skinned potato salad with too much yellow mustard. The three of us would sit at our small dining room table on the southwest side of Detroit, eat and laugh. My father would engage us with tales of his youth and his southern upbringing. My mother was an equally gifted storyteller, and she painted lush and colorful pictures of Zacatecas in the north of Mexico where she was born.

There were, of course, the occasional Chinese carryout or cold leftover dinners we each ate alone in separate and sullen rooms after my mom and dad had argued. Their arguments were few and far between—usually about money, my behavior or grades. They were usually quickly resolved, followed by passionate late-night and early-morning making up that tested the tensile strength of mattress springs while simultaneously scaring and amusing their young son down the hall.

Tonight, I felt like Chinese in a quiet room.

Once Aswan the Rookie dropped me off at home I went out and got some General Tso's, shrimp fried rice and wonton soup from one of the many hole-in-the-wall restaurants near Wayne State University. I was lying on my sofa by the fireplace and eating with chopsticks from the small collection of small white boxes when Skittles called.

"An *amusement park*, man!" Skittles said breathlessly. "Five hours in a damned *amusement park*!"

"Aren't you a little old for cotton candy and tea cup rides?" I said.

"No, see, man, you ain't gettin' it," Skittles said frantically. "An amusement park is an elaborately encrypted heuristic system set up to mask and protect a *real* system. It's got all the mechanisms and mechanics, bells and whistles of a real system. It tells you everything and it tells you nothing. It's a security maze set up for guys like me. But the further you hack in, the more complicated the rides and attractions. Any one of 'em could trigger a rabbit hole— a type of mirror program designed to move backwards through your forward steps, record them steps and obliterate any and every system you used to get in. Only brothas I ever seen use algorithms and encryptions this wicked be some Ukraine dudes that even the Ukraines don't even know about. Dude! I barely got out with my digital nuts!"

"You've dealt with these guys before?" I said.

"Run into 'em once or twice," Skittles said. "They operate out of the Ukraine, Slovenia or Latvia. At least used to. Was known as 'Protocol One.' Then 'The Determinant.' Started out like me—bunch of guys fuckin' around, hackin' for shits and giggles. Moved into hacktivism. Greenpeace and save the mothafuckin' whales kinda shit. Then something happened. Went dark for about a year. Then I'm seein' code from the Protocol One and Determinant days poppin' up all over the fuckin' place. Like it's lookin' for a place to nest and do some real damage. Server-to-server. An hour here, a week there. Worms, Trojans, really nasty malware, spoofed access and cloned security codes—all that shit. I ain't about no real damage, man. I'm a hacktivist, not an anarchist. I'll stir the pot but I ain't about to set the kitchen on fire."

I half understood what he had said, but wholly understood what he was feeling.

Fear.

"So, like, anyway," Skittles continued anxiously, "this Titan system's got traces of Protocol One and the Determinant all up inside it."

"Bottom-line it for me," I said. "In English."

"Bottom line is Titan's got more system than any small bank should ever have," Skittles said. "Rolling algorithm encryptions that maybe you'da seen at Lehman Brothers before the shit went globally bad." Skittles paused. I gave him a few seconds to calm down. Once his breathing settled, he said, "You know what happened when I ran this past a couple like-minded brothas in the Czech Republic? *They hung up on me!*"

"Gotta love the Information Age," I said.

"Bullshit," Skittles said. "Ain't no damned Information Age no more. That died on 9/11. Next day was the birth of the Infiltration Age, Snowman. This is some crazy, scary shit. What inna hell you got yourself into?"

I told him I didn't know.

I thanked Skittles and told him I'd leave his pay at Rocking Horse. Plus the usual two-week supply of Skittles candy. I said I'd also leave some fresh fruits and vegetables from Eastern Market because Man did not live by sugar alone.

"What are you?" he said. "My fuckin' mother?"

He said if I wanted him to go any further, the price was triple. No candy. No fruits or vegetables. Just go-bag cash.

Takes a lot to spook Skittles.

Takes a lot to spook me.

Guess we were both feeling a bit spooked.

10

I'd eaten very little of the Chinese. Being the child of parents who believed wasting food was a sin, I put the leftovers in my new refrigerator, confident it would make for a good, if slightly unorthodox, breakfast. Maybe a General Tso's omelet.

I stared at my new TV suspended over the living room fireplace and listened to Charles Barkley take a hot steaming dump on the Los Angeles Lakers and Kobe Bryant's legacy. Normally, I would have been doubled over laughing at anything that came out of Barkley's bombastic mouth. But I was thinking about Eleanor Paget—a woman who, by all indications and accounts, was a mean-spirited, greedy, dictatorial megalomaniac. Someone capable of turning numerous people to stone by virtue of a simple, unblinking blue-eyed stare.

While vilified and excoriated by many, Paget was equally revered by others: The Detroit Institute of Arts held her in the highest esteem for her multimillion dollar donations and exhibition sponsorships. Her wildly successful thousand-dollar-a-plate black-tie fundraisers and well-publicized speeches acted as a safeguard against anyone who dared think the two billion dollars in art and antiquities at the Detroit Institute of Arts was a quick-sale remedy to the city's mounting bankruptcy debts.

To Children's Hospital she was an angel of mercy for her gifts of money, purchases of state-of-the-art medical equipment and her full payment of hospital bills and funeral expenses for as many as forty children over the past five years. For whatever she may have been behind closed doors, she knew how to smile a Mother Teresa smile and embrace sick kids when the camera shutters clicked or video cameras rolled.

She was good at the theatrics of being magnanimous.

After the ugly and very public death of her husband and his underage paramour, Eleanor Paget needed good PR. Helping sick kids, battered women, an art museum and homeless Iraq and Afghan war vets helped to counteract not only the transgressions of her philandering husband but also the longstanding and very tangible animosity between those with money—who were few, mostly white and ensconced in suburbs like the Grosse Pointes—and those without money, mostly black and Hispanic, who had seen the open sore of Detroit fester year after year.

She was a sanitizing strip of gauze over the deep and bleeding lacerations inflicted by herself and her peers. Barons like her had mined their gold in the heart of a dark-skinned city, then left when the mines were played out.

Ten months after my investigation into her husband's murder/suicide, I'd been fighting for my professional life: Detective Sgt. August Octavio Snow v. Detroit Police Department and the Office of the Mayor. Through an intermediary, Eleanor Paget had offered to pay for a high-powered legal defense team out of Chicago to represent me. I'd declined.

Now she was on a slab in the city morgue with holes to her right temple and the top left of her head.

At nine o'clock I got a call.

"He's clean."

It was Ray Danbury.

"Who's clean?"

"Your boy—this LaJames Lewis Radmon you wanted me to

check out," Danbury said. "Couple minor traffic violations. No arrests, no warrants."

"Thanks, Ray."

"'And if you give yourself to the hungry/And satisfy the desire of the afflicted/Then your light will rise in darkness/And your gloom will become like midday,'" Danbury said. "Isaiah 58:10. Your daddy quoted that more than once at the end of the bible study group at the Fourteenth Precinct. This Radmon kid. He's your charity case, ain't he?"

"Dad was in a bible study group?"

"Lots I suspect you don't know 'bout your daddy," Danbury said, a strange wistfulness in his voice. "Lots I suspect you don't know 'bout me, either." He paused for a moment. Then, his voice normal again, Danbury said, "Anything else I can do for you? Shine your shoes? Pick up your dry-cleaning?"

"A deep-tissue massage might be nice," I said.

Danbury disconnected.

At 3:15 A.M. Monday I found myself awake with a cup of black coffee in my hand, thinking about how Eleanor Paget's death might define me.

My phone rang.

"You awake?"

It was Bobby Falconi from the Wayne County Coroner's Office.

"Seems I am," I said. "What's up?"

In the background I could hear Frank "Honeyboy" Patt's "Bloodstains on the Wall."

"I just finished Eleanor Paget's autopsy and got the labs back."

"And?"

"Yeah, well, it *looks* like suicide," Bobby said. "But there's a couple small things that don't add up, at least for me."

"Such as?"

"Such as she was a diabetic," Jack said. "Type One."

"So?"

"So why would a Type One diabetic take a low-dosage ACE inhibitor and an injection of Humulin, washed down with maybe two ounces of white wine—a Chardonnay—fifteen minutes to a half hour before shooting herself in the head?"

Some diabetics, Bobby explained, were prescribed ACE inhibitors to keep their kidneys healthy and their blood pressure under control. Humulin was simply regular-acting insulin.

"Does that sound like a suicidal?" Bobby concluded.

"What else?" I said.

"Hey, listen." Bobby sighed heavily before speaking again. "Maybe it's late—or early. But the GSR on her right hand? Looks like it was—I don't know—applied. Where you'd expect voids in patterning, there aren't any. I'd never swear to that on a witness stand, though. It's just too inconclusive."

I asked him if he was including this information in his official report.

"Yeah, of course," Bobby said. "You know the routine, August. But everything I've given you is just gonna look like standard stuff on a report. It's not what I put in the report. It's how it's interpreted. Any cross on a witness stand and my balls would be in my throat."

"Tech guys find anything at the scene?"

"Maggie from CSU says they were thorough," Bobby said. "Fingerprints from the house staff, Paget and a couple business associates. A few old, unreadable smudges on the display case the gun was in. Nothing missing. House safe was untouched with forty K in cash, some old bearer bonds, high-end jewelry and unremarkable documents inside. No indications of an intruder."

"You know if anybody called her daughter?" I asked.

"She's got a daughter?" Bobby said.

"Yeah," I said. "Vivian. Maybe in her mid-to-late twenties. I take it you don't know."

"Nope," Bobby said. "That's sad. She look anything like her mom?"

"Spittin' image."

"Well, I guess she's lucky in one respect."

I thanked Bobby and we hung up.

Everybody wanted Eleanor Paget in the ground as quickly as possible: The board of directors at her bank. The Grosse Pointe police. And the Detroit police. The only people worried that she was gone too soon were now quietly panicked that their direct line to her ample wallet might be finally, summarily cut off.

Eleanor Paget was now a part of local legend. One gun, three people: her husband, her husband's young mistress and now Eleanor herself.

Apparently I was the only one who had the nagging feeling that Paget had received assistance in her rocket ride to the afterlife. And that maybe—just maybe—I could have helped her instead of walking away.

And at 3:35 A.M. Monday morning, I heard my father's voice echoing in my head.

"We are defined by those we could have helped and chose not to . . ."

11

In Michigan—somewhere between the end of summer and fall's beginning—there are rare days of grace. Noon's warmth lands lightly on the skin and evening's cool air is welcomed through open bedroom windows. Today marked the end of such grace. Today, fall introduced itself with a decisive chill.

The sun was still bright but, not unlike me, it was rising later in the morning. Splashes of color were revealing themselves in the trees along the street. Most telling was the late night frost slowly steaming off the grass as the morning sun crept over the horizon.

Parked outside of my house was Jimmy Radmon's rusting Pontiac.

With a cup of coffee in hand, I walked outside and peered inside the car; Radmon was asleep in the back seat. I knocked on the window. He awoke with a start then, seeing me, rolled the rear window down.

"What the hell are you doing?" I said.

"Well, I *was* sleeping," he said.

"You live in your car?"

Radmon said nothing.

I nodded to the house. "Come on."

Fifteen minutes later Jimmy was hunched over a plate of my *huevos rancheros* with sausages, toast and black coffee. For a skinny kid he could pack it away.

After he ate I asked him what his story was. It wasn't anything you haven't heard or read about a thousand times before: didn't know his father, wished he hadn't known his mother, quit high school, amazingly smart with no prospects.

Welcome to the life of a young black Detroit kid. He told me Carmela and Sylvia were having him start on installing their new kitchen cabinets today. I was still a bit stung over the ladies' opinion of my taste in decor, but it worried me more that I actually cared so much about goddamn kitchen cabinets.

I gave Jimmy another couple hundred and told him to find a semi-decent hotel or motel until he got back on his feet. I would have invited him to stay under my roof, but I was just getting used to my own mostly sober company.

"You mind I axe you somethin', man?" Radmon said.

"Axe away."

"You rich or somethin'?" he said, looking at the money I'd placed in his hand.

"Or something," I said. "Here's the deal, Jimmy. I'm thinking about buying a couple more houses on the street. You play straight with me, you'll make a decent living helping to renovate 'em. You fuck with me or anybody on my street—and this *is* my street, compadre—and I will end you. We clear?"

"You're him."

"What?"

"That ex-cop, right?" Radmon said, his eyes wide as if he'd just met a celebrity. He pointed at me. "I *knew* it! You're *him*! Oh, *damn*!"

"No autographs," I said. I looked at my watch. "I gotta go."

"Shit, I *knew* it was you!" He raised his hand for a high-five.

I didn't high-five him. Instead I gave him a spare key to the house and said, "You can shower, shit and shave here this afternoon after you take care of Carmela and Sylvia. You find something in the fridge you want, have at it. Except for the booze. Don't touch my TV. When I get home, you're gone. And if anything's missing—"

"I know, I know," Radmon said. "You'll 'end' me." Then Radmon narrowed his eyes at me and said, "I don't fuck my friends, man."

"You're like me, kid," I said. "You don't have any friends."

A week had passed since Eleanor Paget's death. People had been interviewed. Official reports had been written, emailed and filed. The local TV news had breathlessly reported her death. She'd been unctuously eulogized in all the newspapers for her generosity and compassion. The new Detroit mayor—the city's first smilin' Irishman in fifty years—had spoken at length about what Eleanor Paget had meant to the revitalization of the city. And various industry leaders had issued statements praising Eleanor Paget for her business acumen and commitment to the Greater Detroit community.

Everyone feigned missing poor Eleanor Paget.

I'd purchased a black Perry Ellis suit, black Cole Haan shoes, white shirt and mourning-black tie. I had requested a few special alterations that seemed to rouse a scowl of curiosity from the short, balding tailor with bushy salt-and-pepper eyebrows and an Eastern European accent. It was, of course, extra to have the suit altered in time for Eleanor Paget's memorial service. But with Marcus at the needle, the suit looked and felt impeccable. With his expert alterations, you wouldn't even know I was packin' heat.

I hadn't been invited to the memorial service, but it felt only right to go and pay whatever limited respects I had for the woman. My appearance might upset a few of the luminaries, but as this was a memorial service at Grosse Pointe Unity Salvation Presbyterian, I doubted anybody would punch, shoot or shout profanities at me. More likely, two or three security guards with the look of inbred Ivy League frat brothers would quietly ask to speak to me outside. I would more than likely look up at them, smile and say "No," leaving them scratching their blond heads and wondering what the hell else to do.

It was a bright, blue-sky day, maybe fifty degrees. There were the occasional white caps on the Detroit River kicked up by a chilled fall wind. A rust-red freighter slogged its way north on the river, past several small aluminum fishing boats. Two sailboats bounced on wakes as they tacked out of the freighter's lumbering path.

Grosse Pointe Unity Salvation Presbyterian was a looming white stone structure set maybe a hundred well-manicured yards off Jefferson Avenue. For decades it had looked less like a church and more like a pristine militarized outpost that said to all outsiders, "This far, no farther."

Still, the Catholic my mother had instilled in me had me automatically making the sign of the cross at the three-story carved marble sculpture of a Brad Pitt-looking Jesus crucified on the front of the church.

Parking was, of course, valet.

I took my valet ticket from a young, chinless guy, bounded up the steps and was stopped at the tall double doors of the church by another young guy who looked like he'd just stepped out of an Abercrombie & Fitch ad. He smiled at me, glanced at his iPad and said, "Your name, sir?"

"He's with me."

I turned.

"Captain Raymond Danbury, Detroit Police Department," Danbury said, grinning at the young man and showing his badge. The Abercrombie-wannabe glanced at his iPad, touched the area by Danbury's name, and said, "Welcome, gentlemen. We have rosebud boutonnières inside for you."

As we ascended the remaining steps, Danbury said under his breath, "Jesus. You got a couple brass ones."

In the white and gold anteroom, two young, freckled women pinned white rose boutonnières to our lapels, gave us nicely printed and leather-bound programs and handed us off to another male model type.

"Do they clone these guys?" Danbury whispered to me.

About two hundred Detroit luminaries had already gathered

in the cavernous church. The memorial service was about ten minutes from starting, so most attendees—all dressed in couture black—were on their smartphones, feverishly checking email and making last minute mission-critical business calls, or collected in small huddles making lunch plans that involved either business, politics or both.

Money-changers at the temple.

In front of the long white marble altar was a large framed photo of a grinning Eleanor Paget exposing perhaps more cleavage than acceptable for a solemn affair. Behind the photo positioned on the center of the altar were her remains in an ornate gold and white enamel urn.

Sonuvabitch.

She'd been cremated.

Instead of walking down the center aisle and finding a pew, Danbury gently placed a hand on my forearm and we stopped walking. I turned to him. He was holding his fake smile admirably.

"Two niggas walk into a Grosse Pointe church," he said quietly. "One nigga says to the other, 'What'chu think Jesus would say about us bein' all up in here?' The other nigga looks around at the white folk staring at them and says, 'I don't know, but I think we 'bout to find out.'"

I grinned. "That's pretty funny."

"Yeah, it is," Danbury said. "But you know what *ain't* funny? You showin' up like you own the goddamn place."

Before Danbury could say anything else, Aaron Spiegelman, Titan's CFO, appeared at Danbury's side. "What is *he* doing here?"

"He's my guest, Mr. Spiegelman," Danbury said. "Miss Paget had great respect for Mr. Snow. I believe she would have—"

"How *dare* you presume what Eleanor—Ms. Paget—would have wanted? You've overstepped your bounds, Captain," Spiegelman said, raising a forefinger to Danbury's nose.

"Mr. Spiegelman," Danbury said calmly. "I don't much like people putting their finger in my face. Now unless you intend to spend the next hour of this solemn service with that finger jammed up your prissy little ass, I'd suggest you remove it right damn now."

Spiegelman lowered his quivering finger. "This isn't over."

"Yes," Danbury said with a smile, "it is."

Spiegelman spun on his heels and rejoined a group of people who had stared with interest at the proceedings.

"Just like old times, huh?" I said brightly to Danbury. "You. Me. An appreciative public."

Danbury scowled at me.

Then he stormed off, finding others to talk to among the mourners, who included Detroit's new mayor, Grosse Pointe's mayor, the police commissioners of both cities, and several chosen representatives of the auto companies, software companies, real estate mortgage companies, hospitals, various charity organizations and the art museum.

A handsome, well-dressed black woman in her late sixties approached me. She smiled a genuinely pleasant smile, extended her hand and said, "Rose Mayfield, Kip Atchison's executive secretary at Titan."

"Yes, ma'am," I said. "We met at Eleanor Paget's a couple weeks ago and once prior to that a couple years ago." I took her hand and we shook.

"My late husband knew your father," she said, smiling up at me. "He often said your father was a man of honor. And I know you by reputation. I'm sorry for what the force and the old mayor's administration did to you, Mr. Snow."

"So am I, Ms. Mayfield," I said.

"Thank you for helping Eleanor out with that awful business with her husband," Mayfield said. "She may have appeared to be a fierce woman, but I know she suffered greatly over it. She appreciated what you did for her. I appreciate it."

After a moment of polite conversation, I asked her if she knew where I could find Kip Atchison. She pointed toward the front of the church. Atchison was tall, handsome, fair-haired and, judging by the rapt attention of the people collected around him, commanding and charming. He was Eleanor Paget's handpicked CEO, maybe a year on the job.

"I take it Titan Securities Investments Group has a policy against hiring ugly people," I said, still looking at the chiseled Adonis that was Atchison.

"Except for me, yes," Mayfield said with a laugh.

I scowled at her and said, "Ms. Mayfield, my knees weaken in the presence of your beauty."

Mayfield laughed, quickly covering her mouth. "Mr. Snow, church is no place for bullshit."

"On the contrary," I said. "Church is *exactly* the place for bullshit."

I asked her if Vivian Paget, Eleanor Paget's daughter and only child, was in attendance. Mayfield lowered her head for a moment, then said no. Since Vivian was a delicate type, she had decided against attending. Crowds made her nervous. Crowds of strangers feigning pity, piety, sympathy and love made her especially anxious. No, Vivian would come down from her home in Traverse City another time for a private service.

Rose Mayfield smiled and said, "I'd better get back to my seat. I just wanted you to know not everybody thinks you're a pariah."

"I appreciate that, Ms. Mayfield," I said.

She gave my arm a gentle squeeze, then made her way to the front of the church to Kip Atchison, who welcomed her back into the fold with an arm around her shoulders. She did not look pleased by it.

I sat in a pew at the back of the church on the aisle. Next to me was an attractive woman—Armenian maybe?—in her forties with short-cropped auburn hair. We traded smiles and she said, "You look like that actor. You know. Oh, what's his name? Dwayne Rocky?"

"The Rock?"

"Yes! The Rock! Only, not as, you know," she fluttered her hands over her shoulders before saying, "big."

"Thanks," I said with a wan smile while thinking, *Not as big? Pound-for-pound I could take that poser anytime, anywhere.* "And you look exactly like—you know."

"Julia Roberts?" she said, laughing.

"Exactly!"

"I get that all the time!" She laughed again, giving my shoulder a light touch. "I mean Julia and I may as well be twins."

We laughed.

She looked nothing like Julia Roberts.

Easiest place for the devil to play and make hay is in church, my father used to say.

A third of the way through the pastor's excruciatingly uninspired sermon, the woman next to me extracted a card from her black sequined clutch and handed it to me.

Brooke R. Bunnell, Director Account Services, Adecker/ McCulkin Public Relations—New York, Chicago, Detroit, São Paulo.

I took it, smiled at Brooke and whispered, "Make that out to your biggest fan, Ms. Roberts—August Snow."

She giggled, wrote, *Best Wishes, August Snow! Brooke a.k.a. 'Julia',* on the card and handed it back to me.

After another fifteen minutes of the pastor's droning, a raised and angry voice filtered in from outside the church.

As the voice grew louder, I was able to recognize it.

Tomás. My old friend and Eleanor Paget's former house manager.

I excused myself and slipped outside the church.

"Before God and the Lord Jesus Christ, I say I am glad you're dead, you bitter old hag!" Tomás shouted in Spanish. "Rot in hell, Eleanor Paget!"

Four young, tuxedoed security guards had formed a tight

semi-circle around Tomás and, without putting their hands on him, managed to back him several feet away from the entrance of the church.

"Gentlemen," I said, walking quickly to Tomás's back and placing my hands gently on his shoulders. "I'll take it from here."

The guards gave each other confused looks then backed off.

Tomás spat on the ground in front of the church and shouted in English, "Burn in hell, you evil fucking bitch!"

"Come on, Tomás," I said. "Let's bring it down a notch, mi amigo."

Danbury and Grosse Pointe's police chief appeared at the door of the church and assessed the situation.

"I got this," I said to Danbury.

"Well, thank God," Danbury replied. "I was beginning to think you were completely useless."

12

Tomás and I sat in my rental car.

He'd been drinking. He was breathing like a bull ready to charge and, from the stench, he'd been favoring tequila. He wasn't out-of-his-skull drunk, but he was lubricated enough to find the courage to call out a dead woman at a high-society memorial service. The tow-haired security boys had no idea how lucky they were that I'd come out and interrupted: Tomás may have been over fifty, lacking in height and slightly overweight, but I'd seen him take on bigger, beefier opponents two and three at a time.

We sat quietly for a while looking out over the silver-flecked Detroit River. A few small boats were anchored near the freighter channel and their occupants had fishing lines in the water. I'd often wondered what kind of mutated excuse for a fish they were hoping to hook.

After a while Tomás said, "You arresting me, Octavio?"

Only a few people called me by my middle name, Octavio—I'd been named after my mother's favorite poet, Octavio Paz. Mostly family friends, neighbors and a few Mexican-American school-mates from the old days used that name.

"I'm not a cop any more, Tomás," I said. "You know that."

He wobbled his head in a nod and said, "Right. Tha's right. *Si.*" He burped a smelly tequila burp, then said, "Just like your old man. Full of pity for an old spic."

When my father was a beat cop, he caught a notorious drug-store and pharmaceutical warehouse thief. A thief who knew how to circumvent top-end security systems. Only certain items were taken—prescription antibiotics, EpiPens, asthma and diabetes medications, prenatal vitamins. Never money. Never Schedule II controlled substances. The thief was Tomás. He distributed to the sick and dying. People without healthcare. People crushed by this recession or that automotive layoff. His clientele was big. His payment? A meal here and there. The occasional neighbor's sofa to sleep on. A rosary blessing from an elderly immigrant Mexican woman. A stone-faced bullshit alibi from an old Mexi-can-American man.

Instead of arresting Tomás, my father treated him to an early morning breakfast. Soon after, my dad put Tomás in touch with a young Mexicantown activist named Elena Montoya. She was a thorn in the side of everyone from the mayor and city council to Michigan's governor. Tireless, persuasive and unafraid, she lobbied for neighborhood clinics, educational initiatives, and a police pres-ence in Mexicantown that was protective, not persecutive. My dad figured Tomás and Elena together would be an unstoppable force for Mexicantown.

He was right.

Soon after, the two were married.

Tomás once told me, "Couple weeks go by and your dad asks me what I think about Elena. I says, 'That's the kind of woman a man takes a bath for.' I can still hear him laughing his black Alabama ass off."

My father had simultaneously broken his oath as a servant of the law and fulfilled its most important precept: to Serve and Pro-tect. And in doing so he opened the doors to Mexicantown for himself and his family.

"That wasn't pity my father felt for you," I said. "That was love for and belief in you."

"He was a good man, your father. I'm sorry." Tomás hung his head.

"What's going on, Tomás?" I said.

It took him a moment to gather his thoughts through the silver fog of tequila. "You know how old I am?"

I shook my head.

"Fifty-four," he finally said. "Fifty-five in December. Worked hard all my life, even when I was a thief. *Especially* when I was a thief. As a kid? Worked every field in Michigan. Asparagus, potatoes, cherries, apples, cantaloupe and watermelon. Only thing I didn't pick was the seeds out of white folk's teeth." Tears formed in his eyes. He paused, wiped his face, then looked out at the river for a long time before saying, "No love lost between blacks and Mexicans in this city. But your father? He worked every day for our respect. We trusted him. Loved him." With red, swollen eyes, he held me in his gaze. "When the metal stamping plant in Pontiac went under, I got unemployment. But you can't eat or raise a family on unemployment. I needed work. Ten years I worked for Eleanor Paget. Maintaining her house. Organizing staff schedules. Helping plan her fucking parties. Listening to her bitch, moan, piss and groan about this, that and the other. All for six-fifty cash a week—and the *puta* hated parting with that." Tomás smiled at me and said, "Ten years. Six in the morning until six at night. Sometimes later. And after ten years, you know how much I was making? Six-fifty cash a week. But it's—"

Tomás took a deep, ragged breath and we stared out at the sparkling river watching the fishermen bobbing in their aluminum boats.

"It's what?" I finally said.

"Respect," Tomás said, still staring out at what life there was on the Detroit River. "How can I respect myself—my wife—after what she did?"

"What did she do, Tomás?"

Tomás locked me in a hard, unblinking gaze. "Last summer," he began. "After her Belle Isle aquarium charity gala at the house. I thought I'd sent the last of the staff home. I'm in the kitchen finishing up. I feel somebody press against me from behind. I turn and it's her—naked. She whispers she wants me to fuck her. Wants to suck my cock. Kisses on me. She can barely stand, she's so drunk. One of the staff walks in. Sees me. Sees us." Tomás unlocked his eyes from mine and looked back out at the river. "I've seen shit, Octavio. Done shit. But I've never once cheated on my wife. Never wanted to. I got the best God ever made even though I might as well have been born to the devil."

"Wha'd you do?"

Tomás offered a crooked smile. "I carried her up to her bed. I'm carrying her and she's threatening to fire me if I don't fuck her. Calls me names. Spits at me. Tries to hit me. Scratches me. I throw her in bed and she passes out." Tomás paused for a moment, then said, "I look at her laying there. Snoring like some drunk casino whore. You know how easy it would have been to push a pillow on her? Snap her neck?"

"You didn't cheat on Elena, Tomás."

"You know what *machismo* means, Octavio?" he finally said. I did. My mother had taught me the true meaning of the word when I was a boy. But I said nothing. I figured Tomás just needed to talk. "White folk, they take a word—an *important* word—somebody *else's* word—and they fuck it up. Twist it. *Macho. Machismo.* For us it means a man who takes care of his family. Stands tall for his family. Loves his wife, his family more than his own life. How'm I supposed to be that man, Octavio?"

"Machismo isn't something that comes and goes with the tides, Tomás," I said. "You've either got it or you don't. You've always had it. Always will."

I wasn't quite sure if what I'd said had gotten through to him, but he nodded. Then he said, "When I saw her body—Eleanor

Paget—*Madre Maria*, forgive me—you know the first thing I thought? I thought, 'Thank God.' Forgive me Jesus, but that's what I thought." He shifted uncomfortably in his seat. "I think—someone else was there. Had been there."

"Why?"

"I don't want to get nobody in trouble," Tomás said. He furrowed his thick black eyebrows at me and smiled. "Not a cop but still a cop, eh?"

"Talk to me, Tomás," I said. "We've known each other for a long time. You trusted my dad. You can trust me. Talk to me."

Tomás inhaled deeply. "There was the champagne flute on the side table next to where she . . . died. But there was a watermark on the side table next to the love seat facing her. Still fresh. Damp. I know that house, August. Every inch of it. Furniture, too. There was a watermark—round like the bottom of another glass—on that side table. Only—"

"Only what, Tomás?"

"Manuela. The one who brought you coffee when you were at the house. She's young, Octavio," Tomás said. "New to America. New to the house. She wanted to make an impression. Worked hard."

"What about Manuela?"

"She cleaned the room before the police arrived," Tomás said. "She didn't want Miss Eleanor to be embarrassed. And she didn't want herself to be embarrassed by the state of the room. So she polished the table. Cleaned up a little bit." He took in another deep breath. "The police already interviewed her. They interviewed all of us. Now Manuela has no job and she's scared she'll be sent back to Mexico."

We were silent for a moment. Then Tomás burped again.

"You sobering up?" I asked.

"A little," he said.

"Good," I said. "Let's get a drink."

After insisting Tomás drive with me, I moved his F-150 truck to the outer edge of the valet parked cars and left the keys under the driver's seat. I texted Danbury and asked him to volunteer a patrolman to drive Tomás's truck back to Mexican Village Restaurant two blocks away from Tomás's home in Mexicantown.

A couple minutes after Tomás and I swung onto Jefferson Avenue heading back to the city from Grosse Pointe, I received a text from Danbury. Tomás read it: OK. BUT YOU OWE ME.

"This Danbury," Tomás said. "He's one of the good guys?"

I nodded. "He's one of the good guys."

A declaration of hope is sometimes as good as a statement of fact.

13

In your quest for good, authentic Mexican food in Detroit's Mexicantown, you've probably driven past Café Consuela's on Bagley north of 24th a thousand times. And frankly, that's okay; the people who *do* know Café Consuela's—people like me—hope you keep on driving. No mariachi bands at Café Consuela's, no bright paintings of matadors dodging Godzilla-sized bulls or busty Mexican maidens carrying baskets of corn. No six-page menus offering eight types of margaritas. It wasn't Cancun cruise-ship food. Café Consuela's was as good as it gets.

Like a lot of buildings in this part of town, this little white house was outfitted with year-round Christmas lights entwined around its red wrought iron porch rails. And like a lot of houses in this part of town, Café Consuela's grew their own peppers, cilantro and tomatoes.

The often irascible Consuela Marquez-Juarez had done it this way for thirty-five years and when she died seven years ago, at the ripe old age of ninety-two, her granddaughters—Martiza, Louisa, Nina, and one sister-in-law, Dani—continued the fresh-cooked authentic Mexican food tradition with the same commitment and passion.

They would never be rich.

They would, however, be welcomed into the Kingdom of Heaven, no questions asked so long as they brought St. Peter a plate of their chicken chorizo tortillas with spicy green salsa.

Café Consuela's had the dubious distinction of having been raided by the Detroit police. On a false tip perpetrated by a competitor, Café Consuela's was raided on suspicion of growing marijuana in the basement. What the police found were sixty tomato plants under grow lights being serenaded by scratchy recordings of Mexican folk music.

The café's owners didn't begrudge the cops. On the contrary: they cooked a massive meal and sent it to the 14th as a thank-you for being vigilant in the fight against drugs and the protection of the neighborhood.

Shortly after the raid, my mother—trying very hard not to laugh—told me that if the police had been a bit more inquisitive and a lot more observant, they would have discovered something was in fact illegal in the basement of Café Consuela's: the tomato plants and even the soil they grew in had been smuggled in from Mexico.

Nothing like a real Mexican tomato.

When the oldest of Consuela's granddaughters, Martiza, saw Tomás and me enter the restaurant, she walked to the four occupants of the restaurant's lone booth and said, "I'm gonna have to move you."

No "I'm sorry" or "Would you mind?"

I'm gonna have to move you.

The occupants of the booth—members of that next wave of young, white, messenger bag-wearing gentrifying class—wasted no time in moving their dishes and silverware to a table. They could still tell their equally trendy foodie friends that they'd eaten at Café Consuela's and, wow, what an awesome—just *awesome!*—experience.

Tomás and I took over the booth. Martiza—a big, strong woman of indeterminate age with a thick black braid—bent down, hugged Tomás and told him how sorry she was about his suddenly being out of work. Then she stood up, pushed her fists into her ample waist, scowled down at me and said, "*Entonces, ¿cuál es tu excusa?*"—What's your excuse?

"I have none," I replied in Spanish.

"I thought so," Martiza said before bending, cupping my face in her strong hands and giving me a wet kiss on both cheeks.

Martiza had always been a good judge of people. And although Café Consuela's didn't have a liquor license, her astute judgment resulted in her bringing a bottle of Cabresto Ultra Silver Tequila, lemon slices and a small blue bowl of coarse salt to the table. She accompanied this with warm, homemade corn chips and a green chili salsa that would have had the devil fanning his mouth and saying, "Ooo! Hot! Hot! *HOT!*"

Tomás gradually loosened up, but he was reluctant to talk any further about his time with Eleanor Paget. He knew that with me if he didn't want to talk, he didn't have to. His reluctance was understandable: For as degrading and nullifying as it is to be pulled over by cops for "driving while black," it is equally degrading and nullifying to be caught "working while brown." Even if you'd been an American citizen for twenty, thirty, a hundred years, you were still a "wet." Somebody who would steal anything and lie about everything. Best not to talk.

This was the conundrum Tomás wrestled with now.

"What you say stays between us, Tomás," I told him in Spanish.

"What's your interest in all this, Octavio?" Tomás prepped his second tequila shot. "I mean, why do you care?"

I told him why I cared.

Tomás laughed. "Even a kindness from the devil must be repaid." He shrugged. "So you think somebody killed her? Jesus, Octavio, let the Anglos get her justice if there's any owed. She was one of theirs."

"I want to," I said. "But I can't."

"Your father's voice again?" he said. He knew the answer. We tossed back our shots.

Martiza brought out beef chorizo tacos, perfectly seasoned refried beans and saffron rice with peas, carrots and jalapeños. She took the bottle of tequila from us and replaced it with freshly made limeade. There were slices of apples, oranges and fresh raspberries floating brightly in the pitcher.

Between the food and sips of limeade, Tomás told me that two days after Eleanor Paget had been found dead in her study, all of the dayworkers were given notice of their dismissal. This included house staff as well as all security. They were given two weeks' severance—thirteen hundred for Tomás, considerably less for others—and a letter thanking them for their service, signed by a Michael Rothman, Eleanor Paget's personal attorney.

Tomás poured himself another tall glass of limeade, then ate two tacos in quick succession. I followed his lead.

The young lions that had been moved from the booth had finished their lunch. They praised Martiza and the food. A blonde girl with a silver nose stud, jute bracelets and tie-dyed blouse tried out her Spanish on Martiza. The girl briefly regaled Martiza with stories of her travels in Mexico and how wonderful the Mexican people and culture were.

Martiza smiled amiably and nodded. At the end of the girl's story, Martiza said in English, "Mexico is a shithole. It's where dreams go to die. Next time you come here, tell me nice things about your travels in America. This is where hope flourishes."

The young girl flushed red, grinned and said *si*, she would do exactly that.

Satisfied that neither Tomás nor I were drunk, Martiza brought the tequila back out. She took out a black Sharpie pen and made a hash mark on the bottle.

"Drink only to here," she said. "Then you go home, got it?"

"*Si*, señora."

After a shot each, I made the big leap and asked Tomás who he thought might have wanted to kill Eleanor Paget.

"Detroit," he said without so much as a sarcastic smile.

"Can you narrow that down a bit?" I said.

"East Detroit?"

I asked Tomás who besides him had all-access gate passes to the house. There was Rose Mayfield, the black woman I'd spoken with at the memorial service. Aside from having once been Paget's personal secretary, Mayfield was the closest thing Paget had had to a girlfriend over the last thirty years. There was Aaron Spiegelman, Titan's chief financial officer, who had known Paget for nearly as long.

"He'll talk tough to guys like you and me. The help," Tomás said, "But all I ever heard out of his mouth was, 'Yes, Eleanor,' and, 'I'll get right on it, Ellie.' A little birdie perched on her finger whistling at her command. Occasionally he'd bring her a bottle of champagne which they'd never have together."

There was her personal attorney, who lived in Chicago and only came in once every couple months. There were a few others—people from the Detroit Institute of Arts and Children's Hospital. But they were occasional guests who still had to clear a meeting with her in advance.

And there was Eleanor Paget's daughter, Vivian.

"Yeah, she had a pass, but she almost never visited," Tomás said. "Not even Christmas. Can't say as I blame her."

I finally asked him if there had been any official visits, specifically from the FBI or bank regulators.

"The FBI?" Tomás was genuinely surprised. "Really?"

"Just spitballin' here, Tomás."

Tomás grinned. "Bullshit. What's going on, Octavio?"

"I'm not sure," I said, licking the back of my thumb and dousing it with salt.

"No," Tomás said. "No visits from the FBI or bank regulators."

He fell silent, casting his eyes down at the table and playing with his empty shot glass.

"If she was murdered," I asked tentatively, "who would you lay odds on?"

"If I was you, mister-not-a-cop-anymore, I'd ask me if I killed her," Tomás said. "And the answer would be no fuckin' way. Did I *want* to kill her—especially after the incident? Hell yes. She'd say things like 'What would I do without you, Thomas?' and 'You're invaluable, Thomas'—then she would count the fucking silverware or Febreze the furniture the kitchen staff sat on to eat their lunch. That *I* sat on. *Puta*."

"Okay," I said. "Let's say you're down on the suspects list. Who's at the top?"

Tomás smiled. But it wasn't a smile of amusement. It was the smile of barely masked contempt. He looked at me for a long time then said, "Two months ago, I was working late. Cleaning up after a little dinner affair she'd had for some mucky-mucks at her bank. Spiegelman was there. So was the new guy, Atchison. Couple others I hadn't seen at the house before. Raised voices. Cussing toward the end. Mostly Paget going nuclear. Don't know what it was about. Don't care. 'Bout an hour after everybody left, I'm in the kitchen. Atchison walks in bare-assed naked. Grabs a bottle of champagne from the fridge. Looks at me. Laughs and says, 'Bitch fucks like a Vegas pro.' Takes the champagne and heads back upstairs." Tomás paused, keeping me in the cross hairs of his eyes. "He had an all-access pass in more ways than one, Octavio. I like him for poppin' a cap in her. But then you have to ask yourself, why would he kill the goose that laid him a golden egg?"

"Bigger goose," I said. "Bigger golden egg."

14

After thirty-two years running her empire, Eleanor Paget had decided to step down. In the past five years, the bank had stagnated under her leadership and the 2008 collapse of the world economy demanded new leadership and fresh ideas. Joseph Dylan "Kip" Atchison was crowned with the task of reinvigorating the bank and future proofing the Paget family legacy.

Atchison was thirty-four—the same age as me. And, not unlike myself, he was tall and good-looking, though his looks were more along the lines of New England private school head-of-the-lacrosse-team while mine were more along the lines of mestizo conquistador with a healthy dash of Mississippi Delta blues. According to Google and LinkedIn, Atchison had graduated with honors from Princeton University with a degree in finance. He went on to get his MBA from Harvard. After a short stint at the now defunct Lehman Brothers in New York, Atchison came to Detroit as the obscenely paid CEO of Titan.

This was another difference between the pedigreed Atchison and me: I got a bachelor's degree in sociology from Wayne State University, which empowered me to pursue lucrative careers in food service, retail or police work.

Atchison was married to Elise deGeorgette Dawe of Cumberland, Maine. Dawe came from pharmaceutical money and met her husband while a student at Princeton, where she got a heretofore unused degree in biochemistry. They had three young children and lived in Grosse Pointe Farms.

After I'd spent thirty minutes researching Kip Atchison on Elena's laptop, their five-year old granddaughter, Juanita—or June, as she was known—forced her head between me and Elena's laptop screen. It was June's parents' Mommy-and-Daddy night out. "Are you done yet?" she said. I had promised June when I arrived that I'd play Candyland with her. "That looks boring."

Tomás had demanded I stay at his Mexicantown house for the evening since they were closer and we'd drunk our fill of tequila.

"It is, honey." I said. "Boring and stupid."

June turned to me, scowled and wagged a finger. "We never say the word 'stupid.' You ready?"

"Why, yes I am, honey," I said, closing the lid of Elena's laptop. "You got the game?"

June grinned and held the game over her head for me to see.

"You gonna let me win?" I said.

June laughed. "No!"

Elena made Tomás and me the blackest of Mexican coffees and served cinnamon and sugar churros. She may have been a bit put off by our drinking, but she was more than glad to know Tomás was home safe.

I struggled against sleep—or passing out—but managed to play three mind-numbing games of Candyland. Then June, Elena and I watched a Blu-Ray collection of SpongeBob SquarePants episodes, made all the more hilarious by virtue of the blue agave state I was in. Reeling from overindulgence and weighed down by the uncertainty of his family's future, Tomás had collapsed in bed thirty minutes earlier.

After the second SpongeBob episode, little June was a limp ragdoll huddled in her grandma's arms. I carried June upstairs and Elena tucked her in bed.

"You can sleep in Manolita's old room, Octavio," Elena said to me. She collected a fresh towel and washcloth from the hallway linen closet and handed them to me.

I thanked Elena for her hospitality and apologized for the condition Tomás and I were in.

She shrugged. "Men are often just little boys in bigger clothes." She paused, looked around the upstairs. "This color. It's so dark. Don't you think, Octavio?"

I had no opinion either way on the hallway color, but I said, "It could be brightened. Maybe Tomás and I can paint it."

"Yes," she said, nodding thoughtfully. "New paint."

As Elena made up the bed for me in her daughter's old room, we talked. She was curious where I had disappeared to for a year. She told me there were rumors that I'd bought a house outside of Cancun and drunk myself to death, which had made her almost unbearably sad. Another rumor had me living like the long ago legend of New York police detective Frank Serpico in a secluded cabin somewhere in the Swiss Alps. As to India, somehow a rumor began (I'm betting Skittles) that I'd converted to Hinduism and lived on a barge aimlessly floating the Brahmaputra River. My favorite rumor was that I'd come out of the closet and was selling real estate in San Francisco.

I told her there were bits of truth to all the rumors save for my sexuality: I'd nearly drunk myself to death in Paris, but that was considered an acceptable—even laudable—way to go, if it involved good wine. I backpacked in Switzerland, but found the Swiss uninteresting and the chocolate better in Belgium. I told her I didn't quite know what to make of India aside from its astounding poverty, unbelievable wealth, pervasive caste system and an odd-tasting liquor called feni. And although I'm not gay, I had considered moving to California, but the thought of being so far away from my parents' graves was, at least for the time being, unacceptable.

I gave her a few highlights from Norway, hoping to conceal

anything about the woman I'd met. Unfortunately, I was over-whelmed by Elena's empathic powers.

"You met someone there, yes?"

"Yes."

"And you like her?" Elena said.

"Yes."

"What's her name?"

"Tatina."

"Oh, that's beautiful!" Elena said.

"Tatina Stadtmueller."

"Okay, the last name, not so beautiful. Still . . ." She was silent for a moment before saying, "Why did you leave her to come back here?"

"I . . . didn't want to leave my parents alone."

Elena placed her hands on mine, smiled and said, "They're gone, Octavio. And what happened to Maureen in the store—she'd want you to move on. I know you, Octavio. Known you since you were small. I know little scares you. Except maybe love and how it can be lost. That's why you're back, si? Not to be here, but to be away from the one thing that scares you."

I wanted to say something.

Anything.

But there was little for me to say except for "Yes."

"Go back to this Tatina, Octavio." Elena sighed. Gave my hand a gentle pat. "It's a fool's sin not to embrace love."

I nodded that I would.

Someday.

Elena asked me about my house and the neighborhood. She hadn't been down Markham Street in years, finding its deterioration a sadness she couldn't bear. She remembered the names of old neighbors, the sounds of their voices, the color of their eyes, the state of their gardens. She remembered my parents, what a wonderful painter my mother was. She spoke of helping my mother in our kitchen preparing food for parties, celebrations and holidays.

"Tomás says you're bringing the old neighborhood back," she said.

"Maybe a little. Couple houses so far. Not much."

Finally she got out what she'd wanted to tell me. "I'm worried about Tomás."

I asked her not to worry. I said everything would be all right. I would make sure of it.

What else was I supposed to do with twelve million dollars?

At 2:30 in the morning I awoke with a start, instantly reaching for my gun.

It was quiet save for my breathing, but a bad feeling crawled over my chest.

I pulled the edge of a curtain aside and looked out at the street. A black Mercedes was parked near Tomás's house.

I got dressed and checked the clip of my gun. No sooner had I slapped it back into the grip than the door to my room opened. I brought my weapon up.

It was Tomás, leveling a Remington .30-caliber rifle at me.

"One's out back," he whispered. "I have my granddaughter here, Octavio."

"Not gonna happen," I said.

We made our way downstairs. I signaled for Tomás to make his stand by the front door. I would take the back. He nodded and we moved in our opposite directions. Tomás may have gone to bed drunk, but a former accomplished thief's sixth sense, fueled by adrenaline, sobered him up quickly.

I got to the back door and glanced out of the window over the kitchen sink: a thickly built man in black slacks and black leather jacket was about thirty feet from making his crouched way to the house.

Like a number of houses in this part of town, Tomás and Elena had a small vegetable garden—lettuce, kale, carrots, peppers, tomatoes. And like other houses around here, the garden had a number of homemade security measures, mostly meant for rabbits, feral dogs and the occasional inner-city coywolf: Empty cans strung together and suspended slightly above ground. Boards painted brown with jagged bottle glass glued to them. Maybe the occasional Home Depot motion sensor light.

It was late in the growing season. Most of the vegetables had been harvested and the earth turned over. But the security measures remained.

The intruder made his way clumsily through the rows of turned-over dirt. He caught a foot in one of the trip wires setting a line of empty cans clanking. Under his breath he cursed.

In his right hand was a nickel-plated handgun.

I carefully unlatched the back door and waited. After a few adrenaline-soaked seconds, the door handle slowly turned. I let it turn and watched the door creak open.

Crouching low by the refrigerator, I let the man get the door all the way open.

When he was two steps in, I made my move.

I brought the butt of my gun down on his face. The bridge of his nose crunched. Without stopping, I brought my knee up once into his balls then again into his head. He grunted and started to go down. Before he dropped I grabbed his gun hand and twisted the gun from it. He was shaken, but not out. I put him in a chokehold and, after a few seconds of him slapping at my forearm and face, felt his body go limp. Quickly grabbing his thumbs in my fists, I jerked them hard and fast back toward his wrists, listening to the bone pop away from the joint. Hard to handle a gun with dislocated thumbs.

I closed and locked the back door and made my way to the front of the house. Tomás was by the bank of living room windows. He looked at me and I nodded.

Quietly he unlocked the front door and, after a three-count, we went through with our guns leveled at the man standing and smoking by the black Mercedes.

The man—lanky with blond-streaked hair and a droopy, dark mustache—saw us, ditched his cigarette, jumped in the car and burned rubber into the cold, black night.

"Get a good look at him?" I said to Tomás. Tomás nodded.

"Abuelito?"

The voice of a little girl behind us. June was standing in her pajamas on the front porch holding a stuffed bunny.

"Can I have a drink of water?" she said.

"Sure, baby girl," Tomás said, holding his rifle behind him, out of her view. "In a minute. Go back inside. I'll bring you some water real soon."

She yawned, turned and toddled back inside the house.

I tied the unconscious man's hands behind his back with one of Tomás's leather belts, wrapped a second one twice around the goon's mouth and neck and a length of clothesline around his ankles. I dragged him outside to the garden. Once outside I asked Tomás to get me a glass of tequila. He did.

I tossed the tequila in the unconscious man's face. Might have seemed a waste of good tequila, but the alcohol seared into his split nose and eyes and brought him jerking and grunting to life. I pressed my thumb on his Adam's apple and brought a forefinger to my lips. When he stopped struggling, I released pressure on his Adam's apple and he gulped in air as best as he could.

I looked at Tomás and whispered, "You know him?"

"No."

"Sorry," I said to Tomás.

"So am I," Tomás said.

Tomás and I hauled the intruder to my rental car and threw him in the trunk. Then we shook hands and I drove off.

15

While the core of Detroit—even through the city's bankruptcy—may have been experiencing a much-needed and dramatic upswing in multimillion dollar businesses, new restaurants, Portland-style mass transit and dynamic entertainment offerings, including Comerica Park, Ford Field and the Fox Theatre, there were still hunched and decaying corpses along the riverfront that had been waiting decades for final burial. Abandoned buildings, half demolished buildings, factories where even the chain link fences had oxidized into oblivion. Some buildings had collapsed under their own water-soaked weight into mountains of stone and steel rubble. Others were soon to be mercifully plowed under as Detroit struggled to reinvent itself.

Not even Detroit's few gangs risked trolling down by the river near historic Fort Wayne. Too many stories of ghosts and demons. Too many night creatures with sharp teeth and ravenous appetites. Then there's the ghost of Oppenheimer's "Little Boy" said to haunt the soil itself.

This is where I brought the man thrashing about in the trunk of my car.

Perfect place for a friendly little chat.

He clumsily kicked at me once I opened the trunk. For this act of belligerence, I pulled him roughly out of the trunk, turned him over on his stomach and dislocated his right forefinger.

It had been a long time since the violence in me had made its dark presence felt. It had always been there, somewhere in the pit of my stomach, in the submerged recesses of my brain. The marines had helped me focus the violence. My time on the Detroit police force had given it a purpose.

Now, it had reemerged. Tangible and unapologetic.

Blessed be the Lord, my rock,
who trains my hands for war,
and my fingers for battle

Before pulling the man up into a sitting position against my car, I rummaged through his pockets and found his wallet. Then I undid the belt around his mouth and neck. While going through his wallet I knelt down and said, "You come for me or Tomás?"

He didn't answer. I motivated him by pressing the barrel of my gun to his right knee.

"I have no compunction about making you a one-legged side-show attraction," I said.

"For you," the man finally said. "You break nose, mother-fucker!" He had an Eastern European or Russian accent. Hard to tell since, as he so eloquently put it, I'd broken his nose. In the pale light drifting across the river from Windsor, Ontario, I made out the name on his driver's license: Bob Franks.

If this guy was "Bob Franks" then I was George Clooney.

Three hundred cash in his wallet, plus a MasterCard, Visa and a gas card for an off-brand gas only sold on the east coast.

And a condom.

Bob Franks: Eternal Optimist.

"Why, Mr. Franks?"

"Who?"

"Bob Franks," I said. "That's you." I showed him the license. He squinted at it. "Remember? Now who hired you?"

"Don't know."

"You don't know why you made a run at me?"

"Just get paid," the man said. He snorted and spat a wad of blood and mucus. "I gonna kill you, you black motherfucker piece of shit! I gonna break you nigger ass in half!"

"Yeah, well so far you're just breaking my heart," I said, pressing the barrel of my gun harder into Bob's kneecap. "Why me?"

"Man say follow you. Give tune-up is all. Easy money."

"Well, Bob, 'easy' has gone exactly the same way as you getting lucky tonight," I said, holding up the condom for him to see, then tossing it into the nearby darkness. "Who told you to put a beat-down on me? The man in the car?"

"No," the man said, still struggling to catch his breath. "Man in car partner. Other man."

"What's the other man's name, Bob?"

"Why you keep calling me 'Bob'!"

I held up his poorly faked driver's license again and shouted, "That's you, asshole! Unless you wanna give me a real name and cut the bullshit."

He gave me a hard look and said nothing.

I asked him again about the other man. The man who had hired him and his partner to scare me. After a quiet-tough-guy moment he said he didn't know. The job came as a phone call. Half the money was left at a bus station in Toledo.

"Why?" I said.

The man shrugged. "Don't know. Don't fucking care. Money's money."

"Are you shitting me?" I said. It was way early morning. It was cold. And somebody had put a lame-assed contract out on me that had put a good friend and his family in harm's way. "You got a partner who leaves you holding the bag. An employer you don't know. And I bet this mystery employer said half up front, other half when the job is done, right?"

The man gave me a sheepish look then nodded.

"Dear God," I said standing and shaking my head. "You make stupid sound like an aspiration."

"A what?"

I might as well have been talking to a freshly cut slab of slaughterhouse beef. Still, I persisted, hoping there was at least one kernel of usable information rattling around in this Neanderthal's skull. "Did your employer happen to mention Eleanor Paget?"

"Who's this?" Bob said.

"Nothing about a bank?"

The man shook his head. Then he laughed and said, "I know about you. Cop who couldn't cut it. Take off with big wad of police money. Maybe some nigger cop buddies hire me. Maybe want money back."

Anything's possible when you don't know a damned thing.

In the faint light I took note of the right side of his neck. A portion of a tattoo. I took the barrel of my gun and pushed aside his shirt collar. Two church steeples. I'd only seen tattoos like this twice, maybe three times before. And every time I'd seen them, they meant trouble.

I pulled out a pocketknife I keep with me and flipped out the two-inch blade.

"Hey!" Bob Franks said squirming. "What you doing!"

I cut a slit in the knee of his slacks and opened it up.

A star tattoo.

"So you bow to no one, huh?" I said to Bob Franks.

Russian prison tats.

"Fuck you," Bob Franks snarled. "I American citizen now! This profiling!"

"Okay," I said, putting my knife away. "I expected better from you, Bob, but you have been a disappointment." I pressed the barrel of my Glock to his broken nose. "If you, your partner or anybody else comes within a hundred miles of that house again, I will kill you. I will shoot you in your star-studded knees. I will shoot you in your hands and your elbows. I will take a hot steaming piss on you while you bleed out. Then I will find your employer and kill him, too. Understand me, Bob?"

I stood, got in my car and started the engine.

The man calling himself Bob Franks struggled to his feet. Thumping his heavy body against the car, he shouted, "You don't leave me here!"

I rolled the window down a bit. "I give you twenty/eighty odds of hobbling back to where the streetlamps work. By the way: a lot of wild dogs come down here at night to feed on ducks, geese and fish chewed up by boat propellers. You're fresh meat, Bob. They're gonna love you."

"Fucking *nigger*!"

I rolled up the window and laughed as my rear tires kicked dirt and gravel in Bob Franks's face.

16

A year away from the job and I'd gotten sloppy.

If I'd been on my game, I would have taken special notice of the black Mercedes parked a block away from Café Consuela's. A Mercedes in Mexicantown warranted special attention, since it was a mostly dirt-under-the-fingernails working class neighborhood.

If I'd been on my game, I wouldn't have put Tomás and his family in danger.

Somehow I was in this thing now. Whatever "this thing" was.

Over the next several days, I worked out at the Y on Broadway. I found a gun range on Gratiot Avenue and fired off boxes of .9mm- and .38-caliber ammo, reacquainting myself with the weight, balance, firing action and accuracy of my two guns. I also reacquainted myself with the smell of gunpowder and hot brass being ejected. I committed what I'd learned so far about Eleanor Paget and Titan Securities Investment Group to paper, scrutinizing my notes, looking for the connections, analyzing the disconnects.

And I made phone calls.

Most of my calls resulted in quick hang ups, threats of legal action or strings of profanity mixed with liberal doses of vitriol. None of Titan's board of directors or their executive assistants spent more than eight seconds talking with me about their personal or professional relationships with Eleanor Paget. They usually ended the conversation with "Let me refer you to the bank's legal counsel" or "Fuck you, ass-wipe." Former employees at Eleanor Paget's home quickly told me they'd already talked to the police and I should leave them alone. This group included the scared young woman Manuela. And my contacts at both newspapers were more interested in what I knew than they were in accommodating me with what they knew. Which was damned little.

It may have been a long-shot, but the thug with Russian prison tats and Bob Frank's license had spooked me a bit when he said maybe it was someone on the force looking to give me a twelve-million-dollar beatdown. I called Ray Danbury and asked him if he'd heard anything.

"Couple guys on the job still got it in for you," Danbury said nonchalantly. "Think you sold 'em out—sold *us* out—with the trial and the money. Cops you took down are either serving time in Jackson or Huron Valley. One of 'em—Kirby—served ten months and found Jesus in Atlanta. Got his own public-access halleluiah TV show. Jacoby—Martin Jacoby—ate a bullet eight months ago. Left a fuck-you suicide note. It's still in evidence if you ever wanna catch up on your reading. The mayor and his crew? Mayor's trading cigarettes and cookies for TV time at Parnall and his contractor buddy's stamping license plates in Jackson. Most still on the job just don't give a shit about you anymore. That said, I'll keep you posted I hear anything."

"Thanks, Ray," I said.

"Still," Danbury said. "I wouldn't be callin' 911 down here any time soon, ma brotha. Might just go unanswered."

"And that would be different from any other day how, Ray?"

Jimmy Radmon had made inroads with some of my other neighbors, fixing old hot-water radiators, doing drywall work and some electrical. He wasn't quite sure what to charge so he told my neighbors they'd get a bill from me. Tips, however, were acceptable.

"You find a place to stay?" I asked him over coffee and crullers in my kitchen.

"The Monterey Inn," Radmon said, munching a cruller I'd picked up from LaBelle's Soul Hole donut shop on Michigan Avenue near the old train station. I'd never seen anybody so skinny eat with this kid's appetite. "Over on Mt. Rainier. Nothing glamorous, but it's pretty clean and they got cable. Front desk dude's mostly high, so he don't know if I've paid or not—which works out for me."

"Karma's a bitch, Jimmy," I said. "High or not, pay the man."

Radmon nodded. "Yes, sir."

I asked Radmon if he was enjoying the honest life and he shrugged and said it beat the alternative—which was me dumping his lifeless body in an abandoned house. He said the neighbor across the street—Carlos Rodriguez—was always staring at him when he worked at Carmela and Sylvia's house. Giving him the "evil eye."

"You didn't do much to win his confidence with your first visit to the 'hood." I eyed the last of the crullers but knew Radmon would soon inhale it. "Plus, you're black. Mexicans and blacks have never really embraced each other in this town."

"Looks like somebody done did *some* embracing," Radmon said.

When I realized he was talking about my mixed heritage I fell out laughing. I told him I'd talk to Mr. Rodriguez.

Radmon asked if I was planning on buying any of the other houses on the block; there were four others that were up for sale. Houses that in a northern suburban market would have brought in six-digit sales figures. In Mexicantown? Four figures. Maybe five tops.

"Hadn't thought about it," I said.

"Well, you should, man," Radmon said. "This city's comin' 'round, dude. All them rich hipster kids from West Bloomfield and Birmingham, they buyin' up shit down here left and right. Why not have a brotha—or *whatever* you are—be they landlord?"

"Interesting proposition." I wasn't really interested in being anybody's landlord.

After crullers and coffee, Jimmy Radmon strapped on his tool belt and walked to Carmela and Sylvia's house to work on their kitchen. I think the old girls had sort of adopted the lanky black kid.

I made a trip north.

The private security guard—Frank—who had once guarded the formidable gates of Eleanor Paget's estate had been fired from Digital Defense Home Security: his former company thought it might be bad for business if they retained a guard who had allowed the gunshot death of one of their wealthiest clients, even if her death had been officially declared a suicide.

Frank was working at a Kroger's in Farmington Hills, twelve miles northwest of the city.

"You're that guy," Frank said as he bagged a squat Chaldean woman's groceries. The woman was busy arguing with the cashier in broken English about a coupon that had expired.

"I'm that guy," I said.

We shook hands and Frank asked the cashier if he could take five. The cashier, a middle-aged black woman who was in no mood to argue with the old woman and was in the process of honoring her expired coupons, nodded and waved us off. Frank told another bagger—a pimply white high school kid with Dumbo ears and a mouth full of steel—he was taking a smoke break. The kid slurred okay over his braces and took over Frank's station.

Frank and I went outside and he lit up a Marlboro Light.

"Work is work," Frank said after exhaling a plume of smoke. "Some ways, baggin' groceries is better than working security. Especially at that crazy bitch's house."

I asked him what would happen to the surveillance recordings from Eleanor Paget's house. He told me the Grosse Pointe and Detroit police had given them a cursory once over. But since her death was declared a suicide, nobody had much time for or interest in a lengthy interview with the gate guard, or sitting through hours of footage of a member of the way-upper class getting her lawn cut.

The company would probably keep most of the recordings for a while, then dump them like a bad first date.

The only thing to remain would be the digitized versions of Frank's security logs. Which read largely like the owner's manual for a cordless drill.

"If you were a betting man—" I began.

"Which I'm not. 'Cept for maybe a stupid lottery ticket now and then."

"Who would you say had the most personal access to Eleanor Paget?"

He sucked the last bit of smoke from his cigarette and snuffed it out in a nearby standing ash bin. Then he looked at me with narrowed eyes and said, "You think she was zeroed, don't you?"

I said nothing.

He smiled.

"If I was a betting man," he said, "which I'm not, I'd say the odds-on favorite was that Atchison guy. The guy who runs the bank. I'm pretty sure he was feeding her a pork roll at least twice a week. Guy gave me the creeps and I don't get the creeps."

Frank and I talked for a few minutes more, mostly about our time in the service, the Tigers being in the postseason playoffs and the Lions' modest if negligible chances at securing a playoff berth. He said working his second job as a janitor at Wayne State was nice because, even though he wasn't enrolled, it showed him what a real school looked like.

At the end of our conversation I took out my checkbook, wrote a check and handed it to Frank. He looked at it and then back at me.

"The fuck is this?" he said. "This a joke or something?"

"No joke," I said. "You've been helpful. I appreciate it."

"And I owe you—what?" Frank said with no small amount of justifiable suspicion. "Nothing," I said. "Paid in full, Army."

Frank smiled, looked at the check again, stuffed it into an inside pocket of his green Kroger's vest and offered his hand.

"Semper fi, Marine," he said.

We shook hands and I left.

On my way home, I got a call from Ray Danbury.

"Well, you've been a busy little beaver, haven't you?" he said brightly.

He went on to tell me that several days earlier a patrol had picked up a badly beaten man on Jefferson Avenue near the waterfront at four in the morning. The man said he'd been beaten and robbed by a man fitting my description. Apparently I had only stolen his driver's license and left him his wallet with three hundred dollars and credit cards. When the interview delved a hair deeper, the man clammed up. Under a little more pressure the man said he didn't want to file a police report and that he just wanted to go home, which I imagined was some cum-stained roach motel on 8 Mile Road near the Lodge Freeway.

"You still looking into Eleanor Paget's death?" Danbury said.

"Just keeping myself busy," I said.

"Yeah, well, get yourself a wood-burning set or take up macramé," Danbury said. "I don't need you up in this Paget business which, if you haven't already gotten the memo, is closed out as a suicide. Anything else and I'll tie you up, August, swear to God and my Sweet Lord Jesus."

He disconnected. A couple seconds later I got another call. The ringtone this time was a Detroit techno classic, Octave One's "New Life." I answered.

"S'up, Snowman?"

"How do you do that, Skittles?" I said, slightly irritated and a bit amused by the fact that he could remotely change my ringtone.

Skittles thanked me for the payment I'd dropped off at Rocking Horse. I'd put a little something extra in the navy-blue gym bag. I'm sure for what I was paying him he could afford to buy his own mountainous supply of Skittles. But this had been our agreement for a while and who doesn't need the occasional warm-and-fuzzy tradition? "Got me a couple new Alienware 20 laptops," Skittles said. "'Course I had to boost 'em up, but still kickass machines, bro."

"Only use them for good, Skittles," I said.

"Yeah, okay, Mom."

He said he'd been reviewing the information he was able to safely capture from the bank's computer systems. The FBI had inserted a worm into the system, but their worm was simply making endless monitoring and reporting loops—"Gordian Knots"—in the "amusement park."

"All my tax dollars," Skittles said, "and that's the best code them FBI mothafuckas can come up with?"

"You don't pay taxes, Skittles."

"A technicality. Let me net it out for you, Snowman. I'll be damned if I'm going back in that system. But I'll give this up for free: The BIOS of their system is the kind of shit a lot of offshore banks have. Wicked exotic steganographic encryptions. My guess? Since offshore banks be under constant FBI, CIA, Homeland Security, MI-6, BND and Interpol microscopes, what better way to protect big-ass pallets of off-the-grid cash than to move offshore *onshore*?"

"Switzerland and the Caymans come to Detroit?"

"Sounds stone-cold crazy, I know," Skittles said. "And that's exactly why it works. Money at that level's just a concept, man. An abstract. Lines of code jumpin', jivin' and jittering through T-1 or T-3 lines, bouncin' off satellites, nesting on this server for an hour or that server for a day. What if while everybody's lookin' at the big banks, the small banks become cash flow servers? It's all just ones and zeroes, baby. Your credit and debit cards. Everything. I mean, *you* got paid, right?"

"Yeah," I said. "I got paid."

"And where you keepin' them millions, Snowman?" Skittles

laughed. "Tens and twenties in your mattress? Little Sears home safe under the floorboards?"

"I get the point, Skittles."

"Good," he said. "'Cause most people don't. Watch your ass out there, Snowman. And start stuffin' mattresses, baby."

17

Mind, body and soul; locked and loaded; forever and always.

We should have had T-shirts made . . .

My mother wore a navy spaghetti-strap dress, navy high heels and a yellow silk floral shawl. She rocked it like a telenovela star on the red carpet at my graduation from the academy. She wept as only a loving mother can at the sight of her child framed in a crowning moment of achievement. My father looked recruitment poster perfect in his DPD dress blues. He gave me a stern look and said, "Well, you've really stepped in it now, jarhead."

At my graduation party at the house on Markham Street he took me aside, sniffed me and said, "Ah, that new cop smell. Like—fresh panties and blooming daffodils." Then with tequila-glazed eyes he said, "What's the mission now, son?"

"To Serve and Protect," I said.

"No," he snarled. "It's the same as it was in Afghanistan: find the enemy, hunt the truth. Kill one, set yourself free with the other. And God help you if you lose focus 'cause that's when some second-rate bagpiper follows your coffin into the boneyard. Ain't no damned grateful public. Ain't no pats on the back. And like our Lord and Savior Jesus Christ, you gonna have a Judas or two in blue. So again, boy—what's your mission?"

"'Mind, body and soul; locked and loaded; always and forever.'"

"Well." My father laughed brightly. "I guess you *did* listen to the old man from time to time."

As a child and adolescent I'd always thought my father was preparing me to be a man. He wasn't. He was preparing me for war. A war waged every day on men, women and children. A war waged on the poor and disenfranchised regardless of race or sex. And a war that would most likely never be won save for the occasional fragile battle victory.

With Eleanor Paget's death there was no enemy in sight. No scent or tracks leading me to an undiscovered truth. All I had was a deep-seated suspicion that death had not come to Paget by her own hand. That, a couple mil, Catholic guilt and my family home in a necrotic part of southeast Detroit.

Meanwhile, FBI Special Agent Megan O'Donnell provided me with the perfect opportunity to brush up on my evasive driving skills.

On my way back to Mexicantown from the suburban grocery store where I'd talked with Frank the ex-security guard, I noticed her navy-blue Chevy Suburban three cars behind me as I drove east on West 12 Mile Road. It was four o'clock and rush hour traffic was at the beginnings of its stranglehold.

Whoever was chauffeuring O'Donnell was doing a pretty good job: Not following too close. Dropping back every once in a while. But being followed by a Chevy Suburban was like Goliath tip-toeing inches behind David.

I threw O'Donnell's driver a curve by making a quick "Michigan left," heading west on 12 Mile Road and taking the first entrance into a subdivision called Barrington Green.

Most of the streets in Farmington Hills subdivisions were narrow and serpentine. If you had a good lead, it was easy to lose a tail in any one of these subs, considering each was its own little Bermuda Triangle. I managed to round a long curve through look-alike early '70s homes, then backed into the tree-shaded driveway of a yellow two-story house with black shutters.

O'Donnell's car—dangerously exceeding the 20 mph speed limit and blowing past a "Deaf Child" caution sign—rounded the curve, its wheels screeching as it passed the yellow house where I sat. Sliding out of the driveway, I eased up behind them and flashed my headlights.

The Chevy Suburban pulled to the side of the narrow subdivision road and I pulled alongside it. The rear driver's side window lowered and I lowered my window in kind.

"Nice fall day we're having, isn't it?" I said to Agent O'Donnell.

"We need to talk," O'Donnell said, once again proving that she either didn't like or didn't understand my particular brand of humor.

"Always a pleasure to chat with the FBI," I said. "Where to? I could fix a nice late lunch at my house. Or maybe a pricey little restaurant out here, your treat. Antonio's is just up the street. Really good Italian."

We settled on my house in Mexicantown.

"You need the address?" I said. "Oh, wait. You're FBI."

Five minutes after I'd lost them on the Lodge and I-75 South they parked in front of my house on Markham Street. A few neighbor curtains edged back, eyes in the shadows carefully assessing the young, petite blonde with the altogether too serious look.

Her driver stayed in the SUV.

O'Donnell looked around the house, nodding approvingly. "Nice digs. Not so sure about the neighborhood, though."

"Where I grew up," I said. "Make yourself comfortable. I've got some leftover Chinese, or I could—"

"I'm not here to eat, Mr Snow," she said. "I'm here as a courtesy to warn you off looking any further into Eleanor Paget's bank. As I'm sure you're well aware, I don't have to be courteous."

I grabbed myself a Negra Modelo from the fridge, flipped the cap off and said, "I'm not looking into Paget's bank. I'm looking into her death—"

"A suicide?" O'Donnell laughed, even though I was beginning to think she thought very little if anything was funny. "Not much to look into there, bucko. Seems the Grosse Pointe police, the state police, the Detroit police and assorted sundry others have quickly concluded she took her own life."

"They're not as smart as me," I said, taking a healthy swig of my beer. Michigan might be at the forefront of making quality craft beers, but so far none even approached a good Mexican beer. "Nor are they as righteously vigilant."

"Wow," O'Donnell said as she scrutinized what few pictures I had hung in the living room. "Is it me that brings out the asshole in you, or is this just you being natural?"

"Don't mind me, Special Agent O'Donnell," I said. "I get ner-ner-nervous around pr-pr-pretty women. Makes me think I have to act movie-star tough. I'm really a nice guy who enjoys poetry and cooking."

"Somehow you don't strike me as a New Age, kale smoothie kinda guy," she said. "Maybe something to do with that sizable callous on your right inner palm, eh, gunny?"

O'Donnell continued her stroll around the living room, running a hand appreciatively along the back of my sofa. "I understand you had a close encounter with a Mr. Kosimer Kolochek several nights ago?" I gave her a look. "A.K.A. Bob Franks."

"Oh," I said. "Him."

"What did you and Bobby talk about?"

"Franks—or Kolochek—and his partner made a run at me." I plopped down on my sofa. I was really beginning to like this sofa. O'Donnell, her head cocked, was evaluating the gravitas—or lack thereof—of my books on the shelves near the fireplace. "I tried to make him understand that such a thing was unwise."

"And you didn't think to call me about this?" she said, stopping at the two pieces of art I'd hung on my walls. One was a 2008 campaign poster for President Barak Obama that had been signed by the artist. The other was an oil portrait of Octavio Paz that my mother had painted.

"Didn't think whatever your investigation is and Mr. Kolochek were connected," I took another pull of my beer. "Are they?"

"Let's just say he's a known low-end felon." Now she was studying my mother's painting. "Jersey mostly. Stops in Cleveland and Nashville. Petty larceny. Some extortion. Small time drugs. Nearly beat a guy to death in Toledo over eighty bucks. Public defenders keep dumping him back on the streets. Any idea why he might be in Detroit, Mr. Snow?"

"Maybe he's here for a ballgame," I said. "You follow the Tigers? They're leading the ALC Central, you know."

"How nice for them." O'Donnell took a step back from Octavio Paz. "Who did this painting?"

"My mother," I said.

"Lady's got talent," she said, nodding approvingly.

"She's dead."

"Sorry to hear that."

"Do you know what an 'amusement park' is?" I said. O'Donnell turned from the painting and, with her arms folded over her chest, captured me in her dispassionate gaze. "Ask your cybercrimes guy what an 'amusement park' is. I bet he'll know. And I'll bet you come real close to lighting his hair on fire after he tells you."

O'Donnell held me in her unblinking ice-blue gaze for several long, hard seconds.

Then she said, "Nice sofa."

"Thanks," I replied. "I picked it out all by myself. Works well with the TV."

"A few more pieces of furniture," she said, "and this place might actually look like somebody lives here."

"Would you like to see the bedroom?" I said, giving my eyebrows a Groucho Marx flex. "It's state-of-the-art."

"Think she'd mind?" O'Donnell nodded to the photo of Tatina

and me near a fjord in Alesund, Norway on the fireplace mantle. Impervious to my charms, O'Donnell left without closing the door behind her.

It would have been easy to dismiss her as a sharp-knuckled, humorless government automaton. Truth of the matter was I was beginning to like O'Donnell, even if the admiration wasn't mutual.

18

Much of Eleanor Paget's considerable personal wealth had been willed to various charities, local hospitals, and the Detroit Institute of the Arts. From what I could gather, her daughter Vivian stood to inherit sixty-five million from her mother's estate, including the Grosse Pointe Estates house, an apartment in New York overlooking Central Park and a small villa in Tuscany.

When my parents passed away, I got my childhood home in a dying part of town, a couple grand from a life-insurance policy, their books and my mother's oil paintings.

Vivian Paget, now in her mid-twenties, lived the quiet, unassuming life of a watercolor artist in Traverse City, four hours north of Detroit. I remembered her as an attractive younger version of Eleanor. As opposed to her mercurial and bombastic mother, Vivian had appeared sullen and self-contained, full of secrets and deeply-rooted fears.

Through a bouquet of condolence flowers, I managed to charm Rose Mayfield into giving me Vivian's telephone number. I also managed to get on Atchison's calendar. It was time the CEO of Titan Securities Investment Group and I sat down and had a little chat about the bank, the board of directors and his professional relationship with Eleanor Paget.

Before disconnecting, Mayfield thanked me again for the flowers and quickly added, "When you call Vivian, be gentle with her.

She's a wonderful, talented young lady but she's—how shall I say?—delicate. Tell her I gave you her number. We've known each other since she was five. She trusts me and I love her."

"Thank you, Ms. Mayfield," I said. "I owe you one."

She laughed. "I may just take you up on that someday."

Just as I was about to make the call, there was a knock on my door, followed by the overly gleeful sing-song voices of two women calling, "Mr. Snoooow!" and "Hello-ke-dokey, neighbor!"

Carmela and Sylvia.

I briefly considered not answering the door, but against my better judgment I did.

Carmela—her eyes glimmering above round, dimpled cheeks—was holding a large plate wrapped in tinfoil. Sylvia, her abundance of silver hair whipping about in the fall breeze, held out a shining wine bag.

"We just wanted to stop by and thank you for everything, Mr. Snow," Carmela said. "Flautas," she said of the plate. "I just made them."

"And what are flautas without sangria?" Sylvia said.

I invited the two old women in.

"I hope we're not interrupting anything," Sylvia said, her eyes darting around me for a more comprehensive view of the house.

"Not at all, ladies," I said. "Just making a few calls."

In the kitchen I got out plates, glasses and some ice from the fridge. Carmela and Sylvia served up the flautas and poured the sangria. It might have been a little early in the day for sangria, but it wasn't exactly like I had any place pressing to be. And I doubted the old girls had very much of anything to do, save for watching *The View*.

"To good neighbors," I said, raising my glass of sangria.

The ladies raised their glasses, then each took a surprisingly big gulp, which was followed by girlish giggles.

We sat at the kitchen island and talked.

As we talked, I felt something I'd not felt in a long time:

Comfortable. Relaxed. At home in my own skin. My mother had always had people in her kitchen. Talking, laughing, eating. And the aroma of Carmela's flautas only further transported me back to those halcyon days of getting my cheeks pinched and jiggled by an endless array of adopted aunts all speaking Spanish at the speed of light.

Both Carmela and Sylvia had retired from the Detroit Water & Sewage Department. They'd been hired on at the same time, became friends and retired the same week. Carmela was born and raised in Mexicantown while Sylvia was from Detroit's Polish enclave, Hamtramck. Carmela had two sons and a daughter and all three jealously laid claim to her upon her retirement. Early in her retirement she split the difference, agreeing to live with each for four months of the year—one in West Bloomfield, one in Farmington Hills and the other in San Diego.

Sylvia had two daughters. She enjoyed her house of thirty years in Hamtramck. After two break-ins, the increasing noise from neighboring clubs and the changing nature of Hamtramck—from shops selling Polish red floral silk scarves to shops selling stylish silk hijabs—she was ready to leave. Not that she had anything in particular against her new Muslim and Chaldean neighbors. It was just that she saw her life—familiar aromas, small stores where Polish was spoken—evaporating. She was ready for a change. She wasn't, however, ready to move in with either of her daughters and their young children.

"Last thing I want in retirement is to be somebody's live-in babysitter," Sylvia said. "Lord knows I love my grandkids. But, God forgive me, two hours a week with them is enough."

And thus hatched the plan between two old friends over too many margaritas and nachos to buy the house in Mexicantown.

"We love it!" Carmela said.

"Apparently, you don't love it enough," I said. Both women gave me a quizzical look. "The kitchen cabinets?"

Sylvia patted my hand. "Oh, now, don't get all upset, dear. You're a man. How are you to know what looks right?"

They giggled. Partially at my overly dramatic reaction, mostly, I suspected, from the sangria.

I asked them how Jimmy Radmon was working out. They spoke of him as mothers speak of loving, accomplished sons: He was conscientious. Considerate. He had manners—"You don't often find that in young people these days." And he was funny.

"He speaks very highly of you, too," Carmela said.

The only concerns the two women had were the two houses to the east of them that were empty. One a foreclosure, the other simply abandoned. So far the empty houses posed no threats. But empty houses in Detroit were always a big draw for vermin of the four-legged and two-legged varieties. Carmela and Sylvia were considering buying one of the houses and renovating it, but they'd have to sit down and see where they were with their pension checks (recently reduced by virtue of Detroit's bankruptcy settlement), investments and savings.

After an hour the ladies said they'd kept me from my day long enough and, buoyant from the sangria, made their way back to their house. Though their walk was only a minute or so, I watched to make sure they got home safely.

Gathering my senses, I finally made the call to Vivian Elizabeth Paget.

Using my most calming and reassuring voice—honed by the many interviews I conducted during my brief and illustrious career as a cop—I said that she and I had briefly met when I worked a case for her mother several years ago. I was sorry about her mother's death and I was not convinced she had committed suicide. And any information she could provide me concerning her mother, the bank and the people surrounding her might be helpful.

"I—I'm uncomfortable with this." Vivian Paget's voice was soft, unsure. "I've already talked to the police. I don't know anything about the bank or the people she associated with. My mother and I weren't exactly—"

In the background another woman's voice bellowed, "Who is it? Who is that?"

Vivian's already soft voice became muffled—a hand lightly held over the speaker.

"Somebody named August Snow," I heard Vivian say. "It's about Mother."

The next voice I heard was not Vivian's. "Who the hell are you?" the woman said. "What do you want?"

I calmly told her who the hell I was and what I wanted.

None of that carried much truck with the woman.

"Listen, jerk-off," the woman said in a hushed voice, "Viv's been through a lot already. Twenty-six years' worth of a lot. And if you knew her piece-of-shit father and her controlling bitch of a mother then you'd know what I'm saying. So do whatever you gotta do without bothering us, okay?"

"I'm sorry," I said. "You are?"

"Gone."

The woman disconnected.

I called back.

"Listen, motherf—" the other woman began.

"Rose Mayfield," I said quickly. "That's how I got your number. Rose Mayfield gave it to me."

After a long pause, the woman pulled away from the phone and said, "He claims Rosey gave him this number." Then her voice came back to the phone and she said in a calmer yet no less stern voice, "This better check out or I will seriously injure you."

"You'll have to take a number and get in line for that," I said.

"Five minutes," the woman said.

"Five minutes."

Then the line went dead.

Five minutes seemed ample time to finish off the bottle of sangria and wonder what the hell I was doing.

A few sips in, the other woman called back. "Sorry to give you a hard time, Mr. Snow."

"August," I said. "Please."

"I'm Colleen," the woman said. "Viv's wife."

"Viv's a beautiful human being," Colleen Belluomo said. "Smart. Incredibly talented. Generous and thoughtful. No thanks to her crappy-assed parents. You've got to understand—I love her and I don't want anything or anybody to hurt her."

"I understand," I said.

"Rosey—Rose Mayfield—was about the only person who came close to being a real mom to Viv," Colleen said. "She's the only reason you and I are talking right now." Then Colleen sighed heavily. "What's your interest in any of this, August?"

"I used to be a cop," I said. "When I was on the job I caught the case with her father's death and the death of his—girlfriend. I got to know Vivian's mom, and yeah, she was tough and nasty and vindictive as hell. She also came to respect me. Who I am, what I did and how I did it."

"You're *that* cop?" Colleen said. "The one who got shit-canned for blowing the whistle on Detroit's old mayor and his dirty cop pals?"

"One and the same," I said. "Vivian's mom recently asked me to help her and I didn't. Two days later she was dead. Probably would have happened whether I helped or not. If it was suicide I want to know what drove her to it. If it wasn't—"

"Jesus," Colleen said. "You think somebody killed her?"

"I don't know. All I know is I failed her trust. I don't like to fail."

"Guilt's a hard way to live," Colleen said.

"I'm Catholic. You get used to it."

There was silence at the other end.

Then Colleen pulled away from the phone and said, "Hey, hon? He seems all right. Come on, baby. Talk to him."

Before she handed the phone over to Vivian, I heard Colleen say, "Any problems, you just hang up. Or you hand him over to me, n'k?"

The sound of a quick kiss, then, "Hello?"

I apologized for bothering her and said I wished I didn't have to. But as I'd said to her wife, this was the only way I knew how to live. The way I'd been taught by my parents, the marines and the DPD. I asked her how long it had been since she had seen or talked to her mother. She said it had been at least two years since she'd seen her mother. About the same time the investigation into her father's death closed and she'd come out of the closet.

Vivian said her mother had found her lifestyle embarrassing. Her embarrassment had nothing to do with perceived political or religious implications. Eleanor Paget created her own constructs of politics and her religion was clearly self-fulfillment. And as to sex—straight, gay or otherwise—I was pretty sure Eleanor Paget equated the act with any business negotiation where all parties vied for the dominance of their own personal interests.

But to have a daughter who, by birth alone, had an "obligation" to the generations-old Paget name, the Paget legacy—and have her turn out to be a lesbian artist was an unnecessary distraction from the business imperative of maintaining an empire.

Sexual opportunism was, Vivian believed, the only reason Eleanor had consented to marry Vivian's father: Maurice Allensworth had risen through the ranks of Detroit's car companies, ultimately and by sheer force of will building his own automotive interior components business.

"She's the one who convinced him to sell his business and put the money into the family bank," Vivian said. "He didn't want to, but—well, you know how forceful she is. Was."

Allensworth caved to Eleanor's considerable will and sold his business, folding the proceeds into hers. Of course had he maintained the business up to the 2008 economic collapse, he would have been bankrupted. Nobody bought cars for the next three years and, as such, parts suppliers were the first to die.

Knowing Eleanor, she probably lorded this over her husband without shame or reservation.

Vivian finally said, "I spent most of my childhood at boarding schools. I—I actually preferred it that way. I didn't want to be around him—her. Sometimes I'd spend several weeks at Aunt Rosey and Uncle Desmond's house."

"'Uncle Desmond'?"

"Aunt Rosey's husband," Vivian said. "He's—he passed away." She took in a ragged breath and exhaled slowly. "Those were really some of the best times. Being with them. I felt safe with Aunt Rosey and Uncle Des. I felt—wanted."

I asked Vivian about the last time she'd spoken to her mother. She said, "Until about eight months ago, we spoke maybe three times a year. Then she started calling more frequently. The last couple months she called at least once every two weeks. She sounded—different. Smaller. Unsure of herself. She'd ask how Colleen was and if I needed anything. How my art was selling. I asked her if everything was all right and she just laughed it off, saying it was the wine talking and everything was fine." Vivian paused. "I'd never heard her sound like that. Ever."

"Tell me a little bit about your mom's relationship with Rose Mayfield."

"Rosey made my mother—human," Vivian said. "She confided in Rosey. Trusted her. And Rosey could see things in my mother no one else could. Good things. You don't think—"

"No," I said. "Frankly, I don't know what to think at this point, Ms. Paget."

"Rosey's a wonderful person, Mr. Snow," Vivian said. "If she's guilty of anything it's taking more of my mother and father's shit than she should have. I blame myself for that. I think the older my mother got, the more she felt replaced by Rosey as my mother. And my mother was never replaced by anybody."

I figured Vivian needed a break, so I asked her about her art.

She was a watercolorist, having studied at Detroit's world renown College for Creative Studies. She loved CCS, but it wasn't far enough away from her parents. She finally studied at the Sorbonne and began selling in small Parisian and Italian galleries.

I told her I'd just moved back to Detroit, that I was decorating my house and would be interested in seeing some of her work.

She surprised me by asking, "Are you simply interested in decorating?"

It took me a second or two to decipher her question, but when I did, I answered, "My mother was a painter. Not professional, but you'd never know it from her work. I'm looking at one of her paintings right now. A portrait of the Mexican poet Octavio Paz. There's a lot of her soul in that painting and it warms me every time I look at it."

There was a long pause at the other end of the line.

Finally, she said, "Go to my website, Mr. Snow. Just pick something out and email me your home address. Whatever you choose, it's yours."

"I couldn't—"

"Please," she said. "Let me do this for you. Because of what you said about your mother. I envy you that. And because—you let me talk. It was hard to talk about this stuff with Colleen. Not because of Colleen—she's fantastic—but—"

"Just think of me as a priest and this is our confessional moment," I said. Then, making the sign of the cross in the air, even though she couldn't see it, I said, "Bless you. Now say three Hail Marys and drink a pitcher of margaritas."

Vivian laughed a bright, clear, lilting laugh.

"Goodnight, Vivian," I said.

"Goodnight, August," she said. "If you're ever up this way, promise you'll stop by. We'll skip the Hail Marys and go directly for Colleen's homemade honey vodka."

"Deal."

We hung up.

I finished my sangria, retrieved a beer from the fridge and flopped on my new sofa. For a moment I stared at the blank screen of my TV over the fireplace. Then, without really looking, my eyes settled on my mother's painting of the Mexican poet.

Something at the very back of my mind. The claw of a small animal scratching on black glass . . .

20

I bought my second new suit in less than a month: a nice Calvin Klein three-button slim-fit in a heather-grey wool blend. Once again Marcus, the Eastern European tailor, was on the case. While fitting me he occasionally consulted a small black notebook and, like a mad scientist, found a passage or note that had him exclaiming, "Ah! Yes!" Then he would make his chalk marks. At one point Marcus stood on tippy toe and whispered, "You buy a new gun, you tell me. Makes difference in measurements, yes?"

When Tuesday morning came, I was looking good and ready to meet Kip Atchison, CEO of Titan Securities Investment Group.

Eleanor Paget was one of the first Detroit entrepreneurs to take an interest in revitalizing the city's business core. Her considerable efforts had little to do with altruism. They had everything to do with money and solidifying her public legacy. Paget had shouldered, elbowed, bit, clawed and bludgeoned her way into the boys' club of other Detroit business luminaries, all millionaires tens and hundreds of times over.

After the riots and "white flight" in the '60s, several crushing recessions and astoundingly bad political management, property in Detroit became dirt cheap. Architectural wonders that had fifty years ago boasted ninety to a hundred percent occupancy had in recent decades gone begging. Four-star hotels went dark and

Michelin-rated restaurants were shuttered. A pall settled over the city, lingering like smog over L.A.

This was the perfect multi-generational storm for entrepreneurs with pockets full of cash, including Paget. Detroit real estate in the early 21st century meant power. The power to shape a municipality to the benefit of the wealthy. It was the Oklahoma Land Rush of 1889.

41781 Titan Place on Woodward Avenue was Eleanor Paget's land grab acquisition: a white skyscraper built in the late '70s, gone into disuse for much of the '90s and brought back to vibrant life in 2000.

The lobby of Titan Securities Investments Group was large and open, with an expanse of polished white marble floors, tall windows, lazily curving black leather sofas and ultra-modern stainless steel coffee tables. There were four dogwood saplings growing up through mulched holes in the marble floor and a modern take on a Japanese garden fountain at the lobby's center. There were expensive sculptures, paintings and three large wall-mounted flat screen TVs.

None of the TVs were showing SportsCenter.

An expansive curved desk sat in front of a two-story marble wall bearing the Titan logo in polished stainless steel. At the desk sat an attractive black woman with short-cropped auburn hair, her expression pleasant but very professional.

The appearance of the lobby was inviting and feng shui. I took note of at least six security cameras. There were three security guards—one of them a big, beefy black guy—dressed identically in well-tailored black suits. One of the guards sat at the end of one of the sofas near the main entrance. A gaunt white guy with brown hair streaked with grey at the temples and wearing wire rim glasses. He was casually flipping through a magazine. It was my guess this guy was in command and on-point. The other two guards—bigger and beefier—were stationed by the elevators behind and to the right of the reception desk.

Looking like a million offshore bucks, I walked up to the good-looking woman at the lobby desk and announced myself.

"August Octavio Snow," I said. "I have a nine o'clock with Mr. Kip Atchison."

The receptionist smiled a perfect hostess smile, welcomed me to TSIG, Inc. and briefly consulted an iPad. She swept an elegant and well-manicured forefinger across the screen, then tapped something. Looking up at me and still holding her perfect smile, she said, "Please have a seat, Mr. Snow. Mr. Atchison's executive assistant will be with you momentarily. Would you like something to drink? Spring water? Cappuccino?"

"Got any single malts back there?" I said.

"Glenmorangie? Glenfiddich?"

"Seriously?" I said.

"I never joke when it comes to providing our guests and patrons with the highest level of comfort and convenience."

I guessed "patrons" meant "customers" or "shareholders." From a credenza drawer behind her, she pulled out a Waterford crystal tumbler and placed it on a rolling tray.

"May I assume you take it neat?" she said.

"It's nine in the morning," I said.

"It's happy hour somewhere," she said with a demure smile.

Inadvertently, I laughed. Then with a raised palm I said, "Pass."

She touched a finger to her ear, said, "Yes, ma'am," listened for a few more seconds and then said, "Ms. Mayfield will be with you momentarily. She apologizes for an unavoidable delay."

I took a seat on one of the leather sofas. On the coffee table in front of me were an assortment of neatly arranged magazines and newspapers: *Barron's, Bloomberg Businessweek, The Wall Street Journal.* There were also magazines like *Architectural Digest, National Geographic Traveler* and *Travel + Leisure.* Nothing with comics except for the most recent issue of *The New Yorker,* and I rarely found their cartoons funny.

In the fifteen minutes it took Rose Mayfield to come and retrieve me, ten people had entered the lobby. Three talked briefly to the woman at the desk before heading to one of the three elevators at the back of the lobby. Five checked in at the desk, nodded and took seats on the other leather sofas, or simply stood and looked out the windows at the crowds and traffic on Woodward Avenue. The remaining two—a well-dressed elderly couple in the middle of a discussion—stopped near me to reassess exactly how much they needed for their annual month abroad.

"I thought we decided?" the elderly man said to the woman I presumed was his wife.

"Well," the woman said hesitantly, "we kind of did. A month's a long time, Jessep. I'm not so sure fifty's going to be enough. And I don't want to put a lot on our cards."

The man shrugged his narrow Harris Tweed-covered shoulders (as I assumed many a man married for over thirty years shrugs when discussing plans with his wife) then proceeded to the desk, where they were unctuously greeted by the receptionist and escorted to an elevator.

Customers of TSIG coming to check on their pirate's chest of gold doubloons.

A minute later the doors of an elevator slid open and Rose Mayfield emerged. One of the two security guards at the elevators started to escort her, but at a briefly raised hand from Mayfield he stopped and went back to his sentry post. As soon as the young woman at the lobby desk saw Mayfield, she stood, smiled and gestured discreetly to me. Mayfield nodded—she knew who I was—and walked toward me.

No sooner had I stood than the security guard with wire-rim glasses and grey-streaked hair quickly approached Mayfield. She held up a palm and he obediently stopped.

"Wow," I said to Mayfield. "You're like a Cesar Millan human whisperer."

Mayfield and I shook hands. She said, "I am so sorry for the delay, Mr. Snow. Every day is a challenge, emergency or test of faith. We've avoided disaster thus far."

I said it wasn't a problem and that I'd been enjoying the ambiance and riveting conversation—"Boxers, briefs or commando"—with the dead-eyed security guard who at this point stood well within earshot of me.

We entered the elevator and the doors slid closed. Mayfield swiped a keycard against a laser reader and we began to ascend.

"How many floors?" I said.

"TSIG has the first ten," Mayfield said. "Eleven and twelve belong to one of our non-profit ventures—LifeLight, Inc. Fourteen through eighteen we lease. Nineteen and twenty are TSIG executive offices."

"What's this LifeLight thing?"

"We buy state-of-the-art streetlights—solar powered LEDs—and install them in neighborhoods that have been without them for ten, fifteen years. We've partnered with some of the car companies as well as DTE and a few others, to offset the costs. We've still got a long way to go. So far we've installed sixty-five with a goal of a hundred and twenty by the end of this quarter."

"I think some of those lights are in my neighborhood," I said.

"Really?" Mayfield said, smiling. "Which neighborhood is that?"

"Mexicantown."

We came to a stop on the twentieth floor and emerged into a large, airy office space decorated with curving glass block cubicles and Scandinavian-styled pearwood furniture. It was mostly well-dressed young people gazing intently into the hypnotic glow of tablet computers or talking the lingua franca of finance on telephones. Others were performing their mission-critical walk along the plush carpeting, consulting notepads, checking emails or texting on smartphones.

"A twelve million dollar settlement from the city and you move to Mexicantown? Isn't that a bit of a risky proposition?"

"I was raised there," I said. "Back then it was a great place. I'd like to see it become a great place again." Then I said, "What's LifeLight's installation goal?"

"The company that makes the streetlamps is a start-up with proprietary technology. It's going to take some time for them to ramp up production capabilities, but we're hoping we can have five hundred installed over the next three years. Lots of people out there living in the dark."

"Lots of carnivores feeding in the dark," I said.

"Plus we've got a couple land development proposals in front of city council," Mayfield continued. "Large-scale urban gardens. Community parks. Wind and solar energy farms. Lots of open land in Detroit these days. Not very surprising considering the population now is about what it was in 1910."

"Your idea or Eleanor Paget's?"

Mayfield was steely and uncompromising in her clipped answer. "Mine." Her chocolate brown eyes held me in their command when she added, "When Elle took over the bank from her father—which she had to wrestle from his cold, dead grip—I was one of the first ten new employees here. And the first black. The only original still standing. Elle and I became friends. I was one of the few people that took little to none of her shit, if you'll pardon my spicy language."

"Being half-black and half-Mexican, I'm quite the fan of spicy language," I said.

As we walked down the long, wide hallway, everyone we passed nodded deferentially and said, "Ms. Mayfield."

We reached a set of tall, brushed steel doors framed in rosewood. Mayfield pushed through the doors and took a seat behind the large rosewood desk. She gestured for me to sit in one of the two high-back red leather chairs.

"Mr. Atchison's office?" I said, looking around and admiring the décor.

"Mine," Mayfield said. She nodded to another set of tall, brushed steel doors to her left. "His office is through there."

Upon closer inspection, there were signs that this was indeed Mayfield's office: Photos of her smiling and being embraced by Eleanor Paget. Photos of Mayfield with the new mayor of Detroit, the governor and Presidents Barak Obama, Bush-43, Bill and Hillary Clinton. There were ornately scrolled citations from the most recent mayor, the governor and the presidents of Wayne State University, University of Detroit and Madonna University. And there were two large framed watercolor paintings directly behind her desk. Vivian Paget's work, I assumed.

"How's it feel to be so close to Titan's heir apparent?" I said.

She laughed. "There were heir apparents before him," she said. "And there will be heir apparents after him. I've signed the checks paying for their office remodels. And I've signed the checks for the movers who have ushered them unceremoniously out. Eleanor went through presidents, vice presidents, CIOs, COOs, directors and managers like a fat man goes through a bag of M&Ms." She smiled. "I, Mr. Snow, am the only constant."

I asked her about former employees and if any of them had been problematic upon their departure.

Mayfield, looking in full command behind her desk, said, "There have been a couple of lawsuits. Settled quickly, quietly and for sums that were regained within the first hour of the next trading day. The others have gone on to other private wealth management organizations. Two months here at Titan, whether they were fired or not, is considered quite prestigious to like firms. And some consider hiring a former TSIG executive a joyous middle-finger to us." Then Mayfield paused, grinned and said, "Have we been enjoying a friendly conversation, Mr. Snow? Or perhaps an interrogation?"

"Bit of both, I suppose," I said. "My apologies."

"I wouldn't have it any other way."

Her desk phone rang and she answered it.

Titan's fair-haired boy was on his way.

21

Tall, trim, athletically built and Hollywood-handsome, Kip Atchison strode into Rose Mayfield's office smiling a multimillion dollar smile. He extended his manicured hand and we shook.

"Mr. Snow," he said. His suit made me feel like I was wearing a burlap sack. Atchison was the magnificently dressed icon for youth, affluence and power. "I apologize for running late."

"No problem," I said, flashing my own dashing grin. "I've been enjoying Ms. Mayfield's company."

He laughed, glanced at Rose Mayfield and said, "Well, I'm glad *somebody* enjoys her company! She's a real taskmaster. Sometimes I do everything I can to avoid her just so she doesn't run me ragged."

"Which reminds me," Mayfield said, "you've got dinner with Fred Dunn and Greg Stafford tonight at seven, Detroit Athletic Club—"

"Cancel it. Tell 'em to get their kneepads on next week."

"And," Mayfield continued, "a presentation prep for the Garrett Trust acquisition—"

"Garrett Trust," Atchison said under his breath. "What an oxymoron—"

"Either way," Mayfield said, forging professionally forward, "they'll be here Thursday. I've already flown in lobster from Goose Rocks to make them feel a bit more—"

"Save the lobster for our acquisitions team," Atchison said

calmly. "Get those Garrett pissants Subway. Six inch, not twelve. No fuckin' chips."

He took long, self-assured strides and I followed him toward the tall brushed metal doors to the left of Rose Mayfield's office.

Mayfield's office was stunning in its space and tasteful appointments. But it was a small anteroom compared to Atchison's office, which was at least three times the size. It afforded a panoramic view of the Detroit city skyline, the meandering Detroit River and Detroit's Canadian neighbor to the south, Windsor, Ontario.

Garish abstract paintings hung on the walls, along with a dramatic black-and-white photo of Atchison's stunning wife and two perfect young children. The photo was the kind you'd see in a successful suburban dentist's office: cover-model white people huddled closely together, all exposing radiant white teeth.

"I understand you have some considerable assets, Mr. Snow," Atchison said as we traversed the expanse of his office. "Ever think about a wealth management firm like us?"

"I'm old fashioned," I said. "My money's in a mattress."

"Mattresses won't get you three point five APR. And travel bonus points. We've got a really fabulous special this quarter: open a two-mil minimum balance savings, checking or investment account and get a two-year Land Rover LR4 lease on us. Something to think about, right?"

"Oh, yeah," I said, unconvinced.

There was a marble fireplace, full bar, large wall-mounted flat-screen TV and assorted other entertainment electronics. And there was his desk: a long oval glass-top desk with glass Corinthian pillar legs. On the desk were three large computer screens, each monitoring the worldwide heartbeat of money.

Near the bar was an electric guitar on a stand and a small amplifier.

Atchison saw me looking. "Recognize that guitar?"

"Can't say I do."

"Ever see that movie *Back to the Future?*" he said. I nodded. I had, a long time ago with my father. "That's the guitar Marty McFly played! Not a replica, but the real thing! Erlewine Chiquita travel guitar. Single humbucker and volume control, Schaller Honduran mahogany bridge, rosewood pickup. You play?"

"No," I said. "You?"

"No," Atchison said. "But that movie? Wow! Best movie *ever*. Classic! Marty McFly is kind of a hero of mine."

"It's good to have heroes," I said, struggling to contain my sarcasm.

"Have a seat." Atchison gestured to an ultra-modern taupe-colored leather sofa with brushed nickel buttons. He took off his suit coat and casually tossed it across the back of a matching taupe leather armchair facing his desk. He proceeded to loosen his tie, unbutton his shirtsleeves and fold them up.

America's Working Man Hero.

He took a seat on the sofa, making a sound that suggested he hadn't sat for quite some time. Then, clapping his hands once, said, "Rosey offer you anything? Coffee? Tea? Maybe a juice or Red Bull?"

"She did," I said. "Nothing for me."

"Hey, Rosey!" he suddenly shouted. Mayfield entered the office seemingly unfazed by Atchison's frat-boy familiarity. Having worked for and befriended Eleanor Paget, I had the feeling it took a lot more than an Atchison type to set a quiver through her inestimable foundation. "Be a dear and get me a double-shot capp and a chocolate chip biscotti, would you?"

"I will get you a half-caff cappuccino and a low-fat yogurt with berries," Mayfield said.

"Jesus, Rosey—" Atchison whined like the child he very nearly was.

"You've already had three double-shot cappuccinos, five chocolate chip biscotti and God only knows what else this morning,"

Mayfield said. "You may call that 'breakfast.' I call it a heart attack waiting to happen."

"Fine," Atchison grumbled, turning to me and adding, "See what abuse I endure?"

"See what lunacy I suffer?" Mayfield said before leaving.

"Okay," Atchison said, again clapping his hands once. I imagined his single handclap was a way of controlling his apparent ADHD. "Eleanor Paget. Great lady. Unfortunate death. Police say suicide. You not so much. How can I help you with any of this, Mr. Snow?"

I briefly wondered how he knew I didn't think she'd killed herself, but decided to file that question away for another time.

"Just a couple questions," I said. "Nothing official."

"Of course."

His multimillion dollar grin just would not go away and I began to find it patronizing and sanctimonious. It's been my experience that most people who grin this much are either insane, professional liars or vampires. I was beginning to suspect that Atchison might be a hybrid of these.

I emphasized that I was no longer a cop. That this was strictly personal and he had every right to toss me out of his panorama of windows and watch me fall. I gave him an idea of the relationship I had with Eleanor Paget and that in my visit with her, days before her death, she had expressed concerns about her bank's current operations.

I left out details concerning the coroner's autopsy and the fact that the FBI was at this very moment crawling around inside the bank's computer system.

Atchison's sandy blond eyebrows furrowed. He looked intently at me, nodding at each bullet point I ticked off.

"Only six people had all-access security passes to Paget's house," I finally said. "Aaron Spiegelman, your CFO and president of the bank's board of directors. Dr. Harrison Henshaw, director of Detroit

Children's Hospital. Dr. Marleen Clarvineau, a curator at the DIA. Paget's personal attorney out of Chicago. Ms. Mayfield and you. Dr. Henshaw was out of town at a thoracic surgery conference in Atlanta. Her personal attorney was on business in New York. And Dr. Clarvineau was in Portland. That leaves you, Mr. Spiegelman and Ms. Mayfield in town and with access."

"And of course you checked with the company responsible for her home's security?" Atchison said, renewing the lease on his perfect grin.

"Those records can't be obtained without a court order and, since I'm currently considered lower than a snake's hairless ass by the Detroit public safety and legal systems, I don't imagine I'll ever have access. Besides. There's no pending case, ergo no need for those records."

Rose Mayfield brought a silver tray into Atchison's office. On the tray was a white mug bearing the TSIG logo with Atchison's half-caff cappuccino and yogurt. She sat the tray on the coffee table in front of us.

Atchison scowled at the yogurt and said, "I'll be shitting all night if I eat that crap."

"Yogurt and fruit are good for you," Mayfield said. She looked at me and smiled. "You're sure you won't have anything, Mr. Snow?"

I shook my head.

Mayfield glanced at her watch, looked at Atchison and said, "You've got the Stafford and Dunn conference call in fifteen minutes."

Atchison took a loud slurp of his cappuccino, nodded and told Mayfield he'd like his office door closed behind her. Then he brought his wide, faux-innocent eyes to me. "So you're pretty much flying solo, on fumes and looking for a place to land."

"Pretty much," I said.

"Okay," Atchison said brightly, then did his single handclap again. "Let's get to it: Aaron Spiegelman worshipped at the feet of

Eleanor Paget. She carried him around like a miniature poodle in a Louis Vuitton handbag. In all honesty I'd like him gone within the next three to six months. He's not a future-guy. I'm a future-guy. He was Eleanor's little birdie, flying back to her, perching on her finger and chirping about everything he could find out about my initiatives to take this bank into the future."

"Those initiatives being?"

Atchison raised the palm of his right hand to me. "We'll discuss those in a minute. As to Spiegelman, I'm sure the only person he's ever wanted to kill is me. Spiegelman's a wimp who spent his career bowing, kowtowing and taking Eleanor's orders like a Chinese laundry boy. And Rose Mayfield?" Atchison continued unabated. "She and Eleanor were best friends. They'd have their girl chats, girl giggles, girl arguments. Rose is a legacy employee with a titanium-clad employment contract. She's a gimme. A well-paid poster child for diversity with no reason to put Eleanor Paget in the ground. So I think you can safely check that one off. And me?" Atchison sat back, threw his arms to his sides and smiled. "What's my motivation for killing a woman who has given me this?"

"Word has it she gave you a little bit more than this," I said.

For a few seconds, we stared at each other, dueling with our megawatt smiles. Then Atchison said, "Woman could fuck like a porn star. Yeah, I was having an affair with Eleanor. Started two months after I arrived. Her initiation. As I'm sure you may have noticed she was attractive for her age. We understood each other. For people like us there's no division between business and pleasure. The two are intertwined."

I thought about what Tomás had told me about a naked Atchison retrieving a bottle of champagne from Eleanor Paget's refrigerator.

"Sure, we had our disagreements," Atchison said, "but at this level, the future isn't created by yes-men or sycophants. You ever hear of Elon Musk? I'm the Elon Musk of finance."

"Your wife ever meet Eleanor?"

Atchison laughed. "You're asking if my wife could've killed Eleanor?" He shook his head. "Yeah, she knew Eleanor. And yeah, she knew I was screwing Ellie on occasion. Was she angry or jealous? At the level my wife and I operate, jealousy is an antiquated middle-class morality concept: she knows it takes more than a nice pedigree to achieve and maintain my level of success. Plus—she likes the lake house in Charlevoix that came with my contract." He sighed, then leaned forward as if daring me to react. "Does any of this upset your particular moral balance or religious compass, Mr. Snow?"

I shrugged. "What you do with your dick is your business, Mr. Atchison. I could give two shakes of a rat's ass. I'm just trying to determine if you're a killer."

Atchison's grin widened. "And?"

"And," I said, "I think you were probably breast fed by Ayn Rand, raised by L. Ron Hubbard and educated by Malcolm Forbes. I think you're a vindictive narcissist deluded by his own self-worth. I think you're probably capable of killing someone if, in your assessment, they impede your vision of a more powerful future. I also know for a fact that if you did kill Eleanor Paget, I would take you down hard, ugly and fast."

Again, we stared at each other for a moment.

Suddenly Atchison roared with laughter, rolling back on the sofa like a child and clapping vigorously.

"That was so freakin' *cool*! 'I will take you down hard, ugly and fast,'" he repeated through his laughter. "Mind if I use that for this conference call I've got?"

"It's trademarked," I said.

He gave me a brief look as if I were serious then, deciding I wasn't, continued laughing for a few more seconds. He wiped tears from his eyes with a linen napkin from the coffee tray. To be honest, I hadn't expected to be granted a meeting with Atchison;

most killers like as much distance between themselves and their accusers as possible. Which all but confirms their guilt. Then there were egocentric head cases like Atchison who enjoyed a game of chess with their potential executioner.

"I like you, Mr. Snow," Atchison said. "Honestly. So let me be completely forthcoming with you: If I'd had Eleanor Paget killed, there wouldn't have been a body. Not a hair. Not a fiber or DNA. It would have been done with me far away sipping a nicely chilled cocktail in front of twenty witnesses. And a gun? No. Something more—feminine for Ellie. Sleeping pills. Valium overdose. And you, Mr. Snow, would have exactly what you have now: a finger up your nose and a thumb up your ass."

I stood. "Thanks for your time, Mr. Atchison."

"Jesus! This was *fun!*" Atchison bounded to his feet. "And think about that Range Rover deal, okay? It's a great deal! And we'll double your money within six to eight months. Guaranteed."

22

On our way out, Atchison told Rose Mayfield he'd be in the executive conference room and that he expected to be there for the next two hours. She was to have champagne chilled in case the meeting went his way. Which, of course, he fully expected it would.

Then he clapped once, told me again how fun our meeting was and rushed off to wherever the executive conference room was.

Mayfield escorted me to the elevator. "It's been a pleasure, Mr. Snow," she said, shaking my hand. "I hope you enjoyed your meeting."

"About as much as a root canal."

"Welcome to my world." She smiled. "As for me, it's been a pleasure."

"Same," I said. The elevator doors opened. I stepped in and held them open with my forearm. I said to Mayfield, "Can't be much fun."

"I'm sorry?"

"Thirty years of watching ass-monkeys like Atchison fly in and out of that office while you take their lunch orders," I said.

"At my age, Mr. Snow, I have little interest in career fulfillment, social justice or workplace fairness," Mayfield said with a soft smile. "I do, however, covet a peaceable stability, quiet contentment and the occasional midwinter escape to a place with palm trees and glow-in-the-dark drinks."

"You mind one more question?" I said.

"Depends on the question."

"Where were you the evening Eleanor Paget died?"

Mayfield held her smile and said, "At a women in business conference at the Detroit Athletic Club. Eighty to a hundred attendees. Of that perhaps fifteen or so black women. And of that, perhaps four or five my age. Shouldn't be hard to verify. Easier if you're a member. Are you?"

"No."

"Shall I look into a membership for you?" she said.

"My dance card's pretty full right now," I said. "Maybe another time."

I thanked her again, lowered my forearm and let the elevator door close between us.

After several seconds of gliding descent, the elevator doors slid open and I emerged into the lobby. The huge security guards at the elevators saw me and the black one said, "Have a nice day, sir." I told him to do the same. The young black woman at the reception desk noticed me, smiled and said, "Have a prosperous day, Mr. Snow." I said that I would and wished her the same. Walking to the glass revolving entrance doors I noticed the two lobby security guards, including the guy with wire-rim glasses, putting me squarely in their sights. I winked at them and said, "Keep up the good work, fellas!"

I liked Kip Atchison for the murder of Eleanor Paget primarily because I thought the guy was an egocentric sack of shit.

Then again, if being an egocentric sack of shit were a prosecutable crime, there wouldn't be a soul sitting in the US Senate.

I walked from Titan Securities Investments Group to Schmear's Deli. It was a bright, cool day and even the polluted city air felt much fresher and more honest than what I'd been breathing in Atchison's office.

I shot the breeze with Ben for a while. He got busy, so I made time with his waitresses. I ate a plate of scrambled eggs with fresh jalapeños, tomatillos and lox, and a toasted salt bagel, and drove home feeling like the only thing I'd accomplished was a good lunch.

On my way home I called Rocking Horse and said I needed Skittles to call me. A young woman with a serious New Jersey accent said there was no one there called "Skittles." I told her I was a little tired of this routine. She thanked me for calling and hung up.

As I drove past the Home Depot near Mexicantown, I saw my neighbor from across the street, Carlos Rodriguez. He, along with four other Mexicans, got out of a white Ford F-250 Crew Cab. After they'd retrieved their tool belts from the truck's bed, the truck drove off, leaving the men, splattered with drywall mud and sawdust, standing in the fall chill.

Five minutes away from my house, my phone rang. The ringtone this time was Eminem's "Not Afraid." Skittles. I answered and, after a brief-to-non-existent greeting, I told him what I needed.

"Seriously?" he said. "You want me to 'visit' Digital Defense Home Security?"

"I'm not comfortable asking you to do this, but—"

"Hey, man," Skittles said. "No problem. It's just—you know— I'm between a couple, uh, you know, things right now." I heard a girl laugh in the background. "Thirty minutes. Forty tops. Home security companies are usually pretty easy to hack. Usual fee. Same place."

"Usual fee. Same place," I said before thanking him.

"By the way," Skittles said. "There's a package at your house, Snowman. Use the red one first."

"Condoms?"

Skittles laughed and hung up.

On my way home, I'd picked up a tail. A black Cadillac Escalade with blacked out windows. Obviously they weren't concerned about subtlety. I was fairly sure it wasn't my FBI friends, who were a little more discreet in their Chevy Suburbans.

About a mile from my house, the Escalade gunned its massive engine, passed me and continued on its merry way.

There was a small box wrapped in brown paper at the foot of my door. No address. No markings or stamps. A small package of Skittles candy taped to the top.

I opened a bottle of Negra Modelo, then I opened the package: it was a shoebox and inside were six prepaid cell phones. Burners: good for two or three calls, outgoing or incoming, then you drop the SIM card in the gutter and the phone in somebody else's garbage. One of them began ringing.

The red one.

I answered it.

"So it works?" Skittles said.

"It works."

"Cool," he said. "We out."

I tossed the red cell phone on my sofa and stashed the rest of them in my upstairs bedroom closet.

Halfway through my beer, I began having misgivings about what I was into. Instead of having Skittles hack into Eleanor Paget's home security company's video and log archives, maybe I should've been sending Digital Defense Home Security a résumé. Maybe I should have been considering being one of the guys in a black suit in the lobby of Titan Securities Investments Group.

Anything but what I was doing.

You like a damned pit bull, Ray Danbury had said. *Teeth sink in, jaws lock and you ain't satisfied until a piece of somebody's ass been chewed off.*

I certainly didn't have to work anymore. Even with the money I'd pissed away on travel, refurbishing my childhood home and several other houses in the old neighborhood, furniture, a few new pieces of clothes, Frank the Grocery Bagger's education, Jimmy Radmon's modest salvation from a life of low-end crime, a couple of sizable offering plate donations to St. Al's Catholic Church and taking care of my friend Tomás, I still had more money than I could ever imagine spending in three lifetimes.

I gave brief thought to what Carmela and Sylvia had said earlier about two of the empty houses east of them on Markham: buy them, renovate them, flip them. I had absolutely no desire to become a real estate mogul, and flipping property these days in Mexicantown was just seeing the other side of a beat-up penny.

But it was something that didn't require a gun and poking around in the business of the dead and the dying.

By early evening I was hungry, so I made a quick fajita, grabbed a glass of orange juice and turned on the local TV news.

It was mostly the same news that I'd left behind over a year ago: Little kids being hit by stray bullets. Worthless mothers crying. Worthless moms' boyfriends in handcuffs. Reporters asking, "How do you *feel* about your dead baby?" There were the same old stories about Detroit's tsunami of financial woes and the city council clowns who were still running the circus. There was the sports report which, when it came to the Detroit Lions, sounded like a dismal passage from Charles Dickens's *Bleak House*. And the obligatory in-depth analysis of why U of M lost to Michigan State instead of why Michigan State had won.

Then there was the wrap-up news story. "More news is coming out of the wealth management and investment firm once run by Eleanor Paget," the news anchor said. "Today, one of the company's longtime officers announced his retirement: Chief Financial Officer Aaron Spiegelman."

They ran video of Spiegelman announcing his retirement. Standing next to him in Titan's downtown headquarters was Kip Atchison. Spiegelman looked like a whipped dog. Frail. Confused. Drained. Certainly not the attack dog I'd met several times. He stood at a podium bearing Titan's logo. He was a small, wiry man but he'd always seemed to be tightly coiled, ready to pounce at any given second. Now, standing at the podium, he looked sunken into his already small frame. His skin was ashen, his eyes red and swollen. He tried to speak but eventually Atchison took over.

"This has been a pretty tough month for our company," Atchison said. "Eleanor Paget's untimely death. And now Mariana Spiegelman's accident. Aaron has been a great friend to the company over the decades. And now he feels the time has come to fully, completely dedicate himself to his wife's recovery."

At one point Spiegelman gave Atchison a furtive glance. It lasted less than a second. But in that half-second I saw something I'd seen before: The guilt of having inadvertently sacrificed a loved one's life on the altar of ego. The desperation of wanting a single fateful moment back. And the unspeakable fear of unimaginable consequences.

I'd seen his look in a thousand people.

I saw it nearly every day in the bathroom mirror.

The station cut to the weather.

I went online and searched for reports on Mariana Spiegelman's accident: She had fallen down a flight of stairs at the family home in Grosse Pointe Park. Broken ribs, punctured right lung, broken arm. The worst of her injuries was bleeding in the brain. She'd had emergency neurosurgery to stop the bleeding and doctors were keeping her in a medically induced coma.

I didn't have to dig much deeper than the *Detroit Free Press* business section to find out that on the night of Mariana Spiegelman's supposed accident Kip Atchison was fifteen miles away at a restaurant in Bloomfield Hills with twelve business associates, the mayor of West Bloomfield and the comptroller of Oakland County.

I was beginning to like Atchison even more for Eleanor Paget's murder.

Over the next couple days I did as much research as possible on Titan's history and recent acquisitions. Most of the information was public knowledge. Quite a lot of it was mired in the cryptic language of the financial world: macro and micro economics, banking analytics and international market trends.

One thing did become clear, however.

Titan, according to a below-the-fold article in *Crain's Detroit Business*, had been working with an acquisitions "consultant" for the past year, hired at about the same time Kip Atchison joined the company.

Apparently no one other than Kip Atchison knew who the consultant was.

I gave all of this information time to simmer and make its own synaptic connections.

I spent the next several days working out, firing off boxes of ammo at a local gun range and flexing my Mexican cooking muscles in the kitchen. I made my mom's chicken with ancho chile and red sesame seed sauce—*Pipian Rojo del Norte*—twice, never quite approaching the soulful perfection of hers. Frustrated after my second attempt, I made my dad's fried chicken (Bisquick with heavy cream and egg mixed with a dash of red peppers, brown sugar and ginger) and mashed sweet potatoes with curry powder and garlic, which turned out much better.

I took some of the food across the street to the Rodriguez house.

Carlos Rodriguez cracked the door open. It wasn't hard to see he had his trustworthy Louisville Slugger at his side.

"*Sí?*" he said.

"I'm your neighbor from across the street," I said. "August Snow."

"Yes," he repeated. "I know."

"We hadn't properly met, so I thought I'd introduce myself."

From behind Rodriguez I heard a young boy's voice say, "*Quién es*, Papa?"

"Nobody!" he told the boy in Spanish. "Go back to your mother! Don't you have homework?"

"Listen," I said, "I don't want to be a bother. I just cooked way more than I can eat, so—"

A young woman appeared behind Rodriguez. In Spanish Rodriguez admonished the woman—apparently his wife—to get away from the door. His wife said it was rude of him to leave me standing there and that he should invite me in. He said she was crazy. And she, once again, called him rude—only this time with a quiet force that overpowered him.

"Come in," he said begrudgingly.

Inside, the house was cold. There were only a few furnishings. Their son—eight or nine—sat on the floor wearing his winter coat and reading a textbook. The boy looked up at me, smiled a megawatt smile and said, "Hi!"

"I apologize for my husband," Mrs. Rodriguez said. "We're new here. We don't know many people. And after that young man—the drug dealer—"

"I understand, ma'am," I said. "There's no reason for apologies. And the drug dealer's no longer dealing drugs."

"See?" Mr. Rodriguez said to his wife in Spanish. "*Los negros* all look out for their own."

"Carlos!" his wife replied.

"Not always, Mr. Rodriguez," I said in Spanish. The two looked at me, stunned that I'd understood. "Neither do Mexicans. I know. I'm half of both. Truth is I just came by to introduce myself." Then I looked at their son and said, "You like fried chicken and mashed potatoes, compadre?"

"*Si*, señor!"

I handed the serving dish to Mrs. Rodriguez. "Didn't mean to start anything. If there's something I can do, let me know."

"We are good," Carlos Rodriguez said curtly.

His wife smiled at me and said, "*Gracias*, Señor Snow. It's good to have you as our neighbor."

I left.

At home I called Tomás and told him about the Rodriguez family. I asked him if he and Elena could drop by and introduce themselves just to make them feel more comfortable in the neighborhood.

"Aw, Jesus, Octavio. I don't know. I hate that smalltalk, meet-the-neighbors bullshit. That ain't me."

"Okay. No problem," I said. "Let me talk to Elena."

"You fight dirty," Tomás said.

He agreed he and Elena would introduce themselves.

Of course, Tomás, being who he was, asked if that was the only reason I wanted them to meet the Rodriguez family.

"Just a feeling," I said.

"Last time you had 'just a feeling,' it cost you your job," Tomás said. "Stop having these goddamn feelings, jefe!"

On an overcast and cool morning, while I was doing a rigorous third set of deltoid reps at the Broadway Y with 140-pound weights, a small, dark room at the back of my brain decided to suddenly throw a shade up and let in shards of blinding light.

I raced back to the house, showered and dressed. Then I got in my car and broke several speed limits getting downtown.

I found FBI Special Agent O'Donnell enjoying a Maurice Salad at Schmear's Deli. On the table in front of her bagel were several newspapers—the *Detroit Free Press*, the *Chicago Sun-Times* and *The Washington Post*.

"Print media is dead," I said, sliding into the booth across the table from her.

"How'd you find me?" she said with some irritation.

"I'm a detective," I said. "I detect things."

"You *were* a detective," she said, putting her fork down and dabbing the corners of her mouth with a napkin. "And seriously—nobody likes you."

"Even you?" I feigned heartbreak.

"Jury's still out. So why are you here giving me agita?"

I leaned forward and whispered, "You give a shit about Eleanor Paget's death." I paused for effect and smiled. There are certain facial tics and eye movements that give a person away when truth or lies, anger or fear have stepped on a nerve. O'Donnell had no tells. And the hand I was playing was a bluff. Still, it was a good bluff and I needed to know what hand she was holding. "You're looking for Titan's consultant."

After several long seconds, O'Donnell said, "Can I buy you an iced tea? They make a nice green iced tea here."

"Thanks, no. My colon's fine. Thanks for the answer," I said with a smile. Then I stood, fully prepared to walk out into the chilly October day.

"Sit," O'Donnell said.

I did

O'Donnell took a couple sips of water, picked up her fork and toyed with half her bagel. Then she looked at me hard and said, "You found me here. Think you can find your way to my office?"

"Drive slow," I said. "I'm not so good at following highly trained professionals."

O'Donnell threw a ten on the table and muttered, "Asshole."

I assumed she was referring to me.

23

O'Donnell's office was on the fourteenth floor of the Federal Building on Michigan Avenue in the city. It was the antithesis of the offices I'd seen at Titan: small and crowded with file cabinets and cardboard boxes, two computer monitor screens flickering and a small flat-screen TV with a continual cable news flow, the sound muted. Still, no SportsCenter.

Mounted on the walls were pictures of felons, critical reports and updates from Washington D.C., Quantico and other field offices. And there were the requisite framed photos of the FBI's director and the president of the United States.

"Love what you've done with the place," I said, looking around.

"Shut up and sit down." She edged past a stack of cardboard boxes and sat behind her OfficeMax metal desk.

"Yes, ma'am."

We sized each other up for a few seconds. I smiled. She, not so much. Then O'Donnell sighed. "You stuck your head into a hornet's nest and I'm not sure if I like it there." She took a moment before picking up her phone and punching three buttons. "Dan?" she said. "My office."

Ten seconds later a young, lanky white guy entered O'Donnell's office. He was in short sleeves, his shirt collar unbuttoned and tie loosened.

"Mr. Snow, this is Special Agent Dan Cicatello," O'Donnell

said. "Dan, you may have gathered Mr. Snow is the pain-in-my-ass I've occasionally referred to in our morning briefings. He's the one who gave us the head's up about Titan's 'amusement park.'"

Dan thanked me for the tidbit on Titan's computer system.

"You have access to a guy named Donell Avalon McKinney," he said. Apparently he saw the blank look on my face. "Skittles."

I'd never known Skittles by his legal name.

"Hacker legend," Dan said with no small amount of admiration. "Guy really, truly knows his stuff. Elegant, innovative, insidious. I mean he's really—God—he's—"

"Dan," O'Donnell said calmly. "Focus."

"Right, right, right," Dan said quickly. "Sorry."

O'Donnell asked him to give me a high-level—read as "redacted"—download on Titan's computer systems and how it related to their investigation.

Because of the information Skittles had provided that I'd passed on to O'Donnell, Dan and two of his cybercrimes cohorts were able to redirect their infiltration efforts and dig deeper into Titan's IT systems. What they found was what Skittles had suspected: there was seriously encrypted code running deep in the bowels of Titan's system with Ukrainian and Romanian digital fingerprints all over it. Fingerprints that had been seen in bits and pieces in the IT systems of small private wealth management firms in New York, Boston, Philadelphia and Nashville.

"A few of these fingerprints first appeared in 2006 at some of the bigger Wall Street investment firms," Dan said.

"The 2008 financial collapse wasn't exclusively tied to an over-leveraged mortgage market, Mr. Snow," O'Donnell said. "In the wreckage the Bureau started finding bits of coding shrapnel from very organized foreign hacking nests. It took us five years to fit the pieces of shrapnel together. It's only been this past year we've been able to create a partial picture of who, what, when, where and why." O'Donnell leaned forward and folded her hands on a pile of papers on her desk. "If you think Americans were panicked by the financial carnage we brought on ourselves in 2008, just think how they would react knowing our banking system collapsed in part because of well-organized, well-funded hacking cells out of Chechnya, Bulgaria, and possibly state-sponsored Iran."

While O'Donnell persisted in scaring the economic bejeezus out of me, I thought of the decades of money my mom had tithed to the Catholic Church and how much of that ended up in the pockets of crooked priests and the Mafia.

"We now believe," Dan chimed in, "that 2008 was something of a stress-test through the establishment of well-seeded shell and shelf corporations by these hackers. A way to determine the amount of infiltration a banking system could take before the intrusion became detectable. I don't think they expected the system to crash as badly as it did. In fact, I don't think they tried to crash it at all. I think they were just looking for banks they could turn."

"With the end game being?" I said.

"Using medium and small banks to nest offshore money in the world's largest economy. Hiding in plain sight," O'Donnell said. "You name it. Drug money, terrorist money, gun running, extortion and illegal gambling profits. All of it housed and protected for nominal fees, dues, and percentages. America's the new offshore, Mr. Snow. No more midnight dead drops in bus station bathrooms. No more undocumented shipping containers arriving in Port Everglades or Savannah. You need money to blow up a bridge, church, synagogue, mosque, office building, or federal building? You want to launder a hundred mil in drug money? Just head to your local mom-and-pop pretend bank. All banks are nothing more than giant washing machines, Mr. Snow.

But now there's a fifty/fifty chance Granny Sinclair's financial bloomers are churning in the same dirty water as money from the Italian mob, the Albanian mob, the Jamaican mob, Chechen separatists, al Qaeda, Islamic State and God-only-knows who else."

We all sat quietly for a moment. O'Donnell and Dan Cicatello were looking at me, watching me take in their download.

"What's any of this got to do with Eleanor Paget's death?" I finally said.

O'Donnell's brow furrowed. "Absolutely nothing. Save for the fact that your investigation into her death has made a lot of people at Titan very nervous. The phone chatter is the most we've heard since this investigation started three years ago in Boston."

"What phone chatter?"

"Accelerated acquisition schedules. Suspicious executive shuffles. Nothing illegal, but all since you've stuck your nose in this whole business."

"Each private wealth management bank that's been turned has employed a consultant or consultants," Dan said. "Nothing unusual considering most financial consulting firms and hedge fund companies out there are cloaked in secrecy. But this is different. We haven't been able to ascertain who these consultants are or flow chart where they stand in the overall management structure. What we are beginning to see are some of the same acquisition patterns."

"This is the closest we've been to finding the consultant," O'Donnell said. "Which brings us to you, Mr. Snow."

O'Donnell gave Dan a look. Dan stood, shook my hand and said it was nice to meet me. Then he left the room, closing the door behind him.

"To begin with, if you talk about any of this outside of this office, I will have you publically hanged before throwing your corpse in a federal prison," O'Donnell said calmly. She waited until I nodded that I understood. "Next, I'd like to thank you for your unsolicited help. Your bumbling around has yielded more info than you can possibly imagine. Lastly, I do believe Eleanor Paget was murdered. Just like I believe Mariana Spiegelman was physically assaulted by someone associated with this case."

"Why?" I said, already knowing the answer. Sometimes it's just nice to have your ingenuity confirmed by someone other than yourself.

"To move her husband out of the CFO position at Titan," she said, "so Atchison could bring in someone hand-picked by the consultant. A nice move to completely control the board of directors and thus the entire bank."

I sat quietly for a minute, trying to organize everything O'Donnell had revealed to me in her cramped, seemingly disorganized office. I also tried to figure out what my next move was. Or if there was a next move. I had inadvertently positioned myself between the FBI and mostly invisible bad guys who would kill one woman and put another in the hospital to motivate her husband to quit his job.

And then there was the Detroit Police Department.

Even with the department's endless internecine wars, one thing seemed to unite them in the cause of vendetta: Me.

Any move I made that shook the DPD tree would come under very special, very heated scrutiny from the department and possibly the mayor since I'd pocketed several million dollars of their money. Prosecution. Jail time. Vindication for the department and the city that had destroyed my career. It was all on the table. And my new amigos at the FBI would simply watch from the sidelines, quietly thankful for my help with their case and eternally grateful I was gone.

"You need to do something for me," I finally said.

O'Donnell said stoically, "Nothing I can do."

"Oh, I think when you hear what I'm about to offer, you'll

want to do everything you can to make me happy," I said. I told her what I was proposing and that I wanted an agreement in writing and signed by her director.

Gradually, O'Donnell's impassive face changed. She looked very interested.

24

There should be a Senate subcommittee investigation into why the FBI's coffee always tastes like lukewarm ass.

After choking down two cups of brown sludge at the FBI's Detroit office I had a signed agreement. It took considerable back-and-forth haggling, including a conference call between O'Donnell's director in Detroit—a tall, slim guy named Phillips—and their bosses in D.C.

O'Donnell proved she could be quite persuasive. She was 110 pounds of C-4 plastic explosive with a strawberry-blonde ponytail. And nobody wanted to yank the ponytail.

"We've looked into this Snow guy," one of her Washington bosses barked through the phone's speaker. He knew I was in the room and spoke as if he gave a shit. "Former marine. Honorable discharge with citations. Good record as a cop—impetuous, but a good cop. Until he sued his department and walked off with twelve mil in city funds. I don't like cops who sue their own. And a year pretty much off the grid? He sounds troubled, Megan. Conflicted. I don't like troubled and conflicted people, especially when we have to rely on them."

"Sir," O'Donnell said, "I understand your concerns—and frankly I share some of them. But the fact of the matter is we rely on troubled, conflicted people all the time for information." O'Donnell's ice-blue eyes suddenly lifted from the speaker at the center of the conference table and burrowed into me. "Snow seems considerably less troubled and conflicted than a lot of people. And my gut tells me he's solid."

I grinned and gave her a thumbs up, which was ignored.

There was a long pause at the Washington, D.C. end of the line. Then the man said, "It won't be your gut hangin' out on this one, Megan. A lot's riding on what you do in Detroit. You'd better be right about this guy."

"He'll deliver, sir."

O'Donnell's boss here in Detroit—Phillips—ended the conference call by assuring the honchos in D.C. that he'd keep a tight rein on me and the operation. After the call disconnected, Phillips said, "You don't have to worry about me, Mr. Snow. It's Special Agent O'Donnell who should give you the heebie-jeebies."

"She is pretty scary, isn't she?" I said.

"You have no idea," Phillips said, smiling. He nodded to O'Donnell, shook my hand and left the room.

When the agreement was emailed to O'Donnell an hour later, I wanted to puke.

But what else could I do?

Before I left O'Donnell's office, she sighed heavily and said, "You're in this now, Snow. Up to your eyebrows. If you don't deliver—"

"The agreement's null and void," I said, tucking my copy into my coat pocket. "I know. Trust me."

"I'm hoping I can."

The drive home was long and uncomfortable.

I parked on the street and sat in the car for a minute thinking about what I'd done, then got out and walked to my house.

Carmela and Sylvia intercepted me on the sidewalk before I reached the house. In addition to their matching purple North Face bubble jackets, they were wearing ugly multi-colored knit hats, which I assumed they had knitted for each other.

"Afternoon, ladies," I said with a slight bow.

"Ooo!" Sylvia cooed. "Mr. Snow!"

We talked about how cold the day was and the unavoidable imminence of yet another brutal Michigan winter. The few neighbors I had on Markham had carved pumpkins decorating their doorsteps. I doubted there would be many kids in costumes walking around giddy at the prospect of receiving free sugar from neighbors. Not even the Rodriguez boy. Halloween had changed a lot since I was a kid.

After a while Carmela and Sylvia said they were taking the day to visit the Detroit Institute of Arts. That visit would be followed by chili dogs at American Coney Island, an old haunt for Detroit Water & Sewage Department employees. We wished one another a nice day and Sylvia said she hoped I had a nice visit with my friends.

"Friends?" I said casually.

"The ones at your house," Sylvia said. "Two gentlemen. Nicely dressed. One was a big fellow."

"Oh," I said. "You mean Coltrane and Stitt. We played football together at Wayne State."

Any fool can tell the truth, but it requires a man of some sense to know when to lie.

As the two ladies strolled away down the street I reached around to find comfort in touching the handle of my Glock.

A man was watching me through the sliver of front door windows.

I smiled at him and bounded up the steps.

The big, squarely built man who opened the door started to say something, but before he could I hit him in the throat with the butt of my gun. He grabbed his throat, made choking noises and stumbled backwards. I dropped him with a left cross to his jaw and a deep, hard punch to his solar plexus. Then I leveled my gun at the well-dressed man sitting casually on my sofa.

"Move and you're dead," I said.

The man on the sofa smiled at me, put his hands up. "We come in peace, Mr. Snow."

While keeping my gun leveled on the man on my sofa, I gave his companion sprawled on the floor a one-hand pat down. He was carrying. I deprived him of his Sig Sauer. He started to move.

"Stay down," I said, giving him another left cross to his jaw.

He stayed down.

I closed the door, stepped over the big man on the floor and made my way to his boss.

The front door creaked open again and I heard, "Hey, Mr. Snow—"

It was Jimmy Radmon.

He froze mid-sentence after seeing the big man on the floor groaning and me holding my gun on the well-dressed man seated on my sofa.

"Not now, Jimmy," I said.

"Cool," Radmon said, quickly backing out and closing the door.

"Stand up, take your coat off," I said to the man on my sofa. He complied. I had him do a slow 360. Nothing. "Lift your pant legs." He did. Still nothing.

"My name is Leslie Brewster." The man had a slight indeterminate accent. "I have no interest in violence, Mr. Snow. I have every interest in conducting business. Smart, mutually beneficial business."

"And him?" I nodded to his gasping business associate on my floor. "He's your accountant?"

The man smiled and said, "Personal protection. Detroit can be—how shall I say?—hazardous to one's health." The man calling himself Brewster gestured to his companion. "He's harmless really."

"He is now."

"May I sit, Mr. Snow?" Brewster said.

I nodded to the sofa. He sat, crossed his legs and casually brushed an imaginary speck of lint from his well-tailored slacks.

"So what's the play?" I said, lowering my weapon but keeping it aimed. Anything I didn't like, Brewster would get a bullet center mass.

"You've been very busy looking into Ms. Paget's unfortunate passing," Brewster said, "which, as I understand it, has been determined by the authorities to be a suicide."

"I have an innate distrust of authority," I said.

"Ah, the vagaries of youth," the man laughed. "Still, you've been talking to people at the bank. Chasing shadows. I might understand all this if you were still professionally associated with the police. Or even if you'd maintained a personal or professional relationship with Ms. Paget. But you hadn't with either. So please help me understand your interest in all of this."

"First of all, this is my home, fuck-nuts," I said. "I don't have to explain shit to you. You do, however, have to explain why the B and E. Which, by the way, I could shoot you dead in the crack of your ass for and not even get a ticket."

Brewster assessed me for a moment. "I'm here to offer you a rather handsome incentive to stop all this silly investigative work of yours. Investigative work, I might add, that skirts the legal lines of intimidation, harassment and impersonation of a police authority."

"What can I say," I replied. "I'm a multitalented guy."

Brewster kept his sleepy eyes and smug smile locked on me.

"Is this the same incentive you offered Eleanor Paget and Aaron Spiegelman?" I said.

"Miss Paget was a suicide." Brewster accompanied his statement with a theatrically heavy sigh. "Mr. Spiegelman's wife? Nothing more than an unfortunate accident." Brewster paused and assessed me once again. "I have considerable personal interests in the bank. And your skulking around, poking a finger in the eye of people associated with the bank, is affecting those interests. All of the bank's patrons are nervous, and on their behalf I'm offering you what we believe is quite fair." He pointed to an expensive aluminum briefcase on the floor by his legs. "We are prepared to offer you a cash incentive to cease and desist with this silly investigation. We will, of course, require certain legal documents to be signed."

Brewster's bodyguard finally stood on wobbly legs, shook his head and glared at me. I pointed my gun at him and said, "Stay, Fido." He glanced at his boss. Brewster held a palm up.

"As I said, Mr. Snow," Brewster continued calmly. "This is a very generous offer. A half-million. We could, of course, pursue legal action. We'd prefer not to. The bank—its customers and employees—have already been through enough."

"May I see the money?" I said.

Brewster grinned widely and brought the suitcase up to his lap. As he unlocked it I strongly suggested he turn it toward me and lift it open from the back. He did. It certainly looked like five hundred thousand dollars, all neatly stacked, wrapped and snuggly fit into the briefcase.

"This is the best option, Mr. Snow," Brewster said with a grand gesture of his hands. "Everyone wins."

He closed the briefcase.

"Of course, I—we—need papers signed and—"

"Take your money and get the fuck out of my house," I said.

Brewster gave me a confused look. "Excuse me?"

"You heard me, asswipe." I brought my gun out to a fully extended firing position. "Get the fuck out of my house. And by the way. My front door? That's genuine oak with original brass and leaded glass. If you fucked that up getting in here, I will either sue you or put a bullet through your eye. I'm kinda leaning toward the bullet."

Slowly, Brewster stood, put on his suit coat, and picked up the briefcase. He gave me a look that suggested I'd made a big mistake and began walking toward the door.

"My gun," his bodyguard said with a hoarse voice.

"Souvenir," I said, showing him his gun and then laying it on the kitchen island behind me.

"You can't—"

"I can do anything I want in my house, pork chop," I said. "Including clipping your fucking raisins. Now get out."

The bodyguard glared at me before opening the door for his boss. Brewster looked back at me and said, "This is, of course, a mistake, Mr. Snow. Your decision could hurt other patrons. People who don't deserve such pain." He smiled a humorless smile and added, "I wonder how Eleanor Paget's daughter will invest her inheritance? Perhaps I should consult with her."

"Go anywhere near Vivian Paget," I said, taking a step closer to Brewster, "and I will finish you."

I followed them out. They got into a black Cadillac Escalade with blacked out windows, which had been parked around the corner.

Brewster turned to me before climbing into the back seat of the vehicle. He held the briefcase up for me to see, smiled and said, "Last chance, Mr. Snow."

"Keep driving until you smell the ocean, asshole," I said.

I stood in the cold, shivering, and watched them drive off, committing the make and model of their vehicle and its license plate number to memory.

I wasn't shivering from the cold.

Once I got back inside I wasted no time calling Vivian Paget at her home in Traverse City. I had hoped Colleen would answer since Colleen appeared to be the emotional rock.

"Hello?"

It was Vivian.

"Hi, Vivian," I said brightly. "August Snow."

"Yes," she said with a light, welcoming voice. "I remember. Have you picked out a painting yet from my website? I'd still love to give you one."

"I've been to your website twice," I said. "You really make it hard to choose. You do incredible work."

"You're kind," she said with a modesty that verged on heartbreaking.

I made up a story about just wanting to apologize for having alarmed her with my last call, which had not been my intention.

Then I asked if I could say hello to Colleen. Vivian said, "Oh, yes! I'm sure she'd be disappointed if I didn't let her talk to you." I heard her call out Colleen's name.

After a second or two Colleen's voice came on the line.

"August?" Colleen said. "Any more news on Viv's mother?"

I asked if she could talk without Vivian hearing. She said, "Just a minute." There was silence for a few seconds before Colleen said, "What's up?"

I told her what was going on, no sugarcoating. I said my investigation into Vivian's mother's death had rattled some very sensitive and dangerous nerves. I recounted my visit from Brewster and his thick-necked bodyguard, which had resulted in a thinly veiled threat. Then I asked Colleen if she could handle herself with a firearm.

"I got no problem with guns," Colleen said. "I was raised on a farm. Hogs and chickens. You didn't kill, you didn't eat. What's this really all about, August?"

"Some people may want to contest a large part of Eleanor Paget's will," I said, choking down the urge to blurt out the full, bloody truth. "And that means maybe friendly, maybe not so friendly negotiations with Vivian."

"And let me guess," Colleen said. "You're the kind of guy who'd rather err on the side of suspicion and paranoia instead of faith in humanity?"

"It ain't paranoia if they really are out to get ya," I said. "You set with guns?"

"Got a Remington Versa Max Tactical and a Browning Citori

Lightning twelve gauge that belonged to my father," she said. "I'm better at fishing, but I can shoot."

"I'd suggest you put the rod and reel away for now," I said.

Colleen also had a Remington 1911 R1 semiautomatic pistol. All of her guns were kept safely locked away. She knew the combination to the locker. Vivian didn't. Vivian didn't like guns, but she understood and respected Colleen's Northern Michigan farming background and her familial association with weapons.

I told her if I got any more information I'd call. In the meantime she should consider herself on alert. Colleen said they had a good relationship with the local and state cops and that she would ask for extra patrols around the house, the adjacent five acres of their land and the woods across the road.

"I'm gonna talk to a friend of mine about coming up," I said. "He's a good guy and he knows how to handle himself."

"You think we need a man to defend our honor?" Colleen laughed.

"I think you're probably well-equipped on a number of levels," I said. "But you have to admit: it's hard to argue with having a fresh set of eyes just as a precaution."

There was silence between us for a moment. Then Colleen said, "You're not telling me everything."

"Hard to trust somebody you don't know," I said. "But sometimes those are the only people you can trust. And if not me, then go with your instincts. What do your instincts tell you?"

There was a sigh at the other end of the line. "I'll get a room ready for your guy. That and extra ammo."

I ended the conversation by telling her that I'd call again with details, but it had to be on her phone. I suggested she do a security assessment of the house and their adjacent land as soon as we were off the phone. She said she would. I apologized again and she said once the air cleared, she and Vivian wanted me up for a visit that didn't involve guns. "Just good food, a few laughs and a lot of homemade honey vodka."

"Wow. Lesbians *and* moonshiners," I said. "Life on the edge."

I asked Colleen how Vivian had been lately in view of her mother's recent death. Colleen said she'd been good. Almost relieved. Free, even.

I lied and said, "That's good."

We hung up.

Then I called Frank, the ex-security guard I'd met at Eleanor Paget's estate.

"How's the exciting world of bagging groceries?" I said.

"Fucking wonderful," Frank said. "S'up, Mr. Snow?"

"August," I said. "How would you like a working vacation?"

"What's the catch?" he said. In the background I heard a muddled voice over a speaker announcing the arrival of fresh strawberries—with your Kroger Plus card, you could get two packages for a deeply discounted price.

I told Frank what the catch was.

"Jesus," Frank said. "You got a talent for lighting fires, August."

I asked him if he had any guns. He did. I asked him if he had any problems with lesbians. He didn't—"Like there ain't enough in this world drive a person batshit." I asked him if he had any problems with any of this. "Only problem I got is my car, man. Fuckin' oh-five PT Cruiser. Thing barely gets me here. I know it ain't up for no trip to Traverse." I told Frank not to worry. I'd have a car ready for him at Hertz.

"Could be something," I said to Frank, "could be a lot of nothing. Just might turn out to be a nice two-week fall color tour for you."

"Ain't known you for too long, August, but I'm betting it's something."

I told him I'd give him a stipend. Frank asked what a stipend was. I told him and he said I'd already given him enough money. And this wasn't about the money anyway.

"In the army," Frank said, "I had real objectives. Clear goals. Actual targets. Easy to lose your way back in the world, man. And I think I been losing mine." His voice moved away from the phone. "Hey, LaKisha? Listen, I just quit, okay? Tell Larry for me. Thanks, babe."

After the call to Frank, I checked out my front door for damage: a few scratches around the brass keyhole. I'd have to look into a little more security.

There was a tentative knock at the kitchen back door. I had my Glock in my hand.

"Mr. Snow?"

Radmon again.

I opened the back door and his eyes scanned around me, looking for the men he'd seen earlier. I invited him in.

"Cable TV sales guys," I explained. "When I say I don't want Premium HD movie channels, I fucking mean it."

I was sitting in one of the visitor's chairs in Ray Danbury's office at the 14th Precinct. He was feverishly flipping through reams of papers that had collected on his desk.

"What are you looking for?" I said.

"The memo that says I fucking work for you," Danbury sarcastically replied.

I'd brought the gun I'd extracted from Brewster's bodyguard to Danbury and asked him if he could run a trace on it. Simple request. Simple task.

"You still looking into this Paget thing?" Danbury finally said, sitting back in his chair. Draped across the back of his chair was a heather-green wool suit jacket. I imagined the jacket added to the sartorial splendor of his slate-grey monogrammed shirt, expensive-looking olive-green silk tie and heather-green pocketed vest. The only thing that didn't go with the ensemble was Danbury's gut spilling out at the bottom of the vest.

"It's gotten a little more interesting," I said.

I told Danbury everything, save for my current dealings with the FBI. As I talked, he nodded and thoughtfully rubbed a forefinger across his bottom lip.

I finished telling him what I knew and where I thought things were heading. When I was done he said, "Close the door."

I did.

For a minute he stared at the gun in the plastic bag I'd brought him. "Sure you've told me everything, August?"

"I may have left out a few details," I said.

"Like any shit involving the FBI?"

I didn't say anything.

"Listen," Danbury said, his voice low and serrated. "I really don't care about you and your fed buddies so long as it doesn't embarrass me or this department. Been through enough the past ten years. But you start giving me or this department the stink eye and you and I are done, amigo. I join the rest of the department in wanting to see you hamstrung and horsewhipped. You see what I'm sayin'?"

I nodded.

Danbury grabbed the plastic bag that held the bodyguard's gun. "We'll talk in a couple days. In the meantime, cool out in Mexican-town. Renovate some more houses. Get yourself a little half-black Latina with big titties. Anything but whatever you're into. You feel me, August?"

I stood, reached across his desk and shook Danbury's hand.

"Nice suit," I said. "Next time you should see if they have it in your size."

25

"They're squatters."

Tomás sat at my kitchen island sipping a beer. He and Elena had made a visit to the Rodriguez family across the street.

"He's legal, his wife and son ain't," Tomás continued. "Been on hard times. Found the house here and moved in, keepin' things on the down-low. Rodriguez does pick-up construction work. I think he's mad you gave this Jimmy Radmon kid work he could use."

"Makes sense," I said. Tomás would drink beer if nothing else was around. Lucky for him I had a fifth of Jose Cuervo Silver cooling its heels in my refrigerator. I poured him a chilled shot. "I'd be mad at me, too."

"He jimmied the electrical," Tomás said. He sipped the shot and nodded approvingly before knocking it back old-school. "Heating's another thing. Cold as hell in there. Not good for anybody, especially the boy. Elena lives for shit like this. They're her mission now."

"And you?"

Tomás laughed. "I'll do what I can when I can. But don't no man want another man trying to show him how to be a man."

I nodded.

Tomás asked how this thing with Eleanor Paget was going and I told him I honestly didn't know. I said I'd had visitors. "Sounds like you could use some backup, compadre," Tomás said.

"Maybe," I said. "If you're up for it."

Tomás grinned. "Got nothin' else to do."

My next stop was Beaumont Hospital in Grosse Pointe.

The emotionally exhausted, sunken Aaron Spiegelman I'd seen on the local TV news a week ago was even more depleted as he sat by his wife's hospital bed.

Mariana Spiegelman lay in the quiet repose of one floating weightless inside a coma. The top of her head was wrapped in gauze and her oxygen came from a clear plastic tube curling from her cheeks to her nostrils. There were monitors near her bed that provided a cold calculation of how alive she was.

Although the room resembled any other hospital room, there were touches that made Mariana Spiegelman's clinical surroundings softer, less sterile: Floor-length white lace curtains over the rectangle of window. A dark wood side table with a vase bearing yellow and orange mums. A Turkish rug, two bentwood rockers and an antique brass Stiffel floor lamp. Someone had done her hair and had applied a tasteful touch of makeup to her face.

Spiegelman sat in one of the rockers wearing a wrinkled pair of khakis, worn Sperry Dockside shoes and a blue Lacoste tennis shirt. He'd been casually rocking back and forth and reading John Bunyan's *Pilgrim's Progress* to his wife: "'The law, instead of cleansing the heart from sin, doth revive it, put strength into, and increase it in the soul . . .'"

I brought flowers and a book: Pablo Neruda's *The Captain's Verses: Love Poems*. Spiegelman saw me and stopped reading. His eyes filled with tears. Quickly he wiped them away and in a low, hoarse voice, said, "Why are you here?"

I walked tentatively into Mariana Spiegelman's room. "I heard what happened. Whatever our history, Mr. Spiegelman, I can't tell you how sorry I am about your wife."

He stared at me through wet, red eyes before nodding to a small table in the corner of the room. "You can put the flowers there. Someone will put them in a vase."

I handed him the book, and he suggested we leave his wife's room and go for coffee in the hospital's cafeteria.

We sat at a table in the cafeteria for a long time without a word between us. Spiegelman looked even worse in the sterile, white light of the cafeteria. He'd been a wiry man, but now he looked gaunt, nearly skeletal. His normally clean-shaven face bore grey stubble. Occasionally he blew away the steam rising from his coffee, but he didn't drink. Just as well. Hospital coffee is often in need of serious nursing.

Just when I was convinced Spiegelman had slipped into his own coma, he looked up at me and said in a thin voice, "Whatever you want to hear from me, you won't. You should leave."

Said like a man who wanted nothing more than to lay bare all secrets and sins on any altar that would have them.

"You don't have to say anything, Mr. Spiegelman," I said. "I just wanted you to know how sorry I am about your wife's accident."

His eye twitched and his lips pursed. The word "accident" settled on his brain like the needles of a thistle.

"Read her some of the poetry," I said, taking a sip of the brown coffee-water. "My father loved reading Neruda to my mother and she loved the way his voice sounded on the words."

Spiegelman nodded.

We sat in silence for a while longer. I thought about leaving, but something told me he needed someone sitting across from him. Someone who, even in silence, could hold the tether and keep him from floating any further into despair. Finally, staring at his coffee, he said, "Do you think it's possible to be in love with two women at the same time, Mr. Snow?"

"Yes."

He nodded, then after a tentative sip of coffee, said, "I loved Eleanor. Very much. I know what people said about her. What she did. How she treated people. But still . . ."

I reached across the table and put a hand on his shoulder. Tears fell from his eyes and splashed on the table. He hunched under the weight of his painful silence. I stood to leave him alone with his grief. I stopped when he said, "I don't know what to do." He drew in a ragged breath then continued. "She—Mariana—she always straightens my tie in the morning. Sometimes she'll laugh and say, 'When will you ever learn to tie a tie?' Then she'll kiss me like I'm—the only one." He looked up at me, his eyes wet. "They'll come for you, Mr. Snow. Eleanor was just the beginning. I—I didn't want to believe her. It wasn't supposed to be this hard. They—they've never had it this hard."

"Detroit's a hard city," I said. In all likelihood "they" meant Brewster and the ex-military security detail nested at the bank.

"I said no the first time," Spiegelman said, staring at his cup of coffee. "A briefcase full of cash. All I had to do was walk away from thirty years of building a business. Threw them out of my house. The second time, same offer, less money in the briefcase. Atchison came with them. I said no. This is the third time. No money and—my wife—here." He paused, then sucked in another breath. "If I'd only—"

"None of this is your fault, Mr. Spiegelman," I said. "The people who hurt your wife—the ones who killed Eleanor Paget—they're going to pay."

Spiegelman gave a laugh that was somewhere between abject defeat and utter absurdity. "What can you do about any of this? These people?"

For a moment dark and bloody thoughts brewed in my mind, the pit of my stomach. Then, an unexpected flutter of light: from somewhere in the cafeteria, the sound of children laughing. I turned and looked: two kids and a woman I assumed to be their mother sat at a table playing a child's card game. As I looked at them, happy in a place I suspected rarely saw happiness, I said almost absentmindedly, "When I was a kid I was pretty lucky at a game called *La Pirinola*. Four or five kids—cousins, neighborhood kids—each brings a bag of nuts or some chocolate, loose change, maybe comic books. One player at a time spins the *pirinola*, which is like a dreidel. When it stops spinning a face-up side tells you *pon*, or take: take one, take two, take zero or *toma todo*—take it all—from the other kids." I returned my attention to Spiegelman. "I'm gonna take it all from these bastards."

Spiegelman slowly nodded as he looked down at his coffee. "I'm sorry."

"For what?"

"Those men. All they were supposed to do was—warn you. Make you leave Eleanor alone. Leave her memory alone."

The men who had come to Tomás's house.

"One of the security guards at the bank said he knew some people," Spiegelman said. "I told him just a warning. Gave him money. Nothing else was supposed to happen. Nobody else was supposed to get hurt."

"Which security guard?"

"Max," Spiegelman said. "No. Dax. Dax Randolph. Brown hair. Grey at the temples. Wire-rim glasses."

I stood and said, "Read your wife some poetry tonight."

Absentmindedly, he nodded.

I left, not knowing what to do or how to feel about Spiegelman. His love for Eleanor Paget inadvertently put me—put Tomás, his wife and their five-year-old granddaughter—in Titan's cross hairs.

On the drive downtown I got a call from Frank.

"Dude!" Frank said. "A Cadillac ATS-V? You *rock*!"

Frank was about forty-five minutes into his four-hour, 260-mile drive along I-75 North to Traverse City. Apparently he was enjoying the car I'd reserved for him.

I asked Frank if he had everything—and by everything I meant guns and ammo. Frank ticked off the short list: A Beretta M9, a Ruger LC9 and a Springfield M1A rifle. He had licenses and ammo for all except the Springfield rifle, which had been his father's and was of more sentimental value than anything else.

"Sentimental value's no value at all right now, Frank," I said. "Anything else that puts us in the winner's circle?"

"Couple good jokes and movie-star looks?"

Frank had called ahead and spoken to Colleen. She'd walked the perimeter of the house, taken some notes and made a hardware store list of supplies needed to beef up security. She'd also walked basement to attic, front door to back. Vivian had asked what she was doing. Colleen had told her the *Farmers' Almanac* had predicted a Midwest winter full of heavy snows and subzero temperatures. She was simply putting things together to winterize the house.

Colleen had also spun a story about her cousin Frankie, who'd just gotten out of the army and needed a place to stay for a while. Vivian was excited by the prospect of meeting another of Colleen's family members. I asked Frank his first impressions of Colleen.

"Oh, yeah, dude," Frank said, "No doubt she can handle herself. Tough as hell. Smart, too. Plus she's a country girl. Bein' a son of Big Sky country I'm partial to country girls. My daddy used to say a country girl's got about as much gold in their heart as they got dirt under their fingernails."

As I drove, I thought about Frank's dad, and then about my dad—about the things our dads had taught us that turned us into military men. While my mother took pleasure in reading poetry to me when I was a child, my father would read me the battlefield psychology and philosophy of Sun Tzu, Thucydides and Carl von Clausewitz.

"What possible reason could there be for a boy—a child!—to know about war?" my mother once said.

"I'm not raisin' a boy," my father replied. "I'm raising a man. And maybe you ain't noticed, baby, but this is a world of men chewin' up boys for sport."

I thought now of Sun Tzu as I drove. *Engage people with what they expect; it is what they are able to discern and confirms their projections. It settles them into predictable patterns of response, occupying their minds while you wait for the extraordinary moment—that which they cannot anticipate.*

At Titan Securities Investments Group, I was greeted by the attractive black woman at the reception desk.

"Welcome back, Mr. Snow."

"I need to see Kip Atchison," I said. "Now."

The three well-dressed security guards who manned the lobby had, not unlike before, taken an acute interest in me. A young guy casually flanked me while the older athletically-built guy named Dax stood fifty feet behind me to the right. Two more guards—a massive black guy with no neck and a slab-of-gristle-beef white guy—stood resolutely by the elevators.

The receptionist nervously searched my eyes for a moment, then quickly dialed four numbers and touched her ear.

"Yes," she said. "This is reception. I have Mr. Snow here. He wishes a few minutes with Mr. Atchison." There was a long pause. A few nods. A couple of furtive glances at me. Then, "Yes, thank you. I'll pass that on."

Of course, I knew what she was going to say but I waited around to hear it anyway: "I'm sorry, but Mr. Atchison is unavailable. If you'd like to make an appointment—"

"You don't mind if I just go up, do you?" I said, moving quickly from the reception desk toward the elevators.

The brown-haired guard with wire rim glasses quickly made his way in front of me and blocked my path. "Mr. Snow," he said. " My name is Dax Randolph. I think we should—"

"You think we should what, Dax?" I said. "Dance? Friend each other on Facebook? Share tapas?"

"To begin with," he said, with a forced smile and dead blue eyes, "I think we should calm down and—"

Instead of listening to Dax's advice, I juked right and moved left around him, continuing my hurried walk toward the elevators.

The slab-of-beef white guard by the elevators took a step toward me.

"I got him, sir," the guard said, moving toward me. Before Dax could say anything, the guard took a swing at me. With over-developed muscles like his, speed and flexibility were severely compromised. Two jabs to his solar plexus, a right-cross to his jaw and a heel to the knee and he was down.

I cut a look of combat readiness to the massive black guy.

"Lousy pay, empty promises, now *yo* ass squarin' off on *me*?" the big black security guard said. He held up the palms of his hands and shook his head. "Oh, hell no. Don't need this shit. I'm out." He yanked off his black clip-on tie, dropped it to the marble floor and walked past me out of the building.

I felt Dax put a hand on my shoulder. I grabbed his hand, locked the thumb back and turned, bringing his arm up and behind his back. I brought my knee up into Dax's kidney twice.

The receptionist gasped and said, "Oh, God!"

Dax wasn't done. "This isn't a smart thing to do, Mr. Snow," he said as I pushed him away. He shook off whatever pain I might have caused and assumed a stance that was somewhere between well-trained karate and nasty Krav Maga.

I deflected his first two quick punches with right and left forearms, absorbing the impact of his knee into the side of my right thigh. I countered with a heel to his left knee and a right hook to his jaw. Both attacks had impact, but not enough to put him down.

"This is going to end badly for you, Mr. Snow," Dax said, recovering quickly.

"Maybe," I said. "Let's give it a go."

The white security guard I'd laid out managed to get to his feet, but Dax held up a hand. "I got this."

I grinned. "Oh, you got this, huh?"

All warfare is based on deception.

Dax smiled at me. "Yessir. I do."

Bank customers who entered the lobby were hustled into a corner by two of the other security guards.

"I would suggest you walk out of here under your own power, Mr. Snow," Dax said, holding his stance, "or get carried out on a stretcher."

"I'd tell you to kiss my ass," I said, "but I don't want you getting that close to me."

"If necessary I will shoot you," Dax said calmly as he circled to my right.

"Not before I break the barrel of your gun off in your ass," I said.

Dax unleashed a flurry of kicks and punches. Some connected with my ribs and chest. I managed to deflect a few, but he was good. Better than I'd been in my prime marine days. And I'd been damned good.

I managed to land a kick to his ribs that would have brought down an average man. Dax was no average man. He took the kick and countered with his own swing kick, which connected hard with my right shoulder and threw me against a marble wall. He didn't waste time, moving in close and landing three high-speed punches to my stomach and one to my face, which he followed by an elbow to my right cheek. I went down on one knee. Dax dropped to a knee behind me, locked my neck in a chokehold and waited for my lights to go out.

"Get the elevator," Dax called out to the big white security guard.

"Let him go."

Ray Danbury.

Dax let me go. He stood, calmly adjusted his tie and smiled. I stayed on my knees for a few seconds, hoping not to pass out, throw up or both.

August Snow: Tough Guy.

"Officer," Dax said, "this man—"

"Quiet," Danbury said. Standing to Danbury's right was Leo

Cowling, resplendent in a navy blue wool car coat and matching fedora. He was grinning ear to ear as he looked down at me. On Danbury's left were two young uniformed cops. I recognized one: Aswan, the young Chaldean fresh out of the academy.

"We'll be filing a complaint," Dax ventured.

Danbury knelt down by me and whispered, "You okay?"

"Lucky for him you got here when you did," I said, catching my breath. The stars popping in front of my eyes dissipated. "I was wiping the floor with this jerk-off."

"Funny," Danbury said. "Looked to me like he was using your face as a mop."

Cowling was smiling as Danbury helped me to my feet.

Then Danbury handcuffed me, handed me over to the two young patrolmen and quietly said to Aswan, "Take him to my car."

The patrolmen nodded and, hands firmly locked on my upper arms, led me outside to Danbury's car. As they were marching me through the lobby, I called out in a voice loud enough for the bank's patrons to hear, "Why won't they give me my money? It's my money! Twelve million! What have they done with my money? What are they doing with *everybody's* money?"

From behind me I heard Cowling shout, "Read him his rights and shut him the fuck up!"

Outside, a small group of noonday onlookers gawked at the proceedings. A few—the ones who weren't homeless—took video on their phones; maybe something other people could "Like" on Facebook, Snapchat or YouTube. I noticed a trash can and said to Patrolman Aswan, "You mind?"

I leaned my head into the trash can and vomited.

Vomiting in public is bad enough. Vomiting with your hands cuffed behind your back is enough to dislocate shoulders. Fortunately for me, I had strong shoulders.

Once I'd completed my business, I stood upright. Aswan asked if I wanted a breath mint. He opened a tin and tossed two curiously strong mints into my mouth like a trainer tossing fresh herring into the mouth of a seal.

"'When you are the anvil, be patient—'" I said, chewing the mints.

"'—And when you are the hammer, strike hard,'" Aswan finished, then repeated the proverb in its original Arabic.

I winked at him with my good eye, then got in Danbury's car.

Danbury didn't say a word as Cowling drove us back to the 14th Precinct. Cowling kept looking back at me in the rearview mirror. If it were up to him, he would have driven me down to the river, given me a double tap to the back of the head, then gone to lunch at The Whitney.

When we arrived at the 14th, Cowling pushed me toward a female officer and told her to throw me in lockup.

I was in lockup for more than an hour. I figured Danbury needed to cool out before he saw my face again. In the meantime I made new friends.

"Muhfuckin' five-oh, man," a black man wearing motorcycle club riding leathers grumbled. He had an Afro-mohawk and a variety of ear, nose and lip rings. "Niggah can't catch a break in this goddamn town."

"I feel ya, bro," I said. My right eye was puffing up and closing. My ribs ached and I hadn't quite gotten my legs back.

The large black biker furrowed his bushy eyebrows, glared at me with bloodshot eyes and said, "Wha'd the po-po jack yo ass fo?"

I gave him a hard look and made sure he saw my swollen jaw and slowly closing right eye.

"Killing a librarian," I said. "With kindness."

26

"That's why you called me down there?" Danbury shouted. "See some lame-ass mixed martial arts show?"

"I thought you'd like it," I said. I'd called Danbury just before I entered the TSIG building and invited him to witness a crime. "Especially the part where I got my ass kicked."

"That's it. You just made it official," Danbury said. "You and me? We're done. I been tryin' to keep you stowed away safe. Do what your daddy would've done. But that's it. We're fucking done."

Once again we were sitting in his office. Rather, I was sitting. Danbury paced around me like a lion sizing up the warm carcass of an antelope.

I was still handcuffed.

"This mean I won't be getting the family Christmas card this year?"

"Oh, you goddamn right you ain't gettin' no fuckin' Christmas card!"

The beehive of officers outside of Danbury's office heard the boom and clash of his voice and all widened eyes were suddenly on Danbury. Cowling leaned against a desk, legs crossed at the ankles, arms folded across his chest, smiling contently. This was what he'd been waiting for and now he had a front-row seat.

Danbury walked briskly to the door of his office and shouted,

"Don't y'all niggahs got jobs to do that might—just fuckin' *might!*—involve serving and protecting?"

Then he slammed the door shut.

For ten long, loud minutes Danbury excoriated me. If he'd had access to a blowtorch, I wouldn't have had a face. He said the security guard was adamant about pressing trespassing and aggravated assault charges against me. And with that came another potentially embarrassing episode involving the department.

"I've already had one call from the chief and another from the commissioner," Danbury yelled. "The first call took my left cheek! The second call took my right cheek! You can see I ain't got no ass left!"

"I don't know," I said, leaning sideways in my chair for a better view. "Looks like there's still quite a bit."

"You think this is a fucking joke?" Danbury pounded a fist on his desk. "Does it look like I'm goddamn laughing? You have any idea what I've done to keep your ass above ground while you out there dancin' a minstrel show?"

While Danbury eviscerated me, voices had been rising outside of his office, and now the door flew open. Cowling entered first. "I tried to stop her, boss."

Pushing past the much taller Cowling was FBI Special Agent Megan O'Donnell.

"I'm not interrupting anything, am I?" she said. She flipped out her badge and credentials.

"I know who you are," Danbury snapped.

"Good," O'Donnell said, the set of her mouth hard. "Seems we all know each other."

"Want me to toss the bitch?" Cowling said to Danbury.

O'Donnell turned to Cowling, craning her neck to look at him. "That is an absolutely hideous tie. Who wears Jerry Garcia anymore?"

I wanted to laugh but my cheek hurt like hell.

Danbury gave Cowling a look and Cowling backed down.

"My momma taught me to respect women," Danbury growled. "But you barging in like this? Into *my* house? You 'bout to be the one exception to my momma's rule and I don't give a shit what your badge says."

"Wow," O'Donnell said, channeling the calculating calm of Boudica the Celtic Warrior Queen. "I'd always heard about the hospitality of the Detroit Police Department, but . . ."

"Hey, listen, O'Connell or O'Donnell or whatever-the-fuck-your-name-is," Danbury said, "I don't give a baboon's swollen red ass if you're FBI or not—"

"You should." O'Donnell took a seat next to me in front of Danbury's desk. "You really should."

She unfolded two pieces of paper, one of which was a Chain of Custody Request signed by her director, and laid them neatly on Danbury's desk. Danbury looked at the papers. Then he stared for a very long time at me.

"You bullshittin' me, right?" Danbury said at last.

"I'd very much appreciate you taking the cuffs off this man," O'Donnell said.

"And I'd very much appreciate you kissin' my black ass!" Danbury roared.

After a tense few seconds, Danbury sighed heavily, reached into his pants pocket, extracted the key and tossed it to O'Donnell. O'Donnell unlocked the handcuffs and tossed them onto Danbury's desk. I rubbed my wrists to get blood back to my hands.

"We ain't done," Danbury said pointing a rigid forefinger at me. "You have seriously fucked up, August. We for *damn* sure ain't done here."

As I walked out of Danbury's office with O'Donnell as my escort, we passed Leo Cowling.

"Soon," Cowling said, pointing a forefinger at me and flexing his thumb as if to shoot me.

"Wow," I said in reply. "That really *is* a bad tie."

On the way downstairs, O'Donnell said, "Jesus, Snow. You're playing your friends like suckers and your savior—which would be me—like a get-out-of-jail-free card. I give you a week tops before I'm fishing you out of the Detroit River piece by piece."

"In the meantime," I said reaching into my pants pockets and extracting a wallet, "why don't you run this."

O'Donnell took the wallet and looked at the driver's license.

"Who's Dax Randolph?"

"Randolph is the guy who wiped the floor with me at the bank."

"You picked his pocket?" O'Donnell said. "Jesus. You really *are* a piece of work."

I spent the next two hours in an FBI interview room with Special Agent O'Donnell.

I told her about Dax the security guard. How he fought. She said the guards were mostly ex-military and contracted through a company called Black Tree, a private security contractor out of Oklahoma. Black Tree was deep in the pocket of the Department of Defense, with multimillion-dollar contracts for security work in Iraq, Afghanistan, Somalia, Qatar and the United Arab Emirates. Lately there had been some Capitol Hill concern about how extensive and secretive their financial and recruiting practices were: a Congressional investigation had uncovered information that two of their employees attached to the Army in Afghanistan were ex-Russian FSB looking to make big American contractor bucks. Neither had the proper US immigration and security clearance papers.

"Black Tree ain't what it used to be," O'Donnell said. She eyed me with an air of curiosity and disgust. "That looks like it hurts."

"My eye?" I said.

"Your *everything*," she said, gesturing to my body, head to toe. "While Black Tree's sinking in the shit, a few of their former employees—and I'd bet your Dax Randolph is one of them—moved on, looking for other means of gainful employment."

"Like banking," I said.

O'Donnell nodded. "Like banking. Be nice to know who their recruiter is. Think this Dax guy would give him up if we squeezed him?"

"I think this Dax guy is one hard sonuvabitch," I said, feeling my ribs throb. "Squeeze him and all you're gonna get is tired."

O'Donnell picked up her phone, dialed three numbers and waited for a second or two before saying, "Yeah, Gene? Hey, listen. Can I get a couple cups of coffee in here and an ice pack? Yeah, an ice pack. Thanks."

O'Donnell tossed a bottle of Tylenol over the metal table. I caught it and choked down three.

An anonymous looking white guy in a nondescript navy-blue suit brought in two blue ceramic mugs of black coffee, several packets of sugar, powdered creamer and an ice pack. Quickly determining I was the one in need of the ice pack, Gene offered it to me and I took it. The blue coffee mugs were emblazoned with the FBI logo rendered in gold.

"You guys got a gift shop here?" I said, admiring my mug. "I'd like to pick up a couple of these, Christmas being right around the corner."

O'Donnell ignored my attempt at humor. "You're shaking the tree a little early and a little hard for my tastes. And my tastes are what count."

"Yeah, well, I just keep waiting for you Fed-types to back me up." I took a sip of the coffee. It really wasn't bad this time. "I'm out there getting my ass kicked doing your work."

"We didn't invite you to this party," O'Donnell said, tearing open two packs of powdered creamer and one sugar and sprinkling them into her coffee. "You crashed it. Now you're crying like a baby with a scraped knee? Gee. And I thought you were having such fun."

"You sure know how to hurt a guy," I said.

"Looks like Dax does, too."

I asked her if her cybercrimes guy had gotten any further into Titan's computer systems. She said whatever progress her cybercrimes geeks were making was none of my business. Which I interpreted as little to no progress.

We drank our coffee quietly for a moment, each of us gauging where the other stood on the chessboard. I wanted to think I'd played the sacrificial pawn earlier at the bank, hoping to reveal whether Leslie Brewster was the king, the bishop, or one of several very nasty knights. Then again, I may have just been an emotionally compromised, arrogant pawn who ambled boldly and stupidly into a battlefield sacrifice.

Thanks a bunch, Sun Tzu.

Either way, it appeared O'Donnell was happy I was out there. I was the little whirling dervish kicking up dust devils at the foot of a black mountain of dirty money.

O'Donnell finally said, "Couple years ago we lost the man we believed to be the consultant in Baltimore because we went in too early with our legal guns blazing. They smelled us coming. Next thing we know, the guy's lying on an expensive Persian rug with two in the chest and one in the head. Not a good day for the Bureau. We came close in Boston, but what's that old saying about being close? Something about horseshoes?" O'Donnell sighed and eased back in her chair. "Listen. When these guys get spooked, either of two things happen: We end up with a handful of nothing and threats of lawsuits from legions of bank attorneys. Or people disappear or die and we've still got a handful of nothing. They're gold-plated cockroaches and they sense when light's coming their way."

"If these guys are as serious as you say they are," I said, moving the ice pack from my left cheek to my right eye, "then I should have my lawyer—"

"There won't be any Titan lawsuits brought against you," O'Donnell said. "They may pursue a restraining order, but other than that, these guys want this afternoon to go away, quickly and quietly. Pardon me for putting it this way, but you'll just end up being dismissed as one wacko black man in a city filled to overflowing with wacko black men."

The ice pack felt good against my cheek and eye, though I'd much prefer to lick my wounds at home with a couple ibuprophens and a local brew. Maybe an Atwater Java Porter. Or Motor City dark ale. O'Donnell surprised me when she broke the long silence by telling me she was Catholic and, for as cynical as the job had made her, her faith still meant a lot to her. Just like she supposed it meant for me. She said she was carrying guilt—albeit a negligible amount—about how she was using me. But there was the greater good and ultimately people like her and me were just small cogs in the machinery of protecting that greater good.

I told her I appreciated her candor and that once all of this was over, we could both get back to being good Catholics.

Uncharacteristically, she issued a brief laugh and said, "I don't think it works like that."

"It's gonna have to this time," I said.

I told her about the two guys who had broken into my house. The threats made and the offer literally put on the table. I described the man passing himself off as Leslie Brewster. I told her I suspected he was the same man behind Mariana Spiegelman's near-fatal fall and her husband's hasty exit from TSIG.

With every word I said, O'Donnell edged closer to her desk and held me steady in her blue eyes.

When I finished, O'Donnell said, "You believe this man is the consultant?"

"Tha'd be my guess," I said. "I doubt he's the only one. An operation like this probably has several Brewster types. But my gut tells me he's pulling the strings here." I told O'Donnell I'd be glad to give her sketch artist the same description. O'Donnell smirked and said, "Sketch artist? What is this? 1940s Chicago?" Then she reached into a desk drawer, pulled out an iPad and slid it across her desk to me. "Touch the FaceComp app. There ya go. Now you've got twelve hundred facial structures, chins, cheeks, mouths, eye shapes, eye colors, lips, ears, hair types and colors and skin tones at your fingertips. Tats and piercings we can add later."

"Like an Etch A Sketch," I said. "Or Mr. Potato Head."

"Yeah," O'Donnell said. "Exactly like a sixty-million-dollar Mr. Potato Head linked to local, State and Federal criminal databases and facial recognition programs."

For the next twenty minutes I selected, deselected, composed, fine-tuned and perfected the consultant's face on the iPad. It was a very good likeness. I slid the iPad across the desk back to O'Donnell.

"Goddammit," she muttered.

"You know the guy?"

O'Donnell picked up her phone and punched three buttons.

"Ann?" she said. "He's here. Yeah, Detroit. Get everybody in the main conference room, five minutes."

O'Donnell hung up. As quickly as she hung up, she pulled a file from her desk and handed it to me. Inside were a series of 8"x10" black and white photos. Each photo was stamped INTER-POL, followed by a serial number, location and time.

"What am I looking at?" I said.

"You're looking at how all of this could go south," she said. She reached across the desk and pointed to the small, blurry figure of a man in all of the photos. His face was obscured by a fedora in every single one. "You're looking at a man we believe to be someone we call the Cleaner."

"Cute name," I said. "I take it he's not a janitor."

"Of a fashion," she said. "We believe there have been three or four consultants so far. One in Boston. One in Charleston. The last one we know of at Monroe & Morgan Wealth Management in Baltimore failed. Rare, but it happens. Failures answer to the Cleaner. An assassin. The face you just composed is damned close to the guy from Philly we believe was brought in to kill the Philadelphia consultant, but for whatever reason the trigger wasn't pulled."

I squinted at the blurry photos, unable to ascertain much save for the fact that this Cleaner guy was thin and knew where the CCTV cameras were in a variety of cities.

"Nice photos," I said. "Maybe you've got some of Big Foot?"

"That's the best we've had in five years. We think he's Russian." She paused, swallowed hard, then said under her breath, "Or Czech. Maybe Ukrainian. Possibly German."

"So essentially," I said, handing the file back to her, "this guy is a ghost."

Reluctantly, O'Donnell nodded. "You should've walked away from this when you had the chance."

"And this Brewster guy?"

"We're pretty sure he's the one who staked the initial claim in Philadelphia," she said. "The tip of the spear. He sets up an operation, appoints a man on the ground like Atchison, then moves on. If the consultant or the man on the ground fails, he meets the Cleaner. Sloppy isn't tolerated. Sloppy gets mopped up. At least we're pretty sure that's the structure."

I told her about the threat Brewster had leveled at Vivian Paget and asked if she could send a couple agents to Traverse City until this whole thing was over. She said she didn't have an agent to spare, but she would have a chat with the State Police.

"Keep ice on that," O'Donnell said, pointing in the general direction of my face. "I'd never admit to saying this, but you're much better looking when somebody hasn't stomped the bloody shit out of you."

"So I'm back in the pot, waiting for the cannibals to ring the dinner bell?" I said.

"I'll light a novena candle and say a prayer for you," O'Donnell said. "In the meantime, keep the stars as your guide and the stripes as your shield, patriot."

27

By the time I got back to my house, some of the swelling had gone down on my cheek. My right eye, however, was completely closed. I compelled my good eye to perform overtime duties watching for tails and carefully surveying the neighborhood for any cars or people I didn't recognize.

I popped the cap on a Motor City Honey Porter dark ale, downed three ibuprophens with it and stood at my living room windows staring out at the quiet street. I hadn't felt like this in a long time. Not since my trial. No, even longer—not since a woman I'd loved was gunned down in a goddamn convenience store.

Like someone lashed to the mast of a rudderless ghost ship, whipped by winds and a hard, cold rain from all directions.

"Fuck this," I said to the empty street outside my windows.

I finished my beer, cleaned myself up and went to the local branch of my bank. A bank I'd hoped was at least modestly under its own control. When I returned, I walked across the street to the Rodriguez house and knocked on the door. The Rodriguez boy peered out from one of the living room windows. He saw me, grinned and waved. I heard his father sternly tell him to get away from the window.

The door opened and there stood Carlos Rodriguez, splattered with plaster and drywall mud, Louisville Slugger in hand.

"Yes?" he said.

"We need to talk, Mr. Rodriguez," I said.

"About?"

"Taking control," I said.

Reluctantly, he let me in.

His wife came in from the kitchen. It was cold in the house and they were all wearing winter coats.

"Mrs. Rodriguez," I said, "would you mind taking your son to the kitchen?"

"Why?"

"Because I need an honest word with your husband and I mean not to offend you, your son or the home you're trying hard to make here."

She nodded and gestured for their son—Manolito—to come with her to the kitchen.

Once they were gone, Rodriguez took a tighter grip on the baseball bat's handle and said, "What's this about?"

"It's about you and your family squatting here," I said. "It's about your wife and son being illegals. And it's about you being man enough to accept help." He stared at me for a hard minute. Then I held out an envelope.

Without taking the envelope, Rodriguez said, "What's this?"

"This is what neighbors do," I said.

Tentatively, he took the envelope and opened it. His eyes widened at the sight of the money inside.

"I'm an ex-cop," I said. "I won the lottery. There should be enough to last you folks for a while. Buy some space heaters until we can figure out how to get the heat going. Food. Clothes maybe some toys and books for the boy. Something nice for your wife. And I'd like it if you, Jimmy Radmon—"

"The drug dealer kid?"

"He doesn't deal anymore," I said. "I'd like it if the three of us sat down and talked about what we can do with a couple other houses in the neighborhood. You and Jimmy would be working together. And I'd be the paymaster. We flip the houses, you and Jimmy get a cut. That is, if you're good enough for the job."

"Why—why would you do this?" Rodriquez said. I could see that his grip on the bat had loosened a bit and, imperceptible to most, his defensive stance had relaxed.

"Because I know what it's like to feel like you don't have control over your own life. And if you're like me, you hate it and hate God for the corner you feel you're backed into."

Rodriguez looked at the money once again then back to me. "I'll do this—for my son—"

"Bullshit," I said. "Don't lay this off on the kid. Do it for yourself to be the man your son already sees in you." I paused and we looked at each other for a moment. Then I put my hand out and said, "Deal?"

Rodriguez's strong, work-bitten hand gripped mine. "Gracias."

I'd started to leave when Rodriguez added, "You don't mind my asking, Señor Snow, but what happened to your face?"

I thought for a moment before saying, "Slipped on a bar of soap."

Rodriguez nodded. I left and drove north to visit my parents.

The October day was bright and cold. The cemetery's collection of old-growth oaks and dogwoods caught the light of an increasingly distant sun, their fall colors luminescent. I brought along a copy of Octavio Paz's first poetry collection, *Luna Silvestre*.

I parked in the small circular drive near St. Ignatius Cemetery and walked uphill for a minute or two, turning right at the Kowalski family plot. My parents were buried beneath one of the taller oaks of the cemetery. The tree would soon shed its leaves, covering my parents beneath a red and gold patchwork quilt in preparation for a cold winter.

Small flags were stuck in the ground near the headstones: Near my mother's grave there was an American flag and the flag of Mexico. Near my father's grave was another American flag with the green, black and red broad-striped flag African-Americans had adopted as their own.

I smiled. I could guess who'd put them there—Big Jake the caretaker, whom I'd met on my last visit to the graves.

I sat with my back against the oak and stared at their headstones for a few minutes. I wondered if they could feel my presence. And I wondered what they might think seeing me with a swollen-shut eye and a badly bruised cheek, from a battle I'd brought on myself and had chosen to lose.

I did not look like the success they'd hoped for. The man whom they had worked so hard to raise to loftier heights: A social-worker fighting the good fight of the poor and disenfranchised. A lawyer raging against the machinery of exclusion, bigotry and hate. A teacher inspiring children to dream bigger and imagine the greater heights of their own potential.

Something.

Anything but an ex-cop with a couple bucks in his pocket and no family.

"We are defined by the people we lose . . ."

In the distance, I heard a riding mower giving the cemetery one of its last cuts before the grass slept and the snows came. If it was Big Jake I'd have to thank him for the tiny flags.

After reading two of Octavio Paz's poems to the headstones, I sat wondering if the money I'd given Carlos Rodriguez was simply my way of saying goodbye. A way of defining myself to a stranger. Aside from the sounds of distant traffic and Big Jake grooming the rolling terrain, the cemetery was quiet.

Halfway through another poem—"Between Going and Coming"—I heard footsteps shifting fallen leaves.

I turned and looked, hoping it would be Big Jake. But no: it was the man calling himself Brewster.

I dropped the book, pulled out my Glock, and came to a knee.

Brewster smiled and held up the palms of his hands.

"As good a place as any to drop you," I said.

I quickly glanced around: twenty yards behind him in the eleven o'clock position was a man in a long, black trench coat. It wasn't Brewster's original thick-necked bodyguard who'd become so well-acquainted with my living room floor. His new companion was the wiry brown-haired security guard with wire rim glasses. The man I'd fought. Dax. His coat was open and his hand rested discreetly on what could have been a machine pistol. If he was as good with a gun as he was with martial arts, then equal and deadly forces were now in play.

Dax smiled at me. Nodded.

Where there was one bodyguard, there was likely another. By this time, I'd earned more than one thick-necked, mouth-breathing bodyguard.

"I'm only here to see if you've reconsidered my original offer," Brewster said. "As they say in advertising, for a limited time only."

"Turn around and get back in your car," I said. "Or I'll kill you where you stand."

Brewster was thirty feet away. I hated the thought of using headstones as cover. Seemed a sacrilege. But the dead didn't care and headstones are just rocks.

"I have the money in the car." Brewster gestured over the hill. "Of course, you realize my offers are on a sliding scale; we've deducted twenty percent from the original amount. A countdown of sorts."

"A countdown," I said. "To what?"

Brewster smiled and shrugged.

"You're scared, aren't you?" I stood from my kneeling position. Brewster's smile slowly faded and he looked at me with hard dark eyes. The eyes of a shark, its nose sensing blood in the water. Perhaps his own. "This whole Titan deal is going south and you're scared. Hell, I'd be scared too if I found myself in the cross hairs of an assassin."

"Not unlike most of your black brethren," Brewster said, cracks in his cool façade beginning to show, "you seem never to know when to shut up or walk away."

"I take that as a compliment," I said.

Brewster said nothing. His eyes cut to his left for a split second. The third man. Behind a dogwood. Hand on the stock of his gun. A machine pistol.

"Why'd you kill Eleanor Paget?" I said.

The question shocked and annoyed him. "She was a mean-spirited, selfish old bag who blustered and railed against the prevailing winds of change. But kill her? I had no interest in or incentive to kill a madwoman baying at the moon. What would my payout be? Perhaps one of the board members had her killed. Who knows? Who cares? Patience, persuasion and large amounts of cash are my weapons of choice, Mr. Snow." Brewster's easy-going grin was beginning to quiver at the edges.

"What about Atchison?" I said. "Did he kill her?"

"How should I know!" Brewster shouted, finally revealing his frustration.

"You control him," I said. "It's your business to know."

I was starting to think Brewster might have made one too many deals with a few too many devils. And I was just a minor demon that had tipped already tenuously balanced scales.

Brewster took in a sharp breath of chilled air, then exhaled slowly. "He is an impetuous, solipsistic little prick, yes. But I believe he appreciates the forces he has aligned himself with. Such unsanctioned actions on his part would be dangerously inconsiderate of those forces."

"This is holy ground," a gruff voice boomed.

It was Big Jake, the groundskeeper, obscured by a tight grouping of three old-growth oaks on a slight rise behind and to my left. For a man in his late sixties, Big Jake moved with the agility and speed of a Big Ten college running back. Within a second or two he had the highly polished nickel-plated barrel of a large semi-automatic handgun to the temple of the second bodyguard. "Son, you got a choice: Put the gun down and embrace Jesus. Or get ready to suck the devil's dick. Now, what's it gonna be, boy?"

The man eased his machine pistol from beneath his Navy pea coat and let it drop to the ground.

"Praise Jesus," Big Jake said before cracking the butt of his gun on the back of the man's head. The bodyguard collapsed near a tombstone inscribed BELOVED SON.

"Now I'd suggest y'all be on y'all's way fort I call the po-lice," Big Jake said, his gun level and steady on Dax. "Unless y'all want me to kill you dead right here, right now. And I can guaran-damn-tee ya: when I buries yo ass, it'll be so deep you gonna have to look up to see hell."

Brewster glared at Big Jake, then brought his eyes back to me. "Perhaps another time, Mr. Snow," he said.

"This is my last offer to you, Brewster," I said. "Come at me one more time and I will make you suffer before you die."

Brewster turned away and began walking up the tree-and-headstone-covered incline. Dax closed his coat, showed the palms of his hands and began walking toward us to retrieve his co-worker sprawled on the cold ground unconscious.

"Leave him!" Brewster shouted.

Dax stopped, gave me an easy smile and said, "Be seein' ya."

He turned and walked away. Big Jake and I kept our guns leveled at the two retreating men. Without looking back at me, Brewster said loudly, "I assure you, Mr. Snow—my third offer will not be so generous."

Big Jake and I watched them disappear over the knoll.

"Friends of yours?" Big Jake said.

"How'd you guess?" I said.

I looked at the piece Big Jake held in his thick hand—a renowned limited-edition gun.

"Desert Eagle?" I said admiringly.

Big Jake held up the weapon, gazing fondly at it. "Yessah, it is. First Gulf War. Given to me by General 'Stormin' Norman Schwarzkopf hisself." Big Jake tucked the gun back into its holster, sighed and said, "Lots of us in the sand."

"Nine years in Iraq the second time and thirteen in Afghanistan. That's a lot men in a lot of sand," I said. "Thanks for the help, Big Jake."

"Ah, hell, son," Big Jake said, giving me a slap on the back. It hurt. "Didn't really look like you needed no help. I'm pretty sure you coulda took them white boys." He furrowed his bushy eyebrows and scowled at me. "Just don't be makin' it no habit bringin' shit like that around here, you feel me?" He squinted, assessed my face and said, "Look like you already done had more than your fair share of shit for one day."

I told Big Jake I'd take the machine pistol. I'm sure either the weapon or the man's prints or both would prove useful to O'Donnell. I looked down at the unconscious man lying next to his machine pistol. "I'll clean this up."

"No," Big Jake said. "My cemetery, my cleanup. Plus, I might just got something make this young man repent of his evil ways."

"Should I ask?"

Big Jake winked at me. "No, but I'mo tell you anyways: Put him in a coffin with a pint of MD 20/20 for fourteen hours and pipe in some Winans praise music. That oughta tenderize his soul a bit."

"Extraordinary rendition," I said.

28

Before leaving the cemetery, I wrote out a check and handed it to Big Jake. He stared at the check for a moment, then squinted at me.

"What I'ma do with this?" he said.

"Buy yourself a case of Auchentoshan scotch," I said. "You deserve it."

He scowled. "This ain't no blood money is it?"

"It is," I said. "My blood."

He nodded, shoved the check in the inside pocket of his work coat and said, "Got me some nieces and nephews. Momma's been on hard times since this city done fell off the face of God's green earth. Think fort I get me that scotch, I'mo make me a little trip to Toys "R" Us."

"Sounds like a good idea," I said.

We shook hands and I left.

On the way back to my house, I called Frank. After Brewster's visit to the cemetery, it seemed a good time to get a download on what was happening in Traverse City. Especially since Brewster appeared determined to make good on his threats.

"Oh, man, the colors up here have just exploded, dude!" Frank said. "Colleen made some *awesome* chili. No meat, but really good. Then we went to Traverse City State Park and—"

"Listen," I said, wheeling my rental car into the narrow driveway of my house, "I'm glad your fall color tour is a screaming success,

Frank, but something's just cut loose down here and I need you locked and loaded. I'm coming up."

"Bad?" Frank said.

"Bad enough."

"On the job, boss man," Frank said.

No sooner had I entered the house—hand on the grip of my Glock—than Jimmy Radmon knocked on the door.

I let him in.

"Oh, damn, bro," he said, surveying my face. "Them cable guys again?"

I wasn't in the mood for chitchat. "What's up, Jimmy?"

"That Mexican dude across the street?" Radmon said. "Rodriguez? He come down to Carmela and Sylvia's. Got his tool belt on talkin' 'bout helpin' me out. What's up with that?"

"You two are partners now," I said. "He helps you, you help him, you both get paid."

Radmon nodded. By this time I think I'd earned at least a bit of trust from the kid.

"Listen, Jimmy," I said. "I got things to do, okay? I'm gonna be away for a while. If I'm not back in three or four days, I need you to take a letter to my lawyer."

I quickly wrote out a letter assigning ownership of the house to Radmon, along with a bit of money and a stipulation about him going to school. I didn't let him see it before I stuffed it into an envelope, sealed it and wrote my attorney's name and address on the front of the envelope.

He took the envelope, stared at it for a moment, then looked up at me. "Those weren't the cable guys, were they?"

"No."

Radmon nodded and we stood quiet in the kitchen for a moment. Then he said, "I don't know what you into, man. All I know is you helped me out, so anything—"

"Keep an eye out for Carmela and Sylvia," I said. "You're putting your mark on what's left of this neighborhood. It's yours now. Take care of it."

Radmon nodded again, and I sent him on his way.

It took me less than ten minutes to pack a bag for Traverse City. The same black leather duffel that had seen me through a year in India and Europe was now full of ammo for my Glock and my Smith & Wesson .38. I didn't feel confident with only two handguns; Brewster's men appeared well-equipped. Two guys like Dax strapped like the men at the cemetery would be all it would take to wipe out a village. A beaten up ex-cop, an ex-grocery bagger, a watercolor artist and her wife didn't stand much of a chance against odds like that.

I made a stop by Tomás's house north of me near Bagley Street in Mexicantown.

"Jesus," Tomás said. "You look like crap."

"Yeah," I said. "It's been a crappy couple days. Any other night crawlers?"

Tomás shook his head. No one else had bothered him or his family.

Tomás offered me a cup of strong Mexican coffee and a pastry. I said no to the pastry and yes to the coffee. I was operating on a sleep deficit and could use the caffeine charge to keep the battery going. Elena was with her daughter and Carlos Rodriguez's wife, Catalina, at Home Depot looking at interior paint color chips. Tomás didn't expect Elena home for another two, three hours—he suspected the ladies had made a joyous labor of the paint selection by stopping for a glass of wine or two first.

"You got any weapons I could borrow?" I said, knocking back the coffee and pouring another demitasse.

"Jesus," Tomás said. "Most people borrow a cup of sugar or a fucking lawn mower."

"I'm not most people," I said.

"Ain't that the God's honest truth."

Tomás led me to the basement. In a dark, cobwebbed corner between his workbench and stacks of plastic storage tubs was his gun locker. Tomás pulled the cord of the bare light bulb, illuminating an ancient poster of Emiliano Zapata, the legendary hero of the Mexican Revolution, which he'd taped to the doors of his gun locker, splitting it down the center where the double door seam ran.

"Nice poster," I said.

"Elena didn't like how scary the locker looked." Tomás twirled the combination lock. "So I put the poster on it."

"Oh, yeah," I said, staring at the maniacal dark eyes and imposing black mustache of the legendary Mexican revolutionary. "Nothing says cute and cuddly like Emiliano Zapata."

"Fuck you." Tomás opened the doors of the locker.

Eight rifles, including an AR-15, five handguns and ammo for all.

"Holy shit, Tomás," I said, looking at the cache of weapons. "Preparing for the zombie apocalypse?"

"This wasn't always a safe neighborhood. And I wasn't always an altar boy."

I carefully surveyed the locker's holdings. "Mind if I take the Beretta Outlander and the DPMS?"

Tomás pulled the rifles out of the locker and handed them to me. He reached to a top shelf of the locker and retrieved a small lock box. Opening the lock box, he pulled out the firing pins for both. I put the firing pins in the side pocket of my jacket. Then he handed me boxes of ammo.

"I take it the registration numbers have been filed and acid washed?" I said.

Tomás gave me a sour look. I'd asked the dumbest question he'd ever heard. "Sure you don't want the Winchester Diamond Grade?"

"It's pretty," I said, "but I don't think there's any elephants in Traverse City."

"Handguns?"

"I'm good," I said.

"How 'bout an extra gun hand?"

I put a hand on Tomás's shoulder. He understood and nodded.

As I loaded the weapons into the trunk of my car, Tomás said, "This is a helluva welcome-back for you, Octavio. I'm sorry it's come to this."

I shut the trunk. "It all ends soon."

Tomás said he and his family would pray for me. Which meant Elena would light novena candles and bow her head in solemn prayer while Tomás planned his own miracles.

We shook hands, then I got in the car, navigated my way out of Mexicantown and got on the I-75 North entrance ramp, heading for Traverse City.

29

"I know you're not an idiot. So I guess that just makes you stupid."

Thirty minutes northwest of Detroit I got a call from my accountant, Liz Garshaw. I'd known Liz since we were students as Wayne State. We'd slept together a couple times, but decided we had more going with each other as good friends who talked about who we'd slept with.

Liz had been tracking my expenditures and she wasn't happy.

"Europe and Asia I can understand," she said. "And the St. Al's donations, fine. So are the investment properties, though I'd have to argue your dubious choice of locations. But come on, August. Big checks to random guys? The large cash withdrawals? What's going on? Please tell me these guys aren't bookies!"

"They're not bookies, Liz." I didn't tell her about the check I'd just written to Big Jake.

"Then what?"

"Nothing you need to know about."

There was silence at the other end of the line. Then Liz said, "Are you all right?"

"Never better."

"Liar," she said.

I thanked her for her concern, told her I was on the road and we'd sit down sometime soon over too many cocktails to talk about my fiscal irresponsibility and our love lives.

Once you get past the strip malls, dismal grey sprawl of factories and ugly traffic entanglements, the drive north along I-75 in October can be beautiful. In the clear, cold light of late afternoon, the trees crowding the roadside catch the light and flicker their innumerable tones of red, orange and yellow. The farms, working or not, all look like Currier and Ives lithographs.

My rental Caddy was equipped with Sirius XM satellite radio. A nice option for long drives—no obnoxious ads for divorce attorneys, discount meat shops, energy drinks or—my favorite ad—a titty bar in Romulus, Michigan, called Stump Grinders, "where our proud amputee military veterans always get half-price drinks and buffalo wings."

But this time, instead of listening to satellite radio I brought some of my dad's old CDs: Herbie Hancock, Miles Davis, Stanley Clarke, Marcus Belgrave, Koko Taylor and Etta James and, for the more contemplative moments, Earl Klugh. I also brought along one of my father's Lynyrd Skynyrd CDs—an odd choice for a black man since Lynyrd Skynyrd's often associated with white motorcycle gangs who drink too much bourbon and salute the Confederate flag. My dad was from Alabama and he loved Skynyrd. Took him back to the better parts of his growing-up years. And when things got bad in Bama his favorite Skynyrd song became "They Call Me the Breeze."

Occasionally when I was young, after considerable research on my father's part (including musty old copies of *The Negro Motorist Green Book*) regarding where a black man could safely lay his head in Northern Michigan, my mom, dad and I would pack up and make a weekend journey north in Dad's beloved Oldsmobile 98. We would stop at Hollandbeck's Apple Farm just north of Saginaw and get hot cider, warm cinnamon donuts and a bag of small apples. My dad would bullshit with Mr. Hollandbeck—a squat, blotchy-skinned white man with a Santa beard and belly. My mother would talk with Mrs. Hollandbeck, who was short and round, the perfect Mrs. Claus counterpoint to her husband. My mother's conversations with Mrs. Hollandbeck were halting and filled with impromptu sign language and gesticulations; Mrs. Hollandbeck was proficient at her native Dutch and able to hold her own in German, but English proved a challenge for her and her Spanish was nonexistent. They seemed, nevertheless, to enjoy each other's company.

I was usually left to wander the edge of their property, where the unorganized forest met the perfectly aligned rows of apple trees. Sometimes there were other kids pitching small apples into the forest.

"Maybe you see deer come for dem apples," Mr. Hollandbeck once told me. He smelled like sweat, beef and powerful cheese. "Sometimes—you toss one in, look real hard—maybe you see—a *reindeer*. And maybe he got de *red nose*, yah?"

I was pretty sure I wouldn't be stopping at Hollandbeck's Apple Farm today, searching for Rudolph one small apple at a time. Today the beauty of a fall drive to northern Michigan held no more promise than that of blood spilling on fallen leaves.

A four-hour drive north was four hours too long, so I mostly took the speed limit signs as passive-aggressive suggestions.

I called O'Donnell and told her the situation. That I had seen Brewster, a.k.a the Consultant, at the cemetery. And how, if Brewster were the creature of habit I thought he was, taking a run at Vivian was next on his bloody agenda if for no other reason than to cow me. I gave her the license plate number of Brewster's black Cadillac Escalade and said she could find one of his bodyguard's machine pistols in my house, which she was more than welcome to with the proper warrants. She listened patiently while I gave her what I knew, occasionally saying, "Yeah," "Okay" and "Mm-hm."

Then she said, "Where were you earlier today, August? Around one o'clock."

My stomach knotted. This was the first time she'd called me by my first name. And her question sounded like the beginning of an interrogation.

"I was at a friend's house," I said. "I drove there after visiting my parents' graves and a brief stop at my house." I gave her the name of the cemetery. I did not give her Tomás's name or address. I told her the groundskeeper at the cemetery—Big Jake—would confirm this. "What's going on?"

"What did you and Ray Danbury talk about in his office earlier today, after you were brought in from the bank? Before I got you."

"Goddammit, O'Donnell—"

"Maybe you'd better pull off the road."

"What's going on?" I shouted.

I heard O'Donnell sigh heavily. "At one-fifteen this afternoon, Captain Raymond Lewis Danbury was fatally shot on the city's east side. He's dead. Danbury's gone."

My heart clenched and my vision blurred for a second.

"Considering your bank escapade this morning and the loud horsewhipping he gave you, DPD's laying even money it was you," O'Donnell said. "There's an APB out on you."

"I didn't do it," I said, hearing how shallow and distant my voice was. "He was—Danbury was my friend."

"I know," O'Donnell said. "I had to ask."

"And Cowling?" I said. "Lieutenant Leo Cowling? Danbury's driver?"

"Got off a couple rounds," O'Donnell said. "Took three. Neck graze, shoulder, lower abdomen. He'll live. Says it was a black Cadillac Escalade." She paused. "What do you drive, August?"

"You've followed me enough to know the make, model and license," I said. "And no, I don't have any other vehicles."

O'Donnell said she'd do what she could to calm nerves at the department and have the APB pulled. Realistically there was little she could do. At least without tipping the delicate balance of her single largest case.

"You need to get out in front of this thing, O'Donnell," I said. "You don't, then I will flip the whole cart over and set it on fire."

"August, I'm trying to be your—"

"I don't have any goddamn friends."

I disconnected.

30

I'd killed men and seen men killed before.

Friends.

In Afghanistan.

I'd collected their bodies. Said a prayer over whatever pieces of flesh remained. I'd given sitreps to commanding officers on how men died. And I'd saluted as I watched C-17 Globemaster cargo planes lift into the cold grey air, flying the bodies home. Back to farming communities in Indiana. Fishing communities in Louisiana. The suburbs and ghettos of Chicago and Brooklyn and Detroit and Dallas-Fort Worth.

And after saluting, I collected my gear, took my next assignment, put the enemy in the cross hairs and, between the slowed beats of my heart, pulled the trigger.

I'd known men and women killed on the job in Detroit: Patrolwoman Denise Acosta, shot once in the head as she wrote out a parking ticket. Patrolman Lamont Morris, shot twice accompanying a parole officer to the house of a parolee.

And Duty Roster Administrative Assistant Maureen "Mo" McKnight, killed during a convenience store robbery. She was buying a half-gallon of skim milk. One bullet, two lives. Hers and my unborn son's.

Danbury had known my father. Held him as an example of how good police work was done. When I came on the force, Danbury took me under his wing. Bitch-slapped me when I was wrong. Congratulated me when I was right. Taught me the greater value and nobility of serving a community that was constantly under siege from drugs and assault, rape and murder.

He'd roused me out of bed on weekends and barked over the phone that I was to meet him in twenty minutes at this soup kitchen or that homeless shelter. I would stand next to his wife, his son and daughter, making sandwiches or serving bowls of soup to the legions of homeless. The disenfranchised. The forgotten.

I once attended the northwest Detroit Baptist church where he and his family were members. The pastor had invited him to speak to the congregation where he was highly regarded even in the darkest days of the department.

"You know who's standing right next to Saint Peter?" he'd said from the pulpit. "A Detroit cop. And when Saint Peter asks you about your life he's gonna turn to that cop and ask if everything you said is true. And don't nobody know the truth more than a Detroit cop. So get right with your life! 'Cause God's gonna know! Saint Peter's gonna know! And that Detroit cop standing beneath the wings of Saint Peter will for damn sure know! Praise Jesus!"

Now it was Ray Danbury standing beneath the wings of St. Peter. Right next to Denise Acosta and Lamont Morris.

And Mo.

Now it was my turn to get right with the Lord.

But before I got right with God, I had to get right with Danbury.

About thirty minutes out from the home of Vivian and Colleen, a call came through the car's speaker system.

"Mr. Snow?"

It was Brewster.

Instantly, my heart rate lowered. If I was going to take the shot, firing between heartbeats, I had to contain the rage I was feeling over Danbury's murder.

"I'm so sorry," I said. "August Snow is out of the office at the moment. This is Mr. Snow's secretary, Rosario Dawson. May I take a message?"

"Undoubtedly, you heard of Detroit Police Captain Raymond Danbury's untimely death this afternoon," Brewster said. "Such a shame. He was a family man, am I correct?"

"A wife and two kids," I said, losing the battle to contain my rage.

"Pity," Brewster said. "Such a violent city, Detroit is. Even the police aren't safe."

"The fuck you want, Brewster or whatever your real name is?"

"An offer is still on the table, Mr. Snow," Brewster said. "Though becoming less handsome. Still, nothing to sneeze at."

"Why Danbury?"

"Do you have any idea how expensive college tuition is these days?" Brewster said. "Really a pity. So many parents, so many young people struggling to pay tuition. Especially if two siblings are in university at the same time."

I felt my throat tighten and my eyes flood with tears.

"The money was made to look like scholarships, Mr. Snow," Brewster said. "And when offered, your Captain Danbury took it. All he had to do was control you."

"You bastard—"

"And all you had to do was abide by the wishes of an old friend to stay at home and watch sports," Brewster said. "But your pride—your arrogance—got in the way. And now your friend is dead. It's not too late to repair our relationship, Mr. Snow. In the process you would be saving lives—perhaps even the life of Paget's lovely daughter—and allowing business to proceed in an orderly, non violent manner. Is that too much to ask?"

"You know what I think?" The rage that was brewing in my stomach boiled over. "I think I'm going to scoop out your left eye with a hot spoon, then piss in the socket. I think you're dead and you just don't know it yet. So pack fast and book a flight to wherever is the farthest place on this earth away from me and Vivian Paget."

"Goodbye, Mr. Snow."

It was just after five when I wheeled the Caddy into the long gravel driveway of Vivian and Colleen's Traverse City home.

The house was a white shingle three-story Victorian with a separate four-car garage. Behind the house and garage was a large red and white barn-style shed. The estate rested on five acres of well-tended land with the shed near the forested eastern property line. About a hundred yards to the north was Lake Michigan, slate grey and preparing to swallow the pale fall sun.

There was a flagpole near the meandering walkway leading up to the expansive white-railed porch. Three flags snapped in the wind coming in off the lake: The American flag was the most prominent. Beneath it was a smaller rainbow gay pride flag, then a white flag with a blue peace symbol. I mounted the wide steps leading up to the multi-colored leaded glass front door.

Before I could ring the bell, the door opened.

Frank was wearing a bright floral-print Tommy Bahama shirt and blue Billabong cargo shorts.

"Jesus." He stared at the wreck of my face. "I suppose you're gonna tell me I should see the other guy."

"The other guy's peachy," I said. "I got the shit kicked out of me." I eyed Frank's outfit. "Circus in town?"

Frank held his Ruger .9mm casually at his side. He quickly stashed the gun between the belt of his cargo shorts and the small of his back and ushered me in.

The house was warm and smelled of nicely seasoned chili.

Down a hallway from the foyer where Frank and I stood came Vivian Paget and Colleen. Vivian looked like her mother, the only differences being Vivian's blue eyes were soft and the set of her mouth wasn't hard. Her long blonde hair was unkempt in an alluring way.

As opposed to Vivian, Colleen's face was angular with high cheek-bones. I took her to be in her early to mid-thirties. Her eyes were hazel and probing and her hair was dyed jet-black and cut in a short, spiked style. She was the type of woman young boys fantasized about and young girls wanted to be, preferably while wielding a screaming electric guitar and shouting Pink-style fuck-and-fight lyrics.

Frank introduced us. Vivian and I knew each other from a different life.

Seeing my face, Vivian brought her hands to her chest and in a soft voice said, "Oh, my God. You're hurt."

"Looks worse than it is, Ms. Paget."

"Jesus, I hope so." Colleen scrutinized my face. "'Cause that looks just god-awful."

I forced a smile that brought a sting to the right side of my face. "I'm actually much better looking than my current face would have you believe."

She smiled. "I'm sure you are."

Vivian gingerly touched my black-and-blue cheek and said, "I'll get you some ice."

On beautiful bare feet, Vivian turned and walked back down the wide hallway to where I imagined the kitchen was.

"It's nice to finally meet you, August." Colleen shook my hand. It was a firm handshake. The handshake of someone who had worked the land and held a weapon. She nodded toward Frank. "Too bad you sent this douchebag. I thought you said you were gonna send a *man*?"

"Screw you," Frank laughed, to which Colleen replied, "Yeah, you wish."

"I'm glad you kids are playing well together," I said, "but we need to talk and talk fast."

I told Colleen that this time Vivian needed to hear what I had to say. She'd been protected from the situation for long enough. She needed to know what was going down.

Vivian returned from the kitchen with a large baggy filled with ice and a cup of herbal tea. I took the ice and politely waved off the tea.

Colleen and Vivian led the way through the house, a beautiful nightmare of tall windows and multiple entry ways. Too many ways for bad things to come and go as they pleased. Frank made a few adjustments, including securing the exterior cellar doors and enhancing the alarm systems around first floor windows. He and Colleen had agreed on locking outer perimeter rooms save for the kitchen and the library. Locked doors never stopped bad intentions, but at least they slowed those intentions down.

"She's a helluva shot," Frank said of Colleen as we entered the sunroom. "We've gone to the range twice, and fired off a couple boxes of ammo on open ground a couple times. Viv gets a little jittery, but she's pretty much okay with it."

"She just might have to get a lot okay with it real fast," I said. There was that itch at the back of my brain again—that claw scratching on black glass—as I watched Vivian take a seat on a rattan sofa.

The sunroom was long and filled with all manner of greenery. The glass roof arced down from the second floor into the side window panels, allowing a spectacular view of the lake. Just outside and beneath the tall windows were low shrubs, two willow trees and several cherry trees. There were a variety of sculptures on the grounds; some were Vivian's, the others she had purchased from local artists. Classic sculptures chiseled from marble or granite. A carved and hand-painted wood totem— maybe Potowatami or Sauk. Modern sculptures of welded metal designed to rust and ultimately decompose. Even a chainsaw sculpture of an eagle.

It was a beautiful room with an extraordinary view.

It was also a trained killer's dream come true.

I gave Frank a hard look.

"I was gonna close the room off after you got here," Frank said sheepishly.

"What's going on?" Vivian Paget said, her legs tucked beneath her. Colleen placed a comforting hand on her shoulder. I sat in a high-back cushioned rattan chair across from the two. Frank stood in the doorway of the sunroom, scanning the grounds with eyes trained by the US Army.

"Vivian," I began, "I believe some very dangerous men are coming here to make a point."

"What point?"

"That they can hurt you to hurt me."

Vivian nodded without understanding. I explained about her mother, about the people doing everything in their considerable power to take over the bank. The people who had been hurt since her mother's murder. Everything except Ray Danbury's murder. That was my burden, not hers.

"My mother—did they—"

"I believe they did," I said. "I'm pretty sure it was a man named Dax Randolph who's employed at your mother's bank as a security guard."

"When—when are they coming?" she said hesitantly.

"Maybe tonight. Maybe tomorrow," I said. "My gut tells me soon."

"But they might not come at all, right?" I could tell Vivian instantly recognized the false hope she had voiced.

"That's a possibility," I said. "But in all probability they are coming or are already here."

"You keep saying 'they,'" Colleen said. "Who are 'they'?"

"People whose plans for the bank are very illegal and very dangerous," I said. "So far I've dealt with both amateurs and professionals. I've taken care of the amateurs. We're into professionals now. Highly trained ex-military. Private contractors, some employed at your mother's bank."

"These guys would goose-step straight into hell and not give it a second thought," Frank said.

"So," Vivian began as she looked at Frank, "you're not really Colleen's cousin?"

"No, ma'am," Frank said. "Sorry."

I gave Vivian a long, hard look to make sure my words and Frank's words were having the intended impact. My right eye was starting to open and the vision was good.

"If what I think is going to happen does in fact happen, I need you to know something," I said, leaning closer to her. "It's gonna get loud and ugly and people will be killed. It's the responsibility of everybody in this room to make sure that nobody here is killed."

"Can't you just—talk to these people?"

I sighed. "These people don't talk. They obey orders. They come in hard and leave counting their pay." I took a pause for effect. "There's three of us in this room that can handle ourselves. Four would be better."

There was that itch again . . . that claw on black glass . . .

"You knew about this?" Vivian said, desperately searching Colleen's eyes for answers. "You knew about all of this?"

"Viv," Colleen began tenuously. "I didn't want to—"

"Didn't want to what? Upset me? Scare me?"

"Viv—"

"I'm not a child, Colleen!"

"No," Colleen said. "You're not. You're the woman I love. You're my life. You make me better than I ever thought I could be. And I could never forgive myself if something—anything—happened to you." Vivian's eyes began to flood. "If you want August and Frank gone, they're gone. Right now. We'll take our chances with the cops. Or maybe just—we'll just leave. Today. Wait for things to cool down. You tell me what you want to do, Viv, and it'll be done. I swear."

Vivian said, "This is our home. I don't want anybody scaring us out of our home."

Frank ejected the clip from his gun, ratcheted the remaining bullet from the chamber and knelt close to Vivian. He held the gun out for Vivian to take.

"Here," he said softly. "It's just a dumb, useless piece of metal now."

Tentatively, Vivian took the gun from Frank. She stared vacantly at the weapon.

"Good," Frank said. "Like holding a hammer or screw driver or—you know—a paint brush, right? Just a tool."

Reluctantly, Vivian nodded.

"Viv, this tool is the only thing between you being alive or you being dead. The only tool that can help you protect Colleen. It's that simple. And you've got to be able to use this tool. *We've* got to know you can use this tool. 'Cause whatever's coming for you, Viv, is coming for us, too."

The weapon began trembling in her hand and she shook her head. "No. No, I—I don't think . . ."

Frank sighed heavily. Then, using his thumb, Frank slowly popped the bullets from the clip, each landing on Vivian's lap. Her eyes widened and body stiffened.

"Frank—" I began.

"No, man!" Frank said, glaring up at me. "Seriously. She's gotta know how she's gonna die—how Colleen's gonna die—if she can't hold a gun and pull a trigger. If she can't pull her own weight to save her own life." He looked back to Vivian. "If these guys are pros you'll probably be dead—Colleen'll probably be dead—in four to six seconds. That's the merciful way this goes down."

"That's enough, Frank—" I started.

Frank glared up at me. "Oh, I'm just getting started, man." He quickly turned his attention back to Vivian. "The not-so-merciful way is these guys pop August and me then decide to have some fun with you and your wife. Making you watch each other get raped." Vivian's cheeks were stained with tears. Her body quivered. "Then you can watch them zip their pants up before they put a bullet in each of your brains. And you'd better pray it's your brains." Frank thumbed out the last bullet from the magazine, then stood. Vivian looked up at Frank, tears flowing from her eyes. Before I could say anything, Colleen was on her feet. She brought a solid right cross to Frank's jaw. It rocked him. But it didn't stop him. He snapped his gaze back to Vivian and said, "You wanna die like that—fine. Me? I've seen this horror show before, only with a woman who actually fought for her life. You ain't gonna fight for yours? No sense in me putting it on the line for you. Fuck you."

He walked out of the room.

Colleen grabbed a fistful of the bullets from Vivian's lap and threw them at Frank before wrapping her arms around the weeping Vivian.

"I want you and Frank outta here," Colleen growled at me. "Twenty minutes."

"Your choice," I said. "But I'll give you fifteen minutes to think about it."

I walked out of the sunroom.

I found Frank outside leaning against the back of the house staring vacantly at the shed and smoking a cigarette.

"Two tours in Afghanistan," Frank said, "three combat commendations. Don't hardly seem to add up to my last two years nailed to a desk job in Fort Benning, does it? Last tour in Afghanistan, we took a village maybe twenty clicks southwest of Kandahar. Drove out a few Taliban. Villagers loved us. Pomegranates, grapes, roasted lamb. Good people, man. Two nights later, one of my guys—Vicks—goes twitchy. Tries to rape this thirteen-year-old girl. Me and Hammond—this skinny black kid from Oklahoma; good kid—we try to talk Vicks down. Vicks ain't havin' none of it. Tells me and my man Hammond to join in the fun. The girl's struggling. But he's got her pinned down. She finally scratches the hell out of his right cheek. He grabs his service pistol. Before he can shoot her

I shoot him." Frank crushed his expended cigarette with the toe of his shoe, and then lit another one. "Got my ass fried for wasting a hundred-fifty-'G's of government property. But they didn't want none of that shit hitting the PR fan. I mean, how's it gonna look word gets out we're acting just like them stinkin' Taliban ragheads? So the unit gets broken up, I got hitched to a desk stateside with nothin' to do 'cept count paperclips." Frank drew in a deep lungful of his cigarette. We let the chill of a fall wind wash over us for a moment.

"Would you do it again?" I finally asked.

Frank gave me a hard look. "Bet your sweet ass. In a fucking heartbeat."

"Then do it again."

I started to go back inside the house when Frank said, "You think she can do it, man? You think she can pull a trigger?"

"Something tells me if the time comes, she will."

Smoothing things over with Colleen took some effort. Neither one had any particular reason to trust me or Frank. And I couldn't blame them. But in the end Colleen's only concern was for Vivian's safety. If things didn't pan out the way I thought they might in the next two days, I promised Colleen that Frank and I would be on our merry and she should feel free to report us to an FBI agent named Megan O'Donnell. I gave Colleen O'Donnell's card.

The grey disk of the sun was now nearly submerged in Lake Michigan and a strong wind had kicked up when Frank followed me out to my car.

"Jesus," Frank said, staring at the weapons in the trunk. "You got enough here for a platoon."

We brought the guns inside, put the firing pins in and loaded them with ammo. Then we sat in the library and went over the layout of the house and the surrounding grounds. If anybody was going to make a run at us, it would be either dead-on through the front or from the northern lake side. Maybe both in a pincer move.

Frank said there was a Ducati Streetfighter 848 motorcycle and an old Ford pickup with a broad snow plow in the shed. And while the Ducati was a thing of beauty, the truck would be considerably more useful in blocking either street access or maybe a portion of the sunroom at the northern side of the house. Colleen and Frank, when not eating sandwiches from local delis or drinking expensive coffee, had made several trips to the hardware and farm supply store. They had purchased and unspooled thirty yards of razor wire along the perimeter of the sunroom, hiding it within the still-green shrubbery. Frank had gone so far as to hook the wire up to the power. Low voltage that would stun but not kill. Colleen and Frank had made other security enhancements that might give us a fighting chance. But these guys—the guys Brewster rolled with—could march through a mile of razor wire and not break a sweat.

It was late and Frank said he would take the first watch.

"I'll take the first," I said.

"Bullshit," Frank said. "Aside from having had the shit kicked out of you, looks like you ain't slept in twenty-four. Get some rack time, man." He gave me a look and said, "Something happen you're not telling me about?"

I didn't say anything. I just sat in a high-back leather chair feeling my body begin to quiver from the beating I'd taken earlier and the lack of sleep. I'm sure whatever guilt I was feeling over Ray Danbury's death figured in, too.

Frank said, "Well, whatever it is, I got your back, man. Solid on your six."

I forced a smile. "Army strong."

"Hoo-wah."

We bumped fists.

Frank got up from his chair, went to the library's liquor cabinet and poured me a shot of vodka. I tried to decline, but I discovered Frank could be a hard-nosed bastard. Fucking Rangers.

"Viv and Colleen make it the old-fashion Polish way," Frank

said. "With honey. How her grandma used to make it. Down the hatch, Auggie."

"Call me 'Auggie' again and I'll shoot you in your pecker."

"Down the hatch, August."

I snapped the honey vodka back. It was strong and good.

Colleen entered the library, and glared at us. After a few tense seconds, she nodded to Frank and said, "Pour me a vodka, asshole. Big one. With ice." Frank poured and handed it obediently to her. "You got a jaw like toilet porcelain," she said before taking a long pull on her drink.

"And you got a right cross like a young Mike Tyson," Frank said.

Colleen took several more long pulls off her drink before looking at me and saying, "I hope I'm not wrong about you guys. God help you if I'm wrong."

Colleen knew the land of Northern Michigan. Every twist and turn, nook and knoll, every river, stream, lake and creek. She'd farmed it. Hunted and fished it. I had the distinct feeling that if I proved to be wrong, it would probably be several decades (if at all) before anybody found my body and Frank's buried in the land she knew so well.

"Viv's exhausted, so I made some chamomile tea and put her to bed," Colleen said. "I fucking hated what you did, Frank. But I understand why you did it."

There was silence between us for a minute or so. Then Colleen said, "It's that bad?"

"It's that bad," I said.

"You think they'll come tonight?"

"No," I said. "But soon. Maybe tomorrow. Certainly the day after tomorrow. But no question, they're coming."

Colleen stared at me for what felt like a long time. Finally, she said, "You're hoping they come."

"Sorry to say, I am."

"Nothing to be sorry about," Colleen said. "But if we're gonna work things out between us, we're gonna start with the goddamn truth."

"Yes, ma'am," I said.

Frank poured me another honey vodka shot. I didn't fight him on this one.

I lifted the shot glass up in a toast. "The Three Musketeers."

"The Three Musketeers," the two of them said.

"Hopefully four," Frank added.

We were all silent for a long time, each of us wrapped in our own thoughts. I imagined Colleen was thinking about how much she loved Vivian and how she would take the fight to anybody who threatened that love. And I imagined Frank was thanking God for work that employed not only his military skills, but the true core of who he was: somebody whose sole purpose in life had been the protection of people who couldn't protect themselves.

And me?

I was thinking about Oslo, Norway, and a woman named Tatina Stadtmueller who smelled like jasmine, tasted like warm mango and had breached my walls with a kiss.

And I was thinking about blood.

Lots of blood.

All of it spilled on fallen autumn leaves . . .

31

I awoke with a start: I'd been dreaming about Ray Danbury.

Heart racing and disoriented, I looked around at the unfamiliar surroundings. A white bedroom with a tall single window softened by floor-length white curtains. The sun was already high and the curtains iridescent. There was a tall white armoire with delicate hand-painted green tree branches on the doors and a white dressing bureau with pewter handles.

I was lying in a white four-poster with yards of cream damask wrapped with stylish laziness around the posts and covered with a white goose down comforter. Beneath the comforter I was naked. Nothing unusual, considering men's pajamas are dumb and very learned men's health magazines suggest us guys sleep in the buff. Only problem was I couldn't remember coming upstairs, undressing myself and climbing into bed.

At the foot of the bed on a linen chest was my bag and the clothes I'd arrived in, freshly laundered and pressed. There was also a blue string-handle bag on the floor near the linen chest. The bag was from one of the Traverse City shops and contained a navy-blue terry robe.

On the white nightstand next to the bed was my Glock, an ice pack, a cut-glass pitcher of water, a drinking glass and a bottle of aspirin. I poured some water and downed three aspirin.

I looked at my watch: ten o'clock.

I had started to get out of bed when there was a knock on the door. I tucked back beneath the puffy white comforter and said, "Come in."

There was the rattle of china and silverware before the door opened.

Vivian entered carrying a wicker serving tray and was wearing a loose, off-white linen top and matching linen chimney-leg pants that hung precariously low on her hips. Her whitish-blonde hair was pulled up and secured in back by two red enamel chopsticks. She was barefoot and as she moved toward me her high, ample breasts swayed, punctuating her fluid movements.

She sat the tray on the bedside table and said, "There's form-aldehyde-free decaf coffee, antibiotic-free creamer, a gluten-free blueberry muffin and sliced fruit. If you want a fuller breakfast, there's plenty in the fridge downstairs. Except bacon. Or sausage. We mostly don't eat meat."

Then she turned and started to walk out. Looking at her I was reminded of something my father used to say on occasion as he watched my mother walk away from the dinner table: "It must be jelly 'cause jam don't shake like that."

Vivian stopped near the door and with her back to me said, "Frank was cruel. He scared me. *You* scared me."

"I know," I said. "I'm sorry."

"Colleen explained why he said those—things," she said, her back still to me, "and I suppose I should be grateful. But it was—awful." Then she turned to me. "I love Colleen. Very much. I would do anything for her. To—protect her."

"'Love is fierce/It is the heart, aflame/Ignited in small hands/ Refusing the wasteland/Where such fires burn so few.'"

She turned fully to me, the diffused sunlight of the room drifting through the sheer filaments of her pajamas, revealing the shape of her body. Her pale blonde hair caught the same diffused sunlight and seemed a halo about her head.

"That's beautiful," she said.

"A lesser known poet," I said. "My father. He wrote it for my mom."

Hesitantly, she said, "Do your parents love each other?"

"They did," I said. "They're gone now. They were Tristan and Isolde without the political machinations. Romeo and Juliet without the swordplay. Harry and Sally without the long exposition."

She smiled.

"I'm envious of what you and Colleen have," I said. "And I mean to protect it."

She looked at me with pale blue eyes for a moment, nodded and walked out of the room, closing the door behind her.

I drank the lame-o decaf coffee, had a bite of the muffin, which had the consistency of packed wet sand, and all of the fruit. Then I showered, got dressed, checked the clip and chamber of my gun and navigated my way downstairs, carrying the breakfast tray.

"Well, you look a helluvalot better," Frank greeted me in the kitchen.

"You shouldn't have let me sleep that long." I was irritated with Frank's bright attitude. "This ain't a goddamn vacation."

"Nothing from the hotels or motels," Frank said. Colleen had friends who worked at the local hotels and motor lodges. If anyone suspicious showed up, they would call. "And we did shifts. I did a perimeter check at two, scared off a couple of deer and spooked a vicious gang of raccoons. Now it's morning. I don't think whoever's coming are daylight kinda guys."

"Sorry," I said.

"I know we ain't known each other long, but I gotta ask. You trust me?" Frank folded his muscular arms across his broad chest and casually leaned against the double-doors of the large Thermador refrigerator.

"Yeah," I said. "I trust you."

"Then start fuckin' acting like it." Frank walked out of the kitchen. August Snow: Friend to Mankind.

I caught up with Frank and asked him to take me on a full security tour of the estate. He walked me through the house, floor by floor, room by room, from the long, dark attic to the expansive wine and fruit cellar and mechanical room. We walked the grounds and talked about entry points and escape routes. Frank had been thorough in his security assessment thanks in part to his military experience, security job at Eleanor Paget's estate and his obvious brotherly affection for Vivian and Colleen. It was still a lot of house and a lot of land for three people—or even four—to make a stand, but it was possible.

Then again, I'm sure this is what Jim Bowie and Davey Crockett thought at the Alamo just before General Antonio Lopez de Santa Anna went through the whole drunken lot of them like a hot sabre through warm butter.

On the side porch I stopped Frank and said, "There's something you should know."

I told him about Ray Danbury. From Danbury I backed through the story, giving him everything I knew, everything I'd done, everything that was on the line. I told him that if he wanted out I'd understand and he was free to pack up and bug out. No harm, no foul.

"Man, I loved the army," Frank said after a moment, "except for the—you know—the thing. After those two years nailed to a desk—I had to see what else life had to offer. Imagine my surprise when I found out life back in the world had fuck-all to offer. I don't cry about it 'cause I know who I am. You know who I am, August?"

"Tell me," I said.

"I'm a guy who stands by people who stand by him," Frank said. "Listen, man, I'm sorry about your friend. I really am. But you don't have to go through this alone. You stood by me. Big time. Now it's my turn to stand by you. It's the right time to be at the right place to do the right thing."

"Thanks, Frank," I said, offering my hand, which he took and shook.

"Ain't nothin' to it but to do it, jarhead."

Continuing our tour of the grounds, I asked Frank about how Vivian had conducted herself when the three of them had gone to the shooting range. Frank said she mostly jumped and laughed nervously every time a round went off.

"I think you and me are getting to know each other pretty good," Frank said. "One thing I'm getting to know about you, August, is you don't ask questions just for polite conversation."

"Just a feeling," I said. "Can't really say more than that."

Frank nodded.

We walked back inside the warm house. Frank went to check on Vivian. I found Colleen in a small office connected to the library.

She sat behind an antique cherry desk, a pair of red-framed reading glasses perched on the tip of her nose. Her attention moved quickly between a stack of papers and her laptop. Instead of looking her usual Goddess of Rock self, she looked like an accountant eyeball-deep in the minutia of household and business financials.

Save for the attic and Vivian's studio, the office was the messiest part of the house crowded with stacks of cardboard filing boxes and antique wood filing cabinets. There were photos displayed on the wall and on the uncluttered areas of the large desk: Colleen and Vivian looking happy near the Eiffel Tower. Drinking colorful drinks on a beach beneath a palm tree. Looking spectacular in micro-bikinis.

There were photos of them each as little girls. A few photos of Vivian looking glum in a dark blue school uniform blazer bearing an embroidered emblem.

And there were photos of young Vivian with Rose Mayfield. Vivian was smiling. Laughing. Eating cotton candy or looking messy as they stirred cake batter. Mayfield reading *Goodnight Moon* to a five-year-old Vivian.

Colleen saw me standing in the doorway, smiled and took off her glasses.

"Well, good morning, sunshine," she said. "You look a lot better."

"Somehow I doubt that," I said. "Still feel rode hard and put away wet."

"Well, cowpoke, I'd call you a pussy but I don't like maligning the manna of the goddesses," she said, giving me a wry look.

"Thank God for the healing power of honey vodka," I said.

"My grandma Czewbak's recipe," she said. "And I don't dispute its healing powers. She used to give it to us when we were kids and had colds."

"Grandma's Nyquil," I said.

Colleen offered me a seat and asked me if I still thought the threat was real and I said I did, but I wouldn't make my encampment a permanent thing. I'd see how things played out for another day or two, then leave. But even if nothing happened and Frank and I left, I wanted her and Vivian to be hyper-alert. "So what you got going here?" I asked.

Colleen laughed. "Even true love has its price. Viv's the one with the money. I bring some in, but I'm the chief bottle washer on this yacht."

"Looks to me like you're co-captain," I said.

Like most artists, Vivian didn't have a head for or interest in business. Colleen served as her business manager. She paid the bills, maintained Vivian's website, filled orders for Vivian's artwork, talked to galleries, booked showings and answered inquiries. She also made travel arrangements. Vivian had been invited to show at two galleries the coming spring, one in Milan and the other in Brussels. And she had been contracted to do twenty illustrations for a university press book on women scientists starting with Hypatia, Greek mathematician and astronomer, and ending with Dr. Mae Jemison, astronaut.

"Try to get to Bruges," I said. "Nice town. There's a bar there called L'Estiminet. The owner—Jacques—has an extensive collection of blues and Motown he plays night and day. Tell Jacques I sent you. And watch out for his dog Tampa Red."

"Vicious?" Colleen said with a smile.

"No," I said, "but he's a master sandwich thief."

"There's more to you than meets the eye." Colleen sat back in her chair.

"One could only hope so." Looking at the photos of Vivian as a smiling child, I said, "Tell me a little bit about Viv and Rose Mayfield."

Colleen swiveled her chair to look behind her at the photos, then turned back at me. "You believe in second bites at the apple, August?"

"I believe in a lot of things," I said with a shrug. "Including second, third and fourth bites at the apple. Except for Adam and Eve, of course."

Colleen told me her mother had died when Colleen was in her early twenties. That her mother and her grandmother had been her best friends growing up. She knew she was different in a time when being different was a very lonely and potentially danger- ous thing. Especially in a northern Michigan farming community where life was often narrowly focused on the challenge of tilling fields, tending livestock and fending off predators, all in an effort to wrestle enough money from the earth to endure and survive long, hard Michigan winters.

"I tried to do that straight thing," Colleen said. "The lie I kept telling myself screamed at me every time I had sex with a boy. I figured I just needed to have more sex with more boys before the screaming stopped. It didn't."

On her eighteenth birthday she came out of the closet to her mother and grandmother. Their reaction shocked her: An over- whelming sense of relief, even joy, that Colleen was finally accepting herself. But they warned her that to stay in the town she'd grown up in would kill her.

Lean, quick and bare-knuckle competitive, Colleen found herself on a full-ride soccer scholarship at the University of Southern California. And though she never really considered herself academically inclined, her grades were good enough to get into USC's World Bachelor in Business Program.

It wasn't that she disliked Southern California. She just never really understood what all the fuss was about. Off campus, LA was loud, confusing and smelled like too much tanning lotion on a slowly baking fat man. Having grown up in Northern Michigan, she liked more green around her. More contemplative silence. The smell of a lake in the fall. More stars in the night sky. Whenever she talked about hunting and fishing in Michigan, her soccer teammates and classmates often looked at her as if she were an underprivileged alien from an underdeveloped planet. For her mother and grandmother, however, Colleen in California was Dorothy in Oz.

"Oh, honey, you look like a movie star!" her mother would call to tell her when she sent home a photo of herself. "Are you wearing the sunblock I mailed you? You don't want to get the skin cancer!"

Two months after arriving at the Hong Kong University of Science and Technology for the second stage of her bachelor program, she got word that her mother had died. Heart attack. Within days, Colleen's grandmother was admitted to nursing care, then hospice. Although Colleen rushed home from Hong Kong, two weeks later her grandmother was gone. Colleen felt alone and scared. The two people closest to her had been taken away in the blink of an eye.

"If you're gonna fall into a deep depression, Nin's is the best place to do it," Colleen said. "Little dive lesbian bar just outside of Traverse City. Strong drinks. Fairly good bar food. And women who can lie as well as any man when it comes to fishing and hunting stories. That's where I met Vivian. Made me give her the keys to my truck I was so wasted. Took me to her house. This house. I wake up in the bed you woke up in. Next thing you know we're dating." Colleen paused for a moment to look at a photo of herself and Vivian in a warm embrace. "Rosey—well. When I first met Rosey, I was missing my mother so much. Vivian, she'd never had a loving and caring mother. Rosey gave us what we both missed. If it weren't for Rosey, I think Vivian probably would have—you know—" Tears filled Colleen's eyes. She quickly wiped them away and looked back at the photo of Vivian mixing cake batter with Rose Mayfield. "Rosey's our second bite at the mom apple."

"Hear from Ms. Mayfield lately?" I said.

Colleen said Mayfield called nearly every weekend. She had visited the weekend that Vivian's mother had died and the three of them sat around the kitchen table and cried. Vivian and Colleen had cried less because of Vivian's mother's death and more at seeing how distraught Mayfield was.

There had been letters from Rose Mayfield.

I asked if I could read the letters and Colleen gave me a curious look.

"I miss my mom, too," I said, feeling instantly awful I'd used my mother's passing as an excuse to snoop. "I just want to feel what it's like to read a mother's words again."

Colleen nodded. Standing and walking to an overcrowded book case where such weighty tomes as *Principles of Accounting* and *Management Theory Vol. I* shouldered against *The Illustrated Shakespeare*, Colleen retrieved a small stack of Mayfield's letters from a shelf and handed them to me.

"Always letters," Colleen said, resuming her seat behind the desk. "You don't really appreciate a handwritten letter until you get one. Way more intimate than email or text. Like art."

I spent the next thirty minutes reading the letters. Colleen, having very little interest in watching me read, put her glasses back on the tip of her nose and went back to her business.

In the letters Mayfield's love for Vivian was crystal clear. Her words were those of a doting mother. A proud mother. A worried mother ("As a vegetarian, you're probably not getting enough protein. My friend Bhavna Vishnupathi from the Center for Creative Studies suggests a grain called amaranth for more protein. Please try it, dear. Be healthy so I don't worry as much (smile)!").

It was the last letter that proved to be the most interesting and, while Colleen's eyes scanned spreadsheets, I took the opportunity to pocket it. I handed the remaining letters back to Colleen and thanked her. There was something else I wanted to ask her about Vivian, but the time wasn't right. Sooner or later, though, I would have to ask.

"We'll have lunch in town," Colleen said. "I doubt there'll be any midday assassination attempts. I mean, unless the local Tea Party finds Michael Moore's house."

I walked out of the office, the letter in my pocket and a sizable knot in my stomach.

32

It was a slightly overcast afternoon. The trees' fall colors had become impossibly brighter and, with a cool and persistent breeze, large white caps formed on Lake Michigan.

The four of us made our way to downtown Traverse City. The narrow streets were crowded with fall vacationers and color-tour sightseers eager to spend their money on gooey fudge, cherry-flavored anything and sundry trinkets and trash that had TRAVERSE CITY emblazoned across them. Japanese tourists were always the most fun to watch. They seemed unabashed in their enjoyment of all things Traverse City, from cherry-shaped snow globes to X-rated dolls with cherries for testicles.

Traverse City had always been a beautiful place, but the last thirty or so years had proven to be a real boon for this Northern Michigan town: Emerald-green golf courses, luxury condos and boat clubs, pricey restaurants and upscale retail shops. Multimillion-dollar log cabins hugged the Lake Michigan shoreline. Any one of them would have left Abraham Lincoln speechless.

Traverse City in the fall was to Michigan what Cape Cod in the summer was to Massachusetts: Faux-quaint, crowded, and frantic. An indisputable fact of Traverse City was that increased tourism and the nouveaux riches had been good for the local police: More traffic tickets. More boating tickets. More bail money from drunk-and-disorderlies. More property taxes. Money that could be put to serious use ferreting out the numerous meth labs that continued to pop up in the surrounding backwoods like toadstools after a hard rain.

The four of us went to the Me & Us Cafe, a little Greek restaurant on Front Street near the water. It wasn't the type of eatery that a "foodie" would acknowledge in a masturbatory food blog. But the food was good, the atmosphere friendly and the big-screen TVs were broadcasting a roundtable postmortem on the Tigers' season.

Greek food and American baseball. What else could one hope for?

I was surprised Vivian and Colleen suggested the place since they were vegetarians and the aroma of slowly roasting lamb was inescapable. But they were convinced Frank and I were suffering from "meat withdrawal."

"And besides," Vivian said, "they have the best veggie stuffed peppers and Spanakopita around. Plus we can watch the Red Wings!"

My astonishment apparently showed.

Colleen shrugged. "Don't look at me. I'm a hockey fan only by association. My game's football. Go Lions."

Frank and I ate our fill of lamb gyros and fries. Colleen had a bowl of the lemon-rice soup and a small Greek salad with extra pepperoncini. Vivian surprised us all by making short work of her Spanakopita and stuffed veggie peppers. I guess watercolor painting takes it out of a person.

None of us had booze.

At about five the sun had lost its silver sheen and was starting to sink into the Lake Michigan horizon. We needed to get back to the house. First, though, we stopped at a hardware store. I bought a package of twelve light bulbs, lighter fluid, dish soap and utility rags.

"What's this for?" Vivian said.

I started to answer, but Colleen beat me to it.

"Sticky bombs," she said. "A poor man's grenade. Unscrew the bottom of the light bulb, pour in some dish soap and lighter fluid, screw the bottom back on. You could screw it into a socket; flipping a light switch would explode it. You can also wrap half the bulb in a rag strip that has some lighter fluid on it. Light the rag, throw it against something—the bulb shatters and boom."

"Why the dish soap?"

"So the fire sticks to whatever the bulb shatters against," Colleen said. She gave Vivian a quick kiss. "The product of a misspent youth, baby."

"They won't do much damage," I added. "But they're a helluva distraction."

"Mmmm. You're so dangerous," Vivian said, snuggling closer to Colleen.

"Kids, kids, kids," I said. "What say we focus on the job ahead, awright?"

Near their house, Colleen got a phone call: the night manager at the Ramada on I-31 east of 3 Mile Road North. Two men had just checked in carrying identical black duffle bags. When the manager asked them in her friendly front desk way what brought them to Traverse City, they both hesitated. Finally one of the men said, "Golf."

Colleen turned on the speaker of her phone and we listened.

"You know me," her front desk friend said. "I like talkin' to people. And Lord knows, golfers they loves talkin' 'bout golf! These guys? Not a smile between 'em. Might as well been headin' to a funeral. So I ask 'em, I says, 'Where you fellas golfin'? The Legend, the Bear, Coogan's Bluff?' One of 'em, he says, 'Last one.' You know as well as me, Colleen—there ain't no damned Coogan's Bluff! That's the name of an old Clint Eastwood movie! Plus, these fellas—well, they just give me the creepin' willies if'n ya know what I mean."

They paid for two nights.

Cash.

I would have said two's not bad until Colleen got a second call, this time from the Lakeside Motel on I-72 near I-31: Two men, same deal. It was pretty much the same story from the other hotel. Two nights, cash.

Brewster's men knew that Frank and I were there. I had to assume. Why else a four-man team to take out a watercolor artist and her companion? Then again, Brewster had gotten sloppy by killing Ray Danbury. It was an emotional action. And emotions were dangerous in the game he was running. This time it would be cold, calculated and clean: two women who disappeared in the night. Until, that is, Brewster handed me an ear, an eye, a finger— or worse.

Once inside the house, I stopped Vivian by the door, gave her a hard look and said in a low voice, "Are you ready for this?"

With a catch in her throat, Vivian uttered a barely audible, "Yes."

Frank and I moved our cars into some low bushes at the southwest corner of the property. I unlocked the shed door and made sure the keys were in the ignition of Colleen's old Ford pickup and the attached snow plow's bottom edge was leveled waist high. Then we all sat at the kitchen table making sticky bombs. Colleen and I made the first four, demonstrating the art and science. We lost three bulbs—the metal contact ends were too tightly secured to the glass and the effort of unscrewing them shattered the bulbs. But the hard truth was if we needed more than nine stickies, then we weren't coming out of this. At least not with all our pieces and parts.

Considering the fact that pitch black October nights dropped early and hard up here, I figured the four-man crew was well equipped with night vision goggles. Normally they wouldn't need them; in Traverse City the wealthy year-round residents made sure you could admire their fabulous properties day and night thanks to extensive landscape lighting. At night, the houses shone like coveted jewels. Vivian and Colleen's property was no different.

On my street in Mexicantown we were lucky to get eight streetlamps courtesy of a charity.

We turned off the external lighting but kept the juice flowing to the razor wire on the sunroom side of the house.

Darkness would be our ally.

Of course the key to any good plan is having other plans that have absolutely no association with the original plan.

Colleen made three calls: the sheriff's department, the Staties and the local police. She told them several suspicious men had come into town. She gave them the motel locations where the men had registered. And she said she believed she and Vivian might be the targets of a robbery or worse. All three said they'd send men over as soon as possible, but every local cop seemed to be "busy." Another meth lab bust. Nothing like Michigan wilderness for cooking meth.

"Just keep the lights on and doors locked," the local police chief had suggested.

Exactly the opposite of our plan.

I made one last call to O'Donnell.

"You got a helicopter?" I said.

"Why?"

"Because in about an hour a ton of shit's gonna hit a very small fan up here," I said. "Your consultant guy's got a team coming for Vivian Paget and her partner. If you're lucky, you can get at least one Black Tree guy alive. Otherwise, we'll be obligated to kill 'em all."

O'Donnell cursed at me. It had taken every bit of good will and political capital she had to get the DPD to pull its APB on me. And now this. Against her better judgment she also had pulled several warrants for the bank. They would be going in hot and heavy in a day or two.

"Earlier than I want," O'Donnell said. "But you've kinda pushed the needle into the red zone."

"You don't go in the next forty-eight to seventy-two hours, you won't have anything—including your job," I said.

"Remember our deal, August," she said.

"Signed in blood," I said. "I'm going to hell for this."

"We're all going to hell on this one, August," she said before disconnecting.

By eight o'clock it was, as my Grandpa Snow used to say, "blacker than a coalminer's ass." The only light in the house came from the pale grey disc of moon off Lake Michigan.

"You ever seen any of them Halloween movies?" Frank whispered to me.

"Can't say I have," I said.

"Yeah, well, *I* have," Frank said. "This place looks all Halloween creepy in this light. It's kinda cool."

"Don't freeze your ass off out there, Army," I said.

He saluted, then, carrying the Remington Versa Max rifle, two handguns and his Rangers utility knife, exited the front door. He ran flat out for eighty yards until he disappeared into the undulating shadows of the woods.

The wind was up from the north, pushing down from Canada and carrying with it signs of a bone-chilling winter. Frank was right: in this light, the house was definitely creepy. The wind battering against the shutters didn't help. And the fact that men were coming to kill us definitely darkened the mood.

Frank's voice came in over the walkie-talkie. He was in position. Next was Colleen. I wished them luck and told them to stay sharp.

I made one last check on Vivian, upstairs in a locked bedroom. There was reasonable cover in the bedroom and only one window—a decorative round leaded glass window that would take an average man at least four seconds to squeeze through. Time enough to kill him and let his body plug the hole. I'd given her my Glock. I went over how to shoot the gun and what to do if the door to the room was breached. If the intruders made it to that room, then she was as good as dead, but I didn't tell her that.

"Five minutes, tops," I said to her, "and this will be all over."

I started to leave the room to take my position when she said, "August?"

I turned back to her. "Yeah?"

"Thank you."

"Don't thank me yet," I said. "You remember the safe word, right?"

"Wet burrito."

"That's my girl."

I closed the door behind me and listened for the click of the lock. I tried the door several times. It was secure.

For twenty minutes it was as quiet as a nun's prayer. Aside from the wind buffeting against the house, the only sound was my breathing as I lay in the downstairs hallway facing the foyer and front door, stock of the Browning Citori 12-gauge snug against my shoulder, a walkie-talkie and my Smith & Wesson .32 on the floor next to me.

My phone vibrated.

I quickly extracted my phone from a pocket. The number was UNKNOWN.

"Hello?" I whispered.

"Mr. Snow?"

Brewster.

"Yeah," I said. "I'm kinda in the middle of something."

"There's still time to accept my offer," he said. "But I would suspect very little time. Say, perhaps thirty seconds."

"Listen," I said. "Why don't you call me back in about ten minutes. If I answer, you've lost. If I don't, you've won."

I hung up and shoved the phone back in my pocket.

"Moving, moving, moving," Frank's hushed voice said over the walkie-talkie. "Seven, August, seven! Two, front entrance. Three wide, north. Two, south side."

Four men I was ready for. Four was a battle.

Seven was goddamn a war.

"Flush 'em out, Army."

We'd been betting on a front breach of the house. Frank's job was to come out of the forest shooting. The idea was to drive whatever he missed to the left toward the electrified barbed wire concealed in the bushes beneath the sunroom windows or right to Colleen's shotgun. Any trouble coming through the front door got the barrel of my Browning.

Outside, a rifle exploded.

A second after the rifle fire, the front door of the house blasted off its hinges. A man in head-to-toe black tactical gear rushed into the house, his Street Sweeper automatic with suppressor leveled and ready.

I unloaded my Browning at him, center mass. He went back hard against the splintered door jam, but not before his weapon churned out enough rounds to chew up the hallway wall left of me.

Body armor. Otherwise the rifle I had would have shredded a man into hamburger at close quarters. But the blast had only knocked him off balance. He was hurt. But hurt wasn't good enough.

He struggled to bring his Street Sweeper up at me.

A blast from my rifle and his head blossomed crimson.

"Splash one," I heard Frank's voice say over the walkie-talkie.

"Splash two," I replied, moving quickly to the sunroom.

The party had begun.

33

Shock and awe.

The rifles I'd borrowed from Tomás had done their jobs, temporarily throwing off the intruders with big booms and splatter damage. But for hard men like this, shock-and-awe was a very temporary thing. It just compressed their timeframe and gave their mission imperative more deadly immediacy.

We were in close quarters now and a rifle was no good.

Glass shattering.

I brought up my Smith & Wesson .38 and ran into the sunroom. The third man had been careful not to get hung up in the razor wire concealed in the low shrubbery. By the time I entered the sunroom, he had clambered in. Seeing me, he leveled his gun. He was quick enough to pop off a round that found the flesh of my upper right shoulder.

I fired two shots in quick succession and dropped him.

"Splash three," I said into the walkie-talkie. Outside, the engine of the Ford pickup revved and the house trembled.

"Splash four."

Colleen's voice. She had been in the shed to the back southern end of the house. Her mission had been to jam her foot down on the accelerator of the truck and drive the snow plow hot and heavy into any intruders making entry on that side of the house.

A scream.

It wasn't Colleen or Vivian.

I ran to the office on the opposite side of the house and saw one of the men thrashing about, engulfed in flame. Frank had lit him up with two sticky bombs. I leveled my S&W.

"He's mine!"

I turned.

Colleen.

I nodded to her and ran upstairs. Behind me I heard Colleen shout at the man on fire, "This is *my* house, motherfucker!" Then three loud pops.

Upstairs, automatic rifle fire chewed against wood.

I mounted the steps two at a time.

I wasn't quick enough. The man put a black boot to what remained of the door that led to Vivian. He disappeared quickly into the room. Two, three, four loud pops. Automatic rifle fire. Another single pop.

The man backed out of the room, his rifle at his side. He slumped against the hallway wall, then slid to the floor in a sitting position.

Dead.

Vivian came out, my Glock leveled rock-steady in her right hand. She held it over the dead man.

"Wet burrito!" I yelled.

She didn't hear me. Or chose not to hear me. Instead she knelt by the dead man, whispered into his ear, then fired one more shot into the man's left temple, his body quivering as it took the shot and toppling over on the floor.

"Goddammit—wet burrito!" I yelled again.

Colleen edged past me at the top of the staircase.

"Viv?" she called out. "Baby?"

Vivian stood from the side of the dead man and looked at Colleen. Her eyes were not her own. They were the eyes of a killer. Vacant. Cold. It was the look of someone suddenly absent from their own life, untethered and floating between a moment in an unspeakable past and its present echo.

Vivian leveled the gun at Colleen. Rock steady, finger curled around the trigger. I brought my gun up and put Vivian Paget's chest in my site.

"It's me, baby," Colleen said, walking slowly toward Vivian. "It's Colleen."

"You cool?" I said.

"I'm cool," she quickly replied. "*We're* cool—right, Viv?"

"Colleen?" Vivian finally said.

The gun in Vivian's hand began to quiver. She blinked slowly. Soon the weight of it brought her arm down quickly to her side.

"It's all right, baby," Colleen said, cautiously moving forward. "Everything's all right."

Vivian let the gun slip out of her hand. It landed with a thud to the hallway floor. The two women embraced tightly, Vivian weeping on Colleen's shoulder.

"What's happening?" Vivian asked as she sobbed into Colleen's shoulder. "What's going on?"

I lowered my gun and began breathing again. "So much for goddamn safe words," I muttered to myself. I called out to Colleen, "One more. Get her in another room. Now."

Colleen looked back at me and nodded.

I ran downstairs just in time to see the last man. He was standing in the foyer and had a forearm tightly clamped around Frank's neck, his black Glock pressed hard against Frank's temple.

The man saw me and calmly said, "We get to my car and I leave."

"Sorry, August," Frank managed to say through the man's tight grip. "Now stop fuckin' around and put a bullet in this asshole's eye, Marine."

"Hoo-raa," I said before firing a single round from my S&W. The bullet found the man's left eye, spinning him backwards, away from Frank. He fell hard to the floor, dead.

Frank rubbed his neck, then gave the dead man a kick in the ribs. "We get 'em all?" Frank said.

I nodded. "We got 'em all."

Frank and I put out the fire that was consuming the body of the fifth man. Then we checked each of them for identification, knowing we wouldn't find any. The man Colleen had driven the truck into was mounted on the truck's snow plow, pinned against the side of the house, nearly cut in half. Nothing on him either.

Frank and I found two rental cars parked beneath an old oak near the end of Vivian and Colleen's tree-lined road.

"Jesus," Frank said.

Inside the first car's trunk were eight gallons of hydrochloric acid in plastic containers. Apparently the men had gone in heavy, the objective being to quickly kill them, dissolve them down to sludge then let what had been their bodies flow away in the sluice of the sewer system. Taking souvenirs, of course. Proof of a job well done.

Collected around the kitchen table, I told Vivian and Colleen that Frank and I had to bug out fast. I was reasonably sure the immediate threat to them was over. They would have to explain to the local and state cops what had gone down at the house. Save for the fact that Frank and I had been there.

"You're bleeding," Vivian said to me, a vacuous look in her eyes. "There's so much—blood."

"They're not gonna believe we took these guys out all by our lonesome," Colleen said.

I nodded. "I know, but you'll need to buy time until the FBI gets here. Ask for Special Agent Megan O'Donnell out of the Detroit field office. Tell her everything." Then I drew in a deep breath, slowly exhaled and said to Colleen, "I need to talk to you. In private."

In the hallway outside of the kitchen, I told Colleen what I suspected.

She didn't flinch.

Instead Colleen led me to the attic and turned the lights on. Past the boxes covered in dust and cobwebs, past the furniture huddled in a forgotten corner were paintings covered with sheets and leaning against attic beams. Tentatively, Colleen lifted the sheets.

The first was the most revealing; a watercolor portrait of Vivian's father, his lifeless eyes staring out, blood trailing down from a large bullet hole above his left eye near the temple. His mouth was agape and his canine teeth elongated like those of a vampire.

There were others, always with her father lying naked and dead in the riverfront condo bed in which he was found. And there was one of the young girl who had been found with him, lying in quiet angelic repose, her chest soaked in blood.

"They're maybe five years old," Colleen said, her voice choked and halting. "I—thought they were—just dark fantasies."

"It's the way we found them, her father and the girl." Then I asked, "Any of her mother like that?"

Colleen searched my eyes for a few seconds before shaking her head. "No. I—I don't think so." After a moment's hesitation, she said, "What should I—"

"Burn 'em," I said. "Burn 'em all."

Anger seared across my chest.

Anger at myself for not having put everything together nine years ago. Anger for having gotten caught up in the momentary adulation of peers and superiors—my father—for having closed out my first high-profile case quickly and neatly.

Vivian, then eighteen, had murdered her father. As the lead detective, I watched hours of black-and-white surveillance video from the lobby of the riverfront condo high-rise. I'd cross-referenced everyone who entered and exited with residents and visitors. Everyone save for the elegant woman—long legs, black dress, long black hair, briefcase. The one who charmed the elderly black concierge into using his keycard for the elevator. The woman who had exited the condo thirty minutes later.

"You knew," Colleen said, her voice a trembling whisper.

"I had a feeling," I said, staring at the paintings. "I was the lead investigator. Took my suspicions to my captain. Ray Danbury. He told me I was being reassigned from her father's murder to lead investigator following the money Vivian's father had embezzled. A reassignment that had the stink of politics on it. But I sucked it up. Pretty soon I had media lights in my face and stars in my eyes. I—liked it. Liked the recognition. Danbury told me the woman in the black dress was just a resident who'd mislaid her access card. And you know what? I didn't care about that any more 'cause I gave my dad what I thought would make him proud: his son's face in the newspaper and on TV as the cop who recovered millions of stolen dollars. I'd made my bones." After laying bare the ignominious truth, I looked at Colleen and said, "I'm guessing her father was a sick, miserable bastard. I'd guess Vivian was abused as a young girl."

"God," Colleen said.

"The bullet for Viv's father was deserved," I said. I thought about the sixteen-year-old girl who died at Vivian's father's side. "The bullet for the girl—maybe Vivian shot her to kill what she saw in herself. Two bullets for stolen innocence." I held Colleen's eyes steadily in mine. "Listen, this doesn't change anything between you and Viv—if you don't want it to. But you've got to get her help. Serious help."

Colleen, her eyes watery, nodded.

Sirens were approaching in the distance. We rushed back downstairs.

"Helluva time to take a tour of the house," Frank said with some irritation.

"Helluva house," I said. I turned to Colleen. "How much time?"

"Five minutes," she said. "Six, tops."

Colleen quickly patched up my shoulder. A couple splashes of hydrogen peroxide and a fast gauze wrap. No bullet to dig out, no broken bone. Frank and I threw our gear in our separate cars and said hasty goodbyes.

Frank called me ten minutes after we hit the road, racing south through the cold darkness.

"What was that all about back there?" Frank said, his voice coming through the car's speakers. When I was done explaining what I could, he said, "Holy shit. His own goddamn daughter?"

"There are devils that walk amongst us," I said.

"No shit," Frank said. "So what's that make us?"

"The sword in God's left hand," I said.

34

Around Saginaw midway between Traverse City and Detroit, I pulled off of I-75 South and found a Dunkin' Donuts, its sign lit up like a beacon of high-caloric salvation. Frank followed. The goofy-looking, freckle-faced kid behind the counter saw two big guys, sweaty, slightly bloody and mostly wearing tactical black standing at his register.

"Whoa," he said inadvertently.

"Xbox," Frank said. "Call of Duty."

"Sweet," the kid said.

Frank and I carried a dozen mixed donuts and two large coffees to a table by the window. Killing people had never been easy for me, even when I was a marine and on the job. But two things made the killing easier: Knowing that I'd killed bad people intent on doing harm to others. And knowing there would be donuts afterwards.

"How's the shoulder?" Frank finally said.

I told him it hurt, but the bleeding had stopped.

Halfway through the donuts, Frank said, "You think she'll be all right? Vivian?"

"I think she's had years to compress rape, emotional neglect and psychological abuse into a small, dark corner of her mind," I said. "If Colleen's smart—and I'm pretty sure she is—she'll get Vivian some help."

"And you?"

"I'm good," I said, taking a sizable bite out of an apple fritter.

Frank nodded, slurped at his coffee and resumed looking out the window at the red taillights and white headlights of cars blacked out by the night. Ten minutes later, we got coffee refills from the goofy-looking kid at the cash register.

"I'm NutSack357," the kid said with a disturbingly big, toothy grin. "Maybe we can team up sometime for a little online Call of Duty action."

Frank and I hit the road.

About forty-five minutes from Mexicantown, I got a call.

"I got two women up here—one of them fairly coherent—calling you a hero," O'Donnell said. "You and some generic white guy." She had taken a chopper to Traverse City with two other FBI agents, cutting a four-hour drive by car to a fast forty minutes.

"I am heroic by nature," I replied.

"I've also got seven bodies, some very confused local cops and some very pissed off Staties," O'Donnell said. I asked her if she'd gone over the cars Brewster's team had driven to Vivian Paget's estate. She had. "I'm glad you put these guys down, August, but the mess? Jesus. What do I look like? Your personal janitorial service?"

"What about the IDs I pinched from Dax Randolph and the other guy?"

"Let's get one thing straight, August," O'Donnell said. "I do not now, nor have I ever—nor *will* I ever—work for you. So show a little goddamn gratitude to me for letting you walk around free for the next forty-eight to seventy-two hours."

"Just tie this off, O'Donnell," I said.

She asked me about the "generic white guy." I glanced in my rearview mirror at the car Frank was driving. "He's a good guy with the power of righteousness on his side. And that's all you get."

O'Donnell started to say something, but I disconnected.

I slipped a CD into the car's player and turned the volume up. Herbie Hancock's "Cantaloupe Island."

At around two in the morning, we were in Mexicantown. I called Frank and told him we needed to go in my house fast, locked and loaded. Just in case.

"Is your life always this exciting?" Frank laughed.

"Most of the time it's SportsCenter, nachos and beer. Sometimes I buy a lottery ticket."

We went in hard and swept the house from top to bottom. No evildoers. No undead looking for fresh brains. I told Frank he could rack in the spare upstairs bedroom for the night and he didn't argue. We were both exhausted and the smell of spent gunpowder and hot brass shells was still in our noses.

"Nice place," Frank said, looking around my living room. "Not much in it, but nice."

"Glad you approve," I said. "I grew up here."

"You were a kid once?" Frank said. "Hard to believe."

I got Frank some sheets, a new comforter, a pillow and a couple of towels. Then, after taping a plastic bag over my shoulder wound, I took a long, hot shower. After the shower I disinfected my wound, redressed it and put on a pair of well-worn Wayne State Warriors sweats.

Both of us were tapped, but there were still vestiges of caffeine and adrenaline coursing through us. I fired up the TV. "How come you don't got an Xbox?" Frank asked.

"'Cause I'm not twelve."

Frank pulled a face.

My doorbell rang and instantly Frank and I took defensive positions.

I moved to the door and peeked out.

Jimmy Radmon.

"Jesus, Jimmy," I said, opening the door and quickly ushering him in. "What the hell are you doing?"

"I thought you might want somebody to keep an eye on the place. Saw the lights on and figured I'd check it out," Radmon said. He spotted Frank and looked back at me. "He with the cable company, too?"

I introduced the two, then told Jimmy he could go home—wherever that was.

"I'm up the street at Carmela and Sylvia's," Radmon said, his eyes darting between me and Frank. "Case you need anything."

"You're staying at Carmela and Sylvia's?"

"Yeah," Radmon said. "They got carry-out from El Zocalo's and we just, you know, talked and shit. And don't let them old girls fool you, man. They cheat at poker."

Jimmy left and Frank and I flopped on my new sofa. We found a movie on Netflix—*Prometheus*—and watched it while doing a few shots of honey vodka. Colleen had given Frank two liters of their home-distilled liquor. Even warm it was comforting and transcendent.

"I don't get it," Frank said as the movie's end titles rolled at four in the morning.

"It's a brilliant but flawed study of faith and how far a person will go to discover the weight and validity of their belief," I said.

"Yeah, okay," Frank said. "I still don't fuckin' get it."

At about four-thirty, we both knocked off. Before going to bed, I loaded a fresh clip in my gun, racked one in the chamber and made sure the safety was off. I'm pretty sure Frank did the same.

Just in case.

After a light but fulfilling sleep, Frank and I were up at around nine-thirty. I fixed *huevos rancheros*, chorizo sausages, several toasted bagels and a pot of Gevalia Columbian Roast coffee made in my mom's old percolator. Frank buried his face in two plates of the eggs, devouring six sausages and two Asiago cheese bagels. I would have been amused by the sight had I not done the same.

I got a call fifteen minutes after we'd finished breakfast.

"My God," Rose Mayfield said, sounding genuinely upset. "Are you all right?"

"I'm fine, Ms. Mayfield," I said.

Mayfield had received a late-night call from Vivian telling her everything that had happened. Colleen got on the call and, in a less frantic and more coherent way, gave Mayfield the highlights. That the local police, state police and FBI were there. That they were all right. And that Mayfield shouldn't worry about them if she heard or saw anything on the news.

"Thank God for you, Mr. Snow," Mayfield said. "I—it's unbelievable. Everything. It's all just—"

"Everything?" I said.

She drew in a quick breath and said, "Kip Atchison's disappeared. And Aaron Spiegelman's wife is—she's gone."

I really could not have cared less about Atchison. If he was gone, he was gone. Another floater in the Detroit River or sipping piña coladas and banging brown girls in a country without an extradition agreement with the US. Didn't matter. But for whatever reason, the news of Spiegelman's wife dying was a punch in the gut. The brief relationship I had with Spiegelman was, at best, rough. But at his core I knew he was mostly an honorable, hardworking guy who loved his wife. His only flaw was loyalty to and love for Eleanor Paget.

"We need to talk, Ms. Mayfield," I said.

"Of course," she said. "When would you like to come into—"

"Not your office," I said. "I'm *persona non grata* there."

"Then my house," she said. "I usually take lunch at my house on Tuesdays. How does this coming Tuesday sound? Two o'clock."

"Tuesday at two," I said.

Mayfield gave me her address in northwest Detroit. She thanked me again for helping Vivian and Colleen—"Awful—just awful"—then we hung up.

Frank grabbed the last bagel from the plate on the kitchen's island and leaned against my refrigerator. "Why do I have the feeling this Traverse City thing ain't over?"

"Just stay locked and loaded," I said. "If you want."

Frank analyzed his bagel. "Got nothin' better to do. Besides. The chow on this job has been really outstanding." He destroyed the rest of the bagel, licking the crumbs from his fingers. "Plus you shot a guy for me."

"There is that," I said.

I was always a pretty good judge of character. And Frank's character had quickly revealed itself as impeccable. The last thing I needed fueling my Catholic-guilt was walking a good man into a bad situation because I gave him limited or bad intel. I'd seen enough of that FUBAR shit in Afghanistan. We talked for another fifteen minutes about what the endgame might look like.

I told Frank everything I knew about the major players and one ghost operative—the Cleaner. A hired gun whose sole purpose was to kill any member of the organization that jeopardized the full anonymity of the bank take-over operation. A guy like Brewster.

"Any chance of this Cleaner dude making a run at us?" Frank said.

"Possible," I said. "But I have the feeling his job is very narrowly defined. In and out, quick and clean. Cull an already lean herd. At least that's my theory."

"Kinda like Human Resources," Frank said.

"Couldn't have put it any better myself, Frank."

I excused myself and made a call to Tomás. I let him know that his prayers had worked. Or at least Elena's had.

"So that's it?" Tomás said. "These are the guys who killed Eleanor Paget?"

"No," I said.

"Isn't that how this whole thing started?" Tomás said.

"It's how it started," I said. "It's not how it's going to end."

He asked if I still needed the guns and I said I did because of what could be one last, decisive run at me. This time I could use another gun hand if he was willing. He was. Over the phone I introduced him to Frank.

"Hey—don't I know you?" Frank said. "Eleanor Paget's house? Mr. Gutierrez?"

I heard Tomás's laugh boom through the phone's speaker.

They knew each other, but by voice only. Frank never got up to Paget's house. And by the time Tomás left her house to go home, there'd been a shift change. I got back on the line.

"Sounds like a good, solid man," Tomás said. "Young. But solid. White boy?"

"White boy."

"Damn." Tomás laughed. "Solid *and* white. You don't find that very often. Good with a gun?"

"He is."

"Better than me?"

"Tomás," I said. "Nobody's better than you, mi amigo."

"*Mentiroso*," he said. *Liar.*

We hung up.

I was not looking forward to my next call. But it would get me finally, completely off the FBI hook and clear me with the DPD. At least concerning this situation.

I dug the red burner phone that Skittles had given me out of my bedroom closet and started to dial, interrupted by a knock on my front door. I went downstairs drawing my weapon. Frank's was already drawn.

"Yes?" I said brightly, ten feet from the front door.

"Señor Snow?"

It was the kid from across the street, Manolito Rodriguez.

I signaled for Frank to stash his gun, then I opened the door: the Rodriguez boy stood at the door holding a foil-wrapped plate. He grinned widely up at me and said, "My mother, she made these for you. Her and Señora Elena. I didn't drop any."

I lifted a corner of the foil: homemade cinnamon and sugar churros.

I gave an exaggerated scowl at the plate. "Looks like one's missing."

The Rodriguez boy's wide grin disappeared. I took the plate from the boy, slid one of the churros out and handed it to him.

"There," I said. "*That* looks like the one that's missing."

"Gracias, señor—I mean—*Mr.* Snow," the boy said before bounding down my steps and running happily across the street to his house.

After I closed the door Frank said, "Man, this is a great little neighborhood you got here."

For a second I couldn't help but wonder where the hell Frank lived. Then I looked at the street through my living room window. The few houses where my neighbors lived. The houses where people had once lived and, though now empty, stood strong and resolute. Waiting for families to bring breath back to them. I thought about my house. My childhood home and how it was beginning to feel like home again.

"Welcome to Mexicantown, Frank."

35

Most bad guys don't take weekends off for family, church or chores around the house.

However between the Friday night Frank and I returned from Traverse City and Sunday evening, I'm sure Brewster discovered through various news reports that seven of his men had failed in achieving their objective and were subsequently shot to pieces. Such news might force any self-respecting bad guy like Brewster to take a weekend breather to consider his next play.

Hence, the relative quiet before Monday's shit storm.

Frank, Tomás and I were seated in the single booth at Café Consuela's, huddled over a bowl of warm corn chips and green salsa. In an hour or so the lunch crowd would be pressed against the door awaiting a coveted table or the prized single booth.

An hour earlier I'd received a call from Brewster. The usual lofty arrogance was gone. More of his true accent came through in his voice. Austrian or German. Maybe Swiss. There was a noticeable undertone to his anger. Something vibrating below the threatening words.

"I am done being magnanimous, Snow," he'd said. "This gets done tonight. Midnight. A place called Rocking Horse. I guarantee you will take the offer I present."

My stomach tightened.

Dani, one of the café's co-owners, brought us each a mug of hot black coffee, then sat a plate of tortillas and a large bowl of sliced fruit drizzled with yogurt between us.

"Does he always eat like this?" Tomás said, watching Frank demolish two tortillas in less than a minute.

"Hey," Frank said between chomps, "I grew up near Eureka, Montana—small town a stone's throw from the Canadian border. There weren't any Mexicans or Mexican food there. So excuse me if I love this shit!"

Tomás and I shared dumbfounded looks. Tomás said, "I thought we were *every*where?"

"At least that was the plan," I said.

I'd given Tomás a detailed download on what this whole thing was turning out to be. I didn't want to spring any surprises on a person who was proving to be one of my last living friends. He had no obligation to help me out, especially in light of the breach of his home and the real threat to his family's safety. At the end of my full disclosure, Tomás's only question was, "You buyin' lunch?"

I said I was.

"Cool," Tomás said. Then he furrowed his eyebrows and narrowed his eyes at me. "You know you could just call your FBI girlfriend. Let her handle the heavy lifting tonight. Or maybe your shoulder's not the only thing that was wounded, Octavio."

I didn't say anything but met Tomás's hard look with my own.

"What's he talking about?" Frank said.

"Pride," I finally said, my eyes still locked with Tomás's. "He's saying I'm risking my life—maybe yours—because of a bruised ego."

"Ego," Tomás said. "Pride. The distinction is small but real, *cabron*. Either one can get you killed. So. Give me an honest answer right here, right now, or I walk and pray for the blessings of Christ on you."

I drew in a deep breath, and then said, "My dad used to say, 'The only ground a man truly owns is the two square feet he's standing on at any given moment. And God help him if he gets pushed off of that.' I've been pushed off my two square feet too many times. By this city. And now this. And I want it back. Every fucking inch."

"Okay." Tomás smiled.

"Neither one of you owes me anything," I said. "This is all on me."

"Name the time and the place," Tomás said.

"Twenty-four-hundred hours. A place called Rocking Horse, 221 South Industrial Road—"

"Jesus," Tomás said. "Southeast Mexicantown? Even *I* wouldn't feel safe going there in broad daylight, never *mind* midnight. It's a no-man's-land down there."

"Fifty-yard perimeter. Just in case the studio's a kill box."

"You don't look the type that scares easy," Frank said to Tomás.

"I'm not," Tomás said. "But the biggest part of not being scared is not being a fool, gringo."

"Did you just call me 'gringo'?" Frank said.

"Yeah," Tomás said, his muscles coiling and ready to snap. "So?"

Frank exploded with laughter and slapped the table with both palms. "Jesus! I *love* this part of town!"

"Frank?" I said. "In or out?"

He grabbed a tortilla, looked at me and said, "In, dude. For sure."

"I'm asking you guys to risk your lives for a fight that's mine. Big ask."

"It's only a risk if I die," Frank said, staring at the tortilla like it was manna from heaven. "If I live through this then there wasn't no risk, right?"

If Brewster had sent seven men to handle two women in Traverse City, then tonight would be his version of the Invasion of Normandy, Tet Offensive or Korengal Valley. I had caused his banking enterprise irreparable damage—and that meant his life was on the line. A life, I imagine, that had until now consisted of expensive suits, champagne, beautiful whores and the aphrodisiac of power fueled by other people's money.

We ate a light lunch—at least light for Tomás and me—and agreed on the perimeters of our counterinsurgency at Rocking Horse.

I had some other things to do before the witching hour. Tomás said he would take Frank back to his house and introduce him to Generalísimo Emiliano Zapata Salazar.

I paid for lunch and left Café Consuela's.

Today was Ray Danbury's funeral.

He would be buried with full honors: color guard, twenty-one gun salute, bagpiper playing "Amazing Grace." The mayor would attend, as would the police chief and commissioner. The choir from his church would be there along with several hundred of the church's parishioners.

And there would be his family.

His wife of twenty-five years. His daughter, a sophomore at University of Michigan studying criminal justice. And his son, a freshman at Michigan State University, studying girls. Portions of the funeral would be videotaped from afar and broadcast on the evening news. Ray's face was already on the front pages of the newspapers beneath the bold black headlines FALLEN HERO OF THE THIN BLUE LINE and A LIFE OF SERVICE.

I would not be there.

I would be preparing for war against the man who had killed Danbury.

But first, a side trip.

As I drove north on the Lodge Interchange toward Detroit's northwest side, my wounded shoulder began throbbing more than it had been. I didn't have time to think about the pain so I didn't. Thank you, United States Marine Corps.

I made a call on Skittles's red burner phone. I had been putting off the call, and now there were no more delays.

No answer.

I disconnected.

By the time I was near Detroit's Boston Edison neighborhood, it was nearly two o'clock.

Longfellow Street is one of the major residential arteries in the thirty-six block historic Boston Edison neighborhood. Tall pines and old-growth oaks had over the decades formed dreamlike canopies over many of its streets. Boston Edison was a neighborhood of immaculately preserved and meticulously landscaped Tudor Revival, Mediterranean Villa, Italian Renaissance and English Manor style homes detailed with leaded glass windows, cherry wood libraries and carriage houses that now served as garages. This is where those who brought wheels to the masses and soul to music once lived.

If you moved any one of these homes a quarter of an inch outside of Detroit's northwest Eight Mile Road boundary they would sell for four times their currently assessed value.

Instead they were architectural masterworks surrounded on all sides by the encroaching poverty and decay of a bankrupt city.

I parked in the driveway of a three-story Tudor on Longfellow Street behind a black BMW. The trunk of the BMW was open. I rang the doorbell and waited.

The door creaked open.

"Mr. Snow!" a very surprised Rose Mayfield said. "I—I thought our meeting was tomorrow."

"I was in the neighborhood. Just thought I'd take a chance on you being home."

"I—this is inconvenient," she said, bracing her body against the door. "I have to get back to work. I'm just home for a quick bite."

"I don't think there's any rush to get back to the bank," I said. "The FBI just raided Titan Securities Investments Group with thirty agents and twenty-six warrants. Frankly, I don't think you wanna be anywhere near your office right now." I leaned into the door. "But you do want to talk to me, whether you know it or not."

Reluctantly, Rose Mayfield opened the door and let me in.

The foyer was large and decorated with colorful, hand-painted Spanish tiles original to the home. Behind Mayfield was a winding staircase with a handcrafted wrought iron handrail that led to a landing where a round leaded glass window softly diffused the afternoon light. On the landing were two suitcases. I nodded to them. "Going somewhere?"

"My sister's," Mayfield said hesitantly. "In Cleveland. She's not well and—"

"I thought you were going back to work."

Mayfield looked confused for a moment, then said, "After work. I was leaving directly after work."

"Can we sit?" I said. "I promise not to be long."

After a tense few seconds, Mayfield nodded and gestured to a room off to the left. A large, dark library occupied by hundreds of thick, serious-looking books and a large, ornately carved desk. In front of the desk were two low-back leather chairs. There were framed photos and news clippings on the walls.

"My husband's office," Mayfield said. "I don't really use it much."

"How long has he been gone?" I said.

Mayfield nodded. "Eight years. Would you like some coffee? Tea?"

"No. Thank you. I won't be staying long."

We sat in the chairs facing her late husband's desk.

"What did your husband do?" I said, looking around at the photos. Her husband smiling and shaking hands with several ex-mayors, including the late Coleman Young and Dennis Archer. And there were awards and citations from the NAACP, the National Black Lawyers Top 100, American Civil Liberties Union, United Auto Workers Union and Detroit City Council.

"Criminal law for fifteen years," she said. "Then civil rights litigation. Thirty years of fighting meaningless little skirmishes in a war that will never be won."

"Doesn't sound like you're very proud of his accomplishments."

She gave a short, bitter laugh. "What accomplishments? Dez was an idealist in a world without vision or courage. Did I love him? Yes. Of course. But look around, Mr. Snow. Here we are in the much-lauded 21st century. Fighting the same battles of the 19th and 20th century over and over again. Nobody cares about anything except what color their next iPhone will be."

"Without men like your husband," I said, "I wouldn't be able to eat at the same lunch counter as a white man. Or I'd be picking lettuce fifteen hours a day for twelve cents an hour."

"Eating at a damn lunch counter or sitting at the front of a bus are the little tokens that would have you believe progress has been made," she said. "The lines are still drawn in black and white. Even for the president of the United States. They're just drawn in mostly invisible ink. *Especially* in Michigan. In Detroit. This place—these people—corrupt black politicians and bigoted white business people—it's Louisiana 1965, only with better lakes and more Starbucks."

I held her in my gaze for a moment before she said, "Why are you here, Mr. Snow?"

"What happened to Kip Atchison?"

"I—why are you asking me?" she said, sounding both confused and exasperated. "I have no idea where he is! Check the local whorehouses!"

"Okay, let's try this," I said. "When did you know about Vivian Paget and her father?"

She stared at me hatefully for a few seconds before her eyes filled with tears. She blinked and the tears ran down her cheeks, pooling at the corners of her mouth.

"It wasn't hard to see something—awful—was going on," Mayfield finally said. It took her awhile to compose herself. "How can anybody—*anybody!*—do that to a child? A *child* for God's sakes!" Mayfield took a breath. "I told Eleanor what I suspected and you know what she did? She slapped me! Told me to mind my own damned business!"

"And wha'd you do?" I said.

Mayfield smiled. It was a malicious, self-satisfied smile. "I slapped her back." Her voice was low and coarse. "Then I went to her husband. Told him I knew what he was. What he was doing. He ranted and raved. Called me a 'know-it-all nigger.' Then he collapsed into tears. Said something was wrong with him and he needed help. I told him the only help he could expect was from the police if he ever touched Vivian again. That's the same time Eleanor started getting all this plastic surgery. It wasn't about her daughter being—violated—it was about *her* losing *her* charms."

"And you parlayed what you knew into an iron-clad employment contract?" I said.

"My 'ironclad contract,'" she said with no small amount of disgust. "I didn't ask for it. Didn't use Vivian as a bargaining chip. It was offered and I took it. With conditions. Vivian was to go away to a boarding school. Away from *him*. Away from *her*. Then she was to spend her summer vacations with me and Dez here or in Europe. *We* were that child's parents, Mr. Snow! *Me! I* was her mother." Mayfield took a moment. Then she said, "Eleanor didn't even see it as blackmail. She saw it as an agreement between two smart women." Mayfield paused. "She and her husband deserved each other. They each deserved what they got."

"Which brings us to you," I said.

"I told you—"

"Yeah, I know what you told me," I said. "A women in business conference at the Detroit Athletic Club. Yeah, there was a conference that night. But you showed me to a door you knew I couldn't get through. Even if I was a member. You may not like Atchison, but you learned a lot from him in his short tenure: If you're gonna lie, go big and wear other people like camouflage."

Again, Mayfield slumped back in her chair and after a moment thick with silence said, "When did you know?"

"Couple days," I said. "There was a second glass of wine at her house the evening you killed her. You left without removing the glass. Probably panicked. Lucky for you, a young Mexican house-keeper scared of being deported cleaned that up for you. But I didn't know until Traverse City. Some of your letters to Vivian. Especially the last letter. The phrasing: 'You're free of her now,' or, 'She's gone and now you can get on with your life.' Not exactly the way somebody talks about the death of a friend of over thirty years."

Rose Mayfield's eyes filled again with tears. She wiped them away and stared at me. "'Friend.' I'm embarrassed I ever thought of the Great Eleanor Paget as a 'friend.' She was intolerable, arrogant, vindictive and self-aggrandizing with a penchant for manipulating people, for eating their souls. She ate mine—*feasted* on it!—for over thirty years." Mayfield pointed to the awards and citations on the wall. I stood and walked around the room, closely examining the framed honors and decorations. "All of it—useless," she said.

Some were her husband's, but many belonged to her. An under-graduate degree in Finance from Wayne State University. Master's in Business Administration from the University of Michigan-Dear-born. A Master's Degree in Economics from University of Detroit Mercy. There were photos of her in cap and gown, embraced by her late husband. Photos of her in a different colored cap and different colored gown being hugged by Vivian Paget and Colleen.

"That office should have been mine," Mayfield said as I contin-ued to look at the decorations, degrees and citations on the wall. "Ten years ago, it should have been mine."

I walked back to the chair next to her and sat.

Mayfield told me she'd talked to Eleanor a number of times

about advancing in the company. A management position. A leadership role. Something befitting her years of commitment and her education. She never leveraged what she knew about Eleanor Paget's husband or her daughter. The time was never right or a position "didn't quite suit her."

Instead of a career path, she was given more money, over and above her lucrative contract agreement. And when Mayfield's husband got sick—pancreatic cancer—the extra money came in handy. His agonizingly slow death brought her to the brink of exhaustive collapse. And when he did finally die, Eleanor Paget gave Mayfield an expenses-paid two-week vacation to Paris.

Still, the promotions never came. The professional recognition never materialized.

"The last time I asked her for a promotion to the finance group," Mayfield continued, "she said, 'Oh, honey, let's be honest, shall we? The people we deal with, they're just not comfortable with a black face in front of their money.' Then she laughed!"

"The straw that broke the camel's back?" I said.

"If such an insult were the straw that broke this particular type of camel's back, then I fear every black, brown, red and yellow back in Detroit would've been a hundred years' broken by now," she said. "Was it infuriating? Yes. Humiliating? Most definitely. But a reason for me to kill her?" Mayfield cocked her head and gave me a wry smile. "Mr. Snow, I have advanced degrees in economics and finance and over thirty years at the bank. Time and education enough to acquire twenty million dollars of the bank's money in five offshore accounts. For that amount of money, Mr. Snow, feel free to call me nigger in any language you wish."

"Then why?"

"You really don't know, do you?"

"Know what?"

Mayfield's eyes narrowed and she smiled. "That you've been a part of this particular Paget legacy from the minute you first stepped in her house to inform her that her vile husband and his child lover were dead. She had very little faith in the Detroit Police Department. But you proved her wrong. And for her that was both exhilarating and worrisome. Exhilarating because she had a particular soft spot for handsome young men like you who didn't back down from her bombastic personality. And worrisome because those same traits might reveal the truth of how her husband and his whore died."

"Vivian shot them," I said. "I already know that." I edged forward in my chair. "Are you telling me Eleanor somehow had me taken off the murder investigation because I got too close to naming Vivian as a suspect? She pulled all those strings to protect Vivian?"

"Not protect," Mayfield said. "Use. Your Captain Danbury was deep in her pocket. Her money bought your removal from the murder investigation. Her money bought the early release of the gun. She knew Vivian's fingerprints would probably be on the shell casings still in the gun. And that was her weapon of last resort to bring Vivian into the bank. Family meant little to Eleanor. Legacy, on the other hand, meant everything. And she would not see that legacy die with her."

"Jesus," I said. "She would have blackmailed her own daughter to—"

"*My* daughter!" Mayfield shouted. "Vivian's *my* daughter! *I* raised her! *I* protected her from the horrors of her own flesh and blood!"

"And that's why you shot her?"

Mayfield glared at me for a long time. "That's why I shot her." Her look softened after a moment before she said, "What would you have done?"

I didn't answer.

There was no answer to give.

She was quiet for a long time, staring off into space. And that suited me fine; I needed a moment to process having played an unwitting role in someone else's elaborate game.

After a while, she took in and released a deep, heavy sigh.

"I suppose you're gonna take me in," she said.

I stood and said, "I'm not a cop. Truth of the matter, Ms. Mayfield, is I really don't give a shit what happens to you. You killing Eleanor Paget has unleashed hell on me. My friends. Vivian and her wife. That's all I care about right now."

I turned and started for the door.

I heard the click of a gun hammer behind me.

"Do you believe in God, Mr. Snow?" I heard her say.

I turned, looked at her and said, "In my own way, yes." A snub-nose Smith & Wesson .32 was trembling in her right hand, the barrel pointed at me.

"Not very acceptable for a black woman my age to say," she began, "but I don't. How could there be a benevolent God with children like Vivian being raped by their own fathers while their mothers turn a blind eye? How could a loving God just—just sit back and watch the horror of what people go through every day? Me! What I went through for thirty goddamn years! No, Mr. Snow. You make your bones in the here and now, not the happily-ever-afterlife."

"See, here's the thing," I said, walking towards her. "I've already lost everything I really cared about. My parents. A woman I was going to marry, who was shot while buying a half-gallon of goddamn milk. My job. You killed Eleanor Paget for Vivian and twenty million. Me? I got twelve million bucks and everything I've ever really wanted is either in the ground or wondering why the hell I ran. So, yeah. Do me a favor—pull the trigger. Because God or no God—I just don't fucking care."

The gun trembled in her hands and tears flowed from her eyes.

"Do it!" I shouted. Staring down the black maw of the gun barrel, I realized I really didn't care one way or another if she pulled the trigger. If she did, all the pain, all the disappointment and loneliness would be gone. There would no longer be aching memories of the deaths of Mo and my unborn child. No bloody memories of Afghanistan. No memories of a desired future with Tatina.

If Mayfield didn't pull the trigger, then God or no God, I would make it my life's work to scorch this fucking earth starting with Brewster.

Slowly, she lowered the quivering gun and eased the hammer against the strike plate.

I turned my back to her and said, "Maybe I'll get around to talking about you to the cops in a day or two. All depends on whether or not I'm alive after tonight."

I got to the foyer and looked at the staircase where her two pieces of luggage sat on the landing. Like a zombie, she followed me into the foyer.

"Mouthwash," I said staring at her luggage on the staircase landing.

"What?"

With my back still to her I said, "You probably didn't expect the blow-back when you pulled the trigger. Probably got some blood and brain matter on you. In your mouth. You never quite get rid of that taste. Mouthwash helps. Scotch works better." I held up my wristwatch for her to see, pointed to the dial and said, "Tick-tock, Ms. Mayfield. If you've got a plane to catch, I'd suggest you dry your eyes and drive your car."

Then I opened the front door of her house and left.

As I walked to my car I suspected that in less than thirty minutes, Rose Mayfield would be in the wind. On a flight to where the warm sun shone and palm trees swayed lazily in salt water breezes. Two more flights and she just might be beyond tracking. Her money untraceable.

As I was about to open my car door I heard a single gunshot from inside the house.

I got in my car and drove away.

36

By nine forty-five that evening, I'd eaten six pieces of bacon, two fried eggs, two pieces of whole wheat toast, some raw broccoli and a banana. Simple, unadorned food consumed purely for the energy it would provide for the evening's festivities. Protein, potassium, slowly metabolized sugars.

Everything us natural born killers need for a night's bloody work.

I did a weapons check.

I had my Glock auto and my Smith & Wesson .38. I still had one of Tomás's rifles and plenty of ammo for all three. I'd retrieved my bulletproof vest and marine utility knife from my storage unit.

Before leaving the house, I tried calling Skittles one last time. I tried all six of the burner phones he'd given to me.

Nothing.

It wasn't like Skittles to go dark on me for so long. I'd pulled him into something that computer skills and snappy repartee couldn't get him out of. And unfortunately it was necessary for me to pull him in deeper.

But there would be time enough to worry about getting a hold of Skittles. Right now, it was time to run another bloody gauntlet at a building on the southeastern edge of Mexicantown called Rocking Horse.

I called Tomás. He and Frank were strapped. They had

discussed their plan in detail, primarily flanking me high and low and remaining as invisible as possible. They had nearly emptied Tomás's basement weapons locker. Nothing was off the table. Tomás had introduced Frank to Elena. They sat with her and brought her up to speed on the situation and how they planned to end it.

"How bad?" I said.

"Bad enough," Tomás said, laughing. "I may not be getting any Latina lovin' for a month. Ain't but a minute in married man time. Like the old saying goes, 'Time on the vine makes the fruit sweeter.' She thinks after all this time I'm reverting to the old ways. I told her this time the old ways were the only way to help out a good man."

"That would be me?"

"*Si*, asshole."

"I don't want to mess things up with you and Elena, Tomás—"

"Not gonna happen, jefe," Tomás said. "Elena and me raised a teenage girl in this house. And if *that* shit didn't break us, nothing will, man."

"And Frank?"

"She shouted at him like he was a five-year-old boy caught with a lit firecracker. Tore him a new asshole in Spanish. Then told him after this was done he was going to help me paint the upstairs hallway. All he said was 'Yes, ma'am,' 'No, ma'am' and 'Yes, ma'am' again."

"God bless good parenting and the US military."

"We good to go, compadre?"

"Let's set it off, mi amigo."

It was ten-thirty. An hour and a half before I was to meet with Brewster to hear whatever his unacceptable last offer was. For a party like this, there was no shame in arriving early.

I loaded up my car and headed to Rocking Horse .

Over the past fifty years, all of the nearby factories and shipping docks had been shuttered in this part of Mexicantown. Most of the working-class brown and black neighborhoods collapsed in on themselves from years of neglect or fires long ago burned out. It was a very good place for very bad things to happen.

LifeLight—the charity street lighting organization Rose Mayfield had created through Titan—had yet to make its way this far south. Most of the streetlamps had fallen into disrepair, stripped of any copper wiring, leaning into their demise as monuments to a declining population, a dysfunctional city government, forgotten dreams and lost hopes.

There was a long way to go in this part of Mexicantown: Four hundred yards in any direction from the whitewashed three-story artist studio was devastation. Rusted train tracks overgrown with weeds where freight trains hadn't run for thirty years. Freight roads where no freight had arrived in over forty years.

Chernobyl, American-style.

Even so, there were still the harvesters of the few remaining, barely functioning organs of these five or so abandoned city blocks. The heroin-, meth- and crack-addled vampires who trolled the night in search of new veins in which to sink their yellowed fangs.

I parked several blocks away from Rocking Horse, near a closed dry cleaner and small reopened neighborhood bar that promised good food and local bands (including the infamous "Unicorns over Saigon") on Tuesdays and Saturdays. I checked my phone. A text from Tomás: "No time for RH surveil. Action at NW corner of factory. 5 bogies. F and me inside." I waded through the darkness toward Rocking Horse. It was eleven-fifteen.

The heavy steel security door at the back of the building was cracked open. I brought out my Glock, tripped the safety off and eased my way in.

Save for a few safety lights, the cavernous building was dark. I made my way through the makeshift coffee bar where a broken antique Italian coffee roaster sat on the concrete floor like some fossilized prehistoric beast. A small conference room with an odds-and-ends assortment of old office furniture was to my left and to my right there was an open space filled with the tools of lithography: hand-carved printing blocks, jars of paint, typesetting machines, a few desktop computers and printers.

Still nothing.

Cautiously, I ventured upstairs.

More darkness. More cold wind whistling through cracks in the cement and windows that hadn't been caulked, boarded or duct-taped.

There was a large open space on the second floor. Painters' easels, cages full of supplies, a makeshift library, more printing equipment, lithographs hung to dry on clotheslines, a couple of sofas that had seen better days.

Beneath a safety light was a chair.

Slowly, I made my way to the chair. A lime-green Nike running shoe lay near the chair. On the floor surrounding the chair were blood splatters. And in the shadows near the chair lay the body of a young woman, her wrists and ankles bound with zip-ties. A single gunshot to the center of her forehead. She'd been beaten before her execution. Against all marine and police training, a knot tightened in my stomach. Muscle-memory had me make the Sign of the Cross over her.

On the chair was a walkie-talkie.

I picked up the walkie-talkie and said, "Brewster?"

"Good," Brewster said. "Now we can begin. The abandoned factory fifty yards northeast of the building you're in. If you are not here in sixty seconds then I kill the very young Mr. McKinney. Your time begins—now."

He had Skittles.

I pocketed the walkie-talkie, rushed down the flight of steps and back out into the cold night. The fifty-yard distance from Rocking Horse to the abandoned factory to the northeast was riddled with overgrown weeds, garbage and debris. Several rusting carcasses of automobiles caught what pale moonlight there was, adding to the post-apocalyptic landscape. Navigating to the looming hollowed-out skull of the factory was all the more difficult because of the eight-foot chain-link fence topped with rusting razor wire. It was an obstacle course with the added challenge of a ten-degree rise.

I made it over the fence, ducking and dodging the long, gnarled witch fingers of rebar jutting up from the ground and clawing at the cold black sky. Twenty yards out from the loading dock of the building, I stepped on something ribbed and soft. Something that gave a final discordant wheeze: The body of a pit bull issuing the last gases of its mortality.

Clearing the last hurdle of rubble and clambering onto the factory's crumbling loading dock, I gave very brief thought to today's date: November 1: *el Dia de Los Muertos*. The Day of the Dead. A time Mexicans commemorate the lives of loved ones who had shed their mortal coil.

In the core of Mexicantown, a thousand candles would light up the cold, dark night. Skeleton marionettes and people costumed as skeletons would dance. On this first night, mothers and grandmothers would cry and share stories of the lives of children lost. And tomorrow evening, children would hear stories of their forefathers, stories of the mothers of their blood. There would be sounds of traditional Mexican folk and mariachi music echoing in the cold air. The comingling aromas of *pan de muertos*, roasting chili peppers, grilled beef and chicken, seasoned beans, rice and tortillas.

Any other time, I might have joined in these celebrations. I would have celebrated the lives of my mother and grandmothers. I would have toasted tequila to the spirits of my father and his fathers' fathers.

This was not any other time.

Tonight, I was the sword in God's left hand. And soon there would be blood on the blade.

I brought out the walkie-talkie.

"I'm here," I said into the walkie-talkie. "No more marathons. Let's get this done."

I hoped God was watching over me.

And if not God, then Tomás and Frank.

Brewster radioed the directions I was to take through the abandoned building and I made my way cautiously through the dark cavern of the forgotten factory. Somewhere was the sound of gushing water. A busted water main. No telling how long city water had been rushing in unabated, further weakening an already crippled structure; a day, a year, a decade.

I came to a stop at a large open area next to a toppled forklift: someone was sitting thirty yards away in the center of the floor, breathing hard, hands tied behind their back. There was enough light to see that it was a young black man. He was wearing one lime-green Nike running shoe. Standing next to the man was someone dressed in tactical black and holding what could have been a machine pistol.

"They killed her, man," Skittles said, his voice low and quivering. "Shot her. Like she was—was nothin', man. They shot Jersey Girl—"

Before he could say anything else, Brewster's man brought a quick, decisive fist to Skittles's jaw.

"Let's get to business, Mr. Snow, shall we?" Brewster's voice came through the darkness without benefit of the walkie-talkie. In the dark echo chamber of the building, it was difficult to pinpoint exactly where his voice came from. My best guess was it came from behind Skittles and maybe at the ten or eleven o'clock position.

"You okay?" I called out to Skittles.

"I've been very patient with you, Mr. Snow," Brewster's voice echoed. "Far more than I should have been."

Four red dots appeared on Skittles's chest, the red laser trails streaming down from the open second floor.

"You know it's over, right?" I said. "Your friendly neighborhood FBI dropped in on the bank this afternoon. It's done, Brewster. You and your boys probably have less than an hour to find a small, safe corner of the world."

"For the life of me, I can't figure out why you persist in being such a pain in my ass," Brewster said. "There was never anything in this for you. Why, Mr. Snow?"

Instead of a clear head, my mind was on fire with the image of the dead girl at the Rocking Horse building. And from within the flames I heard Rose Mayfield's voice: *How could a benevolent God just sit back and watch the horror of what people go through every day?* "You know what I can't figure out?" I finally said. "I can't figure out why Eminem isn't the fucking mayor and why there aren't statues of the Supremes, Four Tops, Marcus Belgrave and George Clinton on Woodward Avenue. I can't figure out why there isn't a statue of Aurelio Rodriguez outside Comerica Park or why Moby's such a big fuckin' deal and Juan Atkins and Derrick May aren't. And I for damn sure can't figure out why I'm paying for basic cable but I'm getting premium digital cable plus streaming channels I didn't sign up for—"

"Tha'd be me," Skittles said, his words slurring. It was a sure bet his head had been rocked around by a few brutal punches.

"Insolent to the very end," Brewster said. "Here's my last, generous offer to you: I make you watch while I riddle the young man's body with bullets. Or you die first so you don't have to watch me riddle the young man with bullets."

"How's this for a counter offer, Brewster?" I said. "How 'bout you eat a steaming bag of dicks?"

Then I heard it.

Second floor. Three o'clock. A gurgling sound. The sound of a man's throat being cut and the opened trachea flooding with blood.

One of the red laser dots quivered erratically then disappeared from Skittle's chest.

From the second floor two small fireballs arched down, smashing on the floor, the flames fanning out near Skittles and the man with the machine pistol.

Sticky bombs.

I brought up my Glock and fired three times in quick succession as I ran toward Skittles. I hit the man guarding him twice, knocking him back seven or eight feet. He was wearing a vest. Jesus. Everybody's got a goddamn bulletproof vest these days.

Gunfire erupted overhead. Bullets chipped into the waterlogged concrete floor, sending chunks flying.

The man guarding Skittles regained his bearings and fired the machine pistol at me, missing by inches. I fired again twice and he went down, this time for good. At my heels machine-gun fire continued to blister the concrete. Five single quick succession gunshots from the second story. A man's black-clad body tumbled from above, crashing decisively to the floor behind me.

Skittles had taken one in the forearm and one in the thigh. As I ran I fired my own succession of shots to where I believed Brewster had hidden in the shadows. I reached Skittles in time to yank him out of the chair. The two of us tumbled behind a large concrete column.

I dumped a spent clip and slapped another one in the Glock.

Five more single shots rang out. A blast from a shotgun. More machine-pistol fire chipping away at the column Skittles and I huddled against. I quickly checked Skittles's forearm and thigh wounds. Not bad, but if this wasn't done soon, he would bleed out. Most of the firefight was on the second level, the one-o'clock position on my right, two-o'clock on my left. I ripped off a part of his shirt and tied it around the thigh wound. Sporadic gunfire. More machine-pistols erupting. Then I said, "Stay here."

Skittles nodded anxiously, eyes wide with fear and pain.

Since I hadn't returned fire in the time it took to tie off Skittles's wound, two of Brewster's men got brave. They ran, firing their weapons at the column we were huddled behind. Bravery is often just stupidity, though; I dropped both men fifteen yards out, one bullet for each.

Echoing footfalls. Running. Someone to my right. I spun out from the concrete column and saw him: another shadowed figure with a machine-pistol. Four shots from my Glock. He fell.

"How many?" I yelled. I was cautiously confident the balance of power was about even. I needed to hear the voices of my friends to make sure they were in good standing.

"Three," came Tomás's echoing voice. Second floor.

"Four and a half," Frank's voice joined. Behind me, twenty yards at the four-o'clock position.

"Half?" I said.

"Still alive, but ain't too happy about it," Frank said.

I was pretty sure there were two more inside.

And Brewster.

I ran to another concrete column about twenty feet away. Bullets from another machine-pistol cut into an already weakened and collapsing column. One more hit and the column would go, along with a large portion of the second floor.

The unmistakable click of a magazine being changed out.

I spun out from behind the column just in time to see the man slap in another clip and bring the machine pistol up.

Three shots from my gun and he was dead.

More gunfire from the second floor.

"I could use a little help up here!"

Tomás.

I ran up a flight of steps. Some of the steps crumbled beneath my feet as I pushed forward.

"Where?" I shouted.

"Here."

A familiar voice.

I spun around.

A man dressed in tactical black had Tomás on his knees and was pointing the barrel of his gun at the top of Tomás's head.

Dax.

"Qala Sarkarit, Afghanistan," he said. "Is it true you had a kill four hundred yards out with a five-kilometer-an-hour crosswind, Lance Corporal? That the shot that put you up there with Lyudmila Pavlichenko? Or is that just more jarhead bullshit?"

If anything was going to grab and twist my guts it was hearing this bastard address me by my old marine rank. And reminding me of the one shot I should never have taken.

"Who the hell are you?" I said.

"That doesn't matter," Dax snapped. "What *does* matters is you and your friend walk away right now or more people than you can possibly imagine will die. Drop whatever artillery you've got and I promise—you and the Cisco Kid here can walk away."

"Let my friend go now."

"Not until you agree to walk away," Dax said.

"And if I don't?"

"Then you're betting your friend's life on which of us is the better shot."

"My money's on the home team," Tomás said.

"Mine, too," I said just before the two of us leveled our guns at each other and fired.

I felt the impact of a bullet punch into my upper right rib cage, taking my breath away and knocking me off my feet. I lay on my back trying to force myself to breathe, listening to the echoes of gunfire and thanking God for my bullet-proof vest. Then I heard footsteps approaching me. The shadow of a man standing over me. A hand reaching out.

I took the hand, pulled on it and struggled to my feet.

Tomás.

"I get him?" I said, fighting through the pain.

"One in the throat," Tomás said. "I knew you were good, but damn, amigo."

I didn't have the heart to tell Tomás it was a blind-as-a-bat lucky shot.

From the back of the building we heard more gunfire. Tomás called out for Frank and got no reply. Only more automatic weapons fire.

And that's when we felt it. Heard it.

The second floor groaning. Buckling beneath our feet. Concrete snapping and popping. It was seconds away from collapsing, threatening to bury Tomás and me beneath several hundred tons of rubble.

One option.

Run.

Tomás gathered up his Mossberg shotgun and we ran through the opaque grey. Beneath us, the floor was giving way, buckling, shattering, exploding. We made it to another set of stairs at the back of the building. The second floor came crashing down just as we made it to the loading dock. Plumes of grey concrete dust and shards of debris buffeting against our backs. I hoped—prayed—Skittles had the strength, speed and good sense to make it out of the collapsed building.

The cool and persistent November winds quickly swept away the cloud of concrete dust. Beneath a now brilliant moon, Tomás and I scanned the field between Rocking Horse and the abandoned factory for any signs of Frank. In the middle of the rugged debris field was the last of Brewster's men.

The man had his machine pistol leveled at a collection of boulder sized concrete chunks.

"Come and get some, sugah pie!" the man cackled. "You know you want it!"

"Frank," Tomás said under his breath.

We jumped down from the loading dock and navigated our way

toward the man. Tomás may have been almost thirty years older and a good twenty pounds heavier than me, but his surprising speed and agility over the rugged landscape left me outpaced by at least fifteen feet.

Twenty feet away from the man, Tomás stopped and leveled his shotgun.

"Drop it and turn around!" Tomás yelled.

The man whipped out a .45 and pointed it at Tomás, keeping his machine pistol aimed at the concrete slab that Frank was huddled behind. The man was wounded and bloodied. The "half" Frank had shot earlier.

"I know you," Machine Pistol Man said, squinting at Tomás.

"My home," Tomás said. "You and your partner."

"Oh, yeah," the man said. "Nothing personal, amigo."

"My granddaughter was there—"

"Now you hold on, amigo!" the man said, rocking on his heels. He was losing a lot of blood. "I don't do no kids, border-babies or no, and that's the God's honest truth." The man cut his eyes to me and a smile formed beneath his droopy mustache. "I hear you gave my old partner quite a what-for."

The Russian thug with star tattoos on his knees.

"I did," I said.

"Don't like workin' with no Russians anyway," the man said, wavering on his feet. "Unpredictable. Got that meat-on-the-hoof attitude. And that boy, he wasn't half right, bless his heart."

"Put your weapons down," Tomás said. "Easy."

"Well, now, that just ain't gonna happen, is it?" The man laughed.

"You got three seconds before you die," Tomás said. "One . . ."

The man leveled his .45 for the shot, but it was too late; the blasts from Tomás's shotgun echoed through the night, lifting the man off his feet, throwing him ten feet back. His airborne body came to an ugly end, landing hard and twisted on a pile of concrete rubble.

Tomás walked to the body and gave the man's head a nudge with the still smoking barrels of his shotgun. "Viva Zapata, motherfucker."

Frank emerged from behind the concrete rubble.

"You just made my Christmas list, dude," Frank said extending a hand to Tomás.

"Next time, *cabron*," Tomás said taking Frank's hand and shaking it, "don't kill someone *half*way. Kill them *all* the way."

Behind us was the sound of a man struggling to breathe, clambering over the wreckage of the field.

Brewster.

He was running as best as a wounded man could, falling several times as he tried desperately to escape the debris field.

I got to him after his last spill to the hardened ground.

He was bleeding from the hip. After a right cross to his jaw, I patted him down, stood, pointed my Glock at the bridge of his nose and said, "It's over." Then I made a quick call to O'Donnell and told her part one of our agreement was in hand.

"It was business," Brewster said, his voice trembling. "That's all it ever was!"

I thought about Ray Danbury, Mariana Spiegelman, and Vivian and Colleen. And Skittles's friend, Jersey Girl.

It would have been easy to squeeze one last shot. Very easy. But killing him would have killed a large part of the signed agreement I had with the FBI.

Through the cold moonlit wasteland a voice said, "I would very much appreciate your moving away from Mr. Deubel." A quick-clipped voice. German? Eastern European?

Tomás, Frank and I brought our weapons up and crouched, not knowing where in the soupy darkness to point our guns.

"Please," the voice said. "There isn't much time for any of us."

In the northeastern distance was the growing sound of sirens.

I lowered my weapon.

"You sure?" Tomás whispered to me.

I didn't reply. Following my lead, Tomás and Frank lowered their weapons. The figure of a man emerged from the darkness. He was dressed in what appeared to be a black wool car coat and black fedora. It was hard to tell where the perimeters of his body ended and the night began. He was holding a long-barreled automatic pistol with suppressor and laser scope.

"Please," Brewster said, twisting his body to get a look at the man. Brewster knew the voice. It was the voice of his death. Brewster writhed in pain, but it was more than his gunshot wounds. It was knowing he was at the precipice between what his champagne life had been and the final void he was seconds away from being jettisoned into. He was crying.

"I've done *good* things! Boston! Nashville!"

The man dressed in black flicked his gun at me. "Please move away, Mr. Snow." I took two steps back from Brewster and the man said, "Thank you."

"You *can't do this!*" Brewster shouted.

The man in black pointed his gun at Brewster's head and dispassionately fired two bullets. Calmly, the man collected up his shell casings, then casually leveled his weapon at me. He scrutinized me from head to toe, smiled, lowered his weapon, then turned to walk away.

"You work for these people?" I said to the shadowed man.

In the darkness behind me Frank harshly whispered, "Dude! Just let him walk!"

"An independent contractor," the man said, turning slightly to me. "I have no vested interest in the dealings of the organization." The man paused, then said, "Michigan is such a beautiful state. I especially like Traverse City. You were quite effective there, Mr. Snow."

"Thanks," I said. "Were you there for me or the women?"

"Neither," the man said. "Merely an observer fascinated with your—how shall I say?—obsession with this whole matter. You have certain rare talents, Mr. Snow. Gifts. I admire them."

"Thanks," I said. "I think."

The man paused again for a second before continuing, "This is the most conversation I've ever had on a job. Thank you for that."

"Is this over?" I said. "Are we safe? My friends, are they safe?"

"Safe?" the man said with his erudite continental accent. "I suppose so long as you use seatbelts, exercise and do not eat too much processed food or sugar." Then he sighed heavily and said, "I do not mean to injure your pride, of course, but you realize very little of this had anything to do with you. You were, how shall I say, the wasp stinging the giant's tender underbelly. But my contract was only for Mr. Deubel and Mr. Randolph."

"Dax? Why him?"

"Let's just say one should always be careful of the legends one chooses to believe."

And with that, the night swallowed the man whole. Another devil walking the earth.

From the loading dock we heard someone say, "I ain't feelin' too good, man. Like I'ma throw up or something."

Skittles.

I issued a sigh of relief. And not for the FBI deal I'd made.

Dazed, weak from his wounds and caked head to toe in white concrete dust, he looked like a skeleton reveler at a Day of the Dead celebration.

A choir of police sirens drew closer.

I told Frank and Tomás to bug out. Frank asked if I wanted them to collect up Skittles and get him off-scene. Reluctantly, I said no. We shook hands and they left. Somewhere in the near distance, a car started, its sound system blasting Carlos Santana's song "Soul Sacrifice."

A minute after they hit the road, a police chopper was hovering overhead, its blinding spotlight illuminating the carnage. And me.

The Detroit Police and FBI showed up in force. Before their arrival I dropped to my knees, neatly arranged all of my weapons in a semi-circle in front of me and laced my fingers behind my head. Several uniformed and Detroit SWAT tactical teams cautiously made their way toward me, shouting, "Stay on the ground! Stay on the fucking ground!"

I was tired and my ribs hurt. Old wounds were opening. New wounds were bleeding.

I had no intention of moving.

37

"Wow," O'Donnell said, surveying the carnage around me. I was still on my knees, fingers laced behind my head. "You sure know how to throw a party."

"Ain't no party like a Dee-troit party."

The uniformed and SWAT Detroit cops surrounding me kept me squarely in their gun sites. O'Donnell had shown up with her own small contingency of agents.

O'Donnell looked at the prone body of Brewster. "Kinda looks like the first part of our agreement is null and void."

"Yeah, but since your raid on the bank, the second part trumps the first."

Skittles, his arms draped around the shoulders of two FBI agents, was escorted to an awaiting ambulance. "The fuck's goin' on, man?" he was saying. My stomach knotted and I suddenly felt an uncomfortable kinship with Judas Iscariot. I'd given up Skittles for FBI immunity and protection. The buffer I needed from the Detroit Police Department.

O'Donnell was brought into an impromptu confab with three on-site DPD captains, several lieutenants and the commissioner. She was a good head shorter than the men, but it looked like she was holding her own.

Several of the DPD captains angrily gestured toward me. Other gestures were reserved for Skittles, who was quickly secured in the ambulance and whisked away. O'Donnell calmly nodded in the face of the angry recriminations, accusations and threats. She extracted her phone from her coat pocket and held the phone to her ear. She said a few words, then handed the phone to the DPD commissioner. The commissioner took the phone, held up a hand in front of his staff. The captains and lieutenants instantly fell silent.

Several minutes later I was being lifted to my feet by two FBI agents and escorted to one of the two remaining FBI Chevy Tahoes. Past the Detroit uniforms and SWAT teams. Past the captains, lieutenants and commissioner. Past the gathering of news trucks and reporters suddenly on the scene, jockeying for position and hysterically speculating on what latest war had been fought on this decimated Mexicantown territory.

At the FBI Detroit regional office, I was frisked for the third time, treated for minor lacerations, given several ice packs and a couple of aspirin for my badly bruised but unbroken ribs. The bullet wound I'd received in Traverse City was cleaned and redressed. And I spent the next several hours in an interview room answering variations on the same questions from different agents, including a conferenced-in agent in Quantico.

At 5:30 Tuesday morning, O'Donnell entered the room wearing a tactical black jumpsuit and a very imposing sidearm strapped to her left thigh. She had two big cups of Starbucks coffee, a box of Tim Horton donuts and a non-descript white box. She sat the box of donuts and one of the coffees in front of me.

"Ever have the donuts at LaBelle's Soul Hole?" I said, surveying the box of donuts. "Little place on Michigan Avenue near Rosa Parks Boulevard."

"LaBelle Mason-Dunwitty," O'Donnell said, "Carries a Smith & Wesson 1911 and makes a helluva apple fritter. I'm not the *tourista* you may think I am, Snow."

I grabbed one of the buttermilk glazed donuts and took a hearty bite. It was good.

Seemed all of my weapons and most of the weapons used by Brewster's crew were accounted for. However, several of the weapons that had killed them were unaccounted for. Like Frank and Tomás's weapons. And, of course, the gun used to kill Brewster. I casually speculated that perhaps divine intervention had provided me well-armed angels.

"I'd love to meet these avenging angels," O'Donnell said.

"You know how angels are," I said. "'Unseen, both when we wake and when we sleep.'"

O'Donnell's raid on Titan Securities Investments Group had been performed with swift tactical precision. Like the wrath of God, FBI agents stormed the building, gathering up computers, servers, paper files, office safes, lockboxes, safety deposit boxes, notepads, pens, paper and paperclips. Even the offices of LifeLight were turned over.

O'Donnell filled me in on Atchison's story, which made me nearly choke on a plain donut: The FBI and State Police, unable to serve a warrant to Kip Atchison at his Grosse Pointe Estates home, made the long journey north to his palatial Charlevoix summer home. Atchison was found wearing knee-high leather high-heel boots, expensive panties and bra and a long silk scarf. Dead from auto-erotic asphyxiation. An APB was out for a high-end male escort whose professional name was "Ima Bytchakokoff."

"You brought in Aaron Spiegelman?" I said after laughing for a minute straight. "How's he doing?"

O'Donnell shrugged. "'Bout as well as anybody who was in love for twenty-five years and just lost their partner. Funny thing, though. He asked me if you had any part in bringing Titan down."

"And you said?"

"I told him you were integral to our investigation and left it at that. Then he sang like a castrato choirboy about everything that had been going on at the bank."

O'Donnell and the FBI's legal eagles were getting serious carpal tunnel writing up the various and sundry charges against Titan's board of directors. Of course, O'Donnell wasn't quite sure what kind of charges to lay at Spiegelman's feet save for operating with astounding naiveté and willfully blind arrogance. "And hell," O'Donnell said, eyeing a Boston Cream from the box of donuts, "if I could put him away for that, I could certainly put you *and* most of congress away for life on the same charges." She took a moment to enjoy a bite of her Boston Cream and a sip of coffee, then said, "Tell me about Rose Mayfield."

I did.

When I finished, O'Donnell said, "You're lucky three witnesses saw you by your car when the shot was fired." O'Donnell walked to the single narrow window of the room and looked out at the increasing morning traffic on Michigan Avenue, ten stories below. "McKinney, a.k.a. Skittles, is on lock-down at Henry Ford Hospital. He knows you're his Judas. But I think between the morphine drip and the deal we're offering, he might be forgiving."

"Speaking of Judas," I began, "you ever find out anything about Dax Randolph?"

"Just another mercenary looking for a big pay-out," O'Donnell said unconvincingly.

"Really?" I said. "That's not what the Cleaner told me."

O'Donnell, gazing out at the traffic on Michigan Avenue, suddenly turned to face me. "You talked to the Cleaner?"

"Oh, yeah," I said brightly. "We're thick as murderous thieves. He said his contract wasn't just for Brewster. It was for Dax Randolph, too. Which begs the question: Why would there be a high-end contract out on a glorified bank security guard?" O'Donnell folded her arms across her chest and stared at me dispassionately. "The last thing this Cleaner guy said to me was 'one should always be careful of the legends one chooses to believe.'"

"Meaning?"

"See, that's just it," I said. "I had no idea. I thought maybe he was telling me Dax was some sort of legendary badass. But Dax knew things about me. Knew about a mission I had in Afghanistan. A mission maybe five people knew about."

"How's any of this—"

"Dax Randolph never existed," I said. "He was a fiction. A 'legend'. Somebody who wears and sheds a number of skins. Someone adept at infiltration. Dax Randolph was CIA. What better way to find out where terrorist money's coming in from and going out to? Only problem—I mean if Mr. Gramatins, my ninth-grade civics teacher, was right—is the CIA isn't sanctioned for domestic operations. That would be like a big, bad neighbor taking a steaming hot piss on your rosebush, right?"

O'Donnell walked to the metal table, closed the lid on the box of donuts and started to walk out of the room, taking the remaining donuts with her.

"You forgot something," I said, pointing to the squat white box on the table.

"It's yours," she said standing in the doorway.

I opened the box.

Two navy blue ceramic coffee mugs emblazoned with the FBI logo.

She walked away, leaving the door to the interview room open.

38

"Turn the TV on, compadre!" Tomás said. "Channel eight!"

Standing at a podium that threatened to completely hide her was FBI Special Agent Megan O'Donnell. Behind her, standing like an army of giants, were Detroit's mayor, the Detroit police commissioner, several captains, the State Attorney General and people I didn't know. Reporters and photographers were crowded in front of the podium. Cameras clicked furiously, handheld microphones and digital tape recorders competed for airspace.

"Thank you, Mr. Mayor," O'Donnell said. "Since this is an ongoing investigation, I will provide the press with only bullet points that will not impede our continuing inquiries."

In a matter-of-fact voice, O'Donnell informed the gaggle of reporters that Titan Securities Investments Group had been under investigation for fraud, racketeering, extortion, cybercrimes and a litany of other charges. This was a multistate FBI-organized crime investigation carried out with the complete cooperation and resources of state and local law enforcement.

"Before I introduce FBI Regional Director Hammond Phillips, I'd like to personally thank Detroit's mayor and the extraordinary dedication and cooperation of Detroit Police Commissioner Horace Renard and the brave men and women under his command. Also, a special thanks to a private citizen who, at great personal risk, helped us break this case—"

"That's you, mi amigo!" Tomás shouted in my ear. He began laughing loudly. "My man!"

I was about to turn the TV off when the local news anchor threw the broadcast to the affiliate's national news anchor. With overly serious John Williams-style music throbbing in the background, the national news anchor in the Armani suit introduced the evening's top story: a high-level, closed door meeting which included the directors of the FBI and CIA in front of the Senate intelligence subcommittee.

"Heated speculation has begun in the nation's capitol today as to why directors of the FBI and CIA were seen quickly entering senate chambers. Members of the Senate intelligence subcommittee were also seen entering chambers on the heels of John Morgantraugh, Director of the FBI, and Ben Baker, Director of the CIA. Correspondent Nancy Elwitz has the story . . ."

I had a feeling I knew what the meeting was about . . .

. . . The big, bad neighbor taking a steaming hot piss on their neighbor's rosebush.

For two days I slept like the absolved dead on my sofa with occasional interruptions from Jimmy Radmon, Carlos Rodriguez, the Rodriguez kid, Carmela and Sylvia and my seventy-five-year-old real estate agent I'd called to inquire about purchasing two other houses on the street. After my recuperative sleep, I dressed in my black Calvin Klein suit, white shirt, black tie and black wool overcoat and left the house.

I'd been standing over Ray Danbury's grave for about five minutes when my peripheral vision caught him approaching, dressed in a dark plum-colored wool overcoat and matching wool fedora and walking with a cane. Soon I felt the cold business end of his gun press against my neck.

"I could kill you right here and they'd pin a fucking medal on me."

Leo Cowling.

After several long seconds he slowly lowered his gun and let it dangle at his side, then slipped it into his coat pocket.

I began walking away from Danbury's grave when I heard Cowling say, "I see you here again, maybe things go different."

"You won't see me here again," I said without turning to him. "I'm done with the dead."

3 9

A week went by and nobody tried to kill me.

The only real excitement came Wednesday when my electricity, gas, water and cable all went out at the same time. I would have written this off as just another day in Detroit until I got a call from my credit card company.

"Sir," the overly-serious East Indian man said, "My name is Chet. I see that your card has been used on several occasions by someone named August Octavio Snow. Do you know any such person and have you authorized purchases by this person?"

"*I'm* August Octavio Snow."

"Did you, Mr. Snow, authorize August Octavio Snow to make a recent purchase of male penis enhancement products, a two-year subscription to *Big Beaver* magazine and a subscription to the Internet website www.wackyjizzjackers.com?"

After forty frustrating minutes, I finally convinced the credit card guy that I was, in fact, August Octavio Snow and no, I had not authorized myself to buy any of the stuff he'd listed. He apologized for the call and said he would cancel the existing card and would send me a new one.

A new card wouldn't have made much of a difference: soon after the credit card guy hung up, a burner cell phone stowed away in a shoe box on the floor of my bedroom closet began ringing. The ringtone was "Back Stabbers" by the O'Jays.

"Don't feel too good having yo mothafuckin' life up-ended, do it, Snowman?"

"I did what I had to do, Skittles," I said. In the background I heard water splashing and women giggling. "Where are you?"

"I could tell you, but then the FBI would have to kill you." After a pause, he said, "You hurt me, Snowman. You really hurt me."

"I'm sorry."

"Hey," Skittles said, his voice softening. "Ain't about a thang now. But let this shit be a warning to you, man. I ain't to be fucked with."

"Hey, *dude*—get over here!" a voice in the background said. "Holy shit! Those tits are *phenomenal!*"

I recognized the voice.

"You know Danny Cicatello? FBI cybercrimes dude outta the D?" Skittles said brightly. "Yeah, he's cool for an FBI handler. They got us shacked up at some Miami four-star for a couple days. He wouldn't be cool if he knew I was spoofin' a call to you right now, but—" Then Skittles' voice went low and soft. "You plannin' on makin' some sweet love any time soon at your crib, Snowman?"

"Uh—what the hell does that have to do—"

"Just thought if you was plannin' on makin' that funky beast with two sweaty backs, you might wanna pull them shades way down low, bro," Skittles said. "Them new streetlamps in the 'hood? Them LifeLight streetlamps? Some of 'em tasked to an FBI pilot program called Operation: First Light. Even the manufacturer don't know the fed-fuzz be retrofitting some of them streetlamps with state-of-the-art listening, video and blue-spoof surveillance."

"Why my neighborhood?" I said looking out at one of the Life-Light streetlamps.

"Why not the 'hood, bro?" Skittles said. "Shits and giggles. See if all y'all be happy down on the plantation. But guess where most of them streetlamps be?" I said nothing. "Dearborn, baby. Home of the nation's largest population of Middle-Eastern ex-pats."

In the background I heard Skittles' handler admonish him to hurry up and look at a particular bikini-clad young woman.

"Listen, you boys have fun on your little spring break," I said. "In the meantime, its thirty-four degrees in Detroit, I got no heat, water or light. And I'm missing SportsCenter."

Skittles laughed then disconnected.

Five minutes later I had heat, water and light.

And SportsCenter.

That Saturday I did the unthinkable: convinced that the number of people in Detroit who wanted me dead had gone down dramatically, I threw a party at my house. I was determined to do all the cooking, but Elena and Catalina Rodriguez from across the street inserted themselves into the process, which I was grateful for. With the warm and spicy aromas from the kitchen and the cacophony of talk and laughter between Tomás and Elena, Carlos and Catalina Rodriguez, Carmela and Sylvia, Jimmy Radmon, Frank and FBI Special Agent Megan O'Donnell (rather striking in civilian clothes), an immigration attorney and his wife, whom Elena had invited, and four other neighbors, I could feel the heart of the house—my parents' house—once again beating strong.

I had invited Vivian and Colleen. They were in town for a memorial service for Rose Mayfield. It was painful. The loss of the last mother. Colleen said for as much as they wanted to attend my party, they were leaving from Metro Airport on a much needed vacation to Koh Lipe island in Thailand, where they'd honeymooned. I told her to bring me back a snow globe with a seashell in it.

I'd purchased an Xbox and several G-rated games to keep the Rodriguez boy entertained, knowing what being the only kid at an "old people" party felt like. Of course Frank was sitting next to Manolito with a controller in his hands and, in between the electrically charged glances he shared with O'Donnell, he vowed to take the boy to school on FIFA.

Since Tomás's fifty-fifth birthday was a week away, I also bought two bottles of Tequila Cabresto (Reposado and Silver) and a pair of monogramed Reidel crystal tasting glasses for him. Naturally, I hoped to be the first he raised a glass with.

Halfway through the party I got a call.

It was from a beautiful half-Somali, half-German woman six hours away in Oslo, Norway.

"It sounds like I'm interrupting you," she said.

I told her she wasn't. Tomás, with four tequila shots in him, grabbed the phone out of my hand and told Tatina that I missed her terribly and spent nearly every minute crying like a baby for her. It took me a good three minutes to get the phone back—Tomás had handed the phone off to Elena and Elena tossed it to Frank. Finally in possession of my phone, I went upstairs to my bedroom. As we talked I looked out at my street. Lights were on in houses that hadn't seen light in years. The first of the season's snow began drifting down and catching the light of the streetlamps like flecks of diamonds and pearls. It was what I remembered seeing from my boyhood bedroom. And it was the long-ago anticipation of Christmas and all that it meant in Mexicantown expanding warm across my chest.

"I miss you," Tatina finally said. "I'm sorry if my saying that makes you—"

"I miss you, too," I said, sitting on the edge of my bed.

We listened to each other breathe for a moment.

Finally, Tatina broke the easy silence between us. "So, Mr. August Octavio Snow, ex-policeman. What have you been up to?"

ACKNOWLEDGMENTS

The world would still have its books without the people at Soho and Stephany at Fineprint. Of course, I am of the belief those books wouldn't be nearly as interesting, intriguing, illuminating or lovingly cared for . . .

OTHER TITLES IN THE SOHO CRIME SERIES